Come Again

JIFFY KATE

Books by Jiffy Kate

Finding Focus Series (Complete)
Finding Focus
Chasing Castles
Fighting Fire
Taming Trouble

French Quarter Novels
Blue Bayou
Come Again

Table 10 (parts 1-3)

Turn of Fate
(previously titled The Other One)

Watch and See

I've already had my love and now
that's gone, there's no need to try again.

PROLOGUE

Avery

HARD.

Cold.

Quiet.

As I begin to wake and roll from my side onto my back, I groan. The pain in my head is atrocious and images of an angry Brant flash through my mind. He was drunk when he came home last night and our ongoing argument about him coming home late—and never calling to tell me where he is—escalated.

Slowly, I open my eyes and blink. My right eye is swollen but thankfully I can open it, a little. Craning my neck back, I see the dim light over the stove in the kitchen shining but everything else is bathed in the semi-darkness of early morning.

The living room floor.

That's where I am.

I had been waiting for Brant and fallen asleep on the couch. When he came home, I woke up and asked him where he'd been and why he hadn't answered my call.

I was worried.

Sue me.

Hesitantly, I lift my hand and touch my eye, confirming its swollen state. Tears well, threatening to fall as I gently brush my shaky fingers down my cheek, to my nose, and finally coming to rest on my lips. Crusted, dried blood is covering the skin under my nose. Swiping my tongue out to moisten my parched lips, I immediately regret it as the taste of copper hits my taste buds and makes my stomach roll.

After a few more minutes of taking inventory and gaining my bearings, I finally pull myself up, using the nearby couch for support. The rest of my body is sore, but only from laying on the floor, everything else is intact. No other bruises. Nothing broken.

What the fuck happened?

One second, we were having our typical heated discussion. He was admonishing me for being a needy bitch. I was biting my tongue to keep from lashing out at him.

The yelling isn't anything new, but it's not old either. Back in high school, Brant would've never thought of raising his voice to me. He worshipped the ground I walked on and I treated him like a king. My friends were constantly swooning over him and telling me how they wished they could find someone like Brant Wilson—star quarterback, valedictorian, golden boy. Granted, we lived in a small, rural town in the middle of nowhere Oklahoma, so the competition was limited, but Brant would've been a standout no matter what.

He wanted it.

Life.

Success.

And all my friends thought I was so lucky, because he also wanted me.

When Brant came back after he graduated from college and told me about a job offer he got in Houston, and that he wanted me to come with him, I jumped. Head first. No looking back. Sure, I love Oklahoma. I always will. It's home. But the hustle and bustle of a big city has always called to me, like a beacon to my soul. A few days later, I had quit my job at a local restaurant, packed up my clothes and shoes and a few keepsakes to remind me of home, kissed my mama and daddy goodbye, and drove off into the sunset.

The yelling started shortly after we got settled in Houston. I realized early on, the more stress Brant was under at work, the more he'd dump it onto me when he got home. But I've been patient with him, hoping that my grandmother's favorite line was still true: *this too shall pass.* I've always held onto it and applied to every aspect of my life. Everything is temporary, even this life we've been given.

Recently, things got worse. I took a job working at a boutique with some sweet older ladies, and apparently that was just as good as me slapping Brant in the face. He was offended—incensed. He thought I got the job because I felt he needed my financial help. I won't lie, I had thought the added income would relieve some of his tension and keep him from stressing so much over this latest upcoming promotion. But in all honesty, I was bored. The apartment is small and there's only so much cleaning I can do in a day. We're not married. We don't have kids. We don't even have a dog. I had to do something with my time.

But that was when he started berating and belittling me, especially when I'd offer to take him out to dinner or a movie—always thinking I had an ulterior motive.

"Do you think I can't afford to take you out?"
"Do I not do enough for you?"
"The bills are always paid."
"I take care of you."
"What more do you want?"
And the list goes on and on.

Something has changed. He never takes me seriously anymore and if we talk at all, it's always about how he's going to get to the *next level.* The Brant I knew and loved in high school, and even college, the one who liked to watch movies with me on the couch or go out for pizza is long gone. He's been replaced by a money-hungry corporate asshole.

Tiptoeing down the hall, I walk into the guest bathroom and flip on the light. I squint my eyes until they adjust, blinking several times when my face comes into view.

The tears I let fall have dripped into the dried blood on my lip. Mixed with the smudged mascara from last night, it makes me look like the zombie cheerleader I dressed up as on Halloween a few years back.

How the fuck did I get here?

How the fuck did we get here?

When I think I hear something from down the hall, I pause with my hand on the faucet, holding my breath, listening to make sure Brant's not awake. After a few seconds, I ease the water on and grab a washcloth, lightly dabbing at my lip until the blood is gone, leaving behind swollen, split skin.

My eye is puffy and bruised, but at least the skin is intact.

There's also a purple shadow on my cheekbone.

Staring at my reflection, I allow my mind to hit replay.

"Why do you always need to know where I'm at, huh? Tell me, Avery. Have I ever fucked around on you?" Brant's eyes are hazy, but his words are sharp, cutting deep. "I could." He barks out a harsh laugh. "I could have so much pussy. But I don't. I don't because I know you're here, waiting for me to come home."

For a second, I think he's going to stop there and go pass out in the bedroom, but he doesn't. He keeps going.

"I like that, you know?" His hand brushes over my cheek and my body tries to recoil, but I command it to stand firm. I'm no coward. I don't back down. It's not in my blood.

"I won't be for long," I tell him, putting as much finality into my words as I can muster. "I'm not going to sit around waiting for you my whole life. This isn't the life we talked about. It's not the one you promised."

Anger flashes on his face and it contorts his handsome features to something foreign—something I've never seen before.

"What are you trying to say?" he bellows and for a split second I wonder if our neighbors can hear him, almost hoping they can, because he's kind of scaring me.

Will they call the cops?

Maybe turn us in for disturbing the peace?

"Calm down, Brant," I say, my voice controlled and even, hoping he'll follow suit. When I reach out to tug on his sleeve, a familiar gesture I'm

hoping will help defuse the situation, he slaps my hand away, catching me off guard.

"I'm not calming the fuck down, Avery!" He turns and paces, then stops, taking a deep breath and running a hand down his face, but it does nothing to wipe away the pure rage. "What the fuck are you saying? Am I not good enough for you? What the fuck can you possibly want?" His rapid-fire questions are coming so fast I don't have time to refute or reply. "I bought you a fucking car. I pay for this fucking apartment. I let you have your piddly ass little job. This," he pauses, spreading his arms wide, "this is what you've always fucking dreamed of."

"It's not," I tell him when he stops again to take a breath. "I mean," I pause, trying to think of the right words to say and the right way to say them. "I wanted to get out of Honey Springs and be with you, but not like this. Since we've been here, you've changed. This," I tell him waving a hand in his direction, "is not the Brant I fell in love with and I can't—"

Before I get out the rest of my statement, his first blow hits the side of my cheek.

Pain radiates, making me flinch.

I stumble, my eyes going wide in complete dismay.

Tears begin to fall.

I gape at him, trying to make words form, trying to reconcile the last seconds of my life.

Not my Brant. This is not the Brant I love. The Brant I love would never ever lay a hand on me.

With my hand over my cheek, taking shallow, choppy breaths, I force myself to make eye contact with him, hoping he'll realize what he's done and make all of this go away. Instead of the instant regret and remorse I expect to see, he yells again. "Stop your fucking crying!"

Whack.

Another one.

Right across the side of my head, knocking me off my feet.

It must've been hard enough that I fell and hit my head. Running a hand up into my hairline, I feel the knot, but thankfully, no blood. The resulting headache is there, though, adding to the sick feeling in the pit of my stomach.

He didn't even carry me to bed.

When did he become so callous? How did that happen? How did I let it?

With fresh tears falling, I work quickly as I go into the spare bedroom and grab my backpack from the closet. There's only one thing on my mind: getting out of here as quickly as possible, preferably without another altercation with Brant.

I can't be here, in the same space with him, a second longer than necessary.

Going to the bedroom, I quietly open the closet door and grab my stash of money, money I thought would go toward a vacation or a great pair of shoes. Never in a million years did I think it would be to escape what has become my life.

My mama taught me to never be caught without money stored away. *"You never know when you'll need a rainy day fund."* She didn't warn me about a storm and she'll be devastated when she finds out what happened. My mama loves Brant like her own son. She trusted him to take care of her baby girl.

This will break her heart, just as much as it does mine.

As I leave the room, I allow myself one look back. The mere sight of his sleeping form sends chills up my back, and for once, I'm thankful for the copious amount of alcohol and how late it was when he came home. I doubt he'll be awake for some time, and by then, I'll be long gone.

A few hours later, when the sun starts to peak over the horizon, I set my McDonald's coffee cup down in the center console of my car and punch the button on the screen in front of me.

"Good morning, baby." My mama's sweet voice soothes my soul. She sounds chipper for it being so early, but that's no surprise. She and my daddy are up before the roosters, and I mean that in the most literal sense.

"Good morning, Mama." I try not to get choked up on my words, but it's hard. Now that she's on the phone, I feel the adrenaline that's been fueling my body for the last three hours start to dissipate and the heartache finally take over.

"What's wrong?" I hear a screen door shut behind her, the familiar sound bringing with it a vivid picture of the scene, making me wish I was right there, waiting for her at the kitchen table.

Nothing, Mama. That's what I want to say, but it's a lie, and I don't lie to her.

"Well..." I pause, searching for the right way to say what I need to say. "I'm leaving Houston. Brant and I had a fight and I need some time away."

There's a shuffling sound on the phone as she goes about her business, always multitasking. But when she's finally settled, probably with a cup of coffee, she asks, "Did you say you had a fight?"

"Uh, yeah," I chuckle harshly at the loose use of the word.

"So, you're coming home?" There's hope in her voice. A little sadness, and definitely questions, but a lot of hope.

"No, Mama. I can't," I sigh. "It's the first place Brant will check, and I really need some space right now. I don't want to see him until I've had time to think."

"That bad, huh?" she asks, her tone morphing into concern.

I can't speak for a minute while I swallow down the lump in my throat and force the tears to stay put. "Pretty bad," I tell her.

"Are you all right? You need your daddy to come get you?"

"I'm fine, Mama." *I'll be fine.* "I just need some time away...I need to clear my head and figure out what I wanna do...what makes me happy, you know?" That's what I've been thinking about for the past few hours, since hitting the road. I've spent the last two years living in Brant's world, trying to make him happy...waiting on him to make me happy. Screw that. I'll make my own self happy.

"I really wish you'd just come home," my mama says, exhaling deeply into the phone. "We all miss you. And what's so bad that a little TLC from your mama can't fix it?"

Catching a glimpse of myself in my rearview mirror, I flinch, still not used to seeing my splotchy, bruised reflection. I have no doubt it will get worse before it gets better and it would kill her to see me like this. And don't even get me started on my daddy...or my nana and grandpa. I can't do this to them. I can't bring this—my problems—to Honey Springs.

"I'll call you whenever I get where I'm going," I tell her.

"You sure do know how to make a mama worry."

That makes my stomach hurt for a new reason. I know she worries. She's told me time and time again that it's her job. But I also know she wants me to be happy. "I'm sorry, Mama."

She sighs heavily again. "Don't worry about me. I'll just have to pray a little harder."

"I love you." I love that she lets me be me. She's always done that. She's never forced me into a box or made me be something I'm not. If I pull up in her drive right now, she'd hug me and kiss me and take care of me, but I also know her heart would break.

I'll go home soon, when I've had a chance to process what happened and what I'm doing with my life. And I'll come clean about Brant and what really happened between us. But not right now.

"I love you, baby. Promise me you'll be safe."

"I promise."

"And Avery?"

"Yeah, Mama?"

"You know you always have a place here. No matter what."

"I know."

After I end the call, I pick my coffee back up and take a slow sip, eyes on the road ahead. When I left Houston, I made a spur-of-the-moment decision. I could've gone in any direction. I could've driven to the gulf. Galveston is only a short drive from our apartment. I could've headed to one of the smaller islands, finding solace there. Dallas is a big city and I could've easily driven there and got lost in the crowds of people. But I wanted more than that. I wanted to escape and I needed somewhere that would feed my soul.

I was craving color and life.

There was only one place on my short list of possibilities that offered all of that and more: New Orleans.

When I was in the McDonald's parking lot, I pulled up my Airbnb app I'm always searching through, dreaming of places to go. It didn't take me long to find a room for rent just a few blocks from the French Quarter. With it being the end of July, I knew my chances of finding something was a crap shoot, because it's summertime and that means family vacations and the peak of tourism. When I saw a room available for less than forty dollars a night, I jumped on it. It's only available for the next two weeks, so I'll have to find something else eventually, but it'll work for now.

Hopefully, within a couple weeks, I'll be able to find a job and begin figuring out what I want to do—what makes me happy. The money I had stashed, plus the additional thousand I was able to pull out of the bank at the ATM before I left the city, will get me by until then.

I know Brant. He'll track where I withdraw money.

When he wakes up and realizes I'm gone, he'll be furious.

When he finds out I didn't go home, he'll be livid, but also relieved. Relieved, because he'll be glad everyone else doesn't know I left. Furiously angry, because he won't know where I am.

That won't have anything to do with his concern over my well-being, but everything to do with his need to control me. Plus, he'll see my leaving as a failure, as he should, because if there's one thing in life Brant Wilson isn't good at, it's loving me.

He made the biggest mistake of his life by taking his frustrations out on me.

I'm never going back.

A couple hours later, I'm exiting off of I-10 and onto Rampart Street. After a U-turn and another turn down a side street, the typical city view turns unique as I get closer to the French Quarter.

My heart stops at its first glimpse of the bright colors and old-world exteriors. And then it starts anew, beating stronger and truer than it has in a long time.

I'VE BEEN IN NEW ORLEANS FOR ABOUT FORTY-EIGHT hours and I'm already in love.

The jazz music.

The food.

The people.

So many people. Interesting people. Street performers galore—singers, musicians, wannabe singers, and wannabe musicians, mimes, one-trick ponies. Palm readers, Fortune tellers. Voodoo priestesses.

Now, that one, I seriously considered. The thought of putting some sort of voodoo spell on Brant pleases me greatly.

On my first day, I checked in and crashed on the soft bed in the airy, bright-colored bedroom. Exhaustion didn't allow me to think much, thankfully, because when I woke up yesterday morning, the heaviness of everything hit me hard.

The adrenaline rush was gone.

The fight-or-flight mode had been neutralized with the warm breeze off the Mississippi. I was left with the bruised face and memories of Brant's words and heavy hand. It left a mark that's more than skin deep. Now that my fury has subsided, the pain and insecurities have surfaced.

It hit me, like really hit me.

He hit me.

And he didn't apologize. Not that it would have mattered. The damage was done, but if he cared, at all, he wouldn't have left me on the floor alone. He would've reached out.

My phone hasn't rung since I've been here.

I called my mama once I was in my room and told her where I was, much to her distress and disapproval, and I promised to call her again tonight. She wants to know what happened. She said when Brant called the house yesterday morning he sounded nervous. *"It's not like him, Avery. What happened between you two? You used to be so good together."*

Not anymore, Mama. Not anymore.

She promised she didn't tell him where I was and for that I'm grateful, but I know it's only a matter of time before word gets around. Mine and Brant's families frequent the same places. My mama and his mama are good friends. They'll eventually talk.

When I woke up this morning, I set out for beignets and café au lait. Café Du Monde was calling my name, so I walked there. I had seen it on Instagram, but other people's photos never do anything justice.

The room I'm renting is in Marigny, which is only about a fifteen-minute walk to Jackson Square. It's a great walk. Everything about this city draws me in and makes me breathe better—freer, lighter.

After breakfast, I made my way around the square and poked my head into a few places, asking if anyone was hiring, but came up empty handed. One shop said they might be looking for someone to work weekends. If I'm staying here for a while, I'll need more than fifteen or twenty hours a week, so I told her thank you and continued my search.

Bourbon was intimidating. Even in broad daylight, it's full of people from every walk of life. There are suits and sororities, people of all color and levels of nudity—lots of boobs and butts—and everything in between. A couple of the bars had help wanted signs, but I kept walking, deciding Bourbon would be my last resort.

Actually, I think I passed a bar named that.

Now, I'm approaching Canal Street and when I get there, I stop to take it all in. The passing streetcars, the palm trees, the restaurants—everything is giving me life. Standing on the corner, people brushing by, cars driving in haste, yet everything still feeling slow and easy, I take a deep breath and close my eyes.

This.

I needed this.

Maybe I've always needed this.

The sensory overload is helpful in pushing what happened with Brant and the state of our relationship over the past year to the back of my brain. I don't have to think about his hateful words or angry stares. I don't have to remember the way I can still feel the back of his hand making contact with my cheek, rattling my brain. I also don't have to think about the way my soul shrank each time he belittled me or made me feel unimportant or a burden.

Here, in New Orleans, I feel like I can reinvent myself, be the Avery Cole I've always dreamed of being. The Avery I've always felt inside. The one who came out with crazy hair colors and out-of-the-box clothing choices. Here, I'm just one of the thousands of unique people.

"Excuse me," a lady mumbles, bumping my shoulder and pulling me out of my thoughts. It's then I realize I've been standing on the corner through the light, but that's okay. I don't have any hard and fast plans. Sure, I need a job, but that can wait a day.

"Excuse me," I say back to the lady who pressed past me to get closer to the street. She turns a small smile on her lips. "How do I get on one of those?" I ask, pointing at the cheerful, red streetcar coming our way.

"Where you wanna go?" she asks, keeping one eye on the light and one on me, shifting her head as she watches and waits.

I shrug, taking another deep breath, looking one way and then the next. "Anywhere, everywhere." I can't help the light chuckle that escapes. I just want to absorb my new surroundings, become one with the rich, vibrant city.

"Just hop on over there." She points across the street. "It's a buck twenty-five. You'll need exact change. This one takes you up and down Canal." She glances at me, motioning for me to follow her across the street. "The St. Charles line takes you down into the Garden District. I recommend that. Pretty parks and gorgeous houses." She smiles over her shoulder as she walks quickly in the opposite way. "Bonus: they're air conditioned."

I chuckle, nodding my head. "Thanks!" I call out after her. Air conditioning? They should charge extra, because it's still early in the day and I feel like I'm literally melting. I thought Houston was hot and humid, but it has nothing on this.

Jogging to the corner, I dig in my bag and count out five quarters. I'll start on Canal, then everywhere else. Tomorrow, I'll pick up my job search, but today, I'm exploring.

Waking up to the early morning sun shining through the sheer curtains in my room, I stretch. I intentionally didn't pull the shades last night, wanting to feel like I was surrounded by the sights and sounds, even laying in the quiet, cool bed of the room I rented. It's part of a larger house, with several rooms being rented out, so I'm not alone, but yet, I occasionally feel it. It's not a horrible feeling, just different. I've never been completely on my own. I went from living with my parents to living with Brant.

I always thought alone would feel depressing, but it's actually kind of refreshing.

After my excursion yesterday, riding the streetcar up and down Canal Street, stopping at a few places—window shopping, grabbing a bite to eat, getting a coffee. I eventually got off and walked back to the French Quarter, finding myself across from Jackson Square standing next to the Mississippi. The Mighty Mississipp'. The Ole Miss.

I can't help singing, *"Deep River"* in my head, doing my best Clark

Griswold impersonation.

Blame that on my daddy. He's a *National Lampoon's Vacation* junkie.

Today, I'm going to take the St. Charles line down into the Garden District. I've always wanted to see the big, beautiful houses, and there's no time like the present. In a couple days, I should have a job, and I won't have the luxury to walk around like a tourist all the time, so I'm making the best of my freedom.

After showering and tossing my damp hair into a messy bun, because humidity, I opt for some cutoffs and a flowy top. Slipping into my flip flops and grabbing my sunglasses to finish off my ensemble, I head out the door with my trusty backpack in tow.

Being in a rented room, I haven't felt comfortable enough to stash any of my money, so I've been carrying it around with me everywhere I go. It feels safer in a backpack.

The walk to Canal Street takes me by a small, local coffee shop, so I stop in and grab an iced coffee. When I step back out onto the sidewalk, I smile at the contents in my hands—a coffee and scone. A buzzing city surrounding me. I feel alive.

It's not until I get onto the streetcar at St. Charles and slip into the bench across from an older gentleman and he gives me a sympathetic smile that I remember my face. I guess I should've used some concealer, but really, I'm not trying to hide it.

Who is there to hide it from?

It's not my fault Brant decided to be a world-class asshole and take out his frustrations on me.

It's not.

I've had to convince myself of that a time or two over the last few days. I didn't do anything to deserve this. I'm not to blame. I don't think it was too much to ask to know when he was coming home late.

After I finish my scone and crumple up the wax paper it had been served on, I take a drink of my coffee and offer the older man a smile.

It says *I'm okay.*

"Nice day today," he says with a nod of his head.

I smile a little wider. "It is. Hot, but nice."

"Hot should be New Orleans' middle name." He chuckles to himself, looking out the window.

I sit back and watch the big, beautiful houses go by. The Garden District is enchanting. I can't think of another word to describe it. The trees are huge and dripping with moss and some have beads in them, which I assume are leftovers from Mardi Gras. Most of the houses have large columns and shutters. Some have a porch on the second story. All of them have character and seem full of wisdom, like they have a story to tell.

I want to sit on one of those porches. And drink sweet tea. Maybe rock in a chair.

Sighing, I scoot closer to the window and lean my cheek against the glass.

The streetcar eventually comes to the end of the line and I hop off and look around. The area is more modern, more suburban. Not seeing anything that strikes my fancy, I decide to turn and start walking back the way we just came from. I remember seeing a park not too far back the other way and a small café on the corner a little past that.

A stroll in the park doesn't sound bad, so I head that direction.

The park is a lot like everything else in this area—old, green, and charming. I walk through the gardens, sit on a bench, contemplate life, until I've worked up an appetite. My coffee and scone are long gone. So, I make my way to the café.

Crossing the street, I see the sign up ahead. Crescent Moon Café.

It looks appealing and quaint. There are a few bikes parked out front and it makes me want to get one. I can see that being a good way to get around the city. Between a bike and streetcars, I might not even need a car, which is a good thing, because I'm sure Brant will want mine back.

I know I need to call him and make things final between us, but I need a few more days.

"Welcome to The Crescent Moon," a chipper girl, probably my age, calls out. Her high pony tail sways as she walks over and grabs a menu from the hostess stand beside the door.

"Thanks," I tell her, taking inventory of my surroundings—a few booths by the windows and small tables in the center. It's small and cozy. And whatever is being cooked in the kitchen smells amazing.

"Corner," I hear a deeper voice call out as a guy rounds the corner with a tray full of food.

"Will anybody be joining you?" she asks.

"No, just me."

"Right this way."

She takes me to a booth in the corner, the window looking out over the street, lined with large trees with low-hanging branches. "How's this?"

"Perfect," I tell her, my eyes drifting outside, before I toss my backpack into the seat across from me and then slide in.

"Here's the menu," she says, placing it on the table in front of me. "Our specials today are the shrimp po'boy and chicken and shrimp gumbo. Oh, and the dessert is our award-winning bread pudding with warm rum sauce." Her eyes light up. "It's to die for."

I smile, laughing lightly at her enthusiasm. "Sounds great."

"I'll grab you a water. Tripp will be your server."

Picking up the menu, I give it a glance, but the second she mentioned chicken and shrimp gumbo, my mouth started watering. And I plan on saving room for that bread pudding. In a couple weeks, I might be eating ramen and living out of my car, but today, I'm living my best life.

"Hello." The guy who was carrying the tray earlier is standing beside my table with a crooked smile. His hair is longer in the front, swept to the side, giving him a bit of a mysterious vibe, almost like he's trying to hide. But he couldn't. Ever. He's kind of a hottie. Not that I'm looking, but I am a warm-blooded female.

"Hi," I offer back.

"Have you decided what you'd like or do you need a few more minutes?"

"No, I think I'm pretty solid. I'll take the gumbo and a sweet tea," I tell him, handing the menu back. "Oh, and bread pudding."

He gives me the crooked smile again and dips his chin to his chest in acknowledgement. "Solid choices."

But as he turns to leave, I call out, "Could I have the dessert first?"

He turns back, his hair falling over one eye and smiles knowingly, a nod of his head the only response I get.

I don't know why, but I feel the need to eat my dessert first today. Maybe I'm subconsciously comforting myself since no one else is here to do it? It's like retail therapy, but with dessert.

When he disappears behind the doors leading to the kitchen, I turn my attention back to the window, watching as people walk by. For a few minutes, my mind drifts to Houston and Brant and I wonder what he's doing...what is he thinking? Does he miss me? Is he sorry?

I don't care.

I don't.

I can't.

It wouldn't matter.

Part of me feels sick when I think about how unhappy I've been and that I didn't leave. Why did I wait for it all to blow up? It's so stupid. *I* feel so stupid. Another part of me says that if I would've left earlier, Brant would've sweet talked me back into his good graces.

How embarrassing that I was so forgiving of him.

How humiliating that I stayed.

How disconcerting it took him hitting me for me to leave.

What does that say about me?

"Solid, solid choice," the same deep voice says, interrupting my internal debate, as a piping hot piece of the most amazing bread pudding I've ever laid eyes on comes into view.

The rum sauce is literally dripping off the side of the plate.

Melted butter is pooling at the sides.

And my mouth is watering.

"Oh, my God," I groan. "This looks amazing. Like, awe-inspiring." I laugh at my overzealousness, but I can't help it. This bread pudding could very well change my life.

"I promise, you won't regret it. And," he adds, cocking his head to the side. "Wyatt, the owner, he offers a one hundred percent satisfaction guarantee on this. If you're not completely satisfied, even if there isn't a drop left on the plate. You let him know and it's no charge."

"Wow," I reply, nodding my head. "That's confidence I can get behind."

We both chuckle as he walks off, leaving me to my bread pudding. My sweet, sweet bread pudding. Maybe, since I've recently crashed and burned at a relationship, I should consider one with this piece of work in front of me. I mean, he's sweet, warm, delicious, and he doesn't look like he has a mean bone in his body. I smirk at my ridiculousness and dig in, stifling a moan as the decadent goodness touches my tongue.

Just as I'm finishing up my dessert, practically licking my plate—I totally would've had I been alone—my gumbo and crusty bread is served, along with a tall glass of good, southern sweet tea. Everything is delicious and exactly what my shattered psyche needs.

"How was everything?" A curiously dressed gentleman walks up to my table, with genuine interest on his face, just as I'm pushing my clean plate away and setting my napkin on top. His suspenders and seersucker shirt are a unique combination, causing me to peruse the rest of him. I smile when my eyes take him in and notice the scuffed up cowboy boots topping off his ensemble.

Ahh. You gotta love New Orleans.

"It was great. Best meal I've had in a long time. Hands down," I tell him.

His eyes light up. "That's great, just what I like to hear." When he crosses his arms over his chest and continues to stand there, I realize our conversation isn't over and it makes me fidget with the used up napkin.

"Are you new here? Visiting?"

When I look back up at him to respond, because my mama raised me to look people in the eyes when I'm talking to them, he doesn't seem to notice my black eye and split lip. If he does, his expression doesn't change.

"I'm new...not visiting, at least, I don't think I am," I ponder aloud, to him and myself.

"A transplant?" he asks, cocking his head and quirking his eyebrow in curiosity.

"Uh, I don't really know. I'm just..."

"Drifting?"

I bark out a laugh, but he's right. I'm kind of a drifter. Even though I came here intentionally, I don't have much of a plan past getting a job. Clasping my hands together in front of me on the table, focusing on my short nails and chipped bright-blue polish, I think to myself this is a place I'd like to work. Everyone seems so nice and inviting.

"I'm looking for a job," I blurt out, wincing up at him in apology for the abruptness and awkwardness. I can't help myself sometimes. I just say what pops into my head. "You wouldn't happen to have any openings?" I try to sound confident, but my words come out tentative and hesitant, not necessarily what one should be shooting for when soliciting employment.

Fortunately, Wyatt doesn't seem bothered. His expression is neutral as he lets out a loud sigh, his lungs completely deflating as he twists his lips. "I really don't have anything...not even a dishwasher position," he says, looking over his shoulder. "We don't have a high turnover rate here. Most of my employees have been with me for years."

Inhaling, I smile, nodding my head. "I kinda figured. I've worked a lot of odd and end jobs. I always know a good working environment when I see one. Just thought I'd take a chance."

"As you should," he replies thoughtfully. "Always take a chance."

We sit there in silence, not awkward, just contemplative. I turn my attention back toward the window, giving him an out, but he doesn't take it.

"I tell you what." He drops his voice and squats beside the table, getting eye level. "See that guy over there?"

Following his line of sight, I see a man sitting alone at a table in the opposite corner of the café. He has dark hair and equally dark tattoos peeking out from under his shirt. The beard covering his face hides any expression, leaving him appearing even more mysterious than the waiter I had earlier.

"Yeah," I breathe out, still letting my eyes rake over him while he's not looking.

"That's Shaw O'Sullivan. He owns and operates a bar down in the French Quarter. Are you familiar with the area?"

"I'm renting a room off Marigny Street," I offer.

"Perfect. His bar sits off St. Ann. It's called Come Again." He takes out an order pad and jots down information as he continues talking. "He's been known to help people who are looking for a hand up, giving them jobs...taking them in off the street."

"Well, I'm not on the street, yet," I add with a light laugh. "*But* I could really use a job."

His blue eyes meet mine and there's nothing but sincerity there. "I'd give you one if I had anything to offer. And if this doesn't work out," he says, handing me the slip of paper, "come back and see me in a couple weeks. I'll see if I can fit you in somewhere."

Taking the paper, I scan it and look back up at him. "Thank you."

"No problem." He stands from his squatting position and sticks out his hand. "I'm Wyatt, by the way."

"Avery Cole," I tell him, shaking his hand.

"I'd tell you to talk to him today, but he keeps to himself on the weekends—being Sunday and Monday for him. So, I think you'd have better luck if you approached him on Tuesday when the bar opens back up for the week."

"Tuesday," I repeat, unable to take my eyes off the man across the room.

"Good luck, Avery," he says with a tip of his imaginary hat.

"Thanks, Wyatt."

A few minutes later, my waiter, Tripp, I believe is his name, is back. "Can I get you anything else?" he asks, clearing away my bowl and saucer.

"No, I'm stuffed, but everything was delicious."

"That's what we like to hear." Taking a check out of his back pocket, he places it on the table in front of me. "I'll be your cashier when you're ready, but no rush. Can I get you a coffee or anything?"

"No, I'm good." I smile at him, at this place. I think I just found my Cheers.

Reaching across the table, I pull my backpack over and look at the check to see how much I owe. The bread pudding has been marked off with a smiley face and a *Good luck, Avery* written beside it.

Yeah, I love this place.

"Hey, boss," Paulie calls out when I walk through the back door of the bar.

I nod my head in response but keep quiet otherwise. I haven't had my coffee yet, so it's best for everyone if I keep my mouth shut for the time being.

Stepping into my office, I toss my messenger bag onto the floor and flip on the light. Because I'm running a little late, I only have a few minutes before my weekly staff meeting begins, so I use the time to sit at my desk and decompress.

It's a fucking shame that, at nine-thirty on a Tuesday morning, I'm already fighting a personal case of asshole-itis but sometimes it can't be helped. While most people dread and complain about Mondays, my week starts on Tuesday and let me tell you, the name of the day doesn't mean shit. The start of the work week is rough, no matter what.

My weekends fall on Sundays and Mondays. I love my time off and I make a point to spend it wisely, whether it's taking my motorcycle out on long rides or staying home and pigging out in front of my television watching sports. I do whatever the hell I want to do and, usually by Tuesday, I'm ready to get back to work.

But, not today.

Today was predetermined to be a shitty day, for reasons I'm not acknowledging at the moment, but to make matters worse, I ran out of coffee at my house. I pass by some amazing coffee shops on my way to work and thought I could get a cup to go, but everywhere I went was packed. This is New Orleans. People here should either be at work already or still in bed recovering from last night. I mean, what the fuck?

I even contemplated hitting up Café du Monde but knew it'd be full of tourists. Don't get me wrong, I love that place and most days I'm grateful it's located close to my bar, but it's not the kind of place you go to for a quick cup of coffee.

So, here I sit, trying to focus on all the shit I have to do today while fighting off the beginnings of caffeine withdrawal.

"Good morning! Y'all haven't started without me, have you?"

I recognize the sweet voice of my sister and let out a sigh of relief. Sarah is my rock and I rely on her more than I should.

When I walk out of my office, I immediately notice a sweet aroma. Sarah runs the cooking school next door to the bar, so she usually smells like food, but this is different. I know this scent. Picking up my pace, I waste no time in getting to the bar because my sister—the best fucking sister on the planet—has donuts with her.

And coffee.

I grab the large cup from her hand and bring it to my nose, letting the smell of chicory soothe my nerves, before taking a drink.

"Thank you, Sarah, for the coffee and donuts," Sarah says, mocking my bad manners.

"You know how he is before he gets his fix, all grumpy and rude," Paulie says. "He hasn't said one word since storming in here. Shaw's lucky we love him *despite* his moods."

Finally ready to speak, I point to them individually. "You," my finger finding Paulie first, "only love me because I pay you. And, you," I look at my sister, "love me because you have to."

I wrap my arm around Sarah's shoulders and lean down to kiss the top of her head. "Thank you for the coffee and donuts, love. You're a lifesaver." This causes her to blush and swat her hand at me.

"Oh, stop. I didn't do this for you; I did it for those of us that have to work with you." She gives me a wink before speaking quietly so only I can hear. "You doing okay?"

"Yeah," is my quick response before stepping away and grabbing a donut. Sarah knows me better than anyone, and although I know she's not happy with my brief answer, she knows that's all she's gonna get from me.

Two more of my bartenders show up and grab a donut before settling down at the bar, waiting for the meeting to start.

"So, what's on the agenda for this week's meeting? Is this everyone?" Paulie asks.

"No, Jeremy is supposed to be here, too. Today is his first day of training." I look at the front door before glancing at my watch. "If he ain't here in five minutes, he's out."

Paulie chats with the other guys while I finish my coffee, waiting to see if my new hire shows up or not. I won't be surprised if he doesn't show, but I will be disappointed. The guys I hire to work here at Come Again are chosen for a reason and I don't like feeling I'm wasting an opportunity on someone who doesn't want it.

With two minutes to spare, the front door chimes, alerting us to Jeremy's arrival.

"Hey, new kid!" Paulie yells and waves him over to where we're all gathered. Jeremy looks nervous, scared even, and rightly so. I watch as he gingerly sits on a stool, not making eye contact with anyone.

Normally, I would've laid right into him, calling him out on being late and wasting my time, but something tells me to use a different tactic with this kid. All eyes are on me when I grab a couple of donuts and a napkin and walk over to where he's sitting. I drop the food in front of him, ignoring how his body flinches in response.

Speaking only to him, I ask, "Are you clean?"

He glances up at me before nodding his head.

"Good. You're late. I'll allow it this time, but if it happens again, you're out. You got that?"

The speed of his nod increase. "Yes, sir."

I eye Jeremy carefully, taking in his long, stringy hair and dirty clothes. "Eat up," I nod toward the donuts. "After the meeting, I want you to go upstairs and take a shower. Get yourself cleaned up and find some clothes to wear. If you need anything specific, you let me or Sarah know. After that, I'll start your training."

He lets out a shaky breath and looks me in the eye. "Thank you."

I nod before returning to my place at the head of the bar, my good deed for the day taken care of.

The weekly meeting doesn't last long. We go over the schedule for the week and talk about events going on in the city. Come Again isn't far from the infamous Bourbon Street, but we're not really a part of the party scene. While we do get a lot of tourists and stragglers, our clientele consists mostly of local regulars. Still, it's always good to know what's happening around town so we're prepared.

After Jeremy gets cleaned up, I start showing him around the bar. It's not a huge establishment but this place has definitely seen some great times. Opening a bar had been a lifelong dream of mine, so when this space became available back when I was in my mid-twenties, I jumped on it. It was a rough start but after a much-needed makeover and much-appreciated word of mouth, Come Again began to thrive.

"Now, back here is the stock room. It's where we keep supplies, kegs, and the extra bottles of booze. When Paulie or one of the other guys need something, this is where you'll find it. It's imperative we keep this room neat and organized so that when there's a rush and we run out of something, it can be replaced quickly. Believe me, you don't want to make customers wait too long for their drinks. When the natives get restless, things get ugly."

Jeremy quirks a small smile, the first I've seen from him, and nods his head. "Will do...I can do that." His words are quiet, just like his demeanor, and I'm afraid he might get eaten alive if he doesn't show some moxie. I know guys like him, though. Most have been beaten down by society until they can't think further than putting one foot in front of the other.

I slap a hand down on his shoulder, sparing no expense. His whole body shakes but I get his attention. "Listen, all I ask is that you stay clean and show up on time, just like I mentioned earlier, but if you want to thrive, you'll need to dig deep and find your balls." I pause for a second, letting my words sink in and give him a chance to catch my drift. "They're there. I promise, yeah?"

He nods.

"Don't let people walk all over you or make you feel like you're less than them, because you're not. We all put our pants on the same way. So, for anyone who's put you down or made you feel like they're better than you, fuck them."

He swallows before giving me another slight nod. I quirk an eyebrow at him, my face probably looking menacing under the dim light of the storage room. Finally, he tilts his chin up and mutters, "fuck them."

"That's right." I nod my approval, giving him another slap on the shoulder, but not as hard this time, following it up with a squeeze of reassurance.

I'm not the touchy-feely type. I don't hug. I don't have flowery words of motivation. I have real talk and tough love, and it's worked so far. Not for everyone, but those that can be saved, I've saved them.

"Shift starts in an hour." Turning on my heel, I depart the storage room and leave Jeremy behind. My day really hasn't even started yet and I'm already ready for it to be over. Not that I don't love this place. I do. If it weren't for the bar, I'd spend my days doing nothing and that would never work, so I appreciate it for what it is—employment, an outlet, a resource for the less fortunate, and some days, it's the only thing I have to look forward to.

When I approach the front of the bar, I hear the telltale creak of the front door and check my watch. It's early. We always leave the door unlocked once we're all here for the day, even though we don't technically open until later. Every once in a while, we'll get an early straggler—someone having a bad day at work or someone searching for the hair of the dog. We've got remedies for both.

Glancing up, I expect to see a regular, a familiar face, but instead my eyes meet those of a young girl. She barely looks old enough to be in here, legally. "Can I help you?" I bark out, my voice sounding a little rougher than I anticipated.

The way she straightens her back lets me know she heard that too and I inwardly cringe. It's not like I'm intentionally *trying* to be an asshole. For a second, I think my greeting was enough to scare her off, which would've been fine by me, but then she squares her shoulders and clears her throat.

"I'm looking for a job," she says. Her words come out quickly, like she's ripping off a Band-Aid or taking a dive before she chickens out. "I spoke with Wyatt at The Crescent Moon and he mentioned that you might be looking for some help." The more she talks the braver she gets.

"Well, Wyatt was wrong. I'm not looking for anyone."

I'm actually impressed when she takes a couple steps toward me.

Now, there's some moxie.

"He said you help people who are down on their luck," she challenges with a tilt of her head, like she's inspecting me—testing me to see if any of the things she's heard about me are true.

"Are you even old enough to work in a bar?" I ask, squinting my eyes in her direction, but not giving her much of my attention. However, I do look close enough to see the fire in her eyes spark and burn a little brighter, and I have to admit, I like it. But there's no way in hell I'm hiring her. I've never had a female employee...at least, not since...

"I can mix drinks, wait tables, wash dishes—" She starts trying to sell herself and her skills, but I cut her off.

"We don't cook. The only dishes we have are glasses and it's every *man* for himself," I retort, emphasizing the word man.

Her eyes widen and her nostrils flare a little before she huffs, "That's very sexist of you." I watch as her chest rises and falls with deep breaths and she bites down on her bottom lip, as if to keep herself from spewing out any more words of rebuttal.

"Listen, sweetheart, this isn't Bourbon Street. We keep our clothes on here and we don't do body shots," I practically growl out, because she's getting under my skin. How dare she come into my establishment on a Tuesday and challenge me. "If I only want to hire men, then I'll do as I damn well please. Go find yourself a club to work at. That's where the tips are, anyway."

"I'm not a stripper or a...hoochie mama," she says with her arms in the air. I've officially riled this girl up and I don't even know her name. Her hoochie mama comment forces me to fight back a smile. But I can't crack, not now.

When I take a step closer, the sun creeping in the window illuminates her, bringing her pale pink hair into view. It's different. She's different. And so are her eyes. They're dark, coming off nearly black in the dim light, such a contrast from her hair and pale skin. And her accent. She's definitely from the south, but she's not from around here.

She also has a nice shiner and a split lip. Girl fight? Drunken bar fight? Boyfriend? Regardless, she looks like trouble and I definitely don't need any of that here.

"Where're you from?" I ask.

She sticks her chin out in defiance, crossing her arms over her chest. "Why do you care?"

I stand there, stoic, staring at her like she's lost her damn mind. No one ever contests me or contradicts me, except my sister, and on a rare occasion Paulie, but other than that, my word is the end all, be all.

"Oklahoma," she reluctantly mutters after an elongated pause.

"Go back to Oklahoma," I reply, turning around and walking out of the bar, past the storage room, past my office, and out the door at the end of the dark hallway. When the door slams behind me, I let out a few expletives, trying to relieve the sudden buildup of stress.

It doesn't work. Growling, I kick the metal banister, but that does nothing but make me wince in pain. My steel-toed boots took the brunt of it, but it still didn't feel good.

Looking up the rusted staircase to my left, I exhale deeply before taking the steps two at a time. Once I'm at the top, I fling the door open and storm inside.

What the fuck is wrong with me?

No, scratch that. I know the answer and I don't want to think about it. I don't want to think about anything right now. I just want to clear my mind and push myself to the limit and there's only one way I can do that right now.

Scanning the large studio apartment I own above the bar, I verify it's empty and I'm alone before I walk over to my bench press, toss some weights on and get down to business.

I'll need to shower again once I'm finished because after I punish my body into submission, I'm always drenched in sweat, but at least I'll be able to tolerate myself. And I'll be easier to work with.

Inhaling deeply, I bring the bar to my chest. Exhaling, I muscle it up.

Again.

My employees and patrons will thank me for this later.

And again.

And I'll be able to think clearer.

Again.

And Oklahoma will be out of my head.

Who the fuck does she think she is? Coming into *my* bar? And what the fuck was up with her face? Who did that to her?

I pump harder, faster.

I'll also be having a chat with Wyatt about sending a flippant...*girl* to my door, because that's what she is—a girl, maybe twenty-one. He's a lot better suited to employ someone like her, so why would he send her to me? What in the world would I do with her...*in my bar*?

Not happening.

3

Avery

It's been a week. A whole freakin' week. And I still don't have a job. I'm not complaining. I know people search for work for a lot longer and are a lot more desperate than I am. Plus, I've been enjoying my slow mornings, painted in the bright, crisp hues of the early Louisiana sunshine.

While on my job search, I've found interesting spots to stop and hang out. I've walked barefoot through parks and window shopped through the French Quarter. I've drank in the free atmosphere and soaked in the deep culture—street art, jazz bands, second line parades. But my funds are running low and I only have a week before I'll have to find another place to stay, and I was hoping I'd have a job by then and know how much I'll be able to afford.

The dreaded *what ifs* have started to settle in.

What if I can't find a job?

What if I run out of money?

What if I'm forced to go home?

I've decided that when I get down to my last hundred dollars, if I still don't have a job, I'll concede defeat and go home. I won't have another choice.

When I was talking to my mama yesterday, she voiced her concerns and tried to get more information about what happened between me and Brant. Apparently, his mama was at the drug store when she stopped in to get Daddy's blood pressure meds a couple days ago and she mentioned that Brant hasn't been himself and she can't get him to take her calls.

My mama tried to get me to agree to calling him, but that's not going to happen. I know I'll eventually have to talk to him, and I will. I'm not a chicken shit. And, despite what happened, I'm not scared of him.

Okay, maybe I am. A little.

I still can't believe he hit me.

I can't believe he went from someone I would've trusted my life with to someone who'd make me question its safety.

Who is he?

Where did the Brant I used to know and love go?

Thankfully, the split in my lip is almost healed and the bruise below my eye isn't as angry as it was the first few days. It's still there and noticeable, but it doesn't look like I just lost Fight Night.

Pulling myself out of bed, I quickly shower and dress, pulling my hair into a high ponytail. The pink I normally dye it has faded into my platinum blonde. I like it. It's still pink, just not my normal, vibrant fuchsia, but it's pretty. And it'll have to do for now, because after paying up my room for the two weeks and buying gas and food, I'm down to a thousand dollars. It's enough for now, but not enough for long.

I give myself a quick look in the mirror and take a deep breath. Despite everything, I feel lighter and happier than I've been in a while. This city feels good. It feels like somewhere I can be myself.

All the more reason I'm *going* to find a job and I'm *going* to make it. I'm not ready to go home.

Someone out there is in need of someone like me. I just know it.

"Go get 'em, Avery," I whisper to myself in the mirror.

Walking out of the neighborhood I'm staying in and into the French Quarter, I make a beeline for the coffee shop I've already grown accustomed to. I think that's important. Both the coffee and finding a shop that suits you. It's the sign of a good fit. I would go to The Crescent Moon every day, if it was closer. But it's a nice walk, plus a ride on the streetcar, so I'm thinking, it'll be a once a week thing. Maybe later today, after I stop at a few more places and check on job openings, I'll treat myself. I intentionally avoided it on Sunday and Monday because I remember what Wyatt said: Shaw is a regular on his days off. After our showdown in his bar last week, I really have no desire to see him again.

He was surly.

No, scratch that.

He was an asshole. Grade-A, prime choice, top-of-the-line, asshole deluxe.

Just thinking about him pisses me off all over again. *He only hires men?* How sexist can he be?

When I make it to Neutral Grounds, I get the cheerful "hello" I've come to expect.

"Hi, CeCe," I call back with a wave and a smile. Yeah, I'm already on a first name basis with my barista. "Just a drip," I tell her as I walk up to the counter. I'd love to have a cappuccino or a latte, but I'm being frugal. So, fancy will have to wait.

"Any luck finding a job yet?" she asks as she turns to get a cup and fill it up. What's really awesome is if I stay and chat, which I've done a time or two, she'll fill it up as much as I need, which means breakfast is a reasonable two dollars and nine cents.

"No, nothing." Sighing, I lean on the counter and place my correct change by the register.

She gives me a look of pity and genuine disappointment, offering me a "sorry" before setting down my coffee along with the caddy containing the cream and sugar.

"It's okay." Instead of whining like a baby, I set about fixing my coffee just like I like it—four creamers and one sugar. "Something is bound to come up, right?"

"It will," she encourages, busying herself with making a fresh pot of coffee. "Oh, I did see that the bar across the way put a help wanted sign in their window a day or two ago…maybe it was yesterday?" She shrugs, turning around with a contemplative look. "I can't remember, but I bet, if you head over there, it might still be up. That is, if you don't mind working at a bar."

I look out the window, *across the way*, and wonder out loud, "Come Again?"

"Yeah, just on the corner."

I don't know why, but my blood starts to boil and it's not the coffee. "Thanks," I tell her with a smile as I hold up my cup, trying to hide my anger. *What an asshole!* A week after I come looking for work and he puts up a help wanted sign? Like he didn't know he needed help when I was there? Oh, that's right…he only hires men.

"You know, I think I'll head over there now. Catch 'em early."

"Good thinking," CeCe chimes in. "And come back for a refill if you want."

"Thanks," I tell her again, securing my cup with a lid before heading out the door. It's early and I have a feeling the bar isn't open yet, but last week, when I stopped by on Tuesday, even though they weren't technically open, the door was unlocked.

Sipping my coffee, I make my way slowly around Jackson Square, taking the long way to give myself enough time to caffeinate and cool down a little before going back into the lion's den, aka Come Again.

Once I've finished my drink and made two laps around Jackson Square, I'm kind of a sweaty mess. Standing near the bench in front of the bar, I toss my empty cup in the trash and stare at the offending yellow sign in the window.

Sure enough.

Help wanted.

I'm not sure I'm ready for this, but I desperately need a job, so I'm going in. Maybe if he's desperate enough, he'll be a bit more amicable. I scratch his. He scratches mine.

Not like that. I inwardly groan, making a half circle to face the cathedral. Not that scratch. A job. Although, I hate that he does appeal to me on a sexual level. There's just something about him that makes my body react. He's older, mature. The way he walks is more like a stalk, each step intentional. I admit I watched him on his way out of the bar last week, all the way until he disappeared down the long, dark hallway.

Sure, I was fuming.

I was also offended, pissed off, and annoyed.

Digging deep to the pit of my stomach, right down to where my roots live—I pull from the girl who grew up on a farm and was taught to never take no for an answer. A few seconds later, I draw a deep breath and turn my attention back to the bar, storming over to the door. It creaks when I open it, just like last time and I wince at the announcement of my arrival. I could've done without that, maybe had a minute to finish finding my gumption and resolve. But nope, the second I walk through the door, the dark eyes from Tuesday are turned on me and when he sees it's me, he glares.

"I'm here for the job," I demand, a bit out of breath from all the pre-gaming I just did out on the sidewalk, but I find it imperative to have the first word.

"I'm not hiring." Turning his back to me, he goes about his business of stocking the booze behind the counter.

"You're lying," I challenge, placing my hands on my hips and readying myself for a fight.

Slowly, he turns, but only half way, glowering at me from the side. The way the light hits him, it shows off his face and his features aren't as harsh as he makes them out to be. It's the constant scowl that really sets them off. But beyond the scruff, there's a straight nose and a high forehead, which accentuates his dark eyebrows and intense eyes, which are also dark. He's kind of mesmerizing.

"What did you just say?" he finally asks.

"Lying… you're lying," I repeat, swallowing to keep myself from wavering.

He barks out a laugh and I huff out my annoyance. Turning around to the small window beside the door, I tear the yellow sign off the glass and walk over to the bar, slapping it down with force. "Help wanted?" I ask, thinking maybe that'll ring a bell. "I came in last week looking for work, remember?"

"And I told you—"

"Right, I don't have a penis. You made that clear." I roll my eyes and shake my head. "You know how ridiculous that is, right? Let me tell you, I can do just as good of a job as any man. I grew up on a farm. And I might look small, but I'm strong and I can carry my weight." Before I stop for a breath, I'm practically standing on the bar, my pointed finger now in Shaw's personal space, precariously close to touching his chest. The stare he's giving me is lethal, but I'm not scared of him. He might try to intimidate me—and it might work, a little—but he's not running me off this time.

I'm not leaving this bar without a job.

When I continue to hold his gaze, unflinching and unwavering, his expression starts to change. It doesn't soften—*soft* and *Shaw* are two words that don't belong in the same sentence—but it does shift into something resembling surrender, reluctant surrender, but surrender all the same. His lips twitch as his nose scrunches into a snarl. He hates this. He hates that I'm in his space. I can see it written all over his face, but something about what I just said got to him and I can see he's reconsidering.

"Just hire me for a trial basis, maybe a month. If I can't perform up to your specifications, you can fire me, but I'd prefer a notice of some sort. I'm kind of here on my own and I can't afford to be without a job." When I realize I'm starting to ramble, I stop myself from saying more and hold my breath to see what his final decision is going to be. If he wants to go another round, I've got a little more ammunition, but I'm hoping I don't have to use it. "Come on. Give a girl a break."

"Fine," he grits out behind clenched teeth. "Be here tomorrow at noon. You'll start training then."

My eyes widen and I almost ask him to repeat what he just said, unsure I heard him correctly, but then I think better of it. Shaw O'Sullivan doesn't come across as a man who likes to repeat himself and I'm not stupid. I know when to push the limits and when to keep my mouth shut, so all I say is, "Thank you."

Before I open the door to leave, I turn back to him and he's already back to restocking shelves. "You won't regret this," I tell him, or his back rather, which is broad and strong, even under the cover of his black t-shirt.

I see him shake his head and hear a harsh chuckle escape before he mutters under his breath, "We'll see."

When I'm back out on the sidewalk in the New Orleans sunshine, I realize I didn't even ask how much he's going to pay me, but I guess that doesn't matter. I have a job and anything is better than nothing.

Shaw

"So, I HEAR YOU HAVE ANOTHER NEW HIRE STARTING today," Sarah says in her normal, happy tone. My sister is the most cheerful person I know. She's the light to my dark, the joy to my misery. However, she does share some of my physical attributes. All of my siblings have the same dark hair and nearly black eyes.

Black Irish.

Striking.

I've been called that on more than one occasion, usually from women who only want one thing. Occasionally, I indulge them.

"I needed someone," I tell her, hoping to cut off the Spanish Inquisition before it starts. I'm not really in the mood for conversation, which doesn't bode well for today's training session.

Sarah's expression is pleased and intrigued. "Uh huh, *a girl.*"

"Doesn't matter."

"Oh, but it does." She's so fucking good at antagonizing me. If I didn't love her so much, I would tell her to fuck off, but that never goes over well with Sarah. She might be sweet and nice and caring, but she's not afraid to put me in my place, or anyone else, for that matter.

I huff, exhaling harshly through my nose, trying to tamp down the annoyance and frustration. "Please drop it."

"Okay," she sighs, leaning her hip against the barstool. "Want to talk about last week?"

"Nope."

"Didn't think so." The disappointment is evident in her tone, but that's another thing I don't want to get into, not today, besides it was last week—past tense. I made it through, that's all that matters. One day at a fucking time. Story of my damned life. "Well, I can tell you're going to be an absolute pleasure to work with today, so I'm going to leave you with Paulie and the newbie."

About that time, Paulie comes walking into the front of the bar with a crate of clean glasses. "Thanks," he says to Sarah, giving her a side eye and a sly smile.

"How's everything going at Lizzie's?" I ask, feeling the familiar twinge of pain in my chest with the mention of the cooking school next door. It's perfect, though. The only name that would fit the establishment.

"Great," Sarah replies. "This month has been jam-packed, especially with the added evening classes and the increase in tourists. I'm kinda shocked, actually. I didn't think cooking in New Orleans in the heat of July would be appealing, but I guess anything that gets people out of the humidity is a selling point."

"Good." I nod my head, thinking. "You know, if it gets too busy and you need someone, I could always send over one of my guys."

She sighs, standing up straight. "Well, I admit, it's kind of a lot, especially when the classes are in session. What with keeping up with the prep work and cleaning," she says with a sigh. "But I love it, of course, I love being so busy and I'm managing, for now."

"I'll gladly go over and help," Paulie chimes in.

"Thanks, Paulie," Sarah says with a smile. She's got more of a soft spot for the old man than I do, and he has one for her too. "I might take you up on that offer one of these days."

"Anytime," he adds with a nod of his head, retreating to the back for more supplies.

"Well, I've got to get going. I need to shop before tonight's class.

Do you need anything?"

"A shot of whiskey," I tell her. "But I guess I'd settle for a coffee." Giving her my best impersonation of a puppy dog, which probably comes off more like a sad pit bull, she laughs.

"You're on your own today." Walking to the door, she swings it open. "I need to make sure you don't forget how to use a coffee pot."

"Yeah, yeah," I growl, waving her off with a bar towel.

When I hear the front door open just a few minutes later, I call out, "Did you change your mind about the coffee," figuring she forgot something and wanting to give her a hard time.

"Uh," a feminine and newly familiar voice stutters, "well, actually, I did bring coffee."

Turning, I see the new girl standing at the door with a to-go tray of coffee cups and a bag I recognize from the coffee shop on the other side of the square, Neutral Grounds.

"Pastries, too." She offers me a warm smile and holds the bag up, but I can't manage more than a grunt. For some reason, it pains me when people do unexpectedly nice things, maybe because I'm forced to be nice in return and that pisses me off.

She moves toward the bar, depositing the delicious smelling goods in front of me. "I guess I'll set them here? I brought extra, in case—"

"Do I smell coffee?" Paulie asks, walking back into the bar, probably expecting to see my sister changed her mind and retrieved breakfast after all.

The new girl gives him a small smile and a wave, walking toward him with an outstretched hand. "Hi, I'm Avery."

"Paulie," he says with a smile.

Avery. I guess I can quit calling her new girl in my head now.

Like he's in my fucking head, Paulie quirks an eyebrow and adds, "I guess you're the new girl."

"Guess I am," she says with a light laugh. It's not a horrible one. It's airy and girly, much softer and prettier than we're used to around here. And that also pisses me off. This is why I only hire men. It's less complicated. Having a girl around makes things weird and uncomfortable and I don't like having to worry about someone. This is a bar and things get rowdy from time to time. The last thing I want is to have to be concerned about one of my employees' safety.

"Coffee?" she asks, holding up a cup to Paulie, who takes it with enthusiasm. "Help yourself to a pastry." When she offers him the bag, I snatch it from her and open it to check its contents. It's rude and I know it, but I don't want her to think she can buy us with some coffee and donuts.

"What are these?" I ask.

"Danishes—cream cheese and cherry. Oh, and a blueberry scone."

I snarl my disapproval. "Sounds like a bunch of girly shit, if you ask me."

Her demeanor immediately changes—the smile fades and is quickly replaced with an arched eyebrow and pursed lips. "Well, I guess you don't have to eat them, then." She snatches the bag back from me and hands it to Paulie, who's very enthusiastic about these pansy-ass pastries.

Fucking Paulie.

Fucking new girl.

Avery.

What the fuck ever.

"Before you can even start training," I begin, deciding to get down to business and possibly weed her out early, "I'm going to need to see some identification and a social security card. You'll also need to fill out an application."

She looks at me for a moment and I think I might've won the jackpot and she's going to hightail it out of here, realizing this is a legit establishment and we don't employ underage teenyboppers. "Will you need a blood sample too? Or a drug test?"

Paulie snickers around his large bite of danish and I glare at him.

"Don't be a smart ass. That's rule number one," I tell her, walking over to the cash register and reaching underneath to pull out an application and get her a pen. Before I make it back over to where she's standing, she's already pulled out a driver's license and a social security card and slapped them on the counter.

I set the paper in front of her and she quickly starts filling it out, but stops, brushing her pale pink hair out of her face and looking up at me. "Um, I'm staying at a place a few blocks from here, but I'll only be able to stay for a few more days. Should I put that address down for now and then give you a new one when I figure out where I'll be after that?"

"Fine." With her looking up at me like she is, I can't help but notice the faint bruise that's still under her eye and the place on her lip that's still healing. "What happened to your face?"

With her eyes locked on mine, I see the war inside them—hesitation, indecision, and a fierceness that can't be mistaken. Finally, she replies, "My boyfriend."

My back stiffens with that admittance and I feel a surge of anger. She must mistake my change in appearance as something it's not, because she starts to ramble a further explanation.

"He's in Houston...I left him in Houston. So, you don't have to worry about him showing up at your bar and causing problems or anything like that. I haven't talked to him since I've been here, so I doubt he even cares I'm gone."

"I thought you said you're from Oklahoma?" I ask, needing the distraction and a chance to redirect the conversation.

"I am, but I moved to Houston..." she drifts off, probably realizing she doesn't want to tell me—a virtual stranger—her life story.

The sad thing is she doesn't have to finish telling me, I can take a good guess. She probably moved to Houston with her high school boyfriend, maybe college, and he turned out to be an asshole and beat the shit out of her. It's not unheard of and she comes across as a girl who wouldn't go running home. She seems like someone who is independent and adventurous. Maybe it's the pink hair? Maybe it's the tenacity?

After she completes the application, I take her driver's license and social security card to my office and make a copy for my files. In the picture on her license, she looks considerably younger—blonde hair, freckles splattered on her nose, dark eyes full of life and naivety. I look at the date and see it was made a few years ago. She's twenty-three. And like she said, she's from Oklahoma, Honey Springs to be exact. Everything else on her application looks good, so I set the papers on my desk and head back out to the main part of the bar.

Jeremy, my new guy, and Avery, my new girl, are laughing about something when I get there and for some reason, it doesn't sit well with me. I guess, now that I have a female working here, I'm going to have to make a new rule: no flirting or fraternizing.

"Ahem." I clear my throat getting their attention and hand Avery her cards back. "I see you two have met."

"Well, not officially," Avery says, tucking a piece of hair behind her ear and grinning over at Jeremy.

"Jeremy," I say, pointing to the kid. "Avery," I say, pointing to her. "Now," clapping my hands together, "let's get to work. We'll have customers in just a couple of hours, so there's no time for goofing off and mingling. You'll have to do that on your own time. When you're at the bar, that's my time. I'm paying you, so you'll be here on time and do what I say. Is that understood?"

Avery nods her head and replies, "Yes."

I'm glad she didn't add a sir to the end of that. I know it's polite and proper, but this is a bar and I don't ask that of any of my other employees. "We're all on a first name basis around here. Paulie, who you met earlier, is my second in command. If I'm not here, he's who you'll report to and feel free to ask him any questions. He knows this place better than I do."

She nods again and I catch Jeremy staring at her. "Don't you have something better to do?" I ask him, catching him off-guard and making him jump a little. One thing I've learned about the kid is he's a nervous little fucker. It actually pisses me off most days, because if I had to guess, I'd say he's the way he is because someone's beat on him, kicked his ass more than once. Maybe he came from an abusive home?

Maybe he and Avery have a little in common?

Although, unlike Jeremy, Avery comes off as a fighter. Probably a fighter or a flier, and I'm guessing when things got bad between her and her boyfriend, she chose flight and that's how she ended up here.

Jeremy scurries off back down the hallway and I hear Paulie putting him to work, so I continue showing Avery around the bar. She seems to pick it all up quickly, showing she knows her stuff. She wasn't lying about being able to carry her weight. I would never admit that to her, but I'm relieved to know I didn't make a complete mistake by hiring her. At least, not yet anyway.

"How much will I make?" Avery asks with a directness I appreciate.

"I'll start you out at eight bucks an hour and you can keep your cash tips, under the table. All your other tips will be paid on your check."

I watch as her wheels start turning—her big, dark eyes shift to the side and she pulls her lips between her teeth, thinking. "Okay," she finally agrees with a nod, like she's done the math and it works for her.

I can't help but wonder if that'll be enough for whatever she needs and I also wonder how long she'll be around. "If this is a temporary place of employment for you, I'd like to know that upfront. It doesn't mean I won't hire you, for now, but I'll keep my eye out for someone to take your place when—"

"I'm staying." Her words come out strong and sure.

The defiance I've seen from her rears its head making me believe this girl can and will do whatever she sets her mind to.

Avery

STRONG HANDS GRIP MY HIPS AND PUSH ME UP AGAINST a wall. *The lights are dim but I can still see his dark eyes as they pierce into mine and then he kisses me—hard, passionately, strong.*

My hands grip his strong arms, roaming up to his shoulders, and then finally find purchase in his thick, dark hair. He groans and the flame burns stronger, hotter—straight down into the pit of my stomach making me want—this, him.

"More," I plead.

"Say please."

"Please."

"Please what?"

"I...I," I stutter, falter on the words, on what I want. I know, but I can't say it.

"Say it," he demands, reading my mind, or maybe he's just reading my body.

"I want...more."

"More what, Avery?"

Hearing my name come out of his mouth so seductively practically has me coming, without touch or the friction I desire, and it gives me courage. "I need to feel you. Touch me, please."

His hands slide around my backside, squeezing hard and making me moan out the pleasure I feel. "Like this?" *he asks.* "Or like this?"

When he uses his knee to spread my legs and pushes his hard length against my center, I see stars and the wanton pleas fall. "Yes, please. That. I want that."

"So responsive, Avery." *The tickle of his beard as he kisses along my jaw and down to my neck sends shivers up my spine. It's foreign, something I've never felt before and I love it. The added friction and sensation brings an awareness I didn't know was missing from my life. I didn't know he was missing from my life, until now.*

Unbuttoning my jeans, he slips a finger under the edge of my panties...

Oh, God.

Oh, God.

My legs are tangled in the sheet when I wake and there's a throbbing ache between my thighs.

What the hell was that?

Shaw. And me. And...

"No," I groan, covering my head with the pillow. "Ugh." He's such an asshole. Why would I have a dream like that about him? And why was it so hot?

My pulse is still beating rapidly as I try to tame my breathing, but the need for a release isn't going away. After a few moments of trying to get the vision of me and Shaw out of my mind and failing, I slip my hand under the waistband of my sleep shorts and give in to the need, mimicking the moves from my dream. I can't help that when I close my eyes, I still see him.

It doesn't take long to get myself off, which is no surprise, seeing as how I haven't had sex in a long freaking time. Brant and I haven't been intimate in forever. With him working and spending most evenings at dinner meetings, we haven't had a chance. On the weekends, he was always tired or in a foul mood from the week. The fact that I woke up to a sex dream about my new boss is disconcerting, but I'm not hating the release.

Throwing the covers back, I roll out of bed, feeling somewhat pissy for post-orgasm. Normally, I feel lighter, blissful. But I'm supposed to be at work in a few hours for my first official shift at Come Again, and the fact that I can't get Shaw's gruff voice or the feel of his facial hair brushing my skin out of my head is a problem. After a dream like that, I'm afraid all I'll be thinking about today is *me* coming again, and that's just wrong and bad...and WHAT. IS. WRONG. WITH. ME?

My phone ringing from the nightstand where I have it plugged in causes me to jump, pulling me out of my lusty haze. I know it's not my mama. We spoke last night when I called to tell her about my new job. She was happy for me, of course, but still leery of my new location. Also, she mentioned Brant has been calling and that I need to reach out to him. Leaning over to grab my phone, I freeze, my hot blood turning ice cold.

Speak of the devil.

Brant's name flashes on my screen again and my stomach drops. My palms immediately begin to sweat and I have to swallow a lump. I didn't think I'd have this reaction to seeing his name. I honestly thought all I would feel is irritation, but this feels a lot like fear. I drop the phone with a thud back on the nightstand and back away from it like it's a burning flame.

Eventually, the ringing stops and I peer over at it to see if a voicemail shows up. After what feels like forever, and I'm convinced he's not going to leave one or call back, I back away and into the bathroom.

Quickly, I shower and dress, needing coffee and a clear head before I go to work. Hopefully, after a walk to Jackson Square and a stop at Neutral Grounds, I'll be all better. No thoughts of Brant. And no thoughts of Shaw. Or the dream. Coffee fixes everything, right?

Wrong.

A few hours later, when I step inside the bar, I'm immediately hit with visions of my dream causing my cheeks to flush. When Shaw clears his throat to get my attention, I practically leap out of my skin.

"Jumpy, are we?" he asks in his typical grumpy way. "At least you're not late. I'd hate to fire you on your first day."

See, I don't like him. Why would I? He's not nice.

We stand there for a moment, him glaring at me and me trying to avoid eye contact with him so he doesn't see the awkwardness that's creeping into the situation. There's nothing to worry about. It was a dream. He doesn't know what I'm thinking. He has no clue that right now, if I closed my eyes, I could feel his firm grip on my hips.

No, Avery.

Bad Avery.

"Ahem." I clear my throat and take a few steps toward the bar. "What would you like me to do?"

He narrows his eyes and I feel the scrutiny, but I don't know what I did to deserve his ire. Maybe just being here, being me—a girl? Well, he's the one who agreed to hire me, and I think I proved yesterday that I can follow through on my promise of carrying my own weight.

"Go to the storage room and get a bottle of all our bottom shelf liquors. The list is on the wall beside the light switch for reference. After that, the bottled beer needs restocked. Paulie will be in later and he'll have some other things for you to do. Until then, that should keep you busy."

"Okay," I reply with a dip of my chin. Walking past him, I head down the hall, appreciative of the task to distract me and the reprieve from his glare. The storage room is small and dark, but cool, which is nice since the summer heat is still in full force in New Orleans. Thankfully, unlike some of the bars on Bourbon, Shaw keeps the doors of the bar closed, which holds in the bought air, as my grandpa used to say.

Shut the door, Avery! You're gonna let out all the bought air.

With that thought, I make myself busy checking the list by the light switch and filling the crate beside the door with the liquor bottles marked for restock. When the crate is full, I muscle it up, thankful for my days on the farm and that my daddy taught me to *lift with my legs*, and carry it into the bar and behind the counter.

Fortunately, Shaw is nowhere to be seen, so I go about my job in peace, letting the dream fall to the wayside.

"Hey," Jeremy says, walking in from the hallway.

"Oh, hey. I didn't know you were here," I reply with a smile. He seems like a nice guy and it's great having another newbie to take some of the pressure off me. Jeremy told me yesterday that he just started working at the bar last week. So, we're kind of learning the ropes together.

"Shaw's letting me stay upstairs," he says, nodding his head back down the hallway. "Just until I can get on my feet or find somewhere else to stay."

His statement kind of catches me off guard. I mean, I know Wyatt said Shaw helps people, but I just assumed he meant give people jobs. "Wow, that's really...nice," I tell him, unable to hide the hint of shock in my tone.

Jeremy smirks and chuckles. "He's not as bad as he seems."

"Well, he did give me a job, so I guess I can't complain." I return to the shelves and continue to rotate out the bottles, bringing the opened ones to the front and putting the unopened ones in the back, giving the shelves a good cleaning as I go. Two birds with one stone. I like to work efficiently, never putting off until tomorrow what can be done today. There's no sense in that.

Work smarter, not harder—more words of wisdom from my daddy.

"So, what's your story?"

Turning my head toward him, I smile, unsure of what he's asking. "Umm...I don't know. What do you mean?"

"Well, everyone who works here has a story," he says matter-of-factly. "Where did Shaw find you?"

With that statement, I stop and toss the towel over my shoulder. "Shaw didn't find me. I came here looking for work."

"Hmm. Just assumed you were in *the program*." He uses air quotes on the program and I can't help but frown.

"The program?" I ask, keeping myself busy, just in case Shaw walks back in, because I know from yesterday he wouldn't be happy if we were talking when we should be working. I have no desire to get fired on my first day.

"Yeah, Shaw's program. Well, I guess it's nothing official, but pretty much everyone who works here or has worked here in the past has been someone Shaw takes in off the street, cleans up, gives a job, and eventually, sends on their merry way."

"And that's how you ended up here?" I ask, curiosity getting the better of me. Now I need to know everything.

"Yeah, I was hanging out in the alley behind the bar one night." He shrugs, crossing his arms over his chest. "Strung out. Hadn't had a good meal or hot shower in days...weeks maybe. I'd lost count."

The image Jeremy is painting makes my heart hurt. I've always had a soft spot for homeless people—those who are less fortunate or down on their luck. When I was little and my parents would drive into the city for supplies or a shopping trip, the men who would stand at the corners of the busy intersections panhandling for change always made me tear up. I felt for them and wanted to help them. My mama would always make my daddy give them a few dollars out the window.

"I'm sorry you were..." I trail off, wondering what the proper terminology is. Do homeless people like to be called homeless? Displaced?

"Homeless," Jeremy finishes for me. "Don't be." He waves me off like it's nothing, but it doesn't make me feel less for him, not pity, but just bad.

"Well, I'm glad Shaw gave you a job and a place to stay. That's really nice." I mean it now with sincerity and this tidbit of information is making me see Shaw in a new light. He might be an asshole, but at least he's an asshole with heart.

"It was my own fault," Jeremy continues. "I started using a few years ago. My parents kicked me out. They gave me loads of chances, but I always chose the drugs."

"Are you still... using?" I ask. Unfamiliar with drug addicts I don't know exactly what to say. "Is it something you can stop doing?"

"I'm trying."

Loud footsteps coming from the hallway sends us both scurrying back to work.

Shaw glares in our direction and sets a crate of clean glasses down on the bar top. "Put these away," he orders with his dark eyes boring down on Jeremy. When he looks my way, I think he's going to bark a new order at me, but instead, his scowl deepens and then he turns around and walks back down the hall. When he's out of sight, Jeremy releases a heavy breath.

"Dude is intense," he says with a chuckle.

"Seriously."

We continue talking and getting to know each other, but the conversation never turns as heavy, with no more discussion of programs or drugs or being homeless. Jeremy is originally from Texas and used to live in a suburb of Houston, so we have things to talk about. Like, one of my favorite Japanese restaurants happens to be somewhere he and his parents used to go on special occasions when he was younger. After that conversation, we both agree we need to find a good sushi place when we get paid.

"I know I shouldn't splurge on sushi, but..."

"Well, all work and no play is for the birds," Jeremy says with a sigh. "A few pieces of sushi won't break the bank."

"Right," I agree with a laugh. "Besides, I don't technically have a bank account anymore, so..."

"Bank accounts are for the birds too."

We both laugh and I can't say I disagree. I've never been too concerned with money. But, then again, I had plenty growing up. We weren't rich, but we never did without. My grandparents and parents never put much emphasis on it, therefore neither did I. Brant on the other hand, he's different. His mother came from money. They inherited a large piece of land when his grandparents passed away. Maybe that's why he's so consumed with success. Regardless, it doesn't excuse him of his transgressions. In reality, I think I fell out of love with Brant a long time ago. I might've been holding out hope that the spark would reignite, but when he hit me, all of those hopes went out the window.

"So, tell me more about living in Houston," Jeremy says, interrupting my thoughts. "How did you get there?"

"Can we talk about something else?" I ask, not wanting to think any more about Brant. I decided a few days ago I don't want to give him another second of my time, but after the call I didn't take this morning, I know I'll have to. He won't stop. I made the mistake of checking my bank balance yesterday morning and saw that he cleared out what little money I had left in there. Honestly, I'm surprised my phone still works, but that's probably just because he needs a way to contact me. I know I need to talk to him, at least to inform him I'm not coming back and to tell him to go to hell, but I'd rather not discuss it right now.

"Sure," Jeremy says easily, none the wiser to my inward struggles. "Who's your favorite band?"

"Hanson, hands down."

"Han-who?" His look of confusion makes me crack up laughing.

About that time, Shaw reappears and ruins the mood and our friendly banter.

"Paulie needs your help," he says looking at Jeremy. When Shaw leans over the bar, turning his attention to me, Jeremy rolls his eyes behind his back and offers a wave as he departs.

"You can handle the bar until Kevin gets here, right?" Shaw asks.

Why do I feel like this is trial by fire?

"Yep, got it covered," I reply, trying to sound confident.

"If there's a drink you don't know how to make, just tell them it's temporarily off the menu. We're a no-frills kind of bar. Our patrons are used to no one catering to them, so you shouldn't catch any shit. I'll be back at eight."

And just like that, he's gone and I'm left tending the bar all by myself. Granted, there aren't any customers yet, but the fact he's trusting me with it on my first official day makes my chest swell a bit with pride. This feels good—working, fitting in, making a go of things. And I have a new hope that there's more to Shaw than being a grade-A asshole.

Things are looking up, and I realize as I'm standing behind this bar in the French Quarter of New Orleans that I haven't been this happy in a long time.

When the familiar ring from my phone comes from under the counter where I placed my backpack earlier, I freeze, staring at the wood like I have x-ray vision. Somehow, I know it's Brant and now isn't the time for *that* talk. But I also feel safer, here at the bar, feeling Shaw's solid presence even in his absence.

Call me crazy. I know he's an asshole, but I also feel like he wouldn't let anyone come in here and beat the shit out of his employees. Regardless of his surly behavior, he seems like the kind of guy who stands up for those who are weaker than him. Like Jeremy, and the other people he helps.

I'm also at work, which gives me a good out. I won't be able to talk long. Impulsively, before I change my mind, I reach for my bag, unzip it and pull the phone out, just in time for it to stop ringing. Holding it in my hand, I stare at the screen again. This time, a voicemail notification pops up.

With slightly trembling hands, I press my thumb down hard on the screen and swipe to open the message.

"Avery," Brant's rough, thoroughly pissed voice comes through the phone, loud and clear, and it takes me back to eight days ago when I woke up on the hard floor of our apartment—my face bloodied and bruised. Instinctively, I touch the spot on my lip that just recently began to heal.

"Fucking call me," he demands with a growl and I can picture his jaw tensed with his teeth clenched. "I've spoken to your mom and she said you're not at home. If you're there and she's lying, I'm going to be so fucking pissed. You can't just leave without a word. I'll be in Honey Springs this weekend. I expect you to be there as well." There's a long pause and I can hear his labored breaths. "Don't make me look like a fool."

The last statement is laced with intention and ire. He's always been good at threatening me without using words that would make him look like what he truly is—a bully, an abuser.

Don't make me look like a fool sounds an awful lot like *don't make me hurt you...don't make me slap you into submission.* Now that I know what he's capable of, and know he's willing to cross that line, I can't help it. All along, before he ever laid a hand on me, I think he wanted to. His words of belittlement and intimidation were meant to make me feel small. He wanted me to be scared of him so I would fall in line.

My good mood from being left to tend the bar slips away as I place the phone back in my backpack. I was ready to face him and get this over with, but it'll have to wait. Right now, I'm afraid I'd crack. I need time to prepare myself. Tomorrow...I'll call him tomorrow.

6

Shaw

I LOVE THE BAR WHEN IT'S EMPTY. I KNOW, AS THE
bar's owner, I should also love it when it's full of paying customers and
I do, but there's something about being here all by myself that soothes
me. This place means everything to me; it supports me and gives me
purpose.

It also has a killer jukebox hooked up to a kick-ass speaker system.

Running my hand along the top of the machine fondly, I peruse
the music selection. Every song is approved by me and if someone ever
complains about it, they're told explicitly to fuck right off. My place,
my tunes. It's very simple.

Being thirty-eight, and having siblings a good deal older than
me, means I was raised on the classics. I listen to everything from The
Beatles to Zeppelin. The heavier the guitar, the better, but it has to have
soul, too. If music doesn't move you, what's the point?

I push the button for one of my all-time favorite songs and let out
a deep breath. Angus Young's guitar riff fills the room and I can't help
but do a little air guitar of my own. Knowing no one is here, I allow
myself to let loose and sing along as I straighten the tables and chairs
and wipe down the bar for the umpteenth time. I know the cleaning
was all done last night at closing, but it's something I like to do for

myself, even after all these years.

"AC/DC this morning? That's a good sign."

Turning around, I see my sister standing in front of the stock room. She has her hands on her hips and a sly smirk on her face as she looks me over.

"What do you mean?" I ask, going about my business.

"You're usually in a decent mood when you play AC/DC. It makes me almost hopeful, you know? It's when you play Metallica or Pink Floyd that I really want to run and hide."

"I just may have to play *The Dark Side of the Moon* all day," I warn.

"Oh, God, no. That's way too depressing for a bar." She steps behind the bar and starts pulling out glasses and mugs. "One of these days, I'm gonna sneak in some disco on that jukebox, maybe even some hip hop. That'll liven this place right up."

"You wouldn't dare," I say, narrowing my eyes at her.

"No, I wouldn't, not for long anyway, but it'd be funny to see the look on your face if I did."

I shake my head at Sarah, chuckling. I love the playful banter we have. Even though she's ten years older than I am, we've always been close. The fact that she's always stuck by my side and now runs the cooking school next door means the world to me.

"What do you mean when you say hearing me play this kind of music makes you hopeful?" I ask, curiosity getting the better of me. Sarah's one of the few people I can truly let down my walls around and just be myself, or whatever version of myself is left.

Her movements falter a bit but she recovers and faces me with a sad smile. I hate that smile.

She lets out a deep breath and shrugs before speaking. "It makes me hopeful you're finding your way again and becoming the Shaw you used to be." Her voice is soft and I know she means well, but her words still piss me off.

"There's nothing wrong with the Shaw I am now," I growl between clenched teeth.

"No, there's not, but we can all use some improvement from time to time, don't you think? Can you imagine how much easier things would be if you loosened up just a bit instead of building walls all the time? I understand why it's hard for you to let people in but it doesn't mean you shouldn't try. Take Avery for example."

Hearing Avery's name catches my attention, but I school my features, only allowing my eyes to cut over to Sarah. "What about her?"

"She's a great worker, a very sweet girl, and she's scared to death of you. Would it kill you to compliment her, let her know she's doing a good job?"

Hearing that Avery is afraid of me makes my stomach sour. I know I'm a dick around her...well, more of a dick than usual, but I feel completely out of my element with her and I don't know why. I don't even want to try and figure out why I react to her the way I do, but I don't want her to be scared of me. That's just fucking unacceptable.

I run my fingers through my hair, glancing out the front windows, before turning back to Sarah. "You're right, she is a good worker and I don't want her afraid of me." I hesitate, thinking for a moment. "I'll *try* to do better." The gruffness of my words covers up the fact I am a bit remorseful. The last thing I want is for anyone to be scared of me. Helping people is what makes me feel human. Having Avery scared of me feels counterproductive to that effort.

She pats my cheek just like our ma used to do and smiles. "I know you will, Shaw. You're a good man; you should let people see that from time to time."

It's later in the evening when I find myself watching the bar from a corner across the room. Sometimes I'll say I'm taking a break but hide out somewhere on the floor instead, which is what I'm doing now. I like observing how everything runs without me while still being here, to get a feel for how my employees work and behave when they don't know they're being watched. It may sound creepy, but I run a tight ship around here. Since my employees are usually people I bring in off the street, I leave no room for error. I have a one strike policy. I figure after I give them food and clothes and a job, the least they can do is follow orders.

This is definitely not a democracy here. It's a dictatorship. A benevolent one, but a dictatorship, nonetheless. It's for the good of everyone and I'm only looking out for the best interest of my employees and patrons. Being the owner of an establishment like this, in the heart of New Orleans, is a responsibility I don't take lightly. When things get crazy, I shut that shit down. Come Again will never be on the ten o'clock news for a bar fight or riot. Everyone who comes here knows they can have a drink and have a good time, but this isn't fucking Bourbon.

As for my employees, I really enjoy being able to help those in need by giving them a place to work and make money, but I've learned the hard way that not everyone is as honest and hardworking as I'd like. It took me a while to be able to see the difference in someone who wants a handout in life and someone who wants to truly change their circumstances for the better. I specialize in the latter. Although I have no problem giving someone a handout, I'd much rather give them a *hand up* instead.

The crew working this evening seems to be doing well. Paulie, who was the first person I helped out years ago, turned out to be the right-hand man I never knew I needed, so I don't waste time watching him. It's my two newest employees that have my attention, Jeremy and Avery.

I've noticed Jeremy struggling from time to time but I'm trying to let it slide. I don't know all of his story but I know enough to recognize he may need a little extra time to adapt to life here. Living on the streets for as long as he has is fucking rough and you can't expect things to be perfect just because you have a roof over your head and food in your belly. With him being a user, too, I have to pay particularly close attention to his work habits. I was reluctant to hire him when I found out about his drug use because a bar isn't the best place for an addict to be, let's just be fucking honest, but he promised alcohol wasn't his poison and that this job was his only hope, so I caved and gave him a chance.

Speaking of taking chances, I watch Avery greet a customer and quickly fix his order. That girl—sorry, *lady*—really is something else.

She's a quick learner and she hustles better than any of my guys. Of course, I'm still leery about having a woman—her—working here, but she seems to be handling the job just fine.

Remembering what Sarah told me earlier today about being nicer to Avery and giving her some praise and encouragement has me groaning into my beer as I bring the bottle to my lips.

It's not that I don't like her; it's that I'm used to working with men, and men don't seem to give a shit if I'm nice to them or not, they just want to get paid. Besides Sarah, I haven't worked with a woman in a long damn time and I'm rusty, to say the least. It's my opinion that, especially considering the types of men who work here, it's just better if females remain on a customer-only basis.

Shit, am I really that much of a sexist?

Just listening to myself think has me wanting to kick my own ass.

"Hey, stranger," a sultry voice whispers in my ear. "Whatcha doin' lurking in the corner?" Slim fingers and long nails slip around my bicep and I instantly tense. "Relax, Shaw, it's just me. I won't bite...unless you want me to."

I cock my head to the side to see Brandy, a regular, licking her lips while watching me. Relaxing slightly, I turn back to my beer.

"What a charmer you are tonight," she murmurs, her tone quickly turning sarcastic.

"What can I do for you, Brandy? You having a good time?" See, I can be nice. Kinda.

"Funny you should ask, because I was hoping you could turn my good time into an even better one, if you know what I mean." Moving to my side, her hand still on my arm, she winks and it takes all my power not to roll my eyes.

Brandy and I sort of have a past and it's not one I'm proud of. I haven't had a romantic relationship in many years and I'm not interested in having one, but sometimes my hand isn't enough and my needs take over my brain. Brandy just happened to be here at the bar the first time I felt the need to get laid and well, she's been here the other times as well.

It's not that she wants more from me than I'm willing to give, but she does tend to get clingy when she drinks and I'm just not interested tonight.

"Not tonight."

"But, Shaw, baby, you know I can make you feel good. Let's go to your office so I can give you what you need." She drops her hand from my arm to my thigh, but I stop it before it reaches my dick.

"I said no. Find someone else." I stand up quickly, making Brandy teeter in her high heels, and walk away, heading to my office. *Alone.*

I'm almost to the door when I hear another female voice coming from around the corner. I take a tentative step forward and see Avery in the doorway of the storage room talking on her cell phone. Feeling stuck, because she's blocking my way into the office and I don't want to turn around and risk seeing Brandy again, I decide to stay where I am. Surely, she won't be on the phone long and when she's done, I can pretend I was simply walking to my office...which I was in the first place.

I might observe my employees, but I'm not a creeper.

"Brant," I hear her say. "It's over. We're done and that's final."

She's obviously speaking with the asshole who hit her and, although I want to respect her privacy, I'd also like to reach through her phone and fuck him up a little. No one should ever lay a hand on a woman like that. Ever.

But I'd come to the defense of any of my workers—male or female.

Avery is *just* my employee, nothing more.

I'm not sure why I have to keep reminding myself of that or justifying my thoughts. It's infuriating and probably part of the reason I'm so rude to her. She's only been around a few days and she's already under my skin, even though I'd never admit that to anyone else.

"You lost the right to know or have a say about anything pertaining to me the second you hit me." Her tone is firm and strong.

Good for her. I love, I mean, *admire* how she doesn't back down. She didn't back down to me and it's obvious she's not backing down to this Brant guy either. What a fucking douche. It's obvious she doesn't need my help, but I can't help myself, so I keep listening.

"You want your car back?" she asks with a scornful huff as she paces a few steps. With her back still to me, she tightens her free fist and mimics hitting the wall. I'm glad she doesn't really follow through because that would hurt. And then I'd be icing knuckles. I know all about fists meeting walls. "Well, I guess you'll have to find me first. Call the police, I'll happily give the car to them as soon as you send me the rest of my things from the apartment."

Her words are brave but her body language is a mix of emotions. One second, she's nearly punching walls, and now, she's back to pacing and biting at her thumb nail. When she puts her back to the wall, using it for support, I can see her eyes closing tightly and she presses her fist to her forehead, like she's summoning strength. That act alone makes me think her bravado is just that, and in reality, she's afraid of this guy.

That thought puts my whole body on high alert, sending blood pumping forcefully through my veins.

He must be giving her an ear full because she's silent as she stares at the wall in front of her.

I have a feeling this guy isn't done, and if my intuition is right, which it usually is, he'll come looking for her, but I'll be ready if he shows up at my bar. *I hope to God he shows up at my bar.* It'll be a decision he'll greatly regret, that I can promise.

"Fuck you, Brant."

And there's my cue.

When she forcefully hits the end button on her phone, I pretend like I just turned the corner.

"Shit," she gasps when she sees me. Her hand flies up to her chest and I try not to notice the way her tits move in time with her heavy breathing. I try, and I fail.

"Sorry, didn't mean to scare you," I tell her, adopting the cool tone I've come to use with her. "Didn't realize anyone was back here." *Lie.* "You okay?"

She lets out a deep breath, seeming to calm down a bit before answering. "Yeah, I'm fine. I was, uh...talking to my ex." She winces an apology, probably for talking on the phone while she should be working, but I'm not mad about that. "He was just pissing me off." She mutters that last part more to herself than me and I watch as she lets out another breath, trying to gain her composure, I'm sure.

She's not fine or okay, but she is resilient. Like looking in a mirror, I watch her fortify her walls—back straightens, chin lifts, shoulders square.

Her eyes and the way they're looking at me right now, like she's trying to figure me out, have my mouth going dry, so I clear my throat before speaking. "If he keeps bothering you or you need my help in any way, don't hesitate to ask, got it?"

Avery's big brown eyes go wide as she cocks her head at me, surprised by my statement. If I'm being honest, so am I. We stare at each other, and with each passing second, I'm feeling more and more exposed, which makes me extremely uncomfortable. And, yet, I can't seem to break this connection we seem to have.

Finally, she nods her head and softly says, "Okay. Thanks, Shaw," before stepping around me and walking back to the bar.

The second she's out of my proximity, I breathe a little easier and think a little clearer. It's a bizarre feeling I'm not used to, but as the effects of her subside, I feel rage start to bubble up within me. Five minutes alone with her in an empty hallway and I start feeling like I want to let my guard down. Well, fuck that and fuck her.

The walls are there for a reason and no one is going to bring them down, especially not Avery Cole.

7

Avery

"I TALKED TO HIM TWO DAYS AGO, MAMA," I GROAN into the phone, tired of having this same conversation with her regarding Brant and her incessant need for me to *talk it out with him*.

Part of me wants to tell her the truth so she'll back off, but some weird part is holding back. I don't know if I'm afraid she'll take his side, even though that's ludicrous. My Mama loves me and she's always only wanted what's best for me and obviously that's not Brant. But she also loves Brant. So, maybe I'm subconsciously sparing her feelings by not outing Brant for the asshole he really is. I also really hate confrontation.

Sighing, I rub my eyes. "I need to get ready for work," I tell her when she doesn't say anything.

"What are you not telling me, Avery?" she finally asks.

What's that they say about a mother's intuition? Oh, right, it makes her a fortune teller and psychic all rolled into one. Sometimes, I feel like she really does have eyes in the back of her head...and around the world, for that matter. Maybe there's a mom satellite you're only privy to once you birth a child. It gives the Big Brother conspiracy a run for its money.

"It's complicated, Mama."

"I'm a smart woman, Avery. So, how about you tell me and I'll see if I can keep up."

When the snark comes out, I know she's getting pissed. Honesty has always been our policy and she knows I'm withholding the truth, but just thinking about rehashing that night with my mama over the phone has my stomach in knots.

"Fine," she finally says with a resolved sigh. "How's everything else? You like your job? You eatin' good?"

"Everything else is good. My job is good and I'm eating three balanced meals a day." That's bullshit and she knows it, but we both know it's what she wants to hear, so I feed her the white lie and she eats it up, no pun intended.

With a laugh, she continues, "I love you, Avery. You know that?"

"I do, Mama, and I love you too."

"Call me tomorrow."

"I will. Tell Daddy I said hello and I love him too."

"Will do."

A few seconds later, the phone goes dead and I toss it onto the bed.

Looking up at the ceiling, I exhale loudly, my emotions feeling like they're in a damn spin cycle.

I woke up this morning with a nervous stomach. Ever since my conversation with Brant, I've felt on edge, unsettled. But it has nothing to do with where I am. I love this place and this city. I also love the bar I work at, despite my surly boss. But I hate that I still feel like I'm in limbo. I want to feel settled, like I'm building a life here. Another week is all I have in this house and then I'll have to find another room to rent, but I'd like to find something a little more permanent—a small apartment or some roommates. But so far, nothing affordable has come up within a reasonable distance from work.

And I'll soon be without a car, because it's not a matter of *if* but *when* Brant follows through on his threat from the other night. He'll come here and track me down if for no other reason than to make my life hell and force me to face him. I'm sure, somewhere in his twisted mind, he thinks if I see him I'll come crawling back to him. But he's so fucking wrong.

Letting out a frustrated growl, I cover my face with the pillow and force my mind to think about something else, like a place to live. That's something I can control.

I've been fortunate so far, finding a couple of rooms to rent within walking distance to the bar, which I'm grateful for. However, walking five blocks when it's late at night in New Orleans isn't my favorite thing in the world, but I've survived, so far.

What if Brant finds me walking the streets alone at night? What would happen then? Those thoughts bring me to my new contemplation: do I think the night he hit me is an isolated incident?

No.

Yes.

Maybe.

I don't know.

Could he find me?

Yes. I mean, I'm still using the cell phone he pays for. With all of today's high-tech apps, including a specific one I know he has access to that helps you track a cell phone and the person who uses it, it's child's play. My stomach drops at the thought and I chuckle at my melodramatic behavior.

Since when do I let fear guide my life? Never. That's not me.

Although, last night on my way home from work, I did hear my Mama's voice in my head. *"Don't talk to strangers, watch your surroundings, and never get into vans with no windows."*

I thought about asking one of the guys from the bar to walk me home, but I didn't want any of them to think I'm weak or can't take care of myself, especially Shaw. He still seems hell bent on proving me wrong at every turn. Knowing him, he'd probably use it against me and possibly as grounds for letting me go, deeming me a liability.

However, the other night, when I was in the hallway talking to Brant and he overheard my call, I swear something passed between us. The way he looked at me—glared, stared, whatever—it made me feel exposed, like he was examining my soul. When he offered to help me if I ever need it, I believed him. Maybe it's his lack of small talk, but when

Shaw speaks, I believe the words that come out of his mouth.

Pulling myself off the bed, I decide to get ready for work early and go over to Neutral Grounds for a coffee and something to eat. I need to clear my head and CeCe's friendly face always cheers me up.

Making the walk to Jackson Square, I'm thankful for the adrenaline that starts pumping through my veins because it masks the underlying nerves. It doesn't rid me of them completely though, because the reality of my situation is today is Saturday and I know if Brant is planning on showing up in New Orleans, it'll be today or tonight. He's too focused on the promotion he's currently in the running for to take time off work, which was why he was still trying to convince me to come back to Houston. That would make his life easy. If I went back to Houston, accepted his weak apology, he'd be able to pretend nothing happened.

But not me. I could never go back to walking on eggshells, living a lie—Brant's facade of a life. Maybe that's what I was doing all along and Fight Night, as I've come to refer to it in my mind, was a wake-up call to get the hell out of there and get on with my life?

I'm typically a very forgiving person. I tend to see the good in people and overlook their flaws. Like Brant's pride and self-centered attitude, I overlooked those things for years. I also never complained when he left his clothes by the bed, expecting me to pick up after him, along with so many other trivial things that mounted up to a big pain in my ass. I let all of that go, for the sake of love, or what I thought was love.

But the second I woke up on that floor and realized what transpired, it was over.

The switch had been flipped.

My love for him died on that floor.

Maybe it was hanging on by a thread all along.

When I think about him, the only emotions I feel are related to hurt and anger—disappointment, regret—but nothing resembling love or affection.

"Hey," CeCe greets when I walk into the coffee shop.

"Hey." I smile, thankful for the aroma that infiltrates my senses and her happy smile, distracting my busy mind. "You know you're like my favorite person in this city, right?"

"I deliver the goods," she says with a shrug. "Think of me as a legal crack dealer."

We both laugh as she goes about making me a steaming cup of coffee. Now that I'm gainfully employed, I'm back to drinking an iced espresso with two sugars and room for milk.

"So, what's new?" CeCe asks. Unlike Shaw, she's always making small talk, but she also always comes off so genuine with her interest I can't help telling her my life story.

"Ugh," I groan, topping off my to-go cup with the perfect amount of milk, making it a delicious shade of brown. "Well, my ex called and he's—"

She cuts me off by putting her hands up in the air. "Wait. This calls for cake." Walking to the cold case, she pulls out a white porcelain plate with a slice of lemon pound cake on it and sets it in front of me. "It's on the house. Really, you're doing me a favor because I need to get rid of the lemon cake so I can put out a new one today."

I smile and shake my head. "You're kinda perfect, you know that?"

Fluttering her lashes, she folds her hands under her chin and grins. "I know. I'm a catch."

"You are. So, why hasn't someone scooped you up?"

She rolls her eyes as if to say *as if.* "What with all the talk of douchey ex-boyfriends," she says with wide eyes and a sarcastic smile.

"Right," I reply with a nod, taking a healthy pull from my straw and feeling its immediate effect as the liquid gold hits my taste buds. Between the coffee and bite of lemon pound cake, which is rocking my world, I'm instantly feeling more myself. "Well, let's hope not all guys are like Brant Wilson."

"Let us pray," she jokes with a laugh, doing the sign of the cross. "So, what'd douche canoe want?" *Douche canoe* has been her name for Brant from the moment I confided in her about him a couple of weeks ago. It fits.

I sigh, setting my half-eaten cake back on the plate. "Well, he wants my car back, for starters." I frown and exhale through my nose, trying not to let the nerves back in. "But it's in his name, and in his defense, he did pay for it."

"Well, that sucks," CeCe says, wiping down the espresso machine while we talk.

I inwardly roll my eyes when I realize my thoughts turned to Shaw, again, and groan. I swear he just creeps into my thoughts without warning or permission. At least I haven't had any more sex dreams. Actually, I'm not sure if that's a good thing or a bad thing, because it was really hot.

But, I digress.

"Tell me about it," I groan, forcing Shaw out of my brain. "And the really sucky part is that I'm pretty sure he's going to show up here to get it."

CeCe stills with her back to me. "Really? You think he'd come all the way to New Orleans? What's that..." She pauses, turning around with a pensive look. "Like five hours, at least, right?"

"Yeah," I reply, biting on my lip as I let the realness of the situation sink in. Brant. In New Orleans. In all honesty, it scares the shit out of me. As much as I try to not let it, it does. "But I'm *not* going back to Houston, and I don't want to go home right now, so I guess it's the only option. He said he was going to call the cops and file a police report, but I don't see him passing up an opportunity to make the exchange face to face. Especially since he told me to come back to Houston and I told him to fuck off."

"Good for you," she says, giving me a solemn nod of solidarity. "I mean, I hate that you're going to have to face him, but good for you for standing your ground."

"I'll just be glad when it's all over." I exhale loudly and take another drink of my coffee, trying to push down the rush of nausea. "It wouldn't hurt my feelings if I never see him again...ever." I can't help but think there was a time when I thought I'd spend the rest of my life with Brant. I wanted to be *Mrs. Brant Wilson*. I even practiced writing my name, a million times—*Avery Wilson*. I thought it had a nice ring to it. It always made my stomach flip. Now, it just makes my stomach roll.

What if I had married him? I shiver at the thought.

"I don't know, Avery. I just hate that you're by yourself. The thought of you being alone with him again." CeCe voices my own worry. "Not to bring up bad memories or anything, but you looked like shit the first time you walked in here."

"I'll be fine."

CeCe's sad smile tells me she doesn't believe that any more than I do. Squeezing my hand, she says nothing, just transferring as much strength through her touch as possible.

"It'll be fine," I whisper, trying to reassure her while lying to myself.

We stand there for a few seconds, both lost in thought, until CeCe adds, "Maybe he'll decide it's not worth it and forget about it."

I can't help the sarcastic laugh that erupts, thankful for her positive attitude, but knowing it's futile. "Fat chance."

"Yeah," CeCe says with a chuckle, "wishful thinking."

A few hours later, when I show up for my shift at the bar, the nerves are back in full force, but I throw myself into work and try to forget. Fortunately, the weekends are the busiest nights at Come Again. Paulie told me that there are times when Shaw has to turn people away it gets so busy. The last thing any bar or establishment wants is to be over max capacity and get on the fire department's shit list.

"You good with this end of the bar?" Kevin asks, putting a new bottle of Southern Comfort on the shelf in front of me.

"I'm good," I tell him as I mix a simple vodka and tonic for a college-aged guy who I just carded.

With my pink hair and big brown eyes, I know I don't look old enough to card anyone. I've been told I don't look a day over twenty. But surprisingly enough, I don't get much crap for it. I guess people are used to flashing their IDs in a city like this.

"That'll be six," I tell him, slapping down a napkin, dashing it with salt, and then placing the drink down in front of him. The salt helps keep the wet glass from sticking to the napkin. It's a trick I learned from my first waitressing job back in Honey Springs.

"Keep the change," he says with a wink, passing me a ten.

One thing is for sure, tips are good here. Hopefully, they'll be good enough to get me into my own apartment in a few months. I decided earlier as I was walking around the French Quarter, waiting on my shift to start, that I'll save until I have enough for my deposits and a couple months' rent. That way, I won't be stressing over meeting my monthly bills. Until then, I'll keep finding rooms to rent that are close to the Quarter.

"Two beers," another guy says, slapping a twenty in front of me. "Whatever you've got on tap."

Taking the money, I turn and fill up two glasses with Abita Purple Haze, our best-seller. When I return with his beers and his change, my breath catches in my throat.

The hyperventilating starts a split second later.

"Eight's your change," I mumble as I absentmindedly toss the bills onto the bar and take a few steps back until I bump into the counter behind me. My thoughts are no longer on the customer or whether he took his beers or left me a tip.

I can't look up.

My eyes are glued to the scratched, weathered wood of the bar as my hands grip the edge.

Maybe he doesn't see me.

The pink hair kinda gives me away, but maybe there're so many people around the bar that he can't see me.

Thoughts of hiding, running, and turning invisible hit me so hard they paralyze me, locking me in place. Another guy leaning over the bar, snapping his fingers in my direction, is what finally brings me back to the present and out of my fear-driven trance.

"Hey, hot stuff," the blonde-haired twenty-something yells with a sleazy grin as his eyes peruse my chest like it's the menu. "Nice tits. Can I get a whiskey neat? And, uh, whatever else you might be offering."

My eyes narrow as I take a step forward, but I don't get a chance to reply because Shaw's smooth, deep voice slides over me like warm honey. "You can learn to use a little respect or get the hell outta my bar."

"What?" the guys says with a chuckle, throwing his hands in the air, his smile morphing to one of fake innocence. "Can't a guy have a little fun? I was just tryin' to make conversation with this cutie. Where'd you find her? She's nice."

Now it's obvious he's already drunk. I didn't catch that at first due to being preoccupied, but I scowl at him, throwing fire darts with my eyes and again go to defend myself, but Shaw cuts me off.

"You heard me," he says with a familiar shortness to his words and tone, making them bite. "Show some fucking respect or get the fuck outta my bar. Don't come in here and harass my employees."

When I tense, Shaw places a hand on my back and it's hot—searing—shooting electricity through my body. I'm sure he thinks it's the "nice tits" guy that's making me edgy, but he's wrong. I can handle guys like him all day long. If he'd given me a chance, I would've put him in his place myself.

But the tall guy with his blonde hair combed just perfectly, sticking out like a sore thumb in his three-piece suit, is what has me ready to bolt. He's made his way closer to the bar and I recognize the tie he's wearing. I bought it for him on Valentine's Day two years ago.

As he approaches, his blue eyes bore into mine and he glowers when his gaze slides to Shaw standing beside me.

"Avery!" His harsh use of my name causes me to stiffen even more. Flashes of the last time he said my name assault my memory—his hand making contact with my cheek, the sting and disorientation.

"Avery!"

I feel myself physically flinch when he calls out a second time. Knowing I just need to get this over with, on auto-pilot, I step away from Shaw and motion with my head for Brant to follow me to the end of the bar.

Shaw stays behind, filling a couple orders for people, but when I look back over my shoulder, I see him watching me. It's a relief, like I'm walking a tight line, but he's my safety net.

He won't let Brant hit me.

Deep breaths, Avery.

Let's get this over with.

"Avery." This time when he says my name it's a low growl and I can hear the anger over the roar of the crowd. "What the fuck are you doing here? Working in a place like this?"

"What's wrong with this place?" I ask, a bit of my boldness creeping back in as I bristle at his insult. Brant's self-righteousness is one of my least favorite characteristics. It's right up there with condescending asshole, just under abuser. "It's a bar. *You* go to places like this."

"I don't *work* at places like this and neither do you." His jaw clenches as he tries to keep his cool. The tell-tale redness creeping up his neck is the only sign I need to know that his control is slipping between his fingers.

"I do, actually. I've been working here for almost two weeks."

"Does your mama know you're working here?" he asks, cocking his head to the side with a condescending stare. "Man, I bet she'd be so proud. I bet this is exactly what she dreamed for you."

"My mama knows I work here," I tell him, hoping if I show him I'm not intimidated or hiding anything he'll go away. "What else do you have to say, Brant?"

When I go to cross my arms over my chest, his large hand clamps down on my bicep and he begins to pull me through the crowded bar. A few patrons give us speculative stares as Brant plows through them, bumping into one causing the guy to puff his chest. "What the fuck, man?"

"Excuse us," Brant mutters.

Using the distraction, I try to yank my arm back. There's no way in hell I'm leaving here with him. Just as I'm about to dig in my heels, I feel a tall, warm body come up behind me.

"Let go of her," Shaw barks, causing Brant to stop and look.

"Mind your own business," Brant snaps sharply, turning back around and continuing to pull me behind him.

"Let her go. Now." Shaw's voice is harder this time, leaving no room for argument.

Brant stops and turns with a questioning glare, like how dare Shaw talk to him that way. Stuck in the middle, I try to wiggle my arm away from Brant, but his grip is firm, squeezing so hard it feels like he's going to stop the blood flow. Then, Shaw's in my space and his hand covers Brant's.

"This is my bar and she's my employee, so it'd be wise of you to let her go and get the fuck out of here," he warns, low and guttural with a healthy dose of dangerous, like he's begging Brant to give him a reason to physically remove him.

"We have things to discuss." Brant's tone changes minutely. I know him and I know that something he sees in Shaw's glare scares him. He might be big and bad in a normal crowd of people, but he's not so big and bad when he's up against Shaw O'Sullivan. Brant's golden boy, football past doesn't mean shit to Shaw's broad shoulders and well-defined muscles.

"No, I don't think you do," Shaw tells him. "And you *really* don't have any right to put your hands on her." His dark eyes bore into Brant's and I watch as their bodies close in around me.

Brant's sardonic laugh fills the space and he shakes his head. "Oh, this is rich. Are you fucking her?" He looks at me and then at Shaw. "Is that why you came here? Are you whoring yourself out now? I wasn't good enough for you so you thought you'd what?" He shrugs backing up a little as he slowly loses his mind, spouting off ridiculous accusations. "Is he your sugar daddy, Avery? Is that what you want?"

"Brant, stop," I seethe, feeling my blood begin to boil as my face heats with embarrassment.

"How dare you come here after everything that's happened and accuse me of sleeping around? It's none of your damn business, anyway. Like I told you the other day, you lost the privilege of knowing anything about me the moment you..." The realness of the situation washes over me and I have to get it off my chest—say it, out loud. This is my chance. "You hit me! How dare you?"

When I leap for him, Shaw pulls me back and I turn on him, giving him my best death glare, feeling tears prick at my eyes but forcing them away. "Let me go," I demand.

Pulling me into his chest, his mouth is at my ear and his breath is hot against the skin on my neck. "Not happening."

"You know what," Brant huffs. "You can have her. I was done with her anyway."

"Fuck you, Brant!" I half scream, half cry the words, because that cut deep. I was always faithful to him. I loved him. I would've married him. And all he has to say right now is he was done with me? "Fuck. You."

"Where are the keys?" Shaw asks, low and quiet, calmly bringing me back from the edge of my rage, making me think.

"In my bag, behind the counter."

"Go get them," he orders and gently, but decisively places me behind him, urging me toward the bar. For a second, I stare at Shaw's back as he stands in front of Brant with his feet spread apart and his big arms folded across his chest, daring him to make a move.

Numbly, I walk to the bar and kneel behind it, pulling my keys and cell phone out of my backpack. Since he's here, I want him to have everything he can hold over my head. I want this to be the end of it.

While I'm still squatting down behind the counter, I hear a scuffle and raise up just in time to see Brant throw a punch at Shaw, or try to. His fist flies, but it's stopped mid-air, and I watch as Shaw twists Brant's arm behind his back, driving him toward the door.

People are watching, giving the two men a wide berth, and the bar falls silent with only Bon Jovi's *Livin' on a Prayer* playing on the jukebox in the background.

"Don't you ever fucking lay a hand on her again," Shaw says, his voice never raising above its normal even, sharp tone. He doesn't need to yell. The power of his words is in his expression and body language. When I see his fist tighten at his side, I run back around the corner of the bar and toward the two of them, hoping if I can just give Brant what he came for, he'll leave and we can avoid an all-out brawl.

"She deserved it."

Those words make me practically stumble over my own two feet as I pull up just short of Shaw's back. They're also the last words Brant gets a chance to say before Shaw's fist makes contact with Brant's nose.

When I finally get a glimpse of his face, a trickle of blood is the first thing I see, along with a disbelieving look. He's not used to losing, not in life, and definitely not in a fight.

I'm a little ashamed to admit how much it pleases me—seeing the red smear across his face as he wipes the back of his hand across his nose. I don't condone violence, but I, of all people, know Brant had that coming to him. My only regret is that I didn't get to deliver the blow myself.

"Avery," Shaw says calmly, turning in my direction. "Keys."

Placing them, along with the cell phone, in his hand, I breathe heavy, my eyes still wide, as everything feels a bit like an out of body experience—wild and crazy—like I'm watching a movie play out in front of me.

"Here," Shaw says, taking Brant's now bloody hand and turning it over, placing the keys and cell phone in it. "Start walking around, I'm sure you'll find the car. Eventually."

"You're so fucking stupid, Avery," Brant mutters, licking his upper lip, more than likely getting a mouth full of blood in the process. "Your ticket out of Honey Springs was me and now you've blown it. Hope you enjoy rotting in that nowhere town, because I guarantee you'll be back there and now that I'm gone, there's nothing left for you. You better get used to the idea of living a pathetic, lonely life on the farm...where you belong."

"Get out of here, Brant," I tell him, my words losing their fury as he uses my fears against me, spewing words spoken to him in confidence, thinking I was entrusting them to someone who cared about me. "Don't come back."

With one last look, he stuffs the phone and keys in his pocket. Just when I think it's over and he's going to leave without any more of a scene, he solidifies his title of Dick Head of the Year by leaning over to a nearby table and taking some guy's beer. I watch with wide eyes as he chugs it and then slams the empty glass back on the table. Swiping a stack of napkins, he wipes the blood from his nose and tosses them to the ground before throwing open the door and practically knocking over a group of people coming into the bar. They watch him with rapt confusion, wondering what they missed.

The last thing I see of Brant is his retreating form flipping everyone the bird as he storms off down the sidewalk.

"Fucking asshole," Shaw mutters under his breath. "You okay?" The question is for me, but he's giving everyone around us a furtive glance, silently telling them to mind their own business.

"I'm fine," I tell him, suddenly feeling completely drained, but also relieved. Giving a few people an apologetic smile, I allow Shaw to direct me back to the bar.

"Paulie," Shaw yells over the crowd. "Get this guy a beer." He points over his shoulder to the guy by the door who's a beer short thanks to Brant. "Sorry about that." Fortunately, the guy seems fairly good-natured about the whole ordeal, probably enough beers in that he's feeling no pain.

After a few seconds, chatter picks up around us and the bar goes back to a steady buzz.

"You good to work?" Shaw asks quietly as we step behind the bar.

"Yeah, I'm good." I need the distraction and there's no way in hell I'm leaving right now. My luck, Brant would be out there waiting on me. No telling how long it'll take him to find the car.

When Shaw steps back out into the crowd, leaving me to my job, Jeremy and Paulie both give me a tentative smile, but thankfully let everything go. We all go back to the comfortable rhythm of filling drink orders, allowing me a chance to release the pent-up breath I've been holding since Brant walked through the door.

He's gone.

He has his fucking car.

And his fucking phone.

I have neither, but that's okay.

I'd rather be penniless than owe him single damn thing.

The rest of the night flies by in typical fashion—a few spilled beers and a drunk customer who's cut off and given a cup of coffee. Fortunately, nothing rivals the scene with Brant, but I'm left wondering where he's at. Did he find the car? Will that be enough for him?

I hope so.

Paulie and I tag team the front of the bar, wiping down every surface and putting all the barstools and chairs up on the tables so Jeremy and Kevin can sweep and mop the place. Shaw's been MIA since Brant left. For all I know, he went home. It's not like he has to stick around here. Paulie could run this place in a heartbeat.

"I'll wash the glasses," I tell Paulie, taking the full crate of dirties and walking toward the hallway.

"Why don't you go," Paulie urges. "I'll get one of the knuckleheads to wash them when they're finished with the floors."

"Nah, I don't mind."

"You're a good worker," Paulie says with a smile. "I know Shaw doesn't give out many compliments, but just know, you're fitting in nicely around here."

"Thanks, Paulie." I give him a genuine smile, the first I've felt like giving all night. He doesn't know how badly I needed to hear something like that.

On my way to the kitchen, I pass Shaw's office and notice the door ajar. Glancing back over my shoulder, I see Paulie went back out front, so I indulge my curiosity and look inside. My breath hitches when I peek around and see Shaw at the desk. His head is bent as he works on something, concentration drawing his brows together. A weird feeling floods my chest as I watch him. It's like warmth and goodness, which is crazy because Shaw is neither of those things.

Clearing my throat, I get his attention, although it's a slow movement and I wonder if Shaw is ever startled or scared? Does someone like him even truly know the definition? Something about his hard demeanor makes me think he's immune to weak feelings like fear and panic.

"Need something?" he asks, setting his pen down on the desk and leaning back in his chair, folding his big arms behind his head. My eyes trace the tattoos and I have to force myself to look him in the eyes.

"Uh, just wanted to say thank you for...helping me."

Our eyes lock and Shaw holds my gaze for an elongated moment, making me feel apprehensive and fidgety. If it weren't for the large crate of dirty glasses I'm holding, I'd probably be chewing on my thumb nail, but I can't, so I clear my throat again.

"You're gonna stay at the apartment tonight," he declares, relaxing his arms and picking the pen back up like we just had a long, drawn out conversation and it came to a close.

"Uh," I start, but I'm unsure how to finish.

"As soon as you're finished with the glasses, come back to my office and I'll show you up."

"Up?" I ask, dumbly, because I'm having a hard time following him.

"Yes, Avery. Up." He cocks his head to the side and I have to swallow hard because of the extra moisture in my mouth. What the hell? What is wrong with me? "The apartment is up." He points a finger up to the ceiling and it puts those damn tattoos on display again.

In all honesty, I've never been one of those girls who's crazy about every hot guy who crosses her path. That's not me. Maybe it's because I was Brant's girl for so long, as long as I've been allowed to have a boyfriend. But even before then, I don't remember feeling all swoony over guys. I didn't plaster my bedroom walls with posters. I wasn't a boy band groupie. I didn't even like Twilight, so there was never a question of Team Edward or Team Jacob. Sure, I notice when a guy is handsome, but that's usually where it ends. But not with Shaw and for the life of me, I can't make sense of it.

"Why?" I finally ask, readjusting the crate to sit on my hip a little so I can give my arms a break.

"I think we both know there's a very good chance that asshole is still in the city. I'm not letting you go home and get ambushed. Not on my watch," he says, his attention leaving me and going back to the paper in front of him.

My mouth drops open at his high-handedness, but I can't offer a rebuttal because he's right. I hadn't allowed myself to think much past my next task, but now that he's mentioned it, going home, alone, is the last thing I want. Being alone with Brant doesn't sit well with me at all and the thought leaves me feeling nauseated. That might also be my lack of dinner and all of the adrenaline that's been pumping through my veins.

"You okay?" I hear his question before I realize he's out of his chair and walking toward me.

"Yeah, fine," I tell him, taking a deep breath to try and calm the resurgence of unease.

"How about I get one of the guys to finish these," he says, taking the crate from me. "I'll show you up to the apartment and let you get some rest."

"Okay." The fight in me is gone so I let him. Standing in the hallway, I lean against the wall and try take deep cleansing breaths. Now is not the time to lose my shit. It's over. If I was going to freak out, it should've been when Brant showed up...or maybe when he decided I was his own personal punching bag. But not now. Now is the time to suck it up and get on with life.

"Everything'll look better in the morning." I hear my Mama's voice in my head.

Right, Mama. It'll look better in the morning. And Brant will be long gone, on his way back to Houston.

"Ready?" Shaw asks, holding out my backpack to me.

"Yeah."

"I'll call Sarah and ask her if there's any food left from her class tonight. I'm sure there are a few cans of soup upstairs, but you look like you could use something more substantial."

"Soup is fine. It's what I eat every night."

Shaw stops and turns to look at me and it's like it's the first time he's really, truly seeing me. A wall he normally has up is down for a split second and I see him too. He genuinely cares about people. If he didn't, he wouldn't help those guys back in the bar and he wouldn't have stood up to Brant. He also wouldn't be letting me stay at his apartment tonight.

"Thank you," I say quickly, breaking the connection, letting the moment pass. "For everything."

"You're not walking home by yourself anymore either." His words come out unemotional and steady, just like always, like he's offering them in passing.

"I—" I start to say *I'm fine*—my go-to response lately—but he cuts me off.

"It's not up for debate. You shouldn't be walking home alone. I should've thought about that before now."

He opens the door at the end of the hallway and we step out into the blackness of the night. When I see him turn toward me, I back up against the door out of...habit? Fear? I don't know, but it doesn't settle well with Shaw.

"Don't do that," he demands.

"What?" I ask, licking my lips and swallowing hard, trying to keep my voice even like his.

"Act like you're scared of me. You don't have to be afraid of me."

I laugh a little, because it sounds preposterous. Both the way he said the words, in a gruff tone—making his delivery an oxymoron to his statement—and the idea. "I'm not scared of you."

"Why did you just back up like that? Why do you look at me with wide eyes all the time?"

"I don't...didn't...I'm just." I want to say *flustered, unnerved...you ruffle my feathers, Shaw*...but none of that comes out. Instead, I say, "I'm not scared of you."

"Good."

He turns for the set of stairs next to the door taking them two at a time. Since I'm shorter, it takes me a few more seconds to climb the stairs and by the time I get to the top, Shaw is waiting on me like he's been there for hours. With a huff, he sticks a key into the lock and turns it, opening the door wide for me to step in ahead of him.

"It's not much, but there's a bed," he says, walking over by the window and turning on a lamp that illuminates the rest of the small studio apartment. "And there's a bathroom, microwave, fridge, coffee pot." He turns in a circle as he points out all the necessities. "There should be staples in the cabinet and fridge. Sarah keeps the place pretty stocked."

"Who lives here?"

"No one."

"Then why's it so..."

"Some of the guys who come through need a place to sleep for a night or two until I can find them a more permanent place." He sighs and then absentmindedly, without intention, mutters, "And I used to stay here from time to time."

"It's nice," I reply, liking this more open Shaw too much to push for more than he wants to give me.

"There might be some clothes that'll fit you, if you want to shower."

"That'd be great." The thought of a hot shower sounds like bliss right now. I'd love nothing more than to wash away this day.

"I'll, uh, leave you to it, then." Shaw sort of stammers and it's the first time I've ever seen him act like he's unsure of his next move. "I'll, uh...go check and see what's left over from class tonight."

My eyes go wide at the thought of being here all alone and I bite down on my bottom lip to keep from voicing my fears. But I'm sure it's safe. Shaw wouldn't insist I stay here if it wasn't.

"I'll be back," he assures, like he's reading my thoughts. "Bring you something good to eat and make sure you're locked in for the night."

"Okay." I swallow and offer him a small smile, staying glued to the spot on the floor until he closes the door behind him. Once he's gone, I really allow myself to look around. There's a weight bench in one corner with lots of heavy looking dumbbells. Next to that is one of those punching balls that hang from the ceiling. The source of Shaw's muscles, I'm assuming, and this makes my brain take a detour straight to the gutter.

Shaw, sweaty and spent, grunting as he lifts the heavy weights.

Shaw, dripping wet, punching the bag as his muscles coil tightly under his inked skin.

Shaw laying on the bed, naked.

I clear my throat roughly and shake my head. "Get a freakin' grip, Avery," I mutter to myself, setting my backpack by the open door of the bathroom. Well, actually, there's no door to the bathroom. That's interesting, but I guess unnecessary, since people are usually here by themselves.

Or are they?

Does Shaw bring women here?

"Stop," I growl at myself, stomping over to the small chest of drawers by the bed. Pulling the first drawer open, I find a stack of white t-shirts in varying sizes. Picking the smallest one, I go to the next drawer and find men's underwear and boxers, opting for the boxers. Since I'm nosey, I open the other drawer and find jeans and socks.

Interesting.

Seeing all of this for myself makes my heart feel so...I don't know... full? I love people and I love helping them. I always have. The fact that Shaw goes to this extent to care for people who everyone else has discarded makes me feel good. It makes me feel good about Shaw.

I've always been an *action speaks louder than words* kind of person, and Shaw's actions definitely speak loud. He might seem rough and menacing on the outside. His words might come out harsh and bite like a rattlesnake. But his actions...they aren't loud and boisterous, but they are kind and good. He stands up for people who can't stand up for themselves and it makes my heart feel kind of gooey where he's concerned.

Of course, I won't tell him that.

Gathering up my clean t-shirt and boxers, I head for the shower. Hesitantly, I turn on the water and look around the empty apartment before I shed my clothes. Feeling exposed, I quickly jump in the shower like it's going to hide my naked body when in reality there's only a sheer curtain hiding me from the rest of the apartment. I start out fast, finding the shampoo and lathering it in my hair, but somewhere between the conditioner and body wash, which all smells manly, I lose myself to the steam and hot water.

When I hear a thud, I let out a muffled scream and quickly rinse my hair and turn the water off, hiding behind the sheer piece of fabric as I peek out into the apartment. "Hello?"

No response.

My heart is nearly beating out of my chest when I reach over for a towel stacked beside the shower. Wrapping it around my body, I step out of the bathroom and call out again, "hello?"

There's no one there, but I swear I heard something, so I quickly dry off and dress. Just as I'm tossing my hair up in the towel, I hear a knock, followed by Shaw's voice. "Knock, knock."

"Shaw?"

"Yeah, hey," he says, walking in with a to-go box of something that smells amazing.

"Were you just here?"

"Uh, no...I." He pauses, once again sounding flustered and my gut tells me he was here, but he doesn't want to admit it. And then my cheeks flush as I think about what he might've seen when he says, "I just came in."

"Okay." I give him a small, nervous smile and hope my blush isn't giving me away. I mean, what's to be embarrassed about, right? I'm sure if he did see me naked...in the shower...it's nothing he hasn't seen before.

Nope, nothing to see here.

It's just me.

"Hope you're hungry," he continues, obviously wanting to change the subject as much as I do. "Sarah had leftovers. Good ones."

I laugh lightly, folding the waistband of the boxers over a couple times to make sure they stay up. Shaw's eyes follow my movements and now it's his turn to swallow. Hard. Like, visible enough I watch as his Adam's apple bobs. It's hot.

Shit.

"Uh, aren't all of her dishes good?" I ask, searching for safe, neutral territory that won't make me feel like I'm burning alive from the inside out.

"Sure," Shaw says with a shrug. "But some are better than others. I'm not a fan of chicken, so those I could take or leave. But shrimp." His eyebrows dance above his dark eyes and for a split second, I think I'm going to get to see Shaw smile, but then his face changes back to the hard lines it's used to wearing.

"I love shrimp."

"Good, then you'll love this shrimp étouffée."

He's right. I loved it. I loved it so much that I forgot about the events of the day. I forgot I was embarrassed that Shaw might've seen me naked in the shower. I might've even forgot my manners as I moaned my way through the dish.

"Oh my God," I say when I finally push it away. "That was amazing. Tell Sarah I said thank you and compliments to the chef."

Shaw's eyes are on me and like always, his intense gaze makes me feel nervous. "I'll tell her." His words are gruff and his features are hard, but what's new. I'm learning to not let the hardness of his outer expression affect me. "How about you tell me something about yourself?"

It's a question, but I can't tell if it's accusatory or curious, so I play it safe. "What would you like to know?"

"You're from Oklahoma...Honey Springs," he offers.

I nod.

"And you were living in Houston before you came here?"

I nod again.

"What made you want to come to New Orleans?"

I think about it for a moment, not my reasons for coming here but how much of it to tell him and decide that he's already seen me at my worse and I have nothing to hide. "When I woke up, the morning after Brant..."

"Hit you," he offers an extra layer of hardness to his tone.

"Right. After he hit me, I passed out...or he knocked me out. All of that is kind of fuzzy. But when I woke up, I just knew I had to get out of there. I didn't want to be around when he woke up. It was like a fight-or-flight moment and I decided to fly." I shrug, pulling my feet up into the chair and hugging my legs to my chest. "I stopped for coffee shortly after leaving the apartment and considered my options. New Orleans was a place I'd always wanted to visit and never had the chance, so I took it. Plus, when I thought about it, it made me feel happy and alive. That's what I want to feel. Every day."

It's Shaw's turn to nod his head as he continues to watch me with a thoughtful look on his face. "I'm sure New Orleans is a far cry from Honey Springs."

I let out a laugh and smile, just thinking about the small town and the farm I grew up on. "You could say that."

"You like big cities?" he asks.

"I like this big city. Houston seemed like too much concrete and busy streets. I love it here, though. I love the culture and richness of the history, food, people, colors. Something about it just calls to my soul."

"Your soul, huh?" Shaw leans back in his chair and rubs a hand over his short beard.

"Yeah," I reply softly, feeling a bit like I'm being interrogated, but also like he's genuinely interested.

"You like people."

"I *love* people," I correct.

He nods his head again and I almost expect him to admit he does too, but that's not Shaw. He's not one to put himself out on the line like that, so the nod is all I'm going to get.

"What else do you love?" he asks, catching me a bit off guard with the softness in his tone.

"Uh," I pause, swallowing. "Well, I love sunrises and sunsets," I tell him with a small smile. "I also love 80's hair bands, my Mama's meatloaf, December 26th, and riding on the back of a motorcycle." They're all random responses, but the first things that come to my mind, so I just let them all tumble out of my mouth, hoping he doesn't make me regret it.

The raise of his eyebrow tells me I might've mentioned something he also loves and I wonder if he'll tell me or continue to be stingy with information about himself. "You love motorcycles?"

I nod. "Yeah, well, I love riding dirt bikes and four-wheelers. Oklahoma girl, remember?" I smile almost expecting one back from him, but then remember who I'm talking to and continue, "my Daddy and Grandpa always fixed up old motorcycles, mainly Harley Davidsons. We had a few out on the farm and occasionally, I'd get to go for a ride."

"I have a motorcycle," he replies, his face losing a bit of the hardness as he continues. "1995 Fat Boy."

"That's the year I was born."

Shaw gives me his typical huff. It's not a laugh because his mouth doesn't curve up at all, but it's his way of telling me I've said something he finds ridiculous. "Of course it is."

"I'd love to see it...your motorcycle," I tell him, hoping our conversation doesn't end here.

"You should go to sleep."

"We don't work tomorrow," I counter, not liking him telling me what I should and shouldn't do. I'm a grown ass adult.

"Well, I'm sure you have things to do...on your day off."

"Oh, yeah, I'm just loaded. So many social engagements and errands to run." I roll my eyes and huff as I stand from the chair and walk over to the bed. "I've answered a lot of questions about myself, maybe you could tell me something about you."

"Like what?"

I shrug, sitting on the side of the low bed. "I don't know. Anything."

"Why do you like December 26th?" he asks, standing from the chair he was sitting in and moving over to the weight bench which is closer to the bed.

"I said something about yourself, not more questions about me."

"Well, that's a weird thing to say, so I want to know why."

"Because my family is always together and we never have anywhere to go or anything to do. My mama makes breakfast and we watch movies all day. So, it's my favorite."

"My parents immigrated here from Ireland in 1960."

My eyes grow wide. "Like here, to New Orleans?"

"Well, they lived in New York for a while, but then they traveled south, looking for warmer weather and cheaper living."

"They found the warmer weather, that's for sure. I swear some days I sweat so much I feel like I'm going to die from dehydration."

Shaw dips his chin to his chest and I'm afraid I've said something wrong, but then he says, "Yeah, my brother always says we're being conditioned for hell."

"How many brothers and sisters do you have?"

"Three brothers and one sister."

"Are they older or younger?" I ask, keeping him on a roll while he's actually answering my questions.

"Older. I'm the youngest and then Sarah, she's ten years older than me. I was a mistake. None of them let me forget that. Then, there's Shane, Shannon, and Sean."

"Holy crap, your mother was trying to torture herself with all of those names starting with the same syllable."

"Yeah, it was interesting when we were younger, although most of them were out of the house by the time I came around." He shifts on the bench and I almost offer him a spot on the bed, but then think better of it. I like talking to him and I don't want to do anything that'll send him running. "Do you have siblings?"

"Nope, just me," I reply with a shake of my head. "My parents tried for years to get pregnant. They finally had me when my mama was forty-two. They tried again a year later, but lost the baby. So, I'm it."

When I yawn, Shaw goes to stand.

"I should get going and let you sleep."

In a moment of weakness, and maybe from feeling so comfortable after our talk, I ask, "Could you stay? Please."

He continues to stand, but he doesn't move for the door. "I don't think that's a good idea."

"Sure, right." I move up the bed and crawl under the warm, but soft blanket. "Thanks for letting me stay here tonight and for the food. I really appreciate it," I say on another yawn. With my back to Shaw, I expect to hear the door open and close, but it never does. Smiling to myself when I hear him settle in the chair on the opposite side of the room, I close my eyes and let sleep take over.

8

Shaw

I SHOULD LEAVE.

But for some reason, unbeknownst to me, I can't.

The second Avery asked me to stay, my feet felt like cement, so here I sit in this chair staring at her back as she sleeps. I know she's asleep because a few minutes ago, I started hearing a small, soft snore coming from the vicinity of the bed.

Today was a rough day for her, but I can't help and think she's had a lot of rough days in her recent past. The only thing that makes me feel a little better is the fact I got to punch that asshole ex-boyfriend of hers. Man, what a fucking dick head. So pretentious and self-righteous, nothing like Avery, or at least not the Avery I've gotten to know over the last couple of weeks.

She seems grounded, aware of her surroundings, considerate. I've noticed the way she treats people, even though I've tried my damndest not to. I'm an observer. It's what I do. So, catching Avery picking up the slack for Kevin or Jeremy, seeing her take a job off Paulie's hands, and watching her be kind and generous with customers...it speaks volumes about who she is as a person.

When she first walked into my bar, I thought she was a kid looking for a fast paycheck.

But she's no kid.

That was made obvious tonight when I forgot who I was dealing with, used to taking care of guys, and barged back into the apartment unannounced.

Closing in the shower is now a top priority on the apartment renovation list.

No matter how hard I tried not to look, my natural curiosity and desire took over. I didn't look long, not enough for her to notice me or for me to feel like a creep, but it was long enough.

Her petite frame is made up of perfectly proportioned curves in all the right places. Nothing about what I saw behind that shower curtain was a girl.

Luscious tits.

Round ass.

Supple hips.

All the things that get me hard.

Fuck. I let out a quiet groan, trying to alleviate the mounting pressure in my cock. Glancing over at the bed, making sure Avery is still asleep, I immediately regret it because the only thing I can think about doing right now is walking over there, ridding her of that flimsy ass t-shirt and those barely-there boxers, and pushing deep inside her.

"Fuck."

I gotta get out of here. I know she's probably scared and feeling alone, not just in this unfamiliar apartment, but in this city. But I can't. I can't stay here and watch her sleep and not lose my mind or my resolve.

I don't do this shit.

I don't sleep with employees.

I mean, obviously, I typically only employ men and I'm not into dudes. But more than that, I don't sleep with people I have feelings for and as bad as I don't want to have feelings for Avery Cole, as much as I've tried to reinforce every blockade I've spent years building, she's somehow found a way to seep through the cracks.

Unemotional, detached sex.

That's the only thing I allow myself to have, like the sex I have with

Brandy from time to time. I don't give two shits what happens to her. If we fucked tonight and I never saw her again, it wouldn't bother me. She's too clingy, too whiny, too needy. Her fake tits and fake fingernails drive me crazy. But she's a warm, willing body who just so happened to be around the night I caved and gave in to my dick.

That's it.

I think she knows it.

I'm pretty sure she uses me as much as I use her.

The only mention of something more came on our second time fucking. We were in my office and she asked me what I wanted. I told her, honestly, concisely—a warm pussy. She quirked an eyebrow and gave her head a nod, like she was glad we had that discussion. I thought I might never see her again, but I was wrong. A month or so later, she came knocking again. And I fucked her again. Never in a bed, always in my office...the storage room...against the wall in the hallway.

And none of this is helping my painful erection.

Standing from the chair, I pace quietly, or as quietly as I can in this creaky, old apartment. Normally, when I have built-up tension and a hard-on that won't stop, I come up here and work out until I'm so physically spent, I can't even rub one out. But that won't be happening tonight.

Avery's pale pink hair is almost dry now and it has a natural wave to it, so light it almost fades into the white sheets. I almost take a step toward the bed, but stop myself.

What the fuck are you doing, Shaw?

You've done enough.

She's safe and fed.

The big bad wolf is gone.

Step away.

I remind myself once again that the walls are here to stay. I've made it this long without anyone even coming close to breaching them.

Avery Cole poses no threat.

Not if I don't let her.

Turning on my heels I walk to the door and open it quietly, stepping out into the still, humid—even in the middle of fucking October—night air. I pause for a brief moment at the top of the stairs, inhaling deeply. Now that I'm not staring at Avery's sleeping body, I feel like I can finally breathe. Pulling the keys to the apartment from my pocket, I lock the door behind me and make my way down the stairs, stopping halfway down.

"Hey," I call out, the normal gruffness in my tone a bit extra as my hackles raise minutely. A motionless mass at the bottom of the stairs has me firing on all cylinders. I'm used to people sleeping in the alley behind the bar. It's how most of the men who work for me ended up here, but with Avery sleeping in the apartment, I feel an unusual sense of trepidation.

Also, I wouldn't put it past that asshole ex-boyfriend to show back up here.

"Hey." This time, the mass moves and slowly shifts toward the sound of my voice.

"Sorry, man." The guy sounds like he's smoked a carton of cigarettes every day of his life and has a case of walking pneumonia on top of that. "Someone said this'd be a safe place to sleep for the night. Don't mean no harm."

"It's fine," I tell him, taking the last half of the steps quickly, but quietly, because I don't want to wake Avery. Normally, I'd let someone like this stay upstairs for the night until I can get things squared away. I have contacts in shelters and halfway houses around the city, people who will help me place someone in a temporary location until they get back on their feet.

But I can't let him up there tonight and I also can't take the chance of him still being here in the morning when Avery wakes up. It might scare the shit out of her to see me gone and some strange man sleeping at the bottom of the stairs.

"Come with me," I bark.

Just because I do nice things, doesn't mean I'm nice about it. And really, the asshole behavior isn't on purpose. I just can't help it. Call me jaded or cynical, but I treat everyone that comes in my backdoor as the worst criminal and drug addict until I can get a good read on them. I've been burnt one too many times.

I don't look back, but I hear the man following me through the backdoor of the bar. "Shut it behind you," I order, flipping on a couple lights as I go. "You can sleep in here." I motion to the storage room. "There's a bedroll and pillow behind the back shelves. I take inventory every fucking day, so don't even think about stealing my shit, especially the booze. If you're hungry, I'll find you something to eat."

Turning for the door, I call out over my shoulder. "I'll be next door in my office."

Thankfully, I have a futon that pulls out into a bed, if you want to call it that, just for nights like this or late nights at the bar...or nights when I don't want to go home to an empty house.

Walking into my office, I flip off the overhead light and kick out the futon. It's a fucking brick to sleep on, but it'll do. I use a jacket as a pillow and lay back, thankful for the distraction of the guy sleeping next door, because at least I'm not thinking about the girl—*woman*—sleeping upstairs.

Somehow, I manage a few restless hours of sleep—enough to make me functional, but not enough to put me in a good mood. When I wake, the sounds of snoring and heavy breathing from the storage room give me a small sense of peace knowing he's still here. Groaning when I sit, I massage my lower back, desperately in need of a run to stretch my muscles. As much as I hate to admit it, I'm not as young as I once was and my body reminds me of it when I do stupid shit, like sleep on futons.

As I make my way down the hall, I peek inside to make sure everything is intact in the storage room. Outside of the snoring fuck on my floor, everything is just as it should be, so I continue the trek to the bar for some much-needed coffee. While I'm scooping the grounds, thankful for the immediate boost from the aroma alone, I briefly wonder if Avery would like some.

And if I should take her a cup.

But then I mentally kick myself in the dick for even letting myself go there.

No. I'm going to give her time to get up and get the hell out of the apartment, find this guy a place to stay, and then get on with my normal weekend routine. I need my Sundays and Mondays like the Saints need another Super Bowl ring. The respite is vital to my mental well-being. Usually, I don't even cross Canal Street until Tuesday morning. The Garden District is where I live, and all of my favorite places to eat are there. Distinct separation from the bar and the whole busy, touristy vibe of the French Quarter is what keeps me sane.

Once I've given the guy, whose name is Charlie, a cup of coffee and a stale donut leftover from what Sarah brought the day before, I send him on his way, with strict orders to check in at Charity House and to come back and see me on Tuesday. I don't really need another employee or mouth to feed right now, but I also can't turn the guy away.

He can wash dishes and take out the trash. I'll move Jeremy up to the bar. He should be happy about that, since it's where Avery is and he can't keep his fucking eyes off her.

Just the thought has my blood boiling, so instead of taking my bike that's parked in my makeshift shed out back, I decide to jog home. The fresh air, thanks to the streets being hosed down from the night before, is just what I need to clear my head. Paired with the burn of my muscles and lungs, I feel alive, and try not to let the guilt that feeling brings ruin my semi-good mood.

Opening the back door of my house, I look around at the large kitchen, bathed in early morning sunlight, and swallow down the familiar pang.

This is the kind of house you raise a family in, where people grow old together, not for a guy like me. But I can't let myself dwell on thoughts like that because they only lead to drinking too much and wasting my days away in dark rooms.

After a quick shower and change of clothes, I'm back out the door for some much-needed brunch and coffee at The Crescent Moon. For as long as I can remember, I've spent my Sundays, and occasionally Mondays, at the café on the corner just a few blocks from my house.

It's a perfect spot—never too crowded, but steadily busy. The food is great. The atmosphere is low-key. The employees are friends. Wyatt, the owner, is probably the closest thing I have to a friend outside of the bar and my family. We don't speak much, but we can at least commiserate over owning a business in a city like New Orleans. We've both been here through good and bad times—hurricanes, Super Bowls, financial highs and lows...and other things which I'd rather not dwell on at the moment.

When I walk in, I tip my head at Wyatt and walk to my table. That's right, *my* table. It doesn't have my name on it or anything, but everyone who works here knows better than to seat someone at this table between the hours of nine and eleven on Sunday mornings.

It's like my reserved pew at church.

It kinda is like my church, now that I think about it. I come here for solitude and to feed my soul.

Before my coffee can even be served, my service is interrupted in the most unexpected way.

"Hey, Wyatt," a familiar voice says causing me to lift my gaze to the door. Avery walks in and Wyatt actually goes to her, kissing her on the cheek, like their old friends.

What the fuck?

Why is she here?

Why is he touching her?

Why the fuck do I care?

Audibly growling my displeasure, I put my head back down and try to go back to my solitude and ignore the immediate sense of outrage at Avery Cole interrupting my morning. The audacity, after I gave her a safe place to stay last night, she has the nerve to show up here?

My eyebrows are pulled so tightly together it's causing my head to hurt, so I try to relax them and turn my attention to the newspaper I carried in with me. Other people's troubles should do the trick of distracting me from my own, and maybe, if I'm lucky, she'll eat and leave just as quickly as she breezed through the door.

"Shaw."

The way she says my name, in her sweet Oklahoma drawl, makes my heart beat faster and I have no choice but to look up and acknowledge her, even though I don't want to. Turning my head and schooling my features, I snap out, "Avery."

Hers doesn't sound nearly as sweet coming from my mouth. Actually, it sounds more like a curse word and I meet her eyes just in time to see them squint in displeasure and confusion. I'm sure, after our heart-to-heart last night, she probably assumes we're friends or something akin to that. However, I have news for her, my walls are firmly secured and I have no intentions of having any type of relationship with her, friendship included.

She's my employee and I'm her boss.

That's it.

"Just wanted to say thanks again for last night. I know hiring me and letting me work at the bar is out of your comfort zone, so I appreciate you making an exception." She pauses and my scowl deepens with her mentioning my comfort zone. She doesn't know shit about my comfort zone. "Anyway, thanks. I mean it. I appreciate you sticking up for me with Brant and giving me a safe place to stay last night. When I got back to the house where I'm staying...for now..." Another pause and a shift of her feet makes me wonder if something happened. Fortunately, she saves me from being forced to ask and continues. "The car was gone...so, I'm assuming Brant is too."

"Good."

I think she's going to ask to sit or continue to talk, but she just clears her throat and says, "Yeah, good."

Then she turns to leave, but I forgot about something that's been bothering me since last night and I betray my resolve by barking out, "You need a cell phone."

A girl like Avery—young, pretty...fuck that, beautiful—doesn't have any business walking the streets of New Orleans without a cell phone.

She reaches into her backpack and pulls out a small black device, shaking it in the air. "Got one this morning after I left the apartment."

"Good," I say again, turning my attention back to my newspaper.

Without another word, she walks to a table by one of the large windows and takes a seat. Inconspicuously, I watch her...biting her lip, glancing around the entire café, but never letting her eyes land on me. Then, Tripp, one of the waiters walks up to her and her entire face lights up with a big, generous smile. It makes her big brown eyes squint and I notice for the first time that she has a small dimple at the top of her left cheek, right under her eye. When she laughs at something Tripp says, I force my eyes back to the newspaper and make myself appear interested in the bullshit comings and goings of this great city until my coffee shows up and I have something else to distract me.

This is a free country, a free city...free restaurant...anyone can come here, so why am I so pissed off that Avery found this place? It's a great place. It's one of those places where you want everyone to know about it, but you also don't want them to corrupt it and make it something it's not. Not that Avery could ever corrupt anything. She's good. She's a good person, which is why I'm going to continue to make sure my dick doesn't get confused and make a mistake that the rest of me would regret.

9

Avery

"I MADE TWO HUNDRED AND SEVEN DOLLARS IN TIPS
tonight," I exclaim, hopping up on the bar beside Jeremy. Since Charlie,
the new guy, started last week, Jeremy has been promoted to the bar
and it's given us more time to get to know each other. He's a nice guy.
A little rough around the edges, but nice...sweet. He's someone I could
see myself being good friends with. I'm not stupid though, and I know
he still battles with addiction, so I keep it platonic.

"It's those Come Agains I taught you how to make," Paulie chimes
in as he passes by us, setting a few of the barstools back down on the
floor.

The mention of the house drink has me scowling at the corner
where Shaw is sitting, slowly sipping a beer. He's been sitting there
practically all night, scoping out the place like he works for the FBI or
something. I can't believe I've worked here nearly a month and was just
now informed the bar is actually named after a drink. All this time, I
assumed it was a playoff of the parting greeting...*y'all, come again.* But
nope, it's named after a drink that, according to Paulie, has made the
ladies very happy over the years.

Earlier in the evening, someone ordered it and I couldn't
understand what they were saying over the roar of the bar. I thought

they'd asked if this was Come Again, to which I replied loudly, "Yes, this is Come Again." I'm sure the look on my face was like, *duh, didn't you read the sign outside?*

Paulie had stepped in and made the lady her drink, sending a wink over his shoulder in the process.

"Can't believe the boss hired you without teaching you to make the drink," he adds, shaking his head in Shaw's direction.

"He didn't think I'd be around long enough to make it," I shoot back. Over the past week, I've started to feel more and more like my old self. Thoughts of Brant have dwindled down to practically zero. My job has been going well. The tips have been good. *Life* is good. And I can feel the weight of the world slowly easing up off my shoulders.

"Let's go to Bourbon Street," I announce to anybody and everybody. "First round of drinks are on me and my two hundred and seven dollars." Waving the money in the air, I get a chuckle from Paulie and an interested tilt from Jeremy's head. Shaw on the other hand, grunts his displeasure from the corner.

"It's after one in the morning," he says in his typical gruff, even tone. "Everyone there is already three sheets to the wind. It's a bad idea."

"Great idea," I counter, hopping down and grabbing my backpack. "I'm twenty-three and I've been in New Orleans, Sin City of the South, for a solid month and the only time I've been to Bourbon Street was when I was looking for employment, during the day."

"I'll go," Jeremy says, tossing his bar towel on the counter. "I'm not much of a drinker, but I'll come along for the entertainment."

"Yes, Jeremy," I say, pointing to him from across the bar. "That's what I like to hear. We'll go, have a couple drinks, walk the disgusting streets, and maybe sing along to a few bad renditions of 80's hair bands. Then I can at least say I've been to Bourbon."

He smiles, shaking his head at me, but follows me toward the door. "Well, I guess we're going to Bourbon," he calls back, bowing as we leave the bar. I don't miss the furious look on Shaw's face, but I disregard it because he's made it perfectly clear we only have one connection—

he's my boss and I'm his employee. Besides, along with my new sense of self, I've realized that for the first time in all my life, I don't have to answer to anyone—not Brant or my parents, definitely not Shaw O'Sullivan. I'm free, and damn it, I'm going to start living like it.

"So, where should we start?" I ask Jeremy as we make our way across Jackson Square. He shrugs and I can feel him watching me as we walk. "Is this okay?" I stop for a second, realizing that maybe I'm putting him in a bad spot. I know he said alcohol isn't his drug of choice, but I would never want to be that friend—the enabler.

"Yeah, it's great," he replies and that's when I feel it. That long-forgotten knowing, when your self recognizes the awareness of someone else. Maybe it's the softness in his tone or the lingering of his gaze, but I know in that moment that Jeremy might be reading more into this spontaneous outing than I intended.

Clearing my throat and swiping a loose strand of hair behind my ear, I rip the Band-Aid off. "You know we're just friends, right? I might be out of line here. I've kind of been in a relationship for the past six years, but I feel like I'm getting...signals. And I want to make sure we're on the same page. If I am out of line, just chalk this up to the crazy girl from Oklahoma thinking everything is about her, but I swear I'm not really that vain. I just—"

"Just friends." Jeremy interrupts my rambling, thankfully saving me from making a complete fool of myself. "You just got out of a long relationship, like you said, and I'm trying to stay clean. We definitely don't make a good pair right now."

I don't miss the way he says *right now*, but I ignore it. Jeremy is a nice guy. We've bonded over our love of pizza, any kind—pineapple, anchovies, thin crust, thick crust. We haven't found a combination we can't agree on. He's also cute. I can see that. Even under the grit and hardness of living on the street, he's attractive, but I don't feel a spark for him. My skin doesn't tingle when he's near. My heart doesn't beat out of my chest when he looks at me.

If I'm being honest with myself, there's only one person who's made me feel like that in the last month and he's sitting back at the bar wearing a scowl.

I smile at Jeremy and nod my head. "Just friends."

Slowly he stuffs his hands into the pockets of his jeans and tilts his head in the direction we were walking. "Shall we?"

Thankfully, there doesn't seem to be any lingering awkwardness as we continue our walk toward the lights, sights and sounds of Bourbon Street. But as we walk, I can't get my mind off Shaw and the fact that he's brought out feelings I thought were long gone—feelings I thought I'd only experience once in my life, with Brant. I think I'd chalked it up to first love. I was eighteen when I realized I was in love with Brant Wilson. He was all of my firsts. When the spark I felt between us started to die, I thought it was normal.

"I've heard people talk about Hand Grenades from Tropical Isle," Jeremy says as we start passing more and more people, the music and buzz of Bourbon Street oozing out into the New Orleans night.

Taking a deep breath—and immediately regretting it, because *oh my, God*, it really does smell like a toilet—I rid myself of depressing thoughts and tell Jeremy, "Lead the way!"

He grabs my hand, not in a romantic gesture, but more in an effort to not lose me. It might only be a Wednesday, mid-week for most working folk, but it's like a weekend party down here. The neon lights pull your eyes in every direction. There are half-naked girls luring people into bars with open doors and windows, the music from their respective DJs battling it out in the streets.

Finally, Jeremy and I slip into a dim bar and he orders one Hand Grenade. "You're not drinking?" I ask, disappointment lacing my question.

"We're sharing. These things are potent."

"Ohh," I reply, realization hitting me as the bartender places a large grenade-shaped, bong-looking thing in front of us. With the first sip, I also remember how much of a light-weight I am and that half of this might do the trick and have me flat on my ass.

Chuckling, I pass it to Jeremy. "Good call on sharing."

"Right?" He smiles and takes a long pull. "Let's go find some bad renditions of 80's hair bands."

We're not two steps out of Tropical Isle when some guy is yelling from a balcony above us, "Hey, Pinkie, show me your tits!"

"What is it with guys and tits?" I mutter under my breath, giving him my middle finger. Jeremy laughs as we continue walking.

"We've gotta get you to Cat's Meow," Jeremy says, pulling me along the crowded sidewalk.

"Cat's Meow?"

"Karaoke. You're gonna kill it."

On the way to Cat's Meow, we stop off for rainbow-colored shots that only cost three dollars and tasted like battery acid mixed with Kool-Aid. By the time we squeezed our way into the bar on the corner with a neon sign proudly displaying *Cat's Meow*, my head was swimming.

"I'm signing you up," Jeremy yells over the music and singing. "What do you want to sing?"

"You Shook Me All Night Long," I reply without thinking. It's a no-brainer, especially with my good friend liquid courage on my side. I feel ten feet tall and bulletproof.

His eyebrows go up into his hairline. "AC/DC?"

I nod vehemently. "AC/DC. Let's do this," I say, grabbing two shots off a tray that's passing by and toss one back, then the other, before handing the waitress a twenty.

Sometime later, with all the singing and dancing, I kind of lost myself in the crowd. Occasionally, I'd catch Jeremy looking at me and smiling, but I'd just sing louder, letting the alcohol soothe away any embarrassment or inhibitions.

"Avery is going to sing for us," the MC says, squinting past the lights as he scans the crowd of cheering onlookers. "Where are you Avery?"

A sudden jolt of fear strikes me right in the pit of my stomach, but it's followed up with a huge rush of adrenaline, squealing, I squeeze Jeremy's arm before running toward the side of the stage. The throng of people parted like the Red Sea, allowing me to get to the guy holding a microphone. "Ready?" he asks when we make eye contact.

With my head swimming a little, I nod and take a deep breath as he thrusts the mic into my hand. The music starts and I feel a bubble of excitement. Once I'm standing in the middle of the stage, the lights blind me a little, keeping me from seeing all of the eyes watching me. Then, people realize what song I'm singing and begin to cheer and the atmosphere shifts.

I rock that stage.

The place was going wild and I was lost to the music and lyrics, letting my pink hair fly around.

By the time I walk off the stage, arms in the air like a rock star, I'm covered in sweat and met with adoring fans handing me free shots. It's rude not to accept free shots, so I drink. And drink. And pass a few off to my new friends. And drink some more.

Eventually, all the neon lights, booze, and loud music blend into a blur of indecipherability and my body feels too heavy, so I lean on Jeremy for support, laughing at anything and everything.

We stay at Cat's Meow—dancing and singing and sweating our asses off—until I can finally stand on my own again without swaying, but as the initial buzz begins to subside, I realize I need some air.

"Can we get out of here?" I yell over the opening lines of "Baby Got Back." This is the second time this song has been sung since we've been here, so I decide it's a good time to depart.

"Yeah." Jeremy nods and takes my hand as we excuse our way to the open doors.

My vision is still jumpy and I have trouble focusing on one thing at a time. "No more shots," I tell Jeremy, brushing my damp hair away from my face. Now that I can hear myself talk, I notice the slurred, slowness and it makes me laugh, for no apparent reason.

"No more shots," he agrees.

"Holy shit," I murmur. "I think I'm getting drunker." I thought the cool air would help, but it's not. My mind is just as jumpy and out of focus as my eyes.

Jeremy laughs and I feel my head spin.

10

I SHOULDN'T BE HERE.

I don't know why I am.

Half an hour ago, I left my bike in my makeshift shed behind the bar and told Paulie I was walking home. This is *technically* on my way home, but I always bypass Bourbon Street, avoiding it like the plague. So, why am I here now? Why have I walked the length of the street once, dodging drunk people and ignoring jeers and propositions from questionably dressed women, and am now standing at the busiest corner scanning the horde?

Fucking Avery.

She's been under my skin from the moment she walked into my bar. It was something about her innocent yet soulful eyes that made me reinforce my walls the moment I saw her. She was like a surprise storm, something you never expect and can't predict. The pink hair is a contradiction to her true self. You'd think she'd be a bit of a wild child, but until tonight, I've never seen her portray an ounce of debauchery, and believe me, I watch. I watch all the employees at my bar.

Over the years, I've had employees who drink ten times the amount of alcohol they serve, give their friends free drinks, and ones who pocket the cash instead of putting it in the register. I've also had employees who use my bar as a front for drug distribution or prostitution.

People will try anything, but at my bar, they only try it once.

Between me and Paulie, we run a tight ship. He's my eyes when I can't be there. When I am there, he's my backup pair. Which is why I should've taken his advice tonight and gone home. But I couldn't. I still don't trust Jeremy. Something about him doesn't sit well with me and the fact he's out with Avery tonight doesn't either.

Which is why I'm here.

I told myself when I took off walking that I'd make eye contact with him, let him know I'm watching and I'd leave. Avery never has to see me. I just want him to know that someone is looking out for her. And fuck her for making that be me, but I can't let something happen to one of my employees under my watch.

Technically she's not on my watch. I get that. But it's the principle.

I huff in disbelief at my justification. It's bullshit and I know it.

At first, I didn't want to hire her because she's a female and I don't hire females. Then she threw that misogynistic bullshit in my face and I started reconsidering. However, I never thought she'd make it past the first month. What I really thought was that she'd go crawling back to her boyfriend and they'd kiss and make up and I'd fill her place when the time came. But I now know that's never happening.

It appears I'm stuck with her.

And if that's the case, I'm going to make sure she doesn't get herself into trouble. Or let drug abusing dickheads like Jeremy take advantage of her.

Eye contact and then my job here is done.

"Shaw O'Sullivan," a disbelieving, albeit drunk voice slurs behind me and it makes all my cells fire. Avery's laugh forces me to turn around and I'm stuck in her gaze—her glossy, hooded gaze. When she steps into my personal space, peering up at me, I see Jeremy step up behind her, as if to steady her...or pull her back, but I grip her arms and glare at him.

"Why don't you ever smile?" she says almost like she's saying it to herself—thinking out loud. Her eyes flutter closed and I hold onto her a little tighter until she opens them and smiles up at me, giggling. Then she touches me, her hands come up to the sides of my face and she holds my cheeks. "You should smile. I think you'd look nicer, not so mean and surly." She pauses for a second, staring at me. "Surly. That's a funny word. Don't you think that's a funny word, Jeremy?"

Jeremy nods, but stays rooted in place behind her, his eyes also on mine.

"Jeremy took me to Cat's Meow." The meow part is dramatic and she brings a hand away from my face in a claw motion, pawing at the air. But with her other hand, the one that's still planted on my cheek, she brushes softly over my beard and my back stiffens.

Clearing my throat, I take her shoulders and put some distance between us. Her hand falls to her side and her smile goes with it. "Make sure she gets home safely," I instruct, glaring at Jeremy. There's venom in my tone and I know he hears it because he visibly swallows and then nods.

"Yeah, sure."

"Jeremy will. Won't you, Jeremy?" Avery sing-songs her words, now pinching Jeremy's cheek with one of her hands. So, she's a touchy-feely kind of drunk. Good to know. "Me and Jeremy are *just friends*, isn't that right, Jeremy?"

The way she says *just friends* makes Jeremy wince a little, but it makes me feel better. It seems as though there's already been a conversation about boundaries between them. Good for her.

Shitty for Jeremy.

But, good for Avery.

And me.

Now, I can go home and not worry about him putting *things* where they don't belong.

"I'll see you both tomorrow," are my parting words and I turn on my heel and walk away, not looking back. Jeremy will make sure she gets home okay. He needs a paycheck too bad. Plus, he knows I got him off the streets and without me, he'd be right back there. I'm not usually vengeful like that, but I wouldn't be above it.

Walking home, my mind is on Avery, even though I don't want it to be. I've noticed over the past few weeks that she creeps into my thoughts without permission. I'm also pretty sure I can still feel her hands on my face.

Ten hours later, I'm walking back to Come Again, feeling tired and annoyed. I spent the better part of the night unable to sleep due to thinking about things that are not my concern. Avery is none of my business. What she does and who she does shouldn't matter to me.

So, why does it?

Between the lack of sleep and not being able to whip my brain into submission, I'm in a worse than typical mood.

Surly.

Is that what she called me?

I huff my answer to my own mental question and put my key in the lock of the front door, but it's already unlocked, so I open it and step inside. "Hello?" I call out, looking around at the clean, empty bar. Stocking the bar and organizing the shelves, even when they don't need it, is kind of like my own personal therapy. It calms me—allows me to focus on something besides the droning of my mind. It's something I've always enjoyed doing, so the fact that it's done makes me even pissier than when I walked in a few moments ago.

Looking around, I notice that everything is done. Chairs are back down. Napkins are filled. Clean glasses are stacked behind the bar. The smell of coffee is filling the air and a faint sound of jazz is coming from the direction of my office.

Just great.

"Hey." Sarah's voice makes me spin around and I glare at her.

When I don't reply to her greeting, she smiles and shakes her head. "Well, good morning to you too."

"What the fuck? Why'd you clean my bar?" The question is

accusatory and all of my distaste for her actions are present and accounted for.

Sarah barks out a laugh and huffs, leaning her elbows on the shiny bar top. "I think a '*Thank you, Sarah. The place looks great.*' sounds a little better, don't you?" She rolls her eyes when I don't crack and then turns her glare on me. "What crawled up your ass this morning? Or *who*, I guess I should say."

"No one." My eyes drift from one side of the bar to the other and I let out a deep exhale through my nose. "I'm going upstairs," I tell her, brushing past on my way to the back door.

"When you're finished punishing the punching bag, come see me next door."

It's not a request, it's an order, said in a tone that only my older sister can get by with. My mama used to use it with all of us kids when we were younger. Sarah learned it well. Since she doesn't have kids, she uses it on me when she thinks I'm out of line.

I think we can both agree I'm out of line this morning, but I can't help it. I need my routine and she knows that. This bar is the one thing I can control. It's always the same and it never leaves. Without it and without my day-to-day normalcy, I start to feel out of control.

Life feels out of control.

I like order and guarantees. I like for things to be constant. Dependable.

Waving a hand in the air is the only response she gets from me, but she knows I'll be there. Because Sarah is the only thing, besides the bar, that's constant for me. She's been there for me my whole life, even when I'm a complete and utter asshole.

As I step back outside the backdoor, I look around the alley and confirm I'm alone. Walking over to the shed, I unlock it and check on my bike.

It's there, sitting pretty. Even in the darkness she shines.

Instead of going up the stairs to sweat out my frustrations, I decide to take her for a ride. Then I'll come back and punch the shit out of the bag. By the time the bar opens later, I should be semi-cordial. And thoughts of Avery should be long gone.

Later, after the ride and the workout, when I'm showered and redressed in my self-imposed regulation work uniform of white button-down, jeans, and my trusty black boots, I go find Sarah.

She's in the kitchen at Lizzie's Cooking School, in full-prep mode with her sleeves rolled up and hair in one of those ridiculous chef's hats. I can't help the grin when I see her, because she's always been one to take everything to the next level. It's all or nothing with her.

Maybe that's why she's never been married.

If Sarah can't do something with complete excellence, she doesn't want to do it all.

She's the one who sold me on reopening the school. Her pitch was simple, but direct: *It's currently a waste of space, Shaw. Keeping that place closed isn't helping anyone, definitely not you. So, let me run it. I'll be good at it. And it'll be good for you.*

"Sorry for being an asshole earlier," I say when it's apparent she's not going to be the one to speak first.

"I should be used to it by now." She fights back a smile as she puts cellophane over a few stainless steel bowls full of ingredients. "I mean, I'm practically a professional at putting up with your shit."

"Yeah, okay," I reply with a nod and run a hand over my scruff, knowing I've got coming whatever she wants to give me.

"But," she starts and then pauses. "I have to say, you've been extra asshole-ish lately. I thought after the anniversary was past, you'd go back to your more normal level of assholery."

Sighing heavy and loud, I plant my ass on one of the barstools at the prep table. "Sorry," I reply, looking her square in the eyes. Sarah doesn't deserve my wrath. Shit, no one does. But when I get in a funk like this, it's hard to get out.

"Is it Avery?" Sarah asks and just the mention of her name has me straightening and my heart beats a little harder. "I know you didn't want to hire her. Maybe you should let her go?"

Her tone and expression tell me she's testing me, trying to see what my reaction will be, and I try hard to school my features and appear unphased by her suggestion.

Clearing my throat, I start, "I can't afford to be short-handed right now."

"I'm sure you could find someone else—some man, because it's obvious you don't want a woman working in *your* bar."

She's always been so fucking good at playing devil's advocate.

"I could," I reply, calling her bluff. I know it's a bluff because Sarah has expressed how much she likes Avery and I know she wouldn't want her jobless. She knows as much as I do that Avery needs a paycheck. She's all alone in the city, trying to save up enough money to get an apartment. If I fired her, she'd be heading back to Oklahoma in a week. And she doesn't want that.

Not that it matters what Avery wants, but to many people's dismay, I'm not a heartless bastard.

"What's the deal, Shaw?" Sarah's tone is now level and she's giving me her take-no-bullshit stare.

"There's no deal."

"You followed her to Bourbon last night," she deadpans, like it's common knowledge.

My eyes grow wide without my permission and she quirks an eyebrow at the change in expression.

"Why?"

"I didn't," I deny. Deny until proven guilty, that's what my gut is telling me to do.

"So, Paulie's a liar now?" she asks with a tilt of her head.

Fucking Paulie and his big mouth.

At some point in our working relationship, his loyalty to Sarah surpassed his loyalty to me. I don't know when it happened and I know there's not shit I can do about it. With a huff, I look away from her, feeling a tinge of guilt and something else creeping in...embarrassment?

Vulnerability? I'm not sure, but it's fucking uncomfortable and making me want to get up and walk out. It wouldn't do any good though, because Sarah knows all of my hiding places and she'd find me.

"Why'd you follow her?" she presses.

"I didn't." My response comes out defensive and I roll my shoulders in an effort to get myself in check. "I wasn't following her," I start again and this time, my tone is more level, quieter. "I decided to walk home and took the long way around."

"To *Bourbon Street*?" she asks incredulously. "You hate Bourbon Street."

Growling, I stand from the stool and push away from the counter. "Fine, I went to make sure she was okay. She left with the kid and I still don't trust him. Karin, the lady who runs Charity House where he stays, told me last week she thinks he might still be using. I don't want Avery getting mixed up with a guy like him. He's not good enough for her. And I didn't want him taking advantage of her..." I trail off because I've already said enough. The next thing that would've come out of my mouth would've been too incriminating, too telling. The thought alone is enough to make me want to punch walls, because it's happening without my permission—out of my control.

I care about her.

"When did you stop wearing your wedding band?" Sarah asks after a few long, silent moments. Her question isn't accusatory or judgmental. It's knowing and accepting. Maybe that's why my heart doesn't squeeze at the realization. Or maybe because it's time.

"It's been five years," is my response and Sarah accepts it without pause or needing further explanation, and I'm thankful, because I don't think I have the energy or strength to let down the necessary walls for that conversation without them crumbling. Besides that, my answer is a true one. It's been five years. Some days have felt like years and some years have felt like days, but something happened last month...on our fifteenth wedding anniversary...it felt like a release, like the universe was telling me it was okay.

I can move on.

I'm not sure if I'm ready, but taking the ring off was the first step in testing the waters.

"Maybe you should take a night off from the bar? I could use the help," Sarah says, continuing her work as she goes back to slicing some delicious looking bell peppers. "We're making shrimp creole and I know it's one of your favorites."

Sliding back onto the barstool, I decide to take her up on it. Maybe that's exactly what I need—a night off to get my head on straight and refortify my walls.

"Are you gonna feed me?" I ask, stealing a slice of pepper and popping it in my mouth, crunching loudly and earning myself a swat and a laugh.

11

Avery

Yawning, I sit up in bed and rub my eyes.

I'm tired.

It's hard being a natural morning person and working at a bar. I'm up until at least two every morning, but by seven o'clock, my body is telling me to rise and shine. I blame it on being raised on a farm. Every morning growing up, if I wasn't up and dressed, sitting at the kitchen table by seven, my mama was banging on my door. *Are you gonna sleep your life away, Avery?*

Daylight's burnin', my dad would always say.

There's a small tug on my heart that always comes with my mama and daddy's words. Man, I miss them. Homesick isn't really the word for it, but I do miss my parents and grandparents and the farm. At some point, I'll have to go home for a visit, but not until I'm settled here in an apartment. Without a place to call my own, New Orleans still feels like a vacation—temporary. I want permanence.

Thankfully, I've officially saved up a thousand dollars since I've been here. Adding that to the little I have left over from what I started out with, I officially have enough to start apartment hunting. So, that's my agenda this morning. I'm hoping to find something close to the bar so I don't have to depend on public transportation or walk any further to and from work.

Shaw's already gone out of his way to make sure someone walks me home every night. Usually, it's Paulie and I feel bad, but he doesn't seem to mind. It's never Jeremy and I'm not sure why or what to make of that. If I didn't know better, I'd think Shaw is trying to keep me and Jeremy from spending time together outside of work. But that's crazy, because why would he care?

Growling out my frustration, I flip the blanket back and slide my feet to the floor.

Shaw is frustrating.

And maddening.

And confusing.

And difficult.

And opinionated.

And sexy as hell.

I hate it.

I hate that I'm attracted to him. I don't even like to admit it to myself, but I can't help it. It's true. He's got this mysterious vibe that makes me want to know more about him. I want to know what makes him tick. I want to know why he watches everyone from that damned dark corner. I want to know why he's so aloof. I want to know why he hides behind his fierce facade. Because deep under that thick skin of his, I know there's something softer. I've seen it in the way he cares about people, even when he acts like a dick. It's there.

Take Charlie for instance. He's the newest employee at Come Again, and even as an employee, I knew we didn't need another hand right now. The bar is totally covered. Paulie practically runs the place blindfolded. Then, you've got Kevin who's been there a while. He's quiet, keeps to himself, and mans the floor like a champ. Jeremy is turning out to be a great bartender. He's got a great connection with the customers, especially the younger crowd. On most nights, it only takes two of us behind the bar, leaving the rest to keep the place in order and make sure people don't destroy it. So, Charlie's been taking out trash and wiping down tables, but those are things someone else could be doing.

And I know, if someone else showed up in Shaw's alley tomorrow, he'd find them a place to work too. He'd also clothe and feed them and find them a place to live.

Shaw O'Sullivan, while he might seem like an asshole and control freak, is a genuinely nice guy. He's good people, and so is Sarah. I really like her.

She's been coming around the bar more frequently in the past week.

The night after Bourbon Street—which was probably a one and done for me, because holy headache, Batman—Shaw wasn't at the bar. I assumed he was sick or took the night off, but just about the time we were finishing up with the mopping, he and Sarah showed up with shrimp creole for everyone. It was leftovers from the cooking class and it was amazing—easily the best meal I'd eaten since the last time Shaw fed me at his apartment.

Yesterday morning, at our weekly staff meeting, she showed up with donuts.

She's kind, but she also doesn't take shit from Shaw. Their relationship is sweet. I can tell they're close and probably have been their whole lives. I missed out on that kind of relationship because I don't have siblings. When I was little, I'd sometimes pretend I did, somewhat of imaginary friends. My mama thought there was something wrong with me and took me to the pediatrician, but the doctor told her I just had a good imagination.

One thing I've noticed about Shaw when Sarah is around is that he doesn't seem to have his gargantuan walls up. There are cracks in his armor and slivers of a different Shaw shine through.

Enough thinking about Shaw, I sigh, pushing up off the mattress. I have an apartment out there waiting for me to find, so I get up and make my bed, tidying up my small space before showering and dressing for the day.

An hour later, I'm out the door and making my way to Jackson Square. I can't start my hunt without being sufficiently caffeinated.

"There you are," CeCe calls out when she sees me come through the door. "I was starting to think you did something completely insane like sleep in." She makes a mock face of astonishment before her pretty face splits into a smile.

"You know I can't sleep in," I tell her, rolling my eyes. "Lord knows I try, but it's futile. My farm-raised self just can't. When the sun shines, I'm up."

CeCe hands a customer his coffee, smiling as she takes his money. "You should run a coffee shop. It's like you were born for it," she says, handing him his change. "Have a great day," she tells him, before turning back to me. "Me, on the other hand, I could sleep my life away, but alas, I cannot. It's the early bird life for me."

"We should totally switch lives," I tease.

"We should, but I don't think I could work for Shaw O'Sullivan. I swear, that man never smiles. It'd drive me batty."

I laugh, leaning onto the counter. "You know what, it's true. I've never seen it. Maybe he's missing the muscles for smiling?"

CeCe's eyes go a bit out of focus and she sighs dreamily. "Well, he's not missing muscles anywhere else. Maybe he could take some from that amazing six-pack."

My throat suddenly feels tight and I'm forced to clear my throat. "You've, uh...you've seen his, uh, six-pack?" I ask, feeling my cheeks tinge red with heat.

"Oh, yeah." CeCe nods. "A few months ago, my friend, Carys, who owns the Blue Bayou Hotel, was having a grand re-opening. He was the bartender for the evening, and I'd stopped by to drop off some of my coffee equipment, and he was just there, in the courtyard, unloading a few crates of wine and beer...with his shirt off." The way CeCe relays that last part makes it sound scandalous, which according to my overactive imagination, it is.

Shaw without a shirt is probably down right sinful.

I lick my lips because they suddenly feel extremely dry. As a matter-of-fact, my whole mouth is dry. "I'm parched," I squeak out, making CeCe laugh. "I need coffee. Make it iced."

"I think you need to tap that."

My eyes grow wide and I nearly choke on my tongue. "What?" I ask in disbelief and shock. "Why would you say that? I mean...he's my boss, for one...and he's old...-er...than me. And he's surly and rude and confusing." I look at her and watch as she gets pleasure from my discomfort and a knowing smile forms on her lips.

CeCe shrugs. "I'm just saying, someone should tap that."

Someone? As in, just any person? Her statement has me picturing Shaw with a woman—any woman—and my face heats up for an entirely different reason. Something resembling jealousy bubbles up inside me.

Thankfully, CeCe has her back to me as she starts making my iced cappuccino, so she doesn't see my momentary lapse.

By the time she turns back around, I've managed to school my features and put on an unaffected smile as I take the coffee from her and change the subject. "I'm going to look for an apartment today."

"Baby, I'm sure you'll find the perfect place," my mama says gently into the phone. I've been lamenting to her about my unsuccessful apartment hunting trip yesterday. Everything was either too far or too expensive. Even with my thousand dollars that I've saved up, it wouldn't be enough to pay first month's rent and security deposits. "And if you need help, you know all you have to do is ask. I'll send you some money and you can pay me back when you come home for Thanksgiving."

I'm pretty sure that's her way of ensuring I'll be home for Thanksgiving, to which I haven't made any promises.

"No, Mama. I'm an adult. I moved here on my own. I'll figure out a place to live on my own." I huff into the phone, partly from exasperation and partly from exhaustion. I'm running a little late for work, so I've been jogging and talking at the same time, and now I'm breathing hard like I just ran a marathon.

Shit, I need to start exercising more regularly. I walk everywhere, but I miss my trips to the gym. When I lived in Houston, we had a gym at our apartment complex and I went every day and ran the treadmill and did strength training on the machines.

I wonder if Shaw would let me use his exercise equipment? I smirk and cock an eyebrow at the thought, my mind immediately drifting to a visual of him shirtless...working up a sweat.

"Avery?" my mama says, her voice a little loud in an effort to get my attention.

"Sorry," I tell her, hopping up onto the sidewalk out front of Come Again. "I'm at work, Mama. I've gotta go. I'll call you tomorrow."

"Okay, baby. Have a good night and be safe."

"Always, Mama."

"Promise?" she asks in a hesitant tone. It's not like her to linger, so I immediately respond, "Promise," in an effort to ease whatever worries she might be having.

"I hate you walking those streets late at night. I don't like it one bit."

"Mama, I told you, Paulie walks me home."

"But I don't even know this Paulie," she says, her voice rising in volume again.

"He's a good guy, older guy...very honest and hardworking," I assure. "Just think of someone like Daddy, maybe a little younger. Salt of the earth, I swear."

"Okay," she finally says with a sigh.

"Trust me, Mama."

"I trust you. It's everyone else I don't trust. Thanksgiving can't get here fast enough. I need to lay eyes on you and see for myself that you're good."

"Okay, Mama. I really—"

"I know," she says, cutting me off. "You gotta go. I love you."

"Love you."

Pocketing the phone, I pull the handle of the front door and practically dislocate my shoulder.

Locked?

Pulling my phone back out of my pocket, I check the time. It's a little earlier than I thought. I must've been jogging faster than I realized. But someone is still usually here by now. If I had to guess, Shaw is upstairs in the apartment or in his office.

I scan the sidewalk and think about walking down to Café du Monde, but even from here, I can tell there are throngs of people walking around at the corner. But a beignet sounds amazing.

But being late and pissing Shaw off doesn't.

Turning around, I think about sitting on the bench until someone opens the door, but then the sign hanging next door catches my attention.

Lizzie's Cooking School.

Walking over, I peek in the window and see the lights on. When I try the door handle, it opens easily, a tinkling bell rings, signaling my arrival, but Sarah isn't anywhere to be seen.

"Hello?" I call out.

Looking around, I take in the white walls and stainless steel shelving that holds cookbooks and cookware. The faint sounds of jazz filtering in, mixed with a hint of spices, makes me smile. This place is such a contrast to the bar next door.

Feeling comfortable enough in my budding friendship with Sarah, I walk toward the door that I'm assuming leads to the kitchen and prep area. When I swing it open, my heart bounces up into my throat and then plummets to my feet, kind of like when you're on a roller coaster and you get at the top of the giant drop...then *whoosh*.

Shaw is sitting at the stainless steel counter, talking to Sarah...and smiling.

My eyes go wide, eagerly taking in every detail, greedy for the curve of his lips and the way his cheeks push up, making his eyes crinkle on the sides. He's sexy when he's broody. But Shaw is exquisite when he's smiling. The way his lips part, showing off a set of perfectly straight, white teeth, completely transforms his face and makes my body feel like melted chocolate—ooey, gooey, and decadent.

Where has that smile been all my life?

Where has *he* been all my life?

"Avery." It's Sarah who speaks and makes me practically swallow my tongue. "Hi, come on in." Her tone is easy and comfortable, like she was expecting me.

"I'm, uh..." I stutter over my words, pointing over my shoulder, trying to convey what I'm trying to say without speaking. "The bar was locked," I squeak out. "I just was, uh..." I don't know what's wrong with me, but I can't take my eyes off of Shaw and he's now looking at me too, but the smile is gone and I feel an intense loss.

I didn't know I could miss a smile, but I do.

And I want it back.

And I want it to be directed at me.

"Paulie must be running late. He went to pick up a backup keg of the new Abita that was backordered. I thought he'd be back already." Shaw speaks to Sarah, but his eyes still glance back at me, where I'm still frozen in the doorway.

When he finally breaks the contact, I'm able to take a deep breath and get a grip. "I'll just go wait outside."

"No," Sarah insists. "Stay. Are you hungry? I tried out a new recipe this afternoon and Shaw was being my guinea pig, but it'd be great to have a second, unbiased opinion."

I laugh, because I do that sometimes when I'm nervous. "Oh, I don't know about unbiased," I reply. "I already kind of love your cooking."

"Well, you're not as bad as this one," she says, pointing to Shaw who's now standing, towering above the two of us, and backing away toward the door that must lead to the alley that the cooking school and the bar share. It's like he's not sure if he wants to leave Sarah and I alone, but he eventually lets out a huff and walks away.

"Don't mind him," Sarah says, placing a white bowl down in front of me and then ladling in a heaping helping of something mouth-watering. "He's always extra grumpy on Tuesdays."

"Why's that?" I ask, suddenly starving for both the masterpiece in front of me and information about Shaw O'Sullivan.

Sarah shrugs, sighing. "I don't know. I mean, isn't everyone a little grumpy at the beginning of the week? I know I am. It's like you just get into the weekend—letting loose, getting relaxed—and then reality is back and you have no choice in the matter. Shaw's always been moody about things he has no control over."

Her words seem honest, but also like they hold hidden meaning. The way she looks at me with knowing eyes has me feeling like she's asking me to look below the surface or read between the lines, but I'm not sure what I'm supposed to see.

"I guess I get that. I mean, I'm never in a bad mood when the new week rolls around, but then again, I don't have a lot to do over the weekends since I don't have a permanent place to live or...people. Plus, I grew up on a farm and every day was a work day. No time to get all lax and lazy," I tell her, taking my first bite and moaning my appreciation. "Oh, my God. This—"

"Shrimp Malacca," Sarah says with a smile as her eyes grow wide in delight. "You like it?"

"That's not the appropriate word," I mumble around another bite. "It's not sufficient," I add, moaning like a whore.

Sarah's laugh makes me feel good and her smile reminds me of her brother's. Now that I know what Shaw looks like when he smiles, it's easier to see the resemblance between him and Sarah.

"Please know this is not a Meg Ryan moment. I would never fake a foodgasm," I tell her with a smile, laughing a little when she laughs harder.

"Good to know." Sarah's smile is still there, but her eyes change a little, like she's trying to figure me out or something. "So, you grew up on a farm?" The change of topic is casual and easy.

"Yeah, in Oklahoma."

"Shaw mentioned that," Sarah says thoughtfully, her eyes still on me.

I don't know why, but the knowledge that Shaw has said my name in private, while talking to Sarah does something to me. What else has he said about me?

I nod, unsure of what else to say.

"You don't want to farm?" Sarah asks.

"No," I reply honestly with a renewed laugh and a shake of my head, digging in for another bite of this orgasmic Shrimp Ma...calla? "Shrimp Macalla?" I ask, needing to be sure of what I'm putting in my mouth so I can tuck it away for future reference when anyone asks me what the best thing I've ever put in my mouth is.

"Shrimp Malacca," Sarah corrects. "It has curry in it. That's what gives it that extra oomph."

"Delicious," I tell her. "It's my new favorite dish."

"Thanks for the stamp of approval."

"If you ever need an extra taster, I'm your girl."

"I'll remember that," she says with a smile. "Sometimes, I think Paulie and Shaw would tell me a week-old ham sandwich tasted good."

"Paulie's nice."

"He is," Sarah says with a more practical tone, nodding her head. "He's a great asset to the bar and to Shaw."

We sit in comfortable silence for a minute while I finish my bowl. When I'm finished, I pick up my empty bowl and walk over to the large wash station.

"You don't have to wash your own dishes," Sarah says teasingly. "We have a fancy-shmancy dishwasher for that."

"Okay," I reply, setting the bowl on the counter and turning to her, asking something I've been wondering since I started working for Shaw and found out about the cooking school, "Who's Lizzie?"

Sarah's face falls a little before she quickly recovers and takes a deep breath, exhaling with a sigh. "That's not my story to tell," Sarah finally says with a small, soft smile.

"Shaw named the school?" I ask.

Sarah nods and I can tell she's not giving me any more information. Her shoulders are a little straighter, not as relaxed, as she turns around and pours the rest of the food into containers.

Conversation over.

12

HOLY SHIT, WHAT A DAY.

And the night shift hasn't even started.

First, one of the soda dispensers at the bar stopped working and then, one of the toilets got stopped up. The cherry on top, though, was when some asshole blew chunks all over a female customer at the bar. It would seem, his three Come Agains didn't mix well with the room-temp shrimp po'boy he'd eaten while on a business lunch before coming to the bar.

Color me fucking surprised.

After kicking the bastard out for refusing to pay his tab, cleaning up the mess he left, and offering to pay for the lady's dry cleaning, I'm now kicked back on the couch in my office. Best case scenario: I can hide out in here for the rest of the night. In reality, I know I'll be lucky if I'm able to close my eyes for a few minutes before someone needs something.

Just as I start to doze off, there's a knock on my door.

Of fucking course.

Is there a full moon tonight?

When I don't answer right away, hoping they'll go away, they knock a second time and this time the knock is followed by a female voice saying "knock, knock". I recognize the voice right away as belonging to Avery. Part of me wants to answer the door, while another part wants to keep hiding. Yet another part is shaking its head and calling me a "pussy" for, well, being a pussy.

"I know you're in there, Shaw. The light is on and your music is playing."

Son of a bitch.

I can't help but snicker at being called out like that, but I don't do it loudly. There's no reason for Avery to know she made me laugh.

Accepting the fact I've officially been busted, I eventually roll off the couch and open the door. Immediately, I feel like an ass for making her wait so long because her hands are full. Also, she smells delicious.

Wait. No, what she's holding smells delicious...and familiar.

"Here, let me help you." I reach out and take the container from her before she has a chance to argue.

"Thanks." Her voice is a bit timid and her cheeks have a dark pink tint to them.

Is she blushing?

Of course she isn't blushing. That'd be ridiculous. She's probably just overheated from walking to work. Ever since her asshole ex-boyfriend came and took her car, she's been walking everywhere. To say I'm not fond of him, or her walking all over the city, is the understatement of the year.

I look down at the container in my hands and instantly recognize the label. That label plus the mouth-watering cinnamon sugar aroma swirling around can only mean one thing: bread pudding from The Crescent Moon.

Sweet, fucking mother of pearl.

"Is this—" I start to ask but she quickly interrupts me.

"Bread pudding, yeah. Wyatt said it was your favorite. It's mine, too. The best I've ever had, actually, even better than my mama's." A rambling Avery is a cute Avery, even I can admit that. The way she's twisting her fingers and avoiding eye contact, though, makes me wonder if something else is bothering her.

I know she's said she isn't scared of me, but I thought she was relaxing more around here and adjusting pretty well. A healthy amount of intimidation and respect for a boss is fine, but I want her to feel safe around me and know I won't treat her like she's been treated in the past.

"What's this for?" I ask, holding up the container. Before I dig in, I want to know what I'm agreeing to or being swindled into. There's gotta be a catch.

She shrugs before replying. "It's my way of saying thank you. I would've made you something myself but I don't really have access to a kitchen. I thought this would be good enough until I get my own place."

A lot of thoughts fly through my mind at her words, but I need to understand something first. "What are you thanking me for exactly?"

"Well, for taking a chance on me...giving me this job, defending me when Brant showed up, and...uh, just because." She gives me a small smile, brushing a strand of hair behind her ear, and shrugs her shoulders.

So fucking cute.

Now, she's looking directly at me and there's something there. Determination, definitely, but also hope and anticipation maybe? But that can't be and if it is, I have to nip it in the bud. I don't need her following me around like a lost puppy; I thought she was different from all of the other women who come here.

I clear my throat and cross my arms over my chest. "Listen, Avery, I know I haven't made it easy on you but you've proved yourself to be a really good and hard worker and I appreciate that. You don't have to go out of your way to thank me, just continue doing what you've always done while on the clock and that'll be enough."

My stomach drops as I watch the light in her eyes dim. Why can't I just fucking talk to her like a normal person?

"Yes, of course. Feel free to share the bread pudding with the others, if you want." She smiles again, but this time it's fake and it's what I deserve for being such an asshole.

She moves to leave but stops when I ask, "Did you say you can make bread pudding?"

"No, but I used to bake all the time back home." She twists her plump lips to the side as she thinks about it for a second. "I miss being in the kitchen but that's probably because I don't have one yet."

What the fuck?

I mean, her lips *are* plump, but why the hell did I just think that? I clear my throat and she must take it as a sign of irritation because she takes a step back and starts to leave again.

"What, um, would you have made for me if you had a kitchen?"

At this point, my mouth has completely detached itself from my brain and I can't stop the words from leaving. I don't know why I ask. Maybe I'm trying to make up for being such an asshole. Small talk and bullshitting used to be my specialty, but nowadays, I can't seem to hold a normal conversation without sounding like a dick.

A smile that's small but real graces her face and I'm thankful for the relief that floods my body.

"Brownies, probably. Unless you don't like chocolate and if that's the case, I'd make blondies. They're my favorite."

"I've never had a blondie before." I close my eyes and mentally slap the shit out of myself for sounding like such a dumbass.

She laughs, but I try my hardest to ignore how it makes me feel. She's off-limits, end of story.

"Well, here's hoping I find an apartment soon so I can make you some." She gives me a wink then leaves, while I remain standing, wondering what the hell just happened.

I'm so fucked.

The bar closed over an hour ago and I find myself in the same predicament I do every night: waiting to see if Paulie is gonna take Avery home or if I need to step in and make someone— other than Jeremy—do it. I know it's asking a lot of Paulie, since he's usually the one who does it, but I also know he doesn't really mind. Everyone is fond of her and wants her to be safe, just like I do. They also don't mind the extra money I add to their check every week for this special service.

I overheard her telling one of the guys about her adventures in apartment hunting and it doesn't seem to be going well but I'm confident she'll find a place soon and, hopefully, it'll be a safe complex that's not too far away.

"You ready, Avery?" I hear Paulie ask and I'm relieved.

"Sure," is her answer but her voice sounds a little funny, so I look up, catching her watching me. I have a feeling it offends her in some way that I never offer to take her home, but I just can't. I can't even let myself imagine what that would be like.

Just as they're about to leave, Sarah steps in from the storage room. "Hold on, Paulie. I need your help back here," she calls out. "Shaw, you can take Avery home, right?"

I know my eyeballs are bugging out of my head when I turn and look at my sister, but I can't help it. Surely, she's yanking my chain.

"I can help you with whatever you're doing back there. Paulie, go ahead."

"No." Sarah's response is firm and final and it's pissing me off she's doing this in front of *my* employees. "I need Paulie for this and only Paulie. Since everyone else is gone, you can take Avery home and then go home and get some rest. You look exhausted."

Since when did my ma take over Sarah's body? What the fuck is happening here?

My sister turns and leaves with Paulie right behind her, without even a backward glance. I'm so angry I'm afraid to move or speak or do anything right now. Sarah and I will be having words tomorrow, that's a fact. And, if I find out she and Paulie are fucking in the storage room, heads will roll.

That's a long-standing rule around here: no fucking in the storage room.

And, if it's not already, it's getting ready to be the new rule number 1.

Well, except for me. I'm fucking exempt. No pun intended.

"It's okay, Shaw. I can walk by myself." The sound of Avery's soft voice is the cool water that calms the fire in me. Why is she so damn sweet? After all these weeks of me being an asshole on a consistent basis, other than standing up for herself when she needs to, she's never been anything but sweet.

I collect myself and turn her way. "Nah, it's fine," I mutter, shaking my head. There's no way in hell I'm letting her walk alone this late. Not on my watch. "But instead of walking, we're taking the bike."

At least this way, we won't have any awkward silence. We also won't have a chance for any more deep, meaningful conversations like the night she slept in the apartment. That night almost killed me. I can't take another interaction like that. I was on cold shower duty for a week solid getting those images of Avery naked, in the shower, out of my head.

What the fuck, Shaw?

Yeah, now is not the time for that train of thought.

Get your shit together.

I don't turn around to see if Avery is following me as I make my way for the backdoor, but I know she is. I can sense her behind me. And like always, her sweet smell lingers when she's close by. She smells like vanilla and sugar, even after a night at the bar.

When I open the door, I push it wide and check the surroundings. The alley is clear of visitors, so I step aside and let her walk out ahead of me. She pauses when she gets outside and looks around. "Where's your bike?"

"There," I tell her, pointing to the shed.

"Clever," she says, nodding her head in appreciation. "It wouldn't be a good idea to leave something as gorgeous as that bike out in the open. I wondered what you did with it."

"Yeah," I agree, not wanting that small talk I was trying to avoid, and walk to the shed, unlocking the door and sliding it open. Ducking my head, I walk into the darkness and lift the kickstand with my boot, rolling the bike out into the alley.

"Put this on," I tell her, holding out an old helmet I keep on the back, just in case.

She puts the other strap of her backpack on her shoulder, securing it in place, and then takes the helmet from me. Thankfully, she doesn't argue or hesitate. She just puts it on and fastens it below her chin. In the odd lighting of the alley, her hair looks even more muted and subtle, losing the pink hue I'm used to seeing on her. "Your pink is fading," I comment before thinking.

Avery chuckles and shakes her head. "Yeah, I can't decide if I'm going back hot pink or if I'm going to do something different."

I huff my nonresponse, mentally kicking myself for saying anything, and climb onto the bike. "Hop on."

She holds my shoulders and kicks a leg over the back of the bike, not needing any help or instruction, and I have to say, it does something to me. I know she said she's ridden a bike before, but I guess I thought, maybe, she was bluffing. But it's obvious she knows what she's doing, just like everything else.

And that makes me wonder what else Avery Cole might be capable of.

"Ready?" I ask.

"Yes," she replies and it's then I hear the excitement in her voice.

"Hold on."

Avery's hands go from my shoulders to my waist and she doesn't hesitate when she slides them around my torso, holding on tight...just like I told her to.

Why was this a good idea?

Kickstarting the bike, I feel Avery shift behind me as she puts her feet up on the pegs. Trying to direct my focus somewhere besides everywhere Avery is touching me, I take off slowly, until we get to the street. Once there's just open road in front of us, I give it some gas and Avery tightens her grip.

Okay, I did that on purpose. What can I say? I'm a fucking masochist.

She's never told me where she lives, but I know where the house is.

After she moved into another rented room a while back, she gave me the address for her employee file. I've actually driven by just to check it out and make sure it's not some dump. She really does need to find something permanent. I know it's weighing on her that she's a week or two away from being homeless. I would never let that happen, but I would also rather not have to intervene.

I don't take the direct route. Instead, I make the block and then another, avoiding Bourbon Street, because even at two o'clock in the morning, that place is swimming with drunk bastards. Avery doesn't seem to mind. After a few more turns, she's comfortably leaning into me, completely relaxed, as we take the streets of New Orleans.

A few minutes later, I slow the bike down and park against the curb in front of the brightly colored house where Avery rents a room. She doesn't climb off right away or take her arms from around my midsection.

For a second, I think I'm going to have to manually remove her, but finally she lets go and slides off the bike.

"That was really fun." When she takes off the helmet, the smile on her face is as bright as the house she's standing in front of. "Thanks for bringing me home. Now, I'm really going to have to find an apartment so I can bake you some blondies."

I feel my lips twitch. Before I can stop them, a smile is threatening to break and I turn my head away from her. "That's not necessary," I tell her, schooling my features before I turn back around.

"Man, I haven't been on the back of a bike in forever." She lets out a deep sigh and smoothes her hair back. "Makes me miss the farm."

For a second, I just look at her, the realization that she's here in the city alone hits me, not for the first time, but hearing her say she misses home makes it more real. "Do you think you'll ever go back?"

"One of these days," she says with a slow nod. "My mama expects me home for the holidays, but I've gotta find a place to live before I'll agree to that. I need something permanent, so..."

"What?" I ask, wanting to know more—more about her.

"It's kind of crazy, but I feel like if I go back home without having a place to live, it would be easy for my mama to talk me into staying and I don't want that. I love it here. This is feeling more and more like home with every passing day. So, I want my own place and then I'll go back to Oklahoma for a visit."

I nod, understanding what she means.

"Where have you looked?"

"Ha." Avery lets out a laugh. "Where haven't I looked? That's the shorter list. I've been everywhere, but all of the places have either been too expensive or too scary."

I almost laugh again, just barely stopping myself, and I wonder why. For the first time in forever, I want to. I want to laugh with Avery. I want to return one of her killer smiles. But it all seems so foreign. I've spent so many years not doing those things, it's like I've forgotten how.

"That pretty much sums up New Orleans," I tell her, kicking my feet out a little so I can hold my bike up and sit comfortably. "You're wanting to stay close around here, right?" I ask, thinking about any spots I might know.

"Yeah, I need to be within walking distance to the bar," she says. "I also don't mind having a roommate, but I'd prefer a girl. The only roommate ads I've followed up on have been dudes, and nothing against them, but I'm just...I don't know..."

"No," I interject. "That's smart. You either need your own place or a girl roommate...no dudes." I use her terminology and fight another smile. The thought of Avery rooming with some random guy does the trick, keeping my features cool and hard.

"I thought about asking my friend CeCe, but her place is super small. She lives above the coffee shop and there's pretty much just room for her."

I nod, thinking. Everywhere I know is closer to where I live, in the Garden District, but that's too far for Avery to walk all the time. The only plus side is that I could make sure she gets home safe every night, which would also be the negative.

"I'm sure I'll find something." There's worry in her tone this time and it makes me look at her, holding her gaze.

And her worry becomes my own.

Again, here she is, a woman, alone, in a new city...yeah, I admit it. Avery is a woman. I kept calling her a girl—*new girl, the girl*—and Sarah asked me why. Why did I refer to her that way? I don't really know the answer to that. Maybe it helped keep her at a distance if I put her in a category like that. However, I'm well aware that even though Avery is young, she's definitely not a girl. She's all woman and more mature than people ten years older than her. Shit, she's way more mature than I was at her age.

"You're gonna find something," I tell her, trying to sound encouraging. "If you don't, you'll always have a place to stay. The apartment isn't being used on a regular basis. I can clear some stuff—"

"No." Avery cuts me off, shaking her head. "I couldn't do that. I know that's like...your personal space, or whatever," she says, fidgeting with the strap of her backpack. "I couldn't let you give that up."

"Well, I'd still come up there and work out," I tell her, without thinking. "That'd just be part of the deal."

Her eyes go wide and then she's the one schooling her features. When she clears her throat and averts her gaze to the sidewalk beneath her feet, I allow a smirk. I'm pretty sure she's hiding a blush on her pale cheeks. This response from her makes me think she's possibly thought about this before—me working out...in the apartment.

"Of course," Avery finally says, her voice an octave higher than usual, but her eyes are still on the ground. "Right, well, like I said...I'm sure I'll find something. And," she pauses for a second, clearing her throat again, "if I don't, then...well, maybe I could stay at the apartment until I do."

When she looks back up, her big, dark eyes bore into mine, and I feel it in my gut...and my dick...all the way down to my fucking toes.

"Thank you...for offering," she says with a small smile, her expression holding a plethora of emotions—gratitude, confusion, unease, anticipation...maybe even lust.

"Don't," I demand. "Don't thank me and don't look at me like that."

"Like what?" she asks, her eyes growing wider as she swallows hard.

"I don't deserve that look...like you're expecting something from me or grateful for something I've said or done. I'm not the hero here. And I promise you don't want anything from me."

"You're a good person, Shaw." She licks her lips and cuts her eyes away from me, huffing, before continuing. "You just don't want anyone to know. You're covering up something. Pain, hurt, heartache. . . I don't know what it is, but it's okay."

I give her a small smile before I even realize I've done it and I see something else pass over her face—awe, wonder, elation? I'm getting ready to bark out a harsh laugh and turn this interaction around, shut her down with even harsher words, but she starts talking again... shutting *me* down.

"You should smile more often." Her words are a whisper and I instantly regret letting the walls down. I didn't even realize they were down until I started feeling something inside my cold, empty chest. My heart beats faster. My blood feels like it's running warmer, spreading throughout my body.

And it's too late.

Too late to take it back.

Too late to fortify the walls.

Avery has already bulldozed them with her beautiful face and sweet smile and even sweeter smell. The way she's open and inviting and accepting of everyone, even losers like Jeremy and Kevin. She's nice. To everyone. I can't help but feel for her and appreciate her as a human being. Those feelings lead to others that I'm not ready to let myself feel. Not yet. Not with her.

What Avery does next is something that will haunt me forever. She takes a step forward, and before I know what's happening, still lost in my own thoughts, she brushes her lips against mine.

It's fast and soft and sweet. It's everything and not enough all rolled into one.

What I do next is something that will also haunt me...but not doing it would've tortured me, so I reach out and grab the sleeve of her jacket, stopping her from retreating. She swallows, her eyes wide with shock, like she can't believe she just did that.

Oh, but she did.

She started it and I'm going to finish it.

Stepping off the bike, I tower over her, consuming her space. I watch as her chest heaves in anticipation and her eyes grow wide with shock—probably due to her own actions and now mine. Not allowing time for second guesses, I cup her cheeks and tilt her chin, rubbing my thumb along those lips, those fucking plump lips, and then I kiss her back—taking what I've wanted from her since the first day she walked into my bar.

Tasting her.

Feeling her.

Her breath is hot as she exhales sharply when I pull back to give her a chance to tell me to stop, but she doesn't. Instead, she settles into the kiss and opens her mouth, giving me access. Our tongues brush and I feel my cock harden. Between her sweet smell, soft moans, and delicious mouth, I'm ready to mount her, right here on the sidewalk.

When her hands grip my biceps, something about it brings me back to reality.

Pulling away from her, I gain the distance I need to breathe and fucking think. As my eyes trace the features of her face, appreciating her for the first time from this proximity, the reality of what I've done—what we've done—hits me.

Her lips are fuller and swollen.

Her eyes are wide and dreamy.

When her tongue darts out and licks, I force myself to look away.

No, no fucking way.

Climbing back on the bike, I drop my foot down on the pedal barely waiting for it to roar to life before I drive off, leaving Avery standing on the sidewalk.

She's home.

She's safe.

And I've gotta get the fuck out of here before I breach the point of no return.

When I look back and see her still standing there, I know I'm fucked.

I am so fucked.

13

Avery

I KISSED SHAW.

That was the first thing I thought of when I woke up this morning. My second thought was: *Shaw kissed me.* And boy, did he kiss me. Where mine was sudden and quick, more of an outward show of gratitude, Shaw's kiss was demanding and intense, just like him.

And I liked it.

I like him.

I've known this fact for a while, but now that our lips have actually touched, in real life, and not just in my incessant dreams, I know the reality is better than the fantasy. He tasted like mint and a hint of beer, but it wasn't off-putting, just wholly Shaw. His smell, up close, was even more manly and intoxicating than when I pass him at the bar. It's a mixture of clean cotton and leather and some kind of spicy cologne. The combination should be bottled up and sold, because it's damn sexy, just like its owner.

To be honest, I don't know why I kissed him.

Maybe it was a momentary lapse in judgement?

Maybe I was acting on impulse?

Maybe I just don't care anymore?

Besides, it was just a kiss. What's the worst thing that can happen?

Well, besides him firing me, which has crossed my mind.

But, he kissed me back, so I'm not the only one at fault here.

I guess he can still fire me, but that would be a seriously asshole-ish thing to do and I know Shaw can be a serious asshole, but something tells me he wouldn't fire me over a kiss.

And, you know what, I can't be held fully accountable. It's technically his fault, because Shaw smiled...at me. It wasn't big or intentional, but it was something and it did something to me. I forgot myself and who I am and who he is. It made me dizzy with appreciation. I've been wanting to see that smile again since I caught him smiling at Sarah. Now that I know he can and I know how resplendent he is when he does it, I was craving it—needing it like my next breath.

So when he finally did smile at me, I lost my mind.

That's it, temporary insanity.

If he seems angry about it, I'll plead insanity.

All of these thoughts are playing on repeat when I step inside Neutral Grounds, later than usual. My shift at the bar doesn't actually start until eight o'clock tonight. Since we stay open until at least two on weekends, Shaw let's all of us alternate coming in late. Except Paulie. Paulie just gets the shaft. He's always there, probably more than Shaw, but I can tell he loves it...maybe just as much as Shaw.

"Hey!" CeCe calls out when she sees me. There are a few customers in front of me, so I take a seat at one of the tables and wait for everyone to clear out. I ate breakfast in my room before I left, but I still need some caffeine. Since I have the afternoon free, I'm going on another apartment hunt today. Pulling out my phone, I begin scrolling through the screenshots I took of online advertisements. I've decided that if all else fails, I'll just see about renting another room through the holidays, but I'm really hoping I don't have to do that.

"Your usual?" CeCe asks when the bell rings on the door and the last of the customers walks out.

"Yeah, but I'll take it hot today," I tell her. "I know it's still eighty degrees, but that feels like winter compared to last week and it's hard for me to drink iced coffee this close to November."

"How's the apartment hunting going?" she asks as she starts my espresso shots.

The increased aroma of coffee immediately soothes my frayed nerves and calms my mind. I close my eyes and inhale deeply. "Well," I start, letting out a deep breath, "Not great. Everywhere I went last week was too expensive. The one place I thought might be a possibility called back yesterday to say it's been taken. So, the only options left from all the ones I've already seen are ones with male roommates and I just don't think that's the right fit for me."

"Yeah," CeCe agrees. "I don't like that—rooming with some dude you don't know." She frowns, shaking her head. "It'd be different if it was a co-worker or something."

I sigh again, standing and walking to the counter. "That's not happening. The only guy I work with that I'm very close to is Jeremy... well, besides Shaw...and, yeah, neither of them is an option," I say with an exasperated laugh. "So not an option."

"What's that tone for?" CeCe asks, setting my coffee down in front of me.

"What?"

"What happened?" she pushes.

"Nothing. Why?" I ask, my voice going up an octave. I'm a horrible liar. Horrible, horrible liar.

CeCe's eyebrow lifts and she tilts her head to the side. "Something happened."

"I kissed Shaw," I blurt out and then take a tentative sip of my coffee. The near boiling liquid scorches my tongue, but I let it, keeping me from saying anything else I'll regret. The way CeCe's mouth is hanging open and her eyes are wide, I'm going to guess she's thinking what I've been thinking.

"What the hell?"

"I know," I groan, holding my head in my hand. "I know. Such a bad idea. And I can't even blame it on booze. I was totally sober, unless you count being intoxicated on Shaw's smell, which totally doesn't count because it wasn't until I was up close and personal that I got a good, honest whiff, and Holy Jesus, did he smell good. And the kiss. The kiss was...I don't know. I mean, I like went in for a seventh-grade-spin-the-bottle-kiss and then he went in for a push-you-up-against-a-wall-and-fuck-you kind of kiss, which I would've let him do, by the way."

When I finish my dramatic monologue, I hide my face in the crook of my arm and lean on the counter, feeling CeCe's eyes on me without even looking up. "Say something," I finally mutter, afraid to see the judgement on her face. "I'm a salacious floozy who kisses her boss... what?"

Peeking my head up from its hidey hole, I see a small grin shining back at me, which is not what I was expecting. "He kissed you back?"

"Uh, well," I start, stuttering a little at the memory, and then shrug. "He kissed me second."

"And then what?"

I let my eyes dart around the coffee shop, thinking about it all again, for the millionth time. "He started his bike up and drove off."

"Hold up," CeCe says, hands in the air. "Shaw Sexy Ass O'Sullivan, a man with years of experience *and* a six pack, drove you home on his bike?" She's now the one leaning against the counter, fanning herself with a menu. "I'm gonna need a minute."

"Oh, my God," I say with a laugh, appreciating the levity. I needed this. To talk it out, air it out. At least I no longer feel like a Coke bottle that's been shaken up and set on a hot tin roof.

"So, the kiss?" CeCe encourages. "How was it?"

"It was...yeah," I reply with a nod.

"Come on, Avery!" she cries, swatting at me with the menu she's still holding. "I need more than that. I'm in a drought here. A serious, middle of the fucking Sahara drought. I need details."

I laugh again, shaking my head. After a few moments, I finally say, "Good. No, great. Like, best first kiss of my life. Although, I haven't kissed many people, but I think even if I had kissed all of New Orleans, his still would've won top honors."

"Good," CeCe says dreamily. "That's good. Now, I'm gonna need you to go have hot motorcycle sex with him and come back and tell me all about it."

"God, you're a whore!" I laugh and CeCe laughs and it just feels good to have a friend again. It's been too long. In high school, I had a few good girl friends, but after we graduated, most of them got married and are already on their third kid. When I moved to Houston, I lost touch with pretty much everyone except my family. CeCe is a breath of fresh air.

"Hey," she says, when I pass her my money and she puts it in the register. "I know you have to be out of your room soon. So, if you don't have any luck today, you can sleep on my couch until you find something."

"Well, that's the other thing..." I start, pausing. "Shaw offered me the apartment above the bar, if I need it."

CeCe nods, twisting her lips as she thinks. "Well, that's...a possibility."

"Yeah," I reply slowly. "I can't decide if that would be a good idea or a bad idea."

"Well, you'd never be late for work," she says matter-of-factly, nodding.

"True, but I'd also be in Shaw's space. He uses it as a place to work out and get away from things. I'm not sure if me being there would be good...I like him, like *really* like him, and I don't want to complicate things or move too fast. I've seen the way he throws walls up around himself, like he's Fort Knox. It feels like he's finally letting me in a little and letting me see the real Shaw. I don't want to ruin that."

She nods again, watching me thoughtfully. "Well, then, maybe you should stay here, at least until you figure out where your feelings lie for Shaw...and where his lie for you."

"I could help you open up in the mornings," I add. "I know that's not your favorite, so you could teach me how to get everything up and running."

"I couldn't do that. You work until ungodly hours at the bar. I couldn't ask you to get up just a few hours after going to bed."

"Whatever," I tell her. "I'm young. I'll sleep when I'm dead."

"Well, it would be nice having the help."

"And I'll still pay you, of course," I add, not wanting her to think I'm trying to get off cheap.

"No, you save your money so you can get your own place when you find the right one. I'll take you up on the help."

I smile, sticking my hand across the counter for her to shake. "Sounds like a deal."

While I stand at the counter and drink a few more sips of my coffee, CeCe goes about her business and starts wiping down the espresso machine. My thoughts drift back to Shaw and I decide to ask CeCe for her opinion about something else that's been nagging at me.

"Is it too soon to..." I drift off, trying to find the right words.

"Too soon for what?" she asks, tucking a towel that resembles the bar towels we use into the apron that's tied around her waist.

"Too soon to kiss someone."

CeCe cocks an eyebrow and places her hands on her narrow waist. "After Douche Canoe? No. I mean, unless you feel like you're not ready for a relationship." Her expression turns more thoughtful as she contemplates the issue. "I know I've been encouraging this...whatever it is," she says, waving her hands around in the air. "But also, I don't want you to get hurt again. Brant was bad. And I'm sure you might be afraid to jump right into another relationship, but Shaw could be good for you and you could be good for him. I know he seems like an asshole, but I've just never gotten a bad vibe from him. If I had, I wouldn't have been cheering on the sex."

I huff out a laugh and take my lid off my cup to get to the delicious froth that's left in the bottom. "It's kind of strange," I admit. "Brant was my first...everything. First real boyfriend who my dad actually let me date. First sex partner...only sex partner," I mutter. "I mean, there was this one time with Jason Dearmon in Stacey Johnson's basement, but it was on a dare and I only let him slide into third base, if you catch my drift. I freaked out and he told everyone I was a prude."

She laughs lightly and places a hand over mine, forcing me to look at her. "Listen, there are no hard and fast rules about stuff like this. You just gotta do what's right for you. If you like Shaw and you're ready to take the risk again, because let's face it, there's always a risk when feelings are involved, then go for it." She squeezes my hand and I give her a small smile.

After talking a little more with CeCe and feeling lighter, letting out some of my worries and concerns, I spend the rest of the day checking out the potential apartments on my list.

None of them are a good fit.

Once again, they're either too expensive, too far away, or too scary. I did find one place, about ten blocks from the bar. It was basically a studio with the bedroom having a half wall to block it from the rest of the space. Only the bathroom was closed in and it kind of reminded me of Shaw's apartment. But when I walked back down the stairs a guy in a motorcycle vest left the apartment below me and I noticed a gun sticking out of the back of his pants.

Abort. Abort.

I'm sure he could be a very nice guy, but the sketchy feeling I got had me running for the safety of my temporary room. At least the lady I rent it from is nice and she's always home. And no one walks around toting a gun.

I laugh at the ridiculousness of it and think what my mama would say if she knew.

Shaking my head, I run across the street and up the sidewalk leading to Come Again. The night is cool, for New Orleans at least, and everyone is out and about. Even the sidewalk in front of the bar has patrons milling about. A guy opens the door for me when he sees me approaching and I step inside, offering him a smile and a thank you.

I might be somewhat of a feminist, but I can appreciate chivalry and good ol' southern manners.

The place is packed.

Paulie and Jeremy seem to have their hands full at the bar while Kevin and Charlie are clearing glasses and keeping the place in order. I frown when I see how many people are lined up at the bar, waiting on drinks.

"You should've called me," I yell at Paulie when I approach the bar, making my way to the end, so I can slip behind it and get to work. "I've just been walking around. I would've come in if I'd known it was going to be so busy."

"No worries," Paulie says with an irritated tone. "We've been managing."

I pause for a second as I wrap the apron around my waist, wondering if his bad mood is directed at me. Examining his face, I'm about to offer him an apology, even though I don't feel like I owe him one, but then I follow his line of sight.

In the corner, where he normally sits, is Shaw, but instead of sitting at his usual table or helping Paulie handle the bar, he's dancing. Shaw is dancing with a woman, a long neck beer in one hand and her in the other. Her lips are on his neck and his hand is in the back pocket of her jeans. When he tips up his beer bottle, his eyes catch on mine and he holds my gaze.

Pushing me away.

Breaking my heart.

Building the walls back.

Our eyes stay locked as he places his lips on her hair and then her forehead, down to her neck. She wraps her arms around him and he lifts her from the floor, allowing her legs to wrap around his waist. When he carries her down the hall, out of sight, I have to bite down on my lip to keep from saying or doing something I'll regret. There's a sting in my eyes from unshed tears, but I blink them away. I can't. Not here. Not in front of everyone. Not while Paulie's still watching me.

Instead, I dig deep within myself, finding the secret place I first realized was there when I was still with Brant. It's where my hidden strength lies and it allows me to pretend—pretend like everything is fine, pretend like I'm okay, pretend like watching Shaw purposefully hurt me didn't break my heart and stomp on my budding feelings.

Barking out a harsh laugh, I turn to the first customer I see and ask, "What can I get you?"

And to think I thought the worst thing he could do was fire me.

I guess I underestimated Shaw O'Sullivan.

Later, when it's time to go home, my eyes dart to the hallway to see if Shaw will resurface wearing evidence of his sexual escapades with the slut that was wrapped around him earlier.

I shouldn't call her a slut. I'm sure she's a very nice girl, but I can't help it. I'm pissed. Pissed at myself. Pissed at Shaw. And pissed at her for being in the equation.

"You ready?" Paulie asks from behind me making me whirl around, feeling like I've been caught with my hand in the cookie jar.

"Uh, yeah. Yeah, I'm ready," I tell him, grabbing my backpack and taking one last look over my shoulder.

"Jeremy," Paulie calls out, making me jump a little. "Take Avery home. Straight home. And call me when she's there."

Jeremy shows up at my side and eyes Paulie like he's been drinking. "Sure," he says, nodding slowly. "Yeah, I can do that."

"Okay," I draw out, still waiting on Shaw to come out of the woodwork and shut this shit down. He never lets Jeremy take me home. Usually, he keeps him busy until I'm out the door, sending him on stupid little errands. Since our night on Bourbon Street, he's been even worse. I know he doesn't trust Jeremy, but I do. He's my friend.

"Let's go," I say, motioning toward the door, my eyes still on Paulie. He winks and gives me a little smile.

"Good work tonight," he says, pulling the bar towel off his shoulder and going back to wiping down the table he's standing next to.

"Thanks," Jeremy and I say in unison. If it wasn't for Paulie, we'd never have any sort of positive reinforcement.

Walking out of the bar, I wave back at Paulie before letting the door close behind me, my mind still on Shaw and wondering where he's at and what he's doing and who he's doing it with. My active imagination is my worst enemy tonight, filling my head with images of Shaw—

naked, thrusting, heaving, grunting. I can't help it. I keep telling my brain to shut the hell up and try to erase the images, but thanks to my super vivid dreams, I feel like I have a front-row seat.

And then I feel anger and hurt. After the kiss of a lifetime, he goes and does something shitty like that, obviously using that woman to push me away.

"You okay?" Jeremy asks as we cross the street and head down the block.

I shake my head and groan. "Yes, sorry. I'm bad company tonight."

"It's okay," he says, walking slowly with his hands in his pockets. "Wanna talk about it?"

No. No, I do not want to talk about it. There's no way I could tell him how I feel about Shaw and that we kissed last night and then what happened tonight. No, I'll have to save that for a conversation with CeCe. Man, she's going to be pissed. I actually feel bad that I'm going to have to tarnish her view of Shaw.

"Just a long night and I still haven't found an apartment," I tell him, opting for a less personal topic.

"Ah, yeah, I forgot you're still looking for a place to live."

"Yeah, and everything is either too expensive or too far away or too sketchy," I say with a laugh.

"A girl like you doesn't need to be living alone, especially in a city like this."

"I can take care of myself." I feel myself getting edgy over his assumption that I'm weak or vulnerable. "I'm pretty capable."

Jeremy stops, pulling my arm so I'll stop with him. "I know." His voice is low and his eyes are scanning my face. When he licks his lip and brushes a hand through his hair, I recognize the actions as nervous... anxious. "You're one of the strongest girls I've ever met. I admire you, Avery."

It's those words and that tone that tell me it's more than a compliment. He's working up to something more. Just before my heart leaps into my throat, his fingers brush my cheek and he closes the gap between us.

"What are you doing?" I ask, my words coming out shaky, unsure.

When his thumb pulls at my bottom lip, I ask again, "Jeremy, what are you doing?"

"I've wanted to kiss you for a long time, since the first day we met," he admits, and I pull back enough, using the light from the overhead streetlamp to really look into his eyes. They look dilated, weird. He swallows and seems to be lost in his thoughts, stuck in his own mind.

"Jeremy," I say, a little louder this time, getting his attention. "No."

It's the one word that usually works, so I start with that and take a step back. He follows and I put my hand up, pushing back on his chest. "Just friends, remember?"

This time, his eyes finally register my dismissal and he shakes his head. "Don't tell Shaw."

Don't tell Shaw?

Don't tell Shaw. Yeah, that would be bad. Now, I'm the one scanning him from head to toe, wondering if I missed something. I want to ask if he's using, but I don't want to hurt his feelings.

But I also don't want to be a friend who ignores signs.

I ignored signs of abuse with Brant and I see where that got me. I should've left the second he started treating me less than what I deserved. So, I ask, "Are you using?"

"What?" he asks, his voice rising in volume as he scrunches his face in disbelief.

"I'm sorry," I begin, my hands going up to touch his biceps and hold him in place. "It's just, I know we've discussed the fact that we're only friends and I feel like you're not acting yourself..." I trail off and the hurt on his face is evident, making me feel horrible.

"I'm sorry," I whisper.

"I just like you," Jeremy mutters. "I'm sorry."

"We're just friends," I reiterate. "But we *are* friends." I force him to look at me and when he gives me a small smile, I breathe a little easier.

Jeremy nods slowly, biting his bottom lip. "Please don't tell Shaw," he repeats as we start walking again.

"Don't worry, I won't." But, speaking of not accepting less than I deserve, I do have a few things I'd like to say to Shaw O'Sullivan. And now that he's done the worst, I'm not worried about his response. After tonight, I feel like I can handle anything he throws my way.

14

Shaw

I didn't sleep with Brandy.

I didn't even want to.

Never planned on it.

I took her down the hall and walked her straight out the back door. She was stunned and pissed off, but I didn't give a shit. She'd served her purpose and I got what I wanted—Avery saw us together. It was a shit thing for me to do. I know that. I own my fucked up behavior, but after last night and the kiss...no, kisses...I didn't know what else to do.

Emotionally stunted.

That's what Sarah would call me and she'd be right.

Something happened in my psyche five years ago. The day I lost Liz. I regressed, repressed my emotions, and retreated within myself. And now, I can't seem to find my way out.

My feelings for Avery have been building since the first day she walked into my bar and asked for a job. At first, I thought it was pure lust and immediately berated myself for letting my dick respond to a girl her age. However, when she came back and basically called me on my shit and demanded I hire her, something shifted. Sure, I still thought she was the most beautiful, fascinating thing I've seen in a long goddamn time, but I also respected the shit out of her for standing up for herself...standing up to me.

With every passing conversation and every little piece of information I learned about her, I found myself liking her more. *Liking her*. I haven't *liked* someone of the opposite sex in a long damn time.

I love Sarah.

I loved my mama.

I love my sisters-in-law.

They're family.

I loved Liz.

Still do.

But every other female in my life, I wouldn't consider what I feel for them anything resembling admiration. I've felt lust for Brandy, but that's it, nothing more.

Last night, when Avery took the leap and placed her sweet lips on mine, I lost the grip on the restraint I've held onto so tightly since she walked into my life.

The walls crumbled.

And for a brief moment, I let myself feel.

And it was scary.

It was alarming.

It was sudden and life-altering and I had to do something about it.

When Brandy approached me at the bar, my first response was to push her away. I had no desire to be with her. I haven't in a long time, especially since Avery came along. But then I had a thought, and on a spur-of-the-moment decision, I decided to use her, just like she'd been using me all these years.

Never planning on letting it go further than a grope session, I waited, biding my time until Avery came to work. When I saw her and her eyes locked onto mine, I got more than I bargained for.

I expected to find disappointment and maybe a little rejection, but the deep hurt that showed like a beacon in a storm cut me to the bone.

She looked like I had literally ripped her heart out of her chest and stomped on it. I couldn't stick around to watch it. I'm too much of a coward for that. I might talk big and act like a dick, but deep down

I'm not made for that kind of pain. I never wanted to hurt her. Just the opposite. I wanted to turn her away, make her run from me, because I have nothing for her. Everything left inside of me is broken and damaged, nothing someone as bright and alive as Avery deserves.

Nursing a room-temperature beer, I stare down Paulie, who looks like he could pull out my teeth with a set of pliers and shove them up my ass. All the while, my chest aches with a fresh pain, new from anything else I've felt in a long, long time.

"Just say what you want to say," I finally mutter, wanting him to get whatever's eating at him off his chest.

He just grunts his response and brings his own bottle of beer to his lips. When he sets it back down on the table, he shakes his head. "I didn't think you were capable of what I saw tonight."

"What's that?" I ask, playing dumb, forcing him to say it. If he wants to bring it up, we're not tiptoeing in the tulips. We'll talk about it, like men. Paulie's not usually one to broach personal topics, so the fact that he's mentioning it at all is surprising to me.

"That girl..." he pauses, rubbing a hand down his face and scratching at the day old scruff on his jaw. "Avery," he continues, "she likes you." His words are even and matter-of-fact, just like him.

"I'm not a professional on relationships, obviously," he huffs and shakes his head again. "But I'm not stupid and I've watched people my whole life. I know most think I'm just a bum turned bartender, but I've been around the block a time or two, feels like I've lived a few lives, if I'm being honest." When he pauses again, his eyes focus hard on the scratched wood of the table. "She's something special and if I'm not mistaken, you feel a little something for her too."

I bristle at that and twist my neck to the side, avoiding his gaze. When I don't reply or deny, he continues.

"I see it. The way you look out for her, watch her every movement. I've never seen you respond to a woman like that. And I think we can both agree, she's a woman." His knowing eyes go wide in acknowledgement and let out a deep sigh, biting down on my lip to keep from saying something I'll regret later.

"Why'd you do it?" His question is low and laced with disappointment.

"She needs to know what she's dealing with," I reply simply and honestly. "I'm not what she thinks I am. She shouldn't look at me like she does."

"How's that?" Paulie presses, elbows placed firmly on the table.

"Like I'm a good person...like she wants to know everything about me...like I'm some kind of hero. She makes me feel..." I growl and run a hand roughly through my hair.

"What?" he prods, forcing me to voice things I'd rather keep inside.

"Like I want something I shouldn't."

We sit there in silence for what feels like forever. Paulie eventually stands from his chair and kicks it in with his boot, making me look up at him, wondering if this conversation is officially over, but then he stops.

"If you want to die an old, miserable person, that's on you. But I'd suggest you take a second chance when you see it, because they don't come around as often as you think."

"I'm not ready."

Paulie nods, picking at the label on the now empty beer bottle. "Then don't be a dick. Tell her you're sorry and be honest with her, put her out of her misery. Because a girl like Avery won't give up until it's too late and she's been hurt. I think we both know that about her."

We do. Paulie and I both saw what she looked like when she came here. She was bruised and battered. She probably should've given up on that motherfucker long before she did.

I've thought more than once about taking a trip to Houston and hunting *Brant* down, making him sorry he ever laid a hand on her. The punch I got in while he was in my bar wasn't enough. He needs to know that if he ever even looks at her again, I'm going to...

What?

What am I going to do?

As of this evening, I was trying to hurt her bad enough that she'd just leave. When Paulie told me she sucked it up and went about business as usual, I have to admit, I was shocked. I expected her to run, but she didn't.

She's strong.

Stubborn.

Tenacious as fuck.

And now that I know my little ploy didn't work, what now?

"Who walked her home tonight?" I ask, my mind finally feeling clear enough to think about something besides being a dick.

"Jeremy," Paulie answers, walking over and tossing his bottle in the trash.

"What the fuck, Paulie?" I ask, standing up and pushing my chair back with more force than necessary.

His hands go up in surrender. "Hey, you were nowhere to be found and I had a lot of shit to get done. Besides Sarah needed me...so, it was the kid or she walked home alone, and we both know that's not happening."

"Fuck," I groan, raking a hand through my hair again. "I don't trust him, Paulie."

He lets out a sigh and leans against the bar. "Not saying I trust him either, but he's got a boner for Avery. I doubt he'll let anything happen to her."

My frustration rises with the bile in the back of my throat. "That's what I'm fucking worried about."

"So, let me get this straight, you don't want her, but you don't want anyone else having her. Is that right?"

"It's not like that," I mutter, kicking the chair back into its spot.

Paulie lets out a chuckle. "Okay."

"What the fuck?" This time the question is directed more to myself than Paulie, but he just shakes his head and walks to the back, assuming he's taking his leave for the night...morning, what the fuck ever.

When I hear the back door slam, I flip off the lights and walk to the office. Grabbing my jacket and my keys, I follow Paulie, but he's already made his way out of the alley. So, I unlock the shed and back my bike out.

I should drive home seeing it's nearly three in the morning, but I can't. Instead, I drive over to where Avery is staying. When I get to the familiar house, I drive slowly, noticing that all the lights are off. The streets are free of people and I have to hope that she's in there safely.

The thought crosses my mind to call Charity House and see if Jeremy made it back there yet, but I don't.

I do pause for a second, my eyes going to the spot where Avery was standing last night when she kissed me. I let myself feel for a moment, remembering the warmth and electricity that coursed through my body and wonder what the hell I'm doing.

What did I do?

Not the kiss. That I don't regret. But the bullshit with Brandy. Why would I do that? Why would I intentionally hurt someone as good as Avery?

Letting out a frustrated sigh, I roll the bike down the road a little, away from the house, before starting it up and driving off. The cool breeze helps to clear my mind and leads me home.

My quiet, too big house.

Alone, which I normally relish in, enjoying the solitude, but not tonight. Tonight for the first time in a long time, instead of loneliness feeling like an old friend, it's almost too much to bear.

15

Avery

WHEN **I** WALK INTO THE BAR, **P**AULIE RAISES AN expectant eyebrow and tilts his head toward the back of the bar, answering a question I hadn't yet asked. Since no one else is at the bar yet, I take it as a sign and walk with a purposeful gait in the direction of Shaw's office.

"Hey," I say, summoning the bravery I seem to have misplaced the second I stepped into the doorway of his office.

Shaw's head snaps up from his desk, where he's working, and my stomach drops. His eyes are sharp, yet reserved. I can tell whatever walls came down two nights ago have been fully restored, and something about the returned rigidness in his features spurs me on.

"Did you need something?" he mutters as his eyes scan my body, making me feel vulnerable under their scrutiny.

Clearing my throat, I deliver the words I came to say before I lose my nerve. "I just want you to know I know what you're doing. The whole thing with the bimbo in the corner. I know," I pause and swallow, my voice sounding foreign as it comes out of my mouth. When all Shaw does is stare at me, I continue. "You're an asshole. I get it, but I need you to know that I don't play games. So, the next time you have a message for me, just tell me, with words."

A shadow passes Shaw's features and I swallow, wanting to say more, but knowing I'll hate myself for showing my vulnerability. The last thing I want him to know is how much that hurt me.

"I didn't sleep with her," he grits out. There's a tightness in his face and his lips twitch with what I can only assume is guilt or anger, maybe a mixture of both.

"That doesn't make you any less of an asshole."

I turn and walk away, and I keep walking until I'm pushing open the backdoor of the bar. Once it slams behind me, I brace my hands on my knees and take deep, cleansing breaths through my nose, willing myself to not pass out or throw up. Normally, I'm not one for confrontation, but I also refuse to let anyone else treat me like shit. My mind wavers between offering myself a high-five and panicking.

What the hell did I just do?

I told Shaw off.

That's what I did.

And he deserved it.

Yeah, no regrets.

Tentatively, I turn toward the door, expecting it to burst open at any moment and for Shaw to come storming out to tell me I'm fired. After a few minutes, and still no Shaw, I let out a gush of air and place my hands on my head, like I just ran a marathon and I need to catch my breath.

Looking around the alley—up the stairs that lead to Shaw's apartment and then down the alley toward the street—I decide there's no way I can walk back into the bar right now. I need a little time before I have to face him. Besides, my shift doesn't start for another hour. I came in early for the specific purpose of telling Shaw he's an asshole, but I had expected it to take more time than it did.

Now that it's done, my schedule is pretty free for the next fifty-five minutes.

When the backdoor of the cooking school opens, I flinch, spinning around like I've been caught stealing. With my hand over my heart, I let out a nervous laugh. "Oh, my God. Sorry, you scared the shit out of me."

Sarah chuckles and places a hand on her hip. "What are you doing back here?"

"Uh, just...taking out the trash." My statement comes out more like a question and I shoot my eyes over my shoulder to see that the dumpster is empty. Blushing profusely at the lie I just told, I turn back to Sarah and give her an apologetic smile. "Or avoiding my boss?"

"Get in here," she demands softly, opening the door wider for me to step around her. "I need a taste tester and since Shaw is in such a splendid mood, you'll work much better."

I feel like Sarah senses what's going on between the two of us. Her knowing gaze equally sets me at ease and makes me feel exposed. But I like Sarah and she's never been anything but nice to me, so I follow her into her kitchen and take a seat at the counter, waiting for whatever delicious masterpiece she's going to put in front of me.

Within a few days, everything goes back to normal, pre-kiss and Shaw's public display of affection. He's back to being his typical grouchy self, but there haven't been any signs of the bimbo. Paulie seems to be holding some kind of grudge against the grump, but I mind my p's and q's and stay out of that. They can handle their own shit. Sarah takes it upon herself to smooth the waters by offering donuts and free food on a daily basis, which seems to put everyone in a bit of a better mood.

She seems to be a professional peacekeeper.

Over our impromptu dinner a few days ago, she shared stories of Shaw and their other three brothers. Their mother passed away a few years ago and their father a year before that, which makes her the matriarch of the family and a job she takes seriously. When she mentioned their passing, her eyes turned sad and solemn, like I expected, but there was something else she wanted to say, but didn't.

She did say that growing up in their Irish Catholic home was an adventure to say the least. She talked about Shaw being the life of the party, always pulling pranks and getting in trouble. Her stories had me reeling.

Shaw freezing all of his older brothers' underwear.

Shaw dressing up like a girl and crashing one of his brother's dates by claiming the girl was a trifling whore.

I laughed.

He was funny.

Who knew?

The Shaw she spoke of was fun-loving, full of antics and life.

What happened to change him?

What makes someone do a one-eighty like that?

I believe her though, because when the two of them are together, bits of that Shaw come to the surface. He laughs with her and smiles at her. The expression opening up a part of my heart I didn't know existed. It makes me stupid because it makes me want to forgive his shortcomings and disregard his behavior. It makes me want to force him to show me the real Shaw—the one Sarah talks about.

As I'm gearing up to head into work, my phone rings and I answer it.

"Hello."

"Avery." My mama's concerned voice comes over the phone.

"Hey, Mama," I greet, looking around my small room for my hoodie.

"It's raining today," she says, making me smile and shake my head. "Be sure you take an umbrella and maybe some dry shoes. You know how uncomfortable it can be to work in wet socks and shoes. Is there a chance you could catch a ride? Maybe call a taxi? You don't want to get pneumonia."

I roll my eyes at her efforts to mother me even from hundreds of miles away. "I'll be fine, Mama. It's just a little water. I've got a hoodie and an umbrella."

"I just worry about you," she sighs. "Did you hear about that murder? Do you live near—"

"Mama," I say, cutting her off. She's been doing this more and more lately, worrying herself crazy and watching New Orleans news more than her own. "What did I tell you about watching those news stories online. There are murders and abductions everywhere. And I'm careful, you know that. I watch my surroundings and I never walk home at night by myself." I continue my search of my hoodie, finally finding it in the bottom of the suitcase in the closet.

"I know, I know. I just worry."

"I know, but you don't have to. I'm fine and I'm gonna be fine."

"Are you coming home for Thanksgiving?" she asks for the umpteenth time. "It's less than two weeks away and I need to know what to tell your grandparents. They keep asking."

Sitting down on the edge of my bed, I let out a deep breath. "I don't know, Mama. I'm still looking for a place, but I think I'm going to room with my friend CeCe. I have to be out of here in a week, so if I have everything situated by then, I'll see about buying a plane ticket home... or maybe a bus ticket."

It's an expense I really can't afford right now, since I'm still saving up, but I know it's important for me to go home for the holidays.

"Okay, baby."

"I've gotta go. I need to leave myself plenty of time to get to work," I tell her, standing back up and walking toward the door.

Once I end the call, I stuff my phone in my pocket and pull the hoodie over my head. Putting my backpack on, I grab my umbrella and head outside, pausing for a minute when I get to the sidewalk. It's not just raining, it's a freaking downpour. The weather man said this is the remnants of a late season tropical storm and I believe him. The wind is blowing hard enough that the rain is coming in sideways.

So much for an umbrella.

Just when I'm getting ready to turn around and get a dry change of clothes for when I get to work, because I'm obviously going to need them, I hear someone call my name.

Turning around, I look toward the sidewalk and see a large Jeep parked at the curb. It's black and menacing looking, with huge tires.

I pause and look closer, trying to see who's inside before running out into the deluge.

"Avery!"

This time, I recognize the voice, and then I see him.

Shaw is in the driver's seat of the mammoth vehicle and he has the window rolled down just enough for me to hear him call my name again. Without another thought, I run out into the elements and just as I get to the Jeep, the door opens and Shaw offers me a hand.

Once inside, I take a second to catch my breath then glance over to the last person I expected to see at this moment. "Hey."

"Hey," he replies, eyes scanning me like they've been known to do.

"What—" I start at the same time he begins to talk.

"I thought you'd—"

We both pause in an effort to let the other speak, when I huff a light laugh and brush a piece of hair away from my face, I don't miss the way he watches me do it. Something in his dark gaze makes my heart beat pick up the pace. Maybe it's being in this confined space or maybe it's remembering the last time we were this close, in this exact spot.

"I just thought you might like a ride," he continues. "This is definitely no weather to be walking in. If you got pneumonia, I'd feel solely responsible."

Letting out another airy laugh, feeling every bit as nervous as I sound, I tell him, "You sound like my mother."

I glance over to see Shaw wince a little at that, but if I'm not mistaken, there was a hint of a smile on his lips.

"She literally just told me that like five minutes ago."

And that's when it happens.

The corner of his mouth turns up in a lopsided grin and he turns it on me, giving me its full-force, practically knocking me out of my seat. I resist the urge to suck in a deep breath and just swallow down my elation, pretending like him smiling at me like that is the most normal thing on earth.

"Well, thank you," I finally manage, trying to cover up my

befuddlement. I can do this. I can sit in this small space and be normal. Besides, I already know what happens when I act on my impulses concerning Shaw. It ends badly.

"You're welcome."

We don't speak again for the short ride to the bar. I want to ask him if he's planning on giving the rest of the guys a ride, but I don't. I think I know the answer to that. When we pull up into the alley behind the bar and he puts the Jeep in park, we both sit there, still soaking in the comfortable silence.

"I didn't know you had a Jeep," I tell him, running my hand along the leather handle. When he stays silent, I feel stupid for making such a dumb comment. Of course I didn't know he has a Jeep. Shaw and I have only had a handful of real, genuine conversations. It's not like I know everything there is to know about him...but I want to.

"Yep," he says shortly, pulling the keys from the ignition.

When I go to open the door and make a run for it into the bar, he stops me with his words.

"I'm sorry."

I'm sorry.

Two simple words, but they are more profound than a hundred.

With my hand still on the door handle, I look back at him, meeting his gaze. His dark brows are furrowed over his equally dark eyes, upping his intensity and making me feel the depth of his apology.

I should ask for clarification, but I don't because I don't have to. From the way his brows are pinched together in regret, I just know. I don't know where the regret ends, whether he's just sorry about what he did the other night or if he's also sorry for kissing me, but I give him a nod of acceptance.

"Thank you," I tell him again.

A smile and an apology from Shaw, both within a few minutes of each other?

Today must be my lucky day.

16

Shaw

SOMETHING SHIFTED IN ME THE NIGHT OF THE *BRANDY* *Debacle.*

Seeing the hurt on Avery's face cut deep inside my chest, down to a place I thought was dead and gone, along with so many other things...along with Liz. For the last five years, I've felt broken, numb, desensitized to everyone and everything, and I've been okay with it.

I had love.

I had the greatest love.

I had the love of a lifetime.

Enough for two lifetimes.

To expect a second chance would be selfish, and I've never been a selfish person. A dick? Sure. An asshole? Absolutely. But selfish? No. Not until two weeks ago when I made the split-second decision to use Brandy to put Avery in her place—far away from me, somewhere I couldn't hurt her...or kiss her. Because that fucking kiss...that kiss was like an electric shock.

I've thought about kissing her several times—dozens of times—in the past few months, but never allowed myself to move past the fleeting thought, pushing it far from my mind each time it crept in. When she took away the forbiddenness of it all by making the first move and closing the distance between us, I couldn't help but meet her there and take what I wanted, what I've been wanting.

When I drove away from that curb and left her standing there, I felt the need to run, but I also felt revived, like I've been on the brink of death and someone took a defibrillator to my chest.

Alive.

Awake.

Aroused.

Everything I've tried so hard not to feel.

The origination could've been from grief or guilt or pure determination to not live without Liz. I'm not sure, but Avery has somehow changed everything.

To say I was scared as shit would be an understatement.

Since then, and in the following week as I tried to make it right, I've had a change of heart. I realized that no matter what, I couldn't treat her badly, even if I rationalized my behavior by saying I was doing it for her own good. I couldn't be responsible for that look she gave me—disappointment and heartbreak written all over her face.

"So, I was thinking we could have everyone come to the cooking school for Thanksgiving. The guys can watch football here at the bar. The women can hang out in the kitchen. It'll be nice," Sarah says, walking up beside me and resting her elbows on the bar.

"Okay," I tell her, because I know there's no use going against her wishes. She gets what she wants and she knows it, which is why she's telling me what we're doing instead of asking.

Grabbing my coffee cup and helping herself to a sip, she adds, "And I want to invite Paulie and the guys...and Avery."

"Did you just steal my coffee?" I ask in disgust.

"Just a sip. Don't be a baby."

"And left fucking lipstick behind," I groan, pushing the tarnished porcelain her way. "You can have it."

"Thank you," she says cheerfully, once again, getting exactly what she wants. "So, do you want to extend the invite or do you want me to?"

"I'll do it." My response must not be happy enough for her because she gives me a pointed stare over the top of the mug as she takes another drink. When I give her a fake ass smile, she shakes her head and sets the cup back down.

"It's the right thing to do, you know?" Her shoulder bumps into mine and I grunt. "We've never been a family who disregards people with no place to be."

She's right. We haven't. That trait was passed down from our parents. Being immigrants, they were always passing along random acts of kindness. My mother said so many people helped them get here and make a life for themselves and they felt responsible to pass that kindness on.

"You're so much like them," she whispers with a hint of sadness in her tone, the same tone she always takes on when speaking of our parents.

"You are too," I tell her, bumping her shoulder back softly.

"They'd be really proud of you," she adds. "So would Lizzie."

With that statement, I feel my chest tighten like it usually does when her name is mentioned in conversation, but I also notice that the squeeze isn't life-threatening like it used to be. A few years ago, after Lizzie and then the death of my mother and father, I could barely stand to walk past any place Lizzie and I went together. I let the bar go to shit, kept the cooking school in the exact state it had been when we stopped working on it, never ate at the Palace Café, only walked down side streets to avoid places we took daily walks...I avoided life and everything good that was left on this earth.

And any time anyone brought up her name, I died a little inside.

I know it should've been the opposite, I should've loved hearing her name spoken. I should've cherished people's memories of her. I should've wanted to feel like she could walk around the corner at any time. But I didn't. I couldn't.

My therapist told me it was normal, because grief doesn't have a formula.

Everyone is allowed to handle death anyway they want, except for checking out.

He never let me check out.

Neither did Sarah.

She's been my accountability partner for thirty-eight years and she certainly didn't stop when Liz died. She checked on me, cooked for me, and later, when I was ready, she pushed me to move on with life. At first, the movements were small—I took down the Christmas lights that had been up since Lizzie went into the hospital and dumped out the dead plants from her funeral.

Then, together, Sarah and I opened the bar back up.

And more recently, she pushed me to re-open the cooking school. That was partly for me and partly for Sarah, but mostly for Liz. We remodeled it exactly to Lizzie's specifications.

She loved that place and her visions for it. She spent hours talking about it and daydreaming about it. She wrote down recipes and ways she could tweak them and make them her own. She had paint swatches picked out and floor plans drawn. It was the driving force behind her first time in remission.

But then the cancer came back and all of our energy and focus turned to getting her better.

She died six months later.

Three weeks after Christmas.

The fact that date is looming hasn't gone unnoticed, which is probably why Sarah's making even more of an effort to keep me out of my own head and focused on something positive—something I can control.

I can host Thanksgiving and I can invite my employees, even Avery.

"Okay, listen up," I say, clapping my hands together to get everyone's attention. Paulie is talking quietly with Avery. Jeremy and Kevin are cutting up, per usual, and Charlie is watching everyone with a pleased expression on his face. I have to admit, aside from my lingering reserves regarding the kid, which I'm still not ready to let go, the whole crew has really gelled and they're making a great staff. Even after a weekend like we just came off of, which could give Mardi Gras a run for its money, they hung in there, made the customers happy, and in turn, made me pretty proud.

"What's up, boss?" Paulie asks, directing his focus at me and bringing the rest of them in line. They follow him and that's what makes Paulie a great manager. He fills in everywhere and anywhere I need him to, and he helps Sarah out a lot. I couldn't ask for anyone better.

However, Avery definitely gives him a run for his money. For being younger, she's intuitive and smart. She handles the customers and herself with grace and ease. I can't help but appreciate that about her.

"I'm not sure what y'all have going on for Thanksgiving, but I want you to know we'll be having dinner next door and you're all invited."

"Dude, like with turkey and dressing and everything?" Jeremy asks, his eyes growing wide at the prospect.

"And cranberry sauce and rolls and pumpkin pie," Sarah adds, smiling from her spot beside me. "And a full helping of O'Sullivans."

"Yeah, my shithead brothers will be here too," I tell them, in full disclosure. "And their wives and a few kids."

Charlie, the new guy, pipes up. "Man, like a real family Thanksgiving."

That comment fucking tugs at my heart a little, I'm not gonna lie, so I try to lighten the situation back up before I get all emotional about the fact that most of these guys haven't had a real family holiday in a while, maybe never. "If you're into that sort of thing," I tell him, scrunching my face in mock displeasure.

"What can I bring?" Paulie asks.

"Just yourselves," Sarah tells him with a soft smile. "I want you all here and plan on spending the day with us. Let us show you how much we appreciate all your hard work and dedication."

When I breathe sharply out of my nose, Sarah pokes me with her elbow.

"Even though Shaw is a man of few words and even less praise, *we*," she says with a pause and sideways glance my way, "appreciate all of you. And we want you to know you have a place at our table."

I watch as Avery's face softens and she gives Sarah a smile that's equally happy and sad.

"I wish I could come," she says softly. "But I bought a bus ticket yesterday, so I'll be headed home for a few days." She pauses, her eyes going wide. "Oh, shit. I hope that's okay. I'm planning on leaving late Wednesday night. I could work for a few hours. And then I'll be coming back on Saturday morning. I meant to say something, but I hadn't really decided if I was going or not until yesterday."

"That's fine," I tell her gruffly, but I don't mean it to come out like that.

"Okay, well, I guess that does it for our Tuesday meeting." This time, it's Sarah that claps her hands together and dismisses the group, everyone going about their business.

"I'm sorry I didn't say something sooner," Avery says quietly, fidgeting with the tie on her apron. "I should've. I've just been in such limbo and—"

"It's fine," I tell her again, this time a bit softer than earlier. "Take all the time you need."

Her eyes finally meet mine and I hope she sees the sincerity there. It really is fine. We've never been big on policy and procedure around here. If you need a day off, you take it. There's always someone around to pick up the slack and if there's not, I'm happy to step in. I'm definitely not above bartending or bussing tables. I used to do pretty much everything, but lately, my staff has grown and I'm not needed as much.

When she nods her head and diverts her gaze, I feel a small twinge of regret. It's ridiculous though, so I push it down and bury it.

I'm not sure why I wanted Avery to meet the rest of my family, but it's probably a good idea she's going home.

Better for her.

And better for me and my weakening walls.

17

Avery

"I CAN'T THANK YOU ENOUGH, CECE."

She unlocks the door to her apartment and pushes it wide open, allowing me to step in first. "Stop thanking me. It's my pleasure, really. Besides, once you see how tiny it is, you may change your mind."

"Are you kidding? I've spent the past few months living in one room. You have *rooms*, including a kitchen, and actual space to move around. I swear, I'm in heaven."

As I look around the apartment, I can't help the huge grin that spreads across my face. Exposed brick on the walls, windows that face the French Quarter, the already mentioned kitchen, and the fluffy couch that will be my new bed while I'm here all contribute to my joyful mood. Throw in CeCe's eclectic decorating style that obviously spilled into the coffee shop below us and I immediately feel at home. Temporarily, of course.

CeCe lowers my duffle bag to the floor by the couch. "I still can't believe you only have two bags. That bastard better send you the rest of your stuff when you get your own place."

"To be honest, I don't want any of it. I mean, I'd love to have my books and pictures back, but those can be replaced. As for my clothes," I shrug, thinking about how most of my wardrobe in Houston wasn't really *me* anyway, "he can keep them all. He can even wear them, for all I care."

Laughing, CeCe wraps her arm around my shoulders and pulls me in for a side-hug. "You really are better off without him, you know. And I'm so proud of how well you're doing here. This place is better now that you're here."

Her words hit me hard and I bite down on my bottom lip to keep from tearing up.

"Oh, no you don't. None of that crying shit. If you cry, then I'll have to cry and then we'll have to pig out on ice cream and my jeans are tight enough at the moment."

She's full of it, of course, but this time her words make me laugh and all desire to cry is gone.

"So, make yourself at home and help yourself to anything in the kitchen or bathroom you might need. I have to get back to work, but I'll be back in time for us to do an early dinner, okay? You're more than welcome to hang out downstairs if you get bored, but don't feel like you have to. Enjoy your afternoon off work!"

Once CeCe has left, I head straight to the wall of windows and look out. I can make out the cathedral and shops, as well as hear the mixed sounds of people chatting and street musicians playing. People-watching while sitting in an air conditioned space is pretty much the best of both worlds and, again, a rush of gratitude slams into my chest.

CeCe's words about *this place* being better now that I'm here, whether she meant New Orleans or her apartment, was just the validation I needed to know I'm doing the right thing. It seems crazy but, fulfilling my dream and moving here, thriving even, gives me the confidence I need to go home tomorrow. I won't be returning a failure, I'll be visiting my family for the holiday and then coming back to my new home.

I guess that means it's time to call my mama and let her know to be expecting me and that I'll need a ride from the bus station. I could rent a car, but I don't want that kind of expense, besides, my daddy would never allow it anyway, even if I offered.

"Hey, baby, everything okay?"

"Of course, Mama. You sound a little out of breath. Are you okay?"

"Oh, yes, I'm at the grocery store and you know how crazy this place is the week of Thanksgiving. I normally don't wait this long to do my shopping, but I was trying to give you extra time to decide if you were coming or not. I don't suppose that's why you're callin', is it?"

She sounds so hopeful and I immediately feel guilty for waiting until the last minute to make my travel plans.

Before I can give her the answer she wants, she starts talking again. "I almost forgot to tell you, I saw Brant yesterday."

The sound of his name has my blood going cold and my smile fading.

Brant is back home. Of course, he is.

Shit.

"Baby, he looked just awful. I'm sure he's sorry for whatever happened between you two. Haven't you forgiven him by now? It would be very romantic for you two to make up over the holiday. I hope you don't mind, I invited him and his mama and daddy out to the farm for dessert. It's not Thanksgiving without family and friends, right?"

I have to remind myself that she has no idea what she's asking me to forgive before I lash out and say something I might regret. There's no fucking way I can go to Oklahoma now. I don't even care that I just wasted money on a bus ticket.

"Mama, I'm sorry, but I was calling to say I won't be able to be there for Thanksgiving. Also, I'd really like it if you'd stop trying to convince me to forgive Brant. We're over. Like, really over and I don't want to see him ever again."

"Oh" is the only response she gives me. I hate that I'm hurting her but I just can't be where Brant is.

Trying to keep the lump in my throat down, I try to reassure her. "I'll come home soon, I promise. And I'll see you and Daddy at Christmas, okay? You know, y'all can come down here, too. That'd be fun, wouldn't it?"

"I just don't know if we could leave the farm for that long, Avery.

Look, dear, we'll talk more later. I need to get these groceries home. I love you."

"Love you, Mama," I say before hanging up.

I'm flooded with emotions as I curl up on CeCe's couch—sad that I won't be seeing my family tomorrow and terribly guilty for hurting my mama's feelings.

I don't know why I hadn't considered the possibility of Brant going home for Thanksgiving.

I should've prepared for this. I should've known he'd be there. Any other year, he'd have things to do—client meetings or a cruise to the Bahamas. But no, this year, he's already been in Honey Springs for a day.

Of fucking course.

Taking my frustrations out on one of CeCe's eclectic throw pillows, I punch it and then cram my face down into it and scream. If I don't, I'll cry and I can't let Brant have another tear. He doesn't deserve it.

Honestly, I'm more pissed off at myself for allowing him to have any kind of control over me and my actions, whether he knows it or not. I should be able to live my life without worrying about running into him but it's just easier to avoid him for the time being. I'll have to face him sooner or later, I know that, but I'm not ready for that yet.

The excitement and hope I felt just a few moments ago have been replaced with annoyance and disappointment, leaving me feeling crappy and lonely.

Sighing, I look around the small space, needing something to distract me and make me feel better. I can't control Brant, but I can control myself and how I respond to my given situation. I could go hang out downstairs and let CeCe teach me a few things about the coffee making process, but I'm not really in the right frame of mind for that. The only thing that sounds appealing is something I haven't had the chance to do in a long time—baking.

When life hands you shitty ex-boyfriends, you bake.

Hopping off the couch, I head for the door. I need ingredients and CeCe's approval to christen her kitchen. And since it looks like

I'll be making a surprise arrival at the O'Sullivan Thanksgiving Dinner tomorrow, I know the perfect thing to make.

As I head out to the bar, I start worrying that I won't be welcome, but quickly shake that feeling and push it to the back of my mind. Sarah told me the other day that I was welcome if plans changed.

At the time, I didn't expect them to, but then Brant went and ruined everything.

Typical.

The nerves are still buzzing beneath my skin as I approach the sidewalk leading to the bar and cooking school. Regardless of the pep talk I gave myself, they persist. I guess it's a good thing I'm bringing two pans of blondies with me. No one can turn away a girl who comes bearing sweets, right?

CeCe invited me to join her at Blue Bayou, a hotel around the corner. Her friend owns it and apparently that's where she spends most holidays. I considered taking her up on it, but deep down, as much as I wanted to go home, I also wanted to spend Thanksgiving with Shaw and Sarah and everyone from the bar. So, even though I'm sad about not being in Oklahoma, this is definitely the next best thing.

Walking up to the door, I hesitate for a minute, but then the door opens up and a surprised Sarah smiles at me. "Avery!"

The welcoming tone in her voice immediately sets me at ease and I return her smile. "Hi, I'm...well, I didn't go home, so—"

"Come in here," she says, cutting off my awkward rambling. "What's this?"

I look down at the foil covered baking dishes in my hands. "Oh, I baked brownies...well, blondies. I wasn't sure what to bring, but I thought a little more dessert wouldn't go to waste."

"You didn't have to bring anything," she gently scolds as she leads me inside, taking the dishes from me. "But we certainly will not turn down baked goods."

"No, we will not turn down baked goods," a familiar, deep voice says from the direction of the kitchen in the back. When Shaw steps into the main part of the cooking school—which has been transformed into a large dining space with enough chairs to seat what looks like two dozen people—he stops in mid-stride and his face changes from the semi-smile he was wearing to one of indifference.

Or at least fake indifference.

Clearing his throat, he adds, letting his features soften a little. "Turning away baked goods on Thanksgiving would just be sacrilegious."

"Take these and put them with the rest of the desserts," Sarah orders, handing Shaw the dishes. When he goes to lift the foil, she swats his hand.

A small, mischievous smile plays on his lips as he turns and walks away with the blondies in hand, and I relax a little.

"Let me introduce you to everyone. Most of the men are over at the bar, but there are plenty of people to meet in the kitchen." Sarah places an arm around my shoulder and guides me to the back of the kitchen.

When we step inside everyone turns and smiles, awaiting an introduction.

"Everyone, this is Avery. She works at the bar and she's originally from Oklahoma...and she's just an all-around lovely person." I glance over at Sarah and see her smiling at me and it warms me from the inside out—her expression and her words.

When everyone says "hello" in unison, I laugh lightly and wave. "Hello."

"Avery," Sarah begins, pointing to a lady with dark hair and dark eyes, looking every bit like she could be a sibling, but I know she's not because Sarah is the only sister. "This is Amy, she's married to Shane, who you'll meet later, and this is their little one, Brady."

The adorable little boy gives me a wide toothy grin, making his eyes turn into slivers. "Hi," he says with a wave.

"Brady is three," Sarah continues.

"And he's working on giving me all the gray hairs," Amy adds, offering me her hand across the counter where it looks like she's putting the finishing touches on a green bean casserole. "It's nice to meet you, Avery. So glad you could make it."

"Thank you," I tell her before turning my smile to Brady. "It's nice to meet you."

"This," Sarah continues, "is Emily and she's married to Shannon. They have two boys who are also married and are spending the holidays with the in-laws." The way Sarah says in-laws lets me know this has already been a topic of conversation and everyone laughs or gives an eye roll with that statement. I'm gathering this is probably a new thing and change isn't well received, as it is with most tight-knit families, which makes me think of my own and a sharp pain pokes me in my chest.

Ignoring the guilt, I smile apologetically and say, "Sorry, I guess." The laugh I get takes away a little of the ache and instead of a handshake, Emily reaches over and gives me a hug.

"Glad you're here, Avery." She smells good and her honey-blonde hair smells amazing. I think about telling her that, but refrain.

"Thank you," I tell her, admiring the beautiful necklace she's wearing. Now that I get a closer look at her, I can tell she's probably the age of my mother. There are faint aging lines around her eyes and mouth from years of expressing herself. She's beautiful. And motherly. I'm instantly drawn to her.

"This is Cynthia and she's married to Sean. And these are her girls, Molly and Riley." Two girls who look like they're about my age smile and wave along with their mother, who they look just like, except for the jet black hair, which I assume they got from their father if he looks anything like Shaw.

Once I've met the wives and kids, Sarah walks me next door to meet the brothers and a spike of nervousness hits. I'm not sure why. Maybe it's because I want their approval? That thought has me questioning my own sanity because what does it matter if they like me or not?

It doesn't.

This will more than likely be the only time I ever see them, right? So, no harm, no foul.

Thankfully, when we walk inside, the brothers are all just as welcoming as their wives. They all smile and wave, letting Sarah make the introductions. Sure enough, they all look so much alike, give or take a few years. It's obvious in so many ways that Shaw is the baby. Like Sarah, Sean, the oldest of the O'Sullivans, is more like a parental figure than a sibling. When Shannon and Shane, the middle brothers start arguing over a call on one of the three football games playing on the televisions above the bar, Sean is the one to step in and remind them that there will be no brawling on Thanksgiving.

"Next thing you know, you're gonna be telling us to take it outside," Shaw scoffs, rolling his eyes as he takes a pull from his beer, immediately drawing my attention to his lips...and neck and forearms that are on display.

Stop it, Avery.

Get it together.

This is a family get together.

"Yeah, and then he'll make us stand outside until we hug it out," Shannon teases, pushing Shane's shoulder.

"I swear," Sarah whispers. "When they're all together, they act more like they're five instead of fifty-something."

"Speak for yourself," Shane calls out. "And don't think I can't hear ya. Just because I'm older, doesn't mean I'm deaf."

Sarah laughs, shaking her head, "Come on, Avery, let's go back to the land of the civilized."

Paulie, Jeremy, Kevin, and Charlie are all hanging out at the bar, kicked back with beers of their own and enjoying not waiting on customers. I give them all waves and smile as I'm led back next door.

About fifteen minutes later, a spread worthy of a Better Homes and Gardens magazine is laid out on the long table and Sarah calls everyone over. With no specific places to sit, everyone kind of migrates to their spouse, leaving me and the rest of the crew to fill in the other spots.

I end up sitting between Sarah and Jeremy, with Paulie and Shaw sitting across from me. When I realize who I'll be staring at for the entire meal, I consider changing spots with someone, but everyone else is settled, so I guess I can endure Shaw's stares and glares for some turkey and dressing.

Because, oh, my God, does everything look and smell amazing.

It smells like home.

And holidays.

And family.

And everything good in life all rolled into one meal.

"Sean's saying grace," Sarah, announces, doing the sign of the cross and bowing her head. I don't do the sign of the cross, because I'm afraid I would mess it up, but I do bow my head, as does everyone around me. A split second before Sean begins his prayer, I take a peek at Shaw, expecting to see his head down, but find him watching me.

It's no use pretending.

He knows I was looking up to see him.

But I caught him looking at me.

So, we're even.

"Dear Lord," Sean begins and I break my gaze away from Shaw and focus on the table, still feeling his stare on me. "We're so thankful for the family who's here today, those we were given through blood, those we were given through marriage, and those we were given through fate. Bless the hands that made the food and bless those who are about to eat it. Be with all the less fortunate and give us opportunities to show them kindness. Amen."

All the O'Sullivans finish the prayer with the sign of the cross, as does Paulie, before the chatter erupts and plates begin being passed around the table. It's like an organized circus, beautiful chaos, and I'm suddenly filled with so much love...for everyone here who I've met today and for finding this place, along with this family.

Shaw is difficult, but he's also one of the kindest people I've ever met.

When I think of Shaw, I think of something my daddy once told me: integrity isn't about what you do when people are looking, it's about what you do when they're not.

Shaw is the picture of integrity. He's good and trustworthy. And seeing him here today, surrounded by his family, small pieces of his puzzle start to fall into place. However, I'm also left wondering, not for the first time, what happened in his life to change his trajectory? How did he go from being the fun-loving little brother of this big, welcoming family to the Shaw I met a few months ago—brooding, moody, and guarded?

18

Shaw

"Since when did you start hiring women to work

at your bar?" Shannon asks when we're all back over in said bar, catching a few more football games.

"Since I hired Avery," I deadpan, hoping he'll let it go. I really don't want to get into a hundred questions about Avery because I don't know how long I'll be able to keep up the ruse of indifference I try to maintain when she's around.

Thankfully, we left the women, and my brother Shane, next door to gush over the Black Friday sales ads in the newspapers. For whatever fucking reason, he gets a hard-on for cheap electronics.

Once we got all the food put away and take out containers filled to the brim for everyone to take home, the papers came out and we made our exit. It looks like a hurricane hit over there and I want no part of it.

Paulie excused himself a few minutes ago, claiming he had a nap calling his name. Jeremy and Kevin took off right after dinner with a few boxes of food for Charity House, and Charlie slipped out right after them. He's a quiet one, but I like him.

The only people left are my family...and Avery, who has fit in well.

I could barely keep my eyes off her at dinner. She looks beautiful, no more than every other day, but she curled her hair today and her eyes stand out more. Her mouth is fuller and painted a light shade of pink. When I caught her looking at me earlier, I wanted so badly to reach across the table, pull her to me, and kiss her, which is completely insane and out of the question.

But I wanted to just the same.

"She's what? About Riley's age?" Sean's question is benign enough, but it puts my hackles up and feels like a bucket of cold water just got poured on my dick.

I clear my throat and shift on the barstool, taking a much needed drink of my beer. Shrugging, I place the bottle back down in front of me and pick at the label.

"She's cute," Shannon adds, bringing those hackles to full attention.

"A real pretty girl," Sean comments in his fatherly tone.

I know he probably looks at Avery like a kid, due to her age and the fact he has two daughters in their early twenties, but I still don't like it and I want to change the fucking subject.

"Where'd you say she's from?" Shannon asks, earning a groan from me, but I try to curtail it. I don't want to give him any reason to think she's off-limits because that will only make this harder.

"Oklahoma."

"And she moved here all by herself?" he continues.

"She's a grown ass woman. I guess she can move where she damn well pleases."

"You're such a fucking grumpy ass in your old age," Shannon prods, trying to get a rise out of me, but he's not going to get it.

"But she is by herself, huh?"

I swear, he's like an old grandma—nosey as shit and needs to know everyone's fucking business. I don't know how Emily has put up with him all these years. We've always gone back and forth with each other. He was thirteen when I was born and I basically rained on his parade. The hilarious turn of events is that he and Emily weren't planning on having kids, so about five years ago he got the snip. A year later, boom. Pregnant. He named Brady after me, giving the kid my middle name, because we're both 'oops babies'.

I love the kid. Not just because we share a name, but he came along at a time when everything felt dark and depressing. You can't be around Brady and not smile. It's impossible.

"Yeah, she's by herself," I finally answer. "She was actually living in Houston with her asshole ex-boyfriend before she moved here. He beat her up. She wanted a change of pace and a fresh start. I don't blame her, do you?"

"Shit," he mutters under his breath before tipping back his beer.

"What a bastard," Sean chimes in. "Hope he gets what's comin' to him."

"I gave him what I could when he showed his face up here." Just the thought has me wishing he'd show up again so I could finish the job.

"I'm glad," my oldest brother says, patting me on the back, sounding exactly like our father.

"She's a good person," I add, for no other reason than needing to tell someone. "She definitely doesn't deserve to be treated like that."

She deserves only the best things in life, I want to add, but I don't. I stop myself before I show all my cards.

"Who's ready for dessert?" Molly calls out from the direction of the backdoor. "Aunt Sarah told me to tell y'all we're digging in."

After dinner, none of us could even think about pie or cake or brownies, but now that I've had time to let my food settle, I could go for something sweet. And to get away from my brother, the detective.

Maybe if he fills his pie hole with some actual pie, he won't have a chance to grill me about Avery or anything else.

When we all walk into the kitchen, the women are still gathered around the large, stainless steel countertop talking animatedly about various topics. My eye catches Avery's and she doesn't miss a beat, listening to something Sarah and Emily are telling her, but her attention is now split.

Sean, Shannon, and I make our way over to where all of the desserts are spread out like a fucking smorgasbord of deliciousness. I don't indulge in many sweets, outside of the donuts Sarah and the crew bring to the bar in the mornings. Oh, and those dainty, girlie pastries Avery brings every once in a while.

I never told her, but after she walked away that first day, I snuck one and it was amazing.

"We need some more wine," Sarah calls out, holding an empty bottle in the air and looking over my way.

"What do you want?" I ask, unsure of what everyone over here's been drinking.

"I'll get it," Avery says, excusing herself as she walks around the counter and behind Shane and Sean as they compare the pumpkin pie Sarah made to the one Amy brought.

I'll give it to them, pumpkin pie is an art and deserves to be discussed in great detail. But I'm more interested in the beauty who just slipped out the back door. Deciding this is my opportunity to talk to her without the eyes of every one of my family members on my back, I jump on it and nonchalantly slip out the back door behind her.

By the time I make it out into the alley, she's already slipped inside the back door of the bar. Not for the first time, I decide we need an entrance that connects the two establishments. I don't like the idea of her being out here alone, or Sarah, for that matter. When I approach the doorway of the storage room, I give the wood a light tap, hoping to alert her to me being here without scaring the shit out of her.

Calmly, she pulls the bottle of wine off the shelf and turns toward me. "Hey."

If I'm not mistaken, her cheeks instantly tinge pink and she swallows a little harder than necessary, but other than that, she appears unaffected.

"Hey," I reply, willing my heart to calm the fuck down.

Why am I feeling nervous?

Fuck.

"I just wanted to make sure you were having a good time. I know the women in my family can be a little much sometimes, but they mean well."

Avery's lips pull up into a soft smile. "They're wonderful." Her tone is wistful, and I wonder what kind of family get-together she's missing out on today and why.

"I thought you were going home. What happened?" I ask.

She winces and huffs, shaking her head. "It's going to sound stupid and really pathetic," she groans, but continues. "I called to tell my mama I'd be home this afternoon and she informed me Brant was already in town. I freaked out, I guess. I should've just gone and faced him, but I—"

"Don't feel bad about that. You shouldn't be forced to see him if you don't want to and I'd rather you not."

Her lips twist and she gets a curious look on her face. "Yeah, well, I know I can't let him dictate my life, but I just wasn't ready for that. And I still haven't had a chance to tell my parents about why I left Houston in the first place, so..."

"You didn't tell them?"

She takes a deep breath and shakes her head. "No, I haven't...not yet. My mama and daddy love Brant like a son, so telling them...well, it'll break their hearts and I just—"

"You don't want to do that," I finish for her, knowing that her heart of gold is keeping her from shattering her parents' idea of that dickhead. I huff out a laugh when I realize that in a way, she's still protecting him and looking out for him, after everything he's done.

"What's funny?" she asks, brushing a loose piece of hair behind her ear.

I can't help but watch the movement, following her hand to her ear and down her slender neck...

Fuck. I want to kiss her so goddamn bad I can't stand it.

We're quiet for a moment, just locked in a wordless tug-of-war with the familiar electricity buzzing between us. I watch as she licks her lips and I wonder if she's thinking about kissing me too. If I was a betting man, I'd put all my fucking money on it.

But then, she clears her throat and holds up the bottle of wine. "Better get this back to Sarah," she says with a small laugh. When she brushes past me, I close my eyes and inhale greedily, holding onto the small part of her I'm allowed to keep before it dissipates with her departure.

I give her a few minutes to find her way back next door before I head that way, slipping back into the mix of people and listen to Shane give us a play-by-play of what *hot deals* he's getting tonight.

The only *hot deal* I want is standing on the other side of the kitchen, entirely too fucking far away.

Later, when everyone has gone home, even Sarah, I'm sitting in the empty bar with a lingering football game playing in the background. It was a good day. I always love being with my family, even though in the past, being with them has been a constant reminder of the people missing from our dinner table, but today was different. Having the crew from the bar there was great, but Avery made things...different.

I cornered her later before she left, thinking she might need a ride, but she informed me she moved into her friend's apartment across the square. I know CeCe. We've worked a couple events at Blue Bayou together. She's a spunky little thing and I can see where she and Avery would make good friends. It makes me feel a little better that she's closer and not alone.

But, I'll admit, I was really hoping I'd get to walk her home.

Standing from the chair, I push it in and begin shutting the place down for the night when my phone rings.

"Hello?" I answer on the second ring.

"Shaw?"

"Karin?" I ask, recognizing her voice after a second. "Did you get the food I sent over?"

"Yeah, thank you so much. You always go above and beyond," she says, making me grunt and shake my head at her admiration.

"Hey..." She pauses for a second and then continues when I hear a door close in the background. "I just wanted to call and give you a heads up. I'm drug testing Jeremy tonight. I've had my doubts about his sobriety for a few weeks now. If he doesn't pass it, I won't be able to let him stay here. He can check himself into rehab and get clean, and of course, he'd be welcomed back, but I can't have him here when he's using."

I groan and kick the chair I was just sitting in back out and plop back down. Rubbing at my eyes, I try to keep my anger in check. "Fuck," I finally say, knowing Karin understands. We've worked together long enough we've seen everything.

"Yeah, my thoughts exactly. I had high hopes for this one, but something has been off lately and I'd rather nip it in the bud before it gets out of hand. The last thing I need is drugs making their way in and out of the house."

"I don't blame you," I tell her. "I've had my reservations with him and haven't been able to shake them. Last week, he seemed off, but I was giving him the benefit of the doubt."

"Well, I'm just glad we're on the same page," she says, sighing in relief.

"Keep me posted," I instruct, needing to know the outcome so I'll know how to handle things here.

"Will do," she says. "And thanks again for the food today. Everyone loved it."

"Happy Thanksgiving."

"Same to you."

19

Avery

"SINGLE...DOUBLE," CeCe SAYS, HOLDING UP TWO different types of portafilters for the espresso machine.

"To pull a perfect shot, you'll need a grind that's similar to granulated sugar, but that's already set for you too." She engages the portafilter into the grinder and selects the second option for two shots of espresso. The grinder comes to life, filling the quiet space with sound and an aroma that can't be mistaken.

"Ahhh," I sigh when the coffee hits my nose.

"Just wait," CeCe says, pressing the ground espresso down with a small metal object that looks like a big, old-fashioned stamp.

"This is the tamper," she informs. "You want to make sure the grounds are packed in until they're even. Not too hard, but nice and firm."

I snicker like a twelve-year-old at the *nice and firm*, earning a wicked grin from CeCe. "Focus," she says, trying for serious, but failing.

"Next, you place the portafilter into the brew head and turn until it feels tight." She pauses and I lose it.

"For fuck's sake."

Seconds later, the espresso is made and we're onto frothing milk. There's a lot to learn, but I think I'm going to get the hang of it before too long. For today, I'm on regular coffee duty and pastry patrol.

The shop eventually gets busy and I'm completely caught off-guard when the door opens and I call out "good morning" only to be met with a familiar "good morning" in return. Popping up from behind the counter, I'm met with dark eyes and dark hair, darker than usual because it looks wet...from a shower or sweat. Whichever, it sends my heart into overdrive.

"Hey," I say, trying to quiet the butterflies that have taken flight in my stomach.

"Hey," he replies with a small smile that does wicked things to me.

"What, uh...what can I get for you?"

Shaw looks around at the shop and then back up above my head at the menu board. When he crosses his arms over his chest and scratches at his scruff that's grown out a little more than usual, I swallow. Hard. For some reason, my thoughts immediately go to sex.

Sex with *him*.

Him above me.

Him below me.

Him behind me.

I've been thinking about sex all morning. Even the espresso had me thinking about sex. Why should I stop now? It's only natural, if you think about it. If anything gets me hot and bothered, it's Shaw O'Sullivan.

Clearing my throat, he must take it as his cue to hurry up because he huffs and cocks his head to the side like he's thinking but annoyed I'm rushing him. But really, I was doing it for myself...trying to refocus my brain to *not* think about sex...with Shaw.

Right.

Taking Shaw's order.

Giving Shaw what he wants.

What. The. Hell. Is. Wrong. With. Me?

Get it together, Avery.

I smile and surprisingly enough, he returns it. His isn't big or wide, but it's there and it's directed at me, so it feels huge. "Am I not paying you enough?" he asks in a low, husky voice that sounds a lot like bedroom talk.

"What?" I ask, shaking my head slightly, figuring maybe I didn't hear him correctly, what with all the blood gushing through my body thanks to my heart beating so fast.

"I said, am I not paying you enough?" He pauses, his dark eyes devouring mine. "You had to get a second job?"

"Oh." Realization finally dawns and I blush a little at being so scatterbrained and allowing him to affect me like this. "No, I'm just helping CeCe out," I tell him, thankfully being saved by her at that very second as she strolls in from the back.

"Good morning, Shaw," she greets cheerfully, placing a few sleeves of cups under the counter. "Just a black coffee?"

CeCe knows everyone's order. If you've been in once, she miraculously remembers what you like. It's crazy. She's like a coffee wizard. Not that Shaw O'Sullivan's black coffee order is that hard to remember. I've known how he takes his coffee from the first week I started working for him.

"Yeah, and I'll have one of those fancy pastries you like," he says, looking directly at me.

The request isn't what gets me. It's the way he delivers the words, like honey dripping off a spoon, slow and sweet. If this were anyone besides Shaw, I'd think they were flirting with me, but this *is* Shaw and I know he doesn't flirt.

Not with me, at least.

CeCe doesn't miss a beat and goes about pouring his coffee, while I stand there, allowing my eyes to linger on him a little longer than necessary.

"I thought you didn't like them?" I ask, finally pulling myself out of the lust-filled haze. "They're *girly shit*, if I remember correctly."

When his words get thrown back at him, he smirks and it's probably the hottest thing I've seen yet. "Right, well, I decided I like girly shit."

"Okay, so a danish it is," I say with a sweet smile. "Would you like cream cheese or cherry?" I make sure to put extra emphasis on *cherry* because he asked for it and I'm feeling a little naughty today.

When Shaw shifts on his feet and then clears his throat before letting out an obvious breath, I smile inside, feeling like I've won a small battle.

Later that evening, as I'm walking across the square for my shift at Come Again, I have a slight tingle of nerves or maybe it's anticipation. After my encounter with Shaw at the coffee shop this morning, I'm unsure what to expect from him tonight.

Will he be the same flirtatious, easygoing Shaw he was this morning?

Or will I get the Brandy treatment?

I'm hoping for the former.

But when I walk into the bar, he's nowhere to be found. Paulie greets me from behind the bar and Kevin waves from the back, but the table where Shaw usually sits is vacant.

"Hi," I call out to Paulie, placing my backpack under the bar and grabbing my apron.

"Hey," he replies, walking over with a small scrap piece of paper. "Would you mind going to the back and pulling these few bottles. I thought Shaw would be in and I was going to have him do it, but I haven't seen him in a while."

"Sure," I tell him, taking the list. "No problem."

There are only a few people at the bar due to the night being young. I smile at them as I make my way to the storage room. Passing Kevin, I call out a hello. He smiles and gives me another tip of his head.

When I get to the hallway, I notice Shaw's office door is closed, meaning he's either in there and doesn't want to be disturbed or he's not here. Scrunching up my face in disappointment, I punch in the code that unlocks the storage room door and walk inside. Turning on enough lights to see the labels, I grab a crate and make my selections.

As I'm leaving, I hear the backdoor open and I look up, expecting to see Shaw, but it's Jeremy.

"Hey you," I call out, setting the crate down by my feet so I can lock the storage room back up. When Jeremy doesn't reply, I turn to him, noticing he's leaning against the wall just inside the door. "What's up? You okay?"

Grabbing the crate, I walk down to him and feel my pulse quicken when I get a good look at him. Even in the dim light of the hallway, I can tell he's pale. When he looks up at me, or tries to, his eyes don't focus, they squint and then he lets his head fall back to the wall.

"Jeremy."

"Yep," he replies weakly.

"What's wrong? Are you sick?" I want to jump to conclusions. I want to ask him what he took, but I'm trying to be a good friend and give him the benefit of the doubt.

Innocent until proven guilty, right?

"I'm fine," he says, his head snapping up all of a sudden. "You're fine too." His words come out with a bit of a slur and I know then he's on something. I'm not sure what, but when he advances on me and his hands grab my waist, pulling me into him, it's all I can do to not drop the crate of booze on my hip.

"Let go, Jeremy. I'm going to drop this, if you don't." I try to keep my voice calm.

"You like me," he says, his face only inches from mine.

"Yep, we're friends," I tell him with a light chuckle, balancing the crate on my hip so I can push him away gently, without causing a scene. It's a good thing Shaw isn't here. "How about I, uh...call you a cab?" I ask, grasping for a solution to this problem.

Somehow, I need to get Jeremy out of here and sobered up without anyone knowing. Shaw would probably fire him on the spot and that would be the worst thing that could happen. Without this job, Jeremy will be back on the streets and back to...

Drugs.

But I guess it doesn't take him being on the streets to use, because he's obviously been using today.

"What'd you take?" I ask. There's no use beating around the bush. It's obvious he's under the influence of something. Not that him telling me what he's on will help, but it might. Plus, I feel the need to know. I want to help him, but I can't if I don't know what I'm dealing with.

Using the weight of his body, he pushes me against the wall behind me. "I want you. I've wanted you from the beginning."

"Jeremy," I warn, trying to maneuver around him, but between the wall at my back and the crate of booze on my hip and him taking up all the other available space around me, I'm cornered. "Let me set this down, okay?" Opting for distraction, I turn my head when he inches his closer. "I don't want to drop this and cause a scene."

"I want to cause a scene," he murmurs, his mouth brushing my cheek and I recoil, swallowing down the panic as I try to grasp for a solution that doesn't involve getting him fired.

A nervous laugh is all I can manage as I slide the crate down to the floor beside me and effectively move out of his line of attack. When I'm finally able to take a step to the side, I start reasoning. "You don't know what you're saying. How about we go outside and I'll call you a cab. Maybe a coffee or something to eat would help?"

Now it's Jeremy's turn to laugh, harshly, at me. "You're so fucking stupid, *Avery*..." He draws out my name, almost mockingly. "Avery from Oklahoma. Have you ever even been high? Do you know how good it feels? Maybe you should try it, just once." His gaze is invasive, taking me in and for the first time, I'm a little scared, because this isn't the Jeremy I know and all of a sudden I'm having small flashbacks of Brant.

Maybe it's the feeling of being cornered?

Maybe it's feeling like I don't have an escape...or being so caught off guard?

I don't know, but when tears sting my eyes in fear and frustration, I blink them away.

"Well, I..." I don't know what to say. All of my solutions fall flat, so I go with the truth. "I want to help you, but I don't know how."

"Let me have you," Jeremy says, stepping back into my space and grabbing me forcefully, so forcefully I swerve on my feet and fall into his chest.

"Let go," I demand a little louder, no longer caring if someone hears.

Somewhere between those two words and Jeremy trying to lift me off my feet, a booming voice carries down the hallway. "Get your hands off her."

My heart stutters and starts again, practically beating out of my chest. I've never been so equally thankful and scared shitless in all my life. My warring emotions don't stop there. When Shaw pulls Jeremy back, slamming him against the opposite wall, I lunge forward.

"Don't," I say breathlessly, pulling on his strong arm at Jeremy's throat. "He's on something. He doesn't know what he's doing."

I realize as I'm saying the words I'm not making the situation any better.

When Shaw growls, his dark eyes turning on me, I step back.

"Get out of here," he bellows, shoving Jeremy toward the door. "I told you when I hired you that drugs were the one thing that would get you fired. I don't have the time or patience for that shit, and I definitely won't stand for you putting your hands on Avery."

For a second, over Shaw's shoulder, I see the expression on Jeremy's face shift. Maybe Shaw's words sink in and he realizes what he's been doing. Whatever it is, my heart breaks for him and I want to help him even more.

"Shaw," I plead, tugging on his arm again to get him to let go.

"No," Shaw yells, turning his harsh gaze on me again. "This is my bar. I say who stays and he's leaving." Muscling Jeremy the rest of the way to the door, he holds him with one hand while twisting the handle with the other. When he kicks the door open, I hear someone else coming up behind us and turn to see who it is.

"Paulie," I start, walking toward him as panic floods me. "Tell him to let him stay."

He'll listen to Paulie. I've seen it before. When reason fails Shaw, Paulie is the voice in the darkness. So, when Paulie just shakes his head in obvious disappointment, my body sags in defeat. "Please, he's just going to end back up on the streets and what then?" I yell, my voice and plea turning back to Shaw.

"Not my business," Shaw growls.

Jeremy is now stumbling around in the alley, trying to get his bearings but failing miserably.

"Please," I start again. Not thinking, I step toward Shaw, my hands going to his chest and fisting his shirt in desperation. "I'm begging you...please don't do this."

His eyes bore into me and I expect him to push me away, but he doesn't. Instead his hands cover mine and squeeze gently. "I can't help him, Avery. He's made his choices and I'm not going to sit back and watch a bad situation turn worse. Not on my watch."

"Please." I try one more time, willing him to see what I see in Jeremy—someone who has lost his way and doesn't have anyone to turn to. "He's my friend."

The resolve that was firm in Shaw's expression begins to soften as he breathes heavily, his chest rising and falling under my clenched hands. When his eyes dart to the wall and then to the ceiling, I start to realize I have a chance. He's cracking.

"Let me go after him, then." I know it's a cheap shot, one he won't let me take, but I'm out of options.

Growling his frustrations, he lets go of my hands and steps away, kicking the backdoor once again. When he walks out into the alley, I see Jeremy slumped against the wall and I run out behind him.

Shaw, assertively yet gently, pulls Jeremy up to his feet. "You should thank your lucky stars," he mumbles, walking him toward the stairs. When Shaw practically carries him up the steps, I slump against the brick wall in relief. Paulie walks out and stands beside me, letting out a surprised laugh.

"Now, that's one I've never seen before," he muses.

"What?" I ask, confused. "I'm sure y'all have had your fair share of druggies." My eyes are still on the door Shaw and Jeremy just went through as I try to regulate my breathing and chill the fuck out.

"Oh, those are a dime a dozen. Shaw giving one of them a second chance?" I turn to look at him, Paulie's eyes softening as they meet mine. "Well," he continues, "let's just say this is a first."

The meaning behind his statement isn't lost on me. I kind of figured Shaw had never let anyone who came to work loaded stay. As a matter-of-fact, I've heard the spiel he gives on someone's first day of work.

Rule #1 Show up.

Rule #2: Be on time.

Rule #3: No drugs. No booze.

Rule #4: Break rules one through three and you're fired.

And everyone knows, Shaw's rules are non-negotiable.

I don't know what that says about me...or him...or us, but for now, I'm just thankful it's over.

For now, at least.

Jeremy is upstairs, not on the street. Hopefully, he'll sober up and come to his senses and I'll be able to talk Shaw into keeping him around.

20

"HOW IS HE?"

I look up to see Avery standing at the doorway to my office. Checking my watch, I make sure it's not later than I thought and I didn't lose hours of time somewhere.

"I know," she continues, taking a step inside. "I'm not supposed to be in for another two hours, but I was feeling antsy and CeCe didn't need me...and I wanted to check on Jeremy. Ha—have you seen him?" Fidgeting with the strap of her backpack, she looks at me and then around my office, taking in the couch with the blanket tossed to the side.

If it's obvious I slept here, she doesn't say anything, she just brings her eyes back to mine expectantly.

Clearing my throat, I scoot my desk chair back and kick my feet out, resting my hands on my stomach while I try to not let her notice me checking her out. Even though she's obviously worried about the kid, she looks beautiful. Her hair is pulled up in a loose bun on the top of her head, putting her long neck and delicate features on display. Swallowing, I finally answer her.

"He's fine. I've checked on him several times and he's been out. The apartment is stocked, so he's got whatever he needs when he finally wakes up."

She takes a deep breath and bites down on her bottom lip. "I still would like to go check on him. Maybe try to wake him up? I know there's probably nothing I can—"

"There's nothing you can do," I finish for her, confirming her thoughts.

I watch as she squares her shoulders and tilts her chin down to level me with her stare.

"I still would like to go check on him," she repeats with more vigor and determination. Her tenaciousness is one of the things I like most about her but it also drives me bat shit crazy.

"Avery," I pause, choosing my words carefully. "You're not thinking about yourself. I know that's typical of you, but you really need to. Even if Jeremy was high as a kite last night, he was still way out of line with how he treated you. I don't think it's a good idea for you to be around him without setting some boundaries."

She licks her bottom lip and averts her eyes, obviously not wanting to hear what I'm saying, so I make my intentions perfectly clear. "Either you do it or I will."

Avery's eyes squint with my statement, because that's what it is. It's not a threat. It's a promise. I won't sit back and let her care so much for the kid that she gets herself hurt in the process. Not happening. Not on my watch. When she doesn't say anything, I continue. "Are you gonna tell me he's never come onto you before last night?"

It sounds accusatory, but I'm not angry with her. I'm angry with the little dick upstairs. And quite honestly, I don't know if I want her to answer the question, because if he has, I'm liable to go upstairs and kick his wasted ass and not even feel bad about it.

Her shoulders rise and fall with a deep breath before she finally relents. "Once," she admits. "But I told him we're just friends...if he hadn't been high he wouldn't have...done what he did."

"I doubt that," I tell her, my jaw sore from how hard I'm gritting my teeth to keep from losing my cool.

The office is quiet for a moment. I can see her trying to come to terms with what I've said while struggling with her intrinsic instincts to take care of Jeremy. I see the moment her need to help outweighs her need to protect herself. When she turns and makes her way out the door, I jump out of the chair and cross my office in two long strides. There's no way in hell I'm letting her go up to that apartment by herself.

If she won't look out for herself, then I'll have to do it for her.

Jogging down the hall and up the stairs, I'm at her back when she tries the door which is locked. With a frustrated huff, she turns around and crosses her arms over her chest, obvious annoyance on her face. "Can you open it...please?"

A smug smile almost comes out to play but I force it back, realizing that wouldn't help the situation, but I like that she has to ask for my help. Because I want to help. I want to protect her...be there for her... so many things I can't explain and I don't know how it happened, but Avery Cole has somehow become one of the most important people in my life.

Digging the keys out of my pocket, I ignore the way my body feels when she's standing so close and looking up at me with those big brown eyes. I quickly open the door and peek my head inside to make sure Jeremy isn't indisposed, but he's not on the bed.

"Hello?" I call out, looking in the direction of the kitchen.

Avery pushes around me and walks into the apartment, looking from one side to the other.

It's empty.

"Where is he?" she asks, turning to look at me like I did something with him.

I shrug, just as confused as she is. "I don't know. He was just here a few hours ago."

She lets out a frustrated sigh and walks over to the kitchen to look around. "No note, no nothing?" she mutters. "Where could he have gone?"

The disappointment and worry is evident on her face and in her voice, and I wish I could take it away. I hate that this kid has gotten to her and she somehow feels responsible for his well-being.

"You know he's an addict, right?" I ask, biting back my frustration. "You can't force him to change? If he doesn't want to be saved, there's not a damn thing you can do about it."

Avery's beautiful face scrunches in obvious pain over my words, but then she releases a breath. "I know that. I'm not as naïve as you think I am," she says with a huff. "I'm not stupid. I know people can't change unless they want to."

Of course she knows that. Avery might be fifteen years younger than me, but most of the time, her age never crosses my mind unless I'm reminded of it. She handles herself so well and approaches life in a way that's timeless. Her care and concern for others mixed with her strong will and need to experience life to its fullest makes her more mature and aware than people twice her age.

"Jeremy is an adult. He's made his choices in life." I remind her of the same thing I've been telling myself. "You can lead a horse to water but you can't make them drink."

She chuckles lightly, shaking her head. "You sound like my dad."

"Is that a bad thing?" I ask, liking the change in her demeanor. Jeremy doesn't deserve her worry and concern. If he really cared about her, even as a friend, he would try harder, do better.

"No," she says, looking down at her shoe as she toes the rug beneath her feet. "I'm still worried about him, though. I can't help it. He's my friend and he's in trouble."

"I'll tell you what." Pausing, I take a step toward her and she lifts her chin. Her eyes find mine and the depth in them practically knocks me on my ass. "I'll call one of my buddies down at the station and ask them to be on the lookout for him. This is a big city, even if we shut the bar down and all went in separate directions, we'd have a better chance of finding a needle in a haystack."

Twisting her lips to the side to keep from smiling, she whispers, "Thanks."

I nod, feeling my chest expand and warmth spread. We both know I'm only doing this because of her. Sure, I care about what happens to the kid, but I've been through this one too many times and I know how these things go. Truth be told, he's probably already halfway to the next town or headed back home. Most people like Jeremy can only keep it together for so long before they're back to shooting up or popping pills...whatever his drug of choice is.

Early this morning, I got a call from Karin letting me know that she'd asked him to leave yesterday after he failed his drug test, which explains why he showed up lit last night. His period of living a normal life is coming to an end.

With one last look around the apartment, Avery finally walks toward the door. Once we're back in the bar, she heads up to the front to help Paulie and Kevin, while I go to my office and make the call to the station as promised.

"Hello, this is Theo." My old friend answers, his tone brisk and full of business, per usual.

"Theo, it's Shaw."

"Hey, man. What can I do for you?" he asks. "Already causing trouble in the Quarter this early in the evening?"

"Nah, not yet, but I do have a favor to ask."

Theo has always been one to help out when he can. He's broken up fights, escorted belligerent drunks, whatever I need him to do. In return, I give him and any other New Orleans PD drinks on the house when they stop in on a night off. "Shoot," he says without hesitation.

"I have a kid that's been working for me the last few months and he showed up high as a fucking kite last night. I put him up in my apartment to sleep it off, but this afternoon he was gone. Do you think you could put the word out and give me a call if anyone sees him?"

"Sure, man."

"You know I wouldn't normally do this, but...well, if you could find him, that'd be great."

After I've given Theo all the information I've got on Jeremy, I keep myself busy with paperwork for a while. When I can't sit still any longer, I walk down the hall into the bar. It's a quiet night, some of our regulars are here, but for a Saturday, it's pretty mellow. The cooler temps should bring people out, but during the holidays, we don't get as much traffic.

People are off having parties and get togethers.

I watch Avery, but she seems to be fine. Her worry and concern are put away as she waits on customers with her typical cheerful smile and easy way.

When I feel the unresolved tension I've been carrying around bubble to the surface, I make my way next door to check on Sarah and see how everything is going on her side. But before I can open her door, my phone rings from my back pocket.

Pulling it out, I answer without looking to see who it is.

"This is Shaw."

"Hey, man," Theo's voice sounds worried, especially for a seasoned cop like him. There's a hint of dread mixed in with it that makes my stomach drop. "Can you come into the station?"

"Uh, sure," I tell him, pausing and turning back to the door I just walked out of. "Did you find him?"

"Aww, man, Shaw. It ain't good." The heavy sigh on the other end drives home the gravity of the situation, but what he says next isn't what I was expecting. "I've got a D.O.A. that matches your description. We're gonna need an identification before we can go any further."

My stomach that dropped when he called falls to my feet as fear washes over me. A foreboding I can't shake settles where my stomach once was. My first thought is Avery.

What's she going to say?

How will she react?

How badly is this going to hurt her?

The thought of telling her makes me want to hurt something, but not her. Never her.

Fucking druggie.

I let out a growl and punch the door, not hard enough to do damage, just enough to take the edge off. "I'll be down there as soon as I can."

Walking back inside the bar, I make eye contact with Paulie over the heads of patrons.

The crowd has picked up a little and the jukebox is in full swing as life continues around me like nothing is amiss, but everything is fucking amiss. *Fuck.*

"I've gotta run down to the police station," I tell him walking behind the bar. "I'll be back in a while. If I'm not back before closing, lock up, okay?"

Paulie nods with concern etched all over his face. "Everything okay, boss?"

Avery's gaze finds mine and shifts between me and Paulie. When she sees us talking quietly, her brows furrow. "Look out for her," I say quietly, nodding in Avery's direction. "If I'm not back by the time she's ready to go home, make sure she gets there safely."

As I make my way back through the bar, I feel Avery watching me, so when I turn and meet her gaze, full of worry, I hold my phone up and mouth, "I'll call you." Her shoulders rise and fall with each breath and it's like there's an invisible string attached that pulls at me when I turn around and walk away.

Once I'm on my bike and headed to the station, I let my mind go there—thinking about Jeremy, hoping this isn't going to be him, wishing for another chance to knock some sense into him.

For his sake.

For Avery's sake.

For mine.

God, please let this not be the kid.

Me and the Big Guy have a shaky relationship. Ever since I spent two years and three months on my knees in the cathedral across the street, every day, never missing once—lighting a candle and saying a prayer, asking God for the one thing I couldn't do.

Save her.

Let her live.

Take me instead.

But I didn't get that. He took her from me and we haven't talked much since. I remember people coming to the house in the days following Liz's death and they would tell me things like *she's in a better place.* I couldn't believe that. Those words definitely did not help.

Because I knew where she belonged and that was with me.

When I pull up to the station, I park my bike at the curb. Instead of walking straight inside and ripping the Band-Aid off, I pace in front of the lit windows, somehow trying to wish this all away.

"Shaw?"

Glancing up, I see Theo standing there.

"Hey, man." Running a hand through my hair, I let out a pent-up breath. "I guess we should get this over with."

"Yeah," Theo says, holding the door open for me. Once inside, he leads me down a hallway and into a small room with a table and two chairs. It looks like an interrogation room and even though I haven't done anything wrong, my palms feel sweaty and my heart is racing.

"Look, I know this is tough, so let's just start with a few questions."

Exhaling, I flip the chair around and straddle it, leaning against the back as I try to calm my nerves.

"Do you know of any birthmarks or scars this kid might have?"

"No," I tell him, trying to think back and remember seeing anything. "I don't even think he had a tattoo, at least not that was noticeable."

Theo nods, but doesn't give away any signs of whether that goes along with the person they found. "But you did say he's about six one, maybe a hundred and ninety pounds?"

"Yeah, that sounds about right," I tell him.

"Light brown hair?"

"Yeah."

"And he was wearing a blue t-shirt and faded jeans when you last saw him?"

"That's right." I don't have to think too hard about that because the clothes he was wearing were some that I gave him the first night I met him. He'd been sleeping in the alley behind the bar and he was a fucking mess, hadn't showered in days. I gave him fresh clothes, a shower, and a hot meal. Even then, I never got a good feeling about him. Something about his demeanor told me he wasn't ready to let the drugs go.

"Alright," he says with a sigh. "I know this is tough but..." He pulls out a manila folder and opens it. Right on top is a photo of the kid.

The blue shirt, just like I remembered seeing him in this morning.

His eyes closed, again, just like this morning, but there's something different.

Pale.

Lifeless.

My eyes sting as my throat constricts.

"Is this the kid?" Theo asks.

"Yeah, that's him," I confirm, looking up to see the sadness on Theo's face matching how I feel inside. Gone, just like that.

"What a fucking waste, man," I mutter to Theo...to myself. "I tried..." I tried. The words get stuck in my throat and push off the chair and turn to the concrete wall behind me. "Fuck."

"I'm sorry, Shaw. I know you tried," Theo says, his chair scraping against the floor as he stands and walks over, placing a hand on my shoulder. "Can't save them all."

I hate it.

I hate that I couldn't do more.

I hate what I did wasn't enough to save him.

And I hate that the one I couldn't save just happens to mean something to the girl I'm falling for.

Falling for?

Thankfully, I don't have time to dwell on that thought as Theo continues to talk. "I'm gonna need you to fill out some paperwork. We're gonna have to track down his family. Any other information you might have on him would be helpful."

"Yeah," I tell him, the numbness settling in. "Sure, whatever you need."

My words are rote and robotic, as are my movements, as I follow him out into the stark white hallway that leads to a room full of desks. People mill about, answering calls and talking amongst themselves, and all I can think about is Jeremy's lifeless face.

I already know it's going to haunt me, like Liz's. It's going to stick with me and will be waiting for me when I close my eyes to sleep at night.

Once the questions are answered and the papers are finished, Theo tells me he'll call if they need anything else. Jeremy's parents live in Texas, a suburb of Houston to be exact, which helps to explain the instant connection between him and Avery. I don't want to stick around for the phone call. I'm pretty sure I might crack under the pressure of hearing Jeremy's parents learn about their son's untimely death. Although, if I had to guess, it won't come as a surprise.

Along with where he's from, Theo also told me that he'd been picked up on possession before, the first time being before he was even sixteen years old. For that offense, he'd spent a few months in a juvenile detention center and he's basically been wandering since then.

Lost.

Searching.

My heart, albeit calloused, breaks for the kid. I still think he's stupid, but addiction isn't something I've had to deal with and I can't pass judgment on something I don't personally know anything about.

When I'm back on my bike, I consider going home, but I don't want to. Just thinking about the big, empty, too quiet house makes me feel like my stomach is full of lead. So, I drive back to the bar with the intention of sleeping there for the night, somehow preparing myself to break the news to everyone tomorrow.

Sarah probably deserves a phone call tonight, but I just don't have it in me.

After I park my bike, I walk up to the backdoor of the bar and when I go to stick my key in the lock, it turns. Opening it, I see the dim light up front is still on, which means Paulie must be waiting for me.

I'm not surprised. When I was still at the police station, I missed a couple of calls from him.

"Paulie," I call out as I'm walking down the hall, tossing my leather jacket in my office before making my way to where he's sitting at a back table.

With Avery.

"Hey," I say in a softer tone than I've used in a long time.

"Did you find him?" she asks, unfolding her legs from where they'd been tucked under her and sitting up straight in the chair. Her hair that was so beautifully showing off her lovely face is now falling in loose strands and her eyes are tired, worried.

I swallow, nodding my head, still searching for the right way to deliver the news. I expected to spend the night alone, getting a grip on myself before I had to tell someone else.

I wanted those hours to build back up the steel walls that have held me together for five years.

"Where is he?" Avery asks, her quiet voice cutting through the silence of the bar. My eyes meet hers and I will her to understand. When I hear Paulie clear his throat and then cuss under his breath, I know he's interpreted my silence for what it is.

Worst-case scenario.

Avery's eyes dart to him and then back to me. As they begin to fill with tears, I know she now knows too. Leaning against the wall, I absorb its support and meld into it, my legs feeling like they weigh a ton.

"Are you sure?" Her watery question spears my chest.

I nod again, exhaling loudly. "I'm sure. I...I, uh, identified..." I can't finish the sentence because with each word flashes of the kid enter my mind.

Her soft gasp, followed by a barely audible sob fractures my heart wide open.

"Boss," Paulie starts, standing from his chair. As he walks toward me, his strong hand grips my shoulder. "I'm sorry."

Paulie isn't apologizing for the death. Just like the rest of us, he had nothing to do with that, but he's apologizing for the fact I had to witness it. I've confided in him about the nightmares I had after Lizzie died. The one thing I couldn't shake was feeling her skin go cold—all evidence of life leaving her as she left this world...left me.

"It's okay," I tell him, breathing deeply through my nose.

"Do you need anything else?" he asks, glancing back at Avery who's staring out across the empty bar, tears streaming down her cheeks.

"No," I tell him, shaking my head. "We're good."

With one last squeeze on my shoulder, Paulie walks to the front of the bar and leaves, locking the door behind him.

"Let me take you home," I tell Avery, pushing off the wall and holding out my hand to help her stand.

"I don't want to go home," she whispers, wiping the back of her hand across her cheek. "I...I'll just stay here."

"Come on," I insist. She hesitates for a moment before taking my hand. When she gets to her feet, I can't help but pull her into me, wrapping my arms around her shoulders and holding her tightly. The moment she lays her head on my chest and returns the hug, I'm falling.

Any walls that were left standing crumble at her feet.

21

Avery

Standing there, with Shaw's arms wrapped around me, the pain from learning about Jeremy's death subsides. It's still there, but it's no longer dominating my mind and my heart.

Shaw is.

This man who tries so hard to block people out and pretend like he doesn't care is the polar opposite of what he portrays. He's good. He has a huge heart. He cares about other people more than himself.

If I had to guess, Jeremy's death is hitting him harder than anyone, but he's too afraid to show it.

"Let's go for a ride," he murmurs into my hair before leaning back and smoothing it out of my face. My eyes are still leaking tears but I give him a small smile and nod my head.

Taking my hand in his, we walk down the hall and he flicks a few switches, making the bar go dark. On our way out, he stops by his office and grabs his leather jacket and reaches behind the door to grab a denim one.

"Put this on," he demands softly. "It's chilly on the bike tonight."

Slipping my arms into it, I close my eyes and inhale. I feel like I'm in a Shaw O'Sullivan cocoon.

Warm.

Manly.

Fresh.

The smell reminds me of the night he let me stay in his apartment and I used the shampoo and conditioner in his shower and it smelled like him. That night seems like so long ago...so many things have happened since then. So much has changed.

"Ready?" he asks once we're both seated on the bike.

"Yes," I reply, wrapping my arms tightly around his waist, loving the way his body feels beneath my touch. Unlike the first time I rode with him, he's relaxed and pliable, leaning back into me and letting me hold him. As we turn out onto the nearly empty New Orleans street, his hand comes down to rest on my calf. It's a subtle gesture, but it affects me. Making me feel protected and comforted and good.

I'm not sure where we go or how long we ride. I just get lost in the lights passing by and the feel of the wind hitting my face beneath the helmet Shaw insisted I wear. My thoughts drift to Jeremy and I let the tears fall at will.

When the bike slows to a crawl and Shaw turns it into a driveway, I sit up straighter and take notice, looking around at our surroundings. We're parking in the drive of a house. In the dark, all I can tell is it's a large house with a porch on the front. The landscaping is well taken care of and thanks to the light by the back door, I see that it's blue.

I love blue doors.

Call me crazy, but to me, they make a home feel welcoming.

Shaw kills the engine and offers me his hand.

Once I'm off the bike, I unbuckle the helmet and hand it to him, watching as he ambles off the seat with ease.

"Is this your house?"

"You said you didn't want to go home." His deep voice is low and gravelly, making me wonder if he might have shed some tears of his own on our drive.

Shaking my head, all the while keeping my eyes firmly on him, I say, "no, I don't."

"Let's get inside." He motions with his head toward the back door and takes my hand again, something I like very much and could get used to.

When we step inside, I can't help but gawk at the kitchen. This place definitely has a woman's touch. I can't help wondering who. Maybe it was Sarah or one of Shaw's sisters-in-law, but something in my gut tells me it was someone who loved this place as much as him. The pristine stainless-steel appliances are surrounded by granite countertops and white porcelain backsplashes. With the hanging industrial-looking lighting, it's something straight out of a *Better Homes and Garden* magazine. "This is beautiful," I tell him, trying not to think about what woman had a hand in making it so. As I pull my arms out of the denim jacket and drape it over one of the tall bar stools that surrounds the large island in the middle of the kitchen, I glance up to find Shaw watching me.

"Can I get you something?" he asks, walking to the refrigerator and opening it. "Water, tea…"

"A glass of water would be great." My throat feels dry, maybe it's from crying or the bike ride…or maybe it's because Shaw's now taken his leather jacket off and he's standing with his back to me in the white t-shirt and jeans I've come to love.

The way his muscles move under the thin shirt has me swallowing hard and suddenly, out of the blue, I'm hit with the realization that I'm here…in Shaw's home.

With him.

Alone.

I feel the mood shift when he turns around and sets a glass of cold water down in front of me, his eyes scanning my face and then lingering on my lips.

He feels it too.

I know he does when he swipes his tongue along his bottom lip before biting down on it and shaking his head slowly.

"What?" I ask, taking a slow sip of water, hoping it helps regulate my heart that's now beating out of my chest.

"You," he murmurs.

"What about me?"

He shakes his head again, a tentative smile causing his lip to turn up on one side. "I shouldn't want you." It's like a warning to himself and me and he lays the words down between us like a sad, slow love song.

I walk carefully to where he is, leaning against the counter. The way his arms are crossed over his chest gives me a perfect view of the muscles tensing as if they know how tempted I am to reach out and touch them.

"What are these?" I ask, wanting to distract him and pull him out of his head. When I let my finger gently touch the hint of black ink peeking out from under the sleeve of his shirt, his muscles tighten even more.

"Ink," he says flatly, still watching my every move.

"Do you have more?"

He nods his response, not giving me any more than he has to and I wonder if those walls I'm so tired of are creeping back up. Maybe coming here was a bad idea...maybe I should ask him to take me back to CeCe's. Turning to walk back to where I was standing, he grabs my arm and spins me around.

Now, my back is to the counter and he's hovering over me, caging me in with his strong arms.

We stand there for a minute, both of us breathing heavily, inches apart.

"Are you okay?" I ask, wanting to make sure that he doesn't want to talk about Jeremy...what he saw. I don't want him to feel like he has to shoulder that all alone. "If you want to talk, I'm—"

Shaw's hand comes up and he places a finger on my lips.

"I don't want to talk about that right now. Later, but not now."

I nod, relishing in the feel of his finger on my lips...one finger. What would it feel like for him to touch me with more...I want that. I want more. I want all of him, whatever he'll give me.

"I shouldn't want you like this. . .but I do." His words are raw and vulnerable and I feel them whisper across my collar bone. Closing my eyes, I let them wash over me, my body shuddering in their wake.

"Why shouldn't you?" I ask, my voice hoarse and deep and new to my ears.

Shaw runs the tip of his finger along the sensitive skin on my neck, up to my jaw, "too many reasons."

I know I should care about those reasons, that I should demand them, but I don't. I want him too badly to think clearly anymore. I just need this night and then I can let him go.

"You're everywhere," he says like it's a confession. "You're in my thoughts, my dreams...I can't get you out of my head. And to be near you all the time and not be able to touch you like I want, like I need...it kills me." He lifts me by my waist as if I weigh nothing and sets me on the counter, settling himself between my legs.

If he'd just step a bit closer—touch me, feel me—he'd know how wet I am and how much I want him—*need him*—and that scares me. But if he stays where he is—close but not close enough—I just might scream.

His hands remain at my waist and I watch him as he takes in my body with his eyes, like he's committing every inch of me to memory. I feel as though I'm under a microscope and he's studying every shuddering breath I exhale, every goosebump erupting on my flesh, and every fiber of my being responding to him. I hope he finds what he's looking for.

"I want you, Shaw," I tell him, needing him to know I'm all in.

When his eyes meet mine, they're still searching, looking for something. The second he finds it, his lips are on mine—hungry, demanding, devouring. It's an all-consuming kiss, one that steals my breath and makes me weak.

Shaw's hand grips my neck gently, tilting my head back to allow his mouth room to roam.

First my neck.

Then to that sensitive spot again behind my ear.

His fingers tangle with my hair that's now more down than up and he tugs, growling against my skin, "I want you so fucking bad."

"Take me," I plead, desperate for him. "Have me. I'm yours."

When he pulls back, his hooded eyes travel from my eyes and down to my breasts before coming back up and settling on my mouth. After a second of internal debate, he licks his lips like he's planning his assault.

Yes. Please.

The struggle is clear on his face but so is his desire. If I were to look at my own face right now, I imagine I'd see the same desire mirrored back, tinged with impatience.

"Touch me, please," I breathe out, barely keeping the whine out of my voice. His grip on my waist loosens, but he's still moving too slowly, so I grab his hand and place it on my breast. It's not exactly where I want it but it'll do for now.

Finally, *finally*, he snaps out of whatever mind game he's been playing, and he squeezes then rubs his thumb against my nipple, eliciting a gasp from me which spurs him on. When he brings his other hand up and repeats his movements on both breasts, I moan.

My cotton shirt is thin but tight across my chest and I wish he'd just rip it off of me already. I expected Shaw to be intense, but not this calculating. I want out of control. I want a distraction.

"Lower." I'm not above begging at this point.

"If I start this...if I give into this...I won't be able to stop," he warns, his teeth punishing his bottom lip as he fights his carnal impulses.

"I don't want you to stop; I want you to *take me*. Please. I need you." I unbutton my jeans and lean back to move them down my hips, the cool air doing little to tame the heat covering my body.

Shaw's eyes don't leave mine as he helps me discard them onto the kitchen floor. Then, his fingers lightly graze their way back up my legs, landing on my pussy covered only by a thin scrap of fabric. When I spread my legs, I know the second he feels how wet I am. I see it in his eyes which are still locked on mine.

Hunger.

Desire.

Unrestrained passion.

Everything I've wanted from him and he's finally giving it to me in spades.

I've never wanted someone as badly as I want Shaw O'Sullivan.

He makes quick work of removing my panties before sliding his finger along my slit and up to circle my clit. The relief I feel as his finger enters me is short-lived because my core immediately starts to tense in preparation for the release I so badly desire. I'm dancing on the edge of wanting to prolong this feeling but also needing to come so fucking badly as he pumps two of his thick fingers inside me.

"So fucking wet, so tight. Do you like it when I fuck you with my fingers?"

"Yes," I pant, gripping his shoulders. "I'm so close, Shaw."

"I can feel you," he whispers, losing himself in the moment. "Come for me, Avery."

When he curls his fingers, angling them to hit just the right spot as his palm gives my clit the friction it needs, my thighs begin to shake. Gripping his shoulders tighter, my orgasm takes over, making me cry out.

Before I have a chance to catch my breath or remember my own name, Shaw grabs me by my waist and pulls me to the edge of the counter. I watch as he unbuttons his jeans and frees his cock.

It's long and hard as it bounces against his chiseled stomach. At some point, he'd also discarded his shirt and his gorgeous chest is on full display, swirls of black painting his skin.

I want him.

I want him so fucking bad I can't stand it.

Even though I just had one of the best orgasms of my life, I'm still greedy for more.

Reaching for his cock, I stroke it and watch as Shaw's head falls back, a guttural moan erupting from somewhere deep inside him, spurring me on. When I catch a bead of precum and swirl it around the tip, his head snaps up and his eyes look ravenous—like a starved man looking at his first meal in days...weeks.

"I'm on birth control," I tell him, wanting him to know he doesn't have to worry about me.

Shaw's hands are back on my hips, pulling me into him. "I'm clean," he assures me, panting as he leans his forehead against mine. "I swear."

"I trust you."

The next thing I know, my ass is no longer on the cold countertop. Instead, Shaw has me wrapped around his body as he pushes me up against a wall. I feel his cock slide against my wetness as he lines up with my center. He teases for a split second, repositioning his hands on my thighs. Just as I'm getting ready to beg, he nudges my entrance and then slides inside.

It's slow at first, his heavy breaths and weighted stare dominating the space between. I feel every inch, every glorious inch, as he fills me, consuming me from the inside out. When he's buried deep, he pauses for a second and I wonder if something's wrong—worry that he's having regrets or changed his mind. "Give me a second," he pants. "You're...you, oh God. You're so tight and I'm..."

Cupping his cheek, I brush my thumb along the soft skin under his eye, wanting to give him anything and everything he needs. Unable to keep from touching him, my lips are on his. . .my hands are in his dark, thick hair—something I've always wanted to do—drowning in the goodness of being in Shaw's embrace and feeling him inside me. I try to keep my hips still, but after a few seconds, they move on their own accord. With a loud growl, Shaw grips my legs tighter and begins to thrust into me—my back sliding up and down the wall as my hands try to find purchase.

"Ahhhh," I cry out, both in pleasure and delicious pain.

It's desperate.

It's frantic.

It's everything and yet I'm grasping for him, needing more.

"Fuck," I groan when Shaw begins to hit a spot inside me I didn't even know existed. "Oh, fuck."

"God, Avery," he moans. "You feel so fucking good. I'm gonna come, but I want this to..." He grunts and speeds up his pace. "I never want this to end. You feel amazing..."

When his speed increases and his pelvis rubs against my clit while his cock drives into me, I erupt around him, completely coming undone. I'm so far gone that I don't even remember Shaw coming. I wish I did. I wish I could remember every sound and word.

I vaguely remember him carrying me up the stairs and laying me on a bed.

At some point, in the early morning hours as the sun is barely peeking through the sheer curtains, I'm awakened by soft kisses on my shoulder. The feel of Shaw's beard on my skin does tantalizing things to my body, waking me up better than my favorite cup of coffee.

This time, when Shaw rolls me over and slips between my legs, it's slow and sensual.

It's savoring and soft.

And I get a front-row seat to Shaw's orgasm, soaking up every nuance—the way his neck elongates as he comes, the vein that becomes more prominent, his perfect white teeth capturing that full bottom lip I love to suck on.

Later, I'm not sure how long, I wake up again to the bright New Orleans sunshine painting the room a beautiful golden color. Lifting my head off the softest pillow I've ever laid my head on, I sleepily look around the room, letting the events of earlier sink in.

I'm here.

At Shaw's.

With him.

And I had the best sex of my life.

I can't help the smile that splits my face and I'm kind of glad Shaw's nowhere around to see it, because it's so big I wouldn't be able to hide it. Rolling over, I sit up in bed and bring the grey quilt with me, pulling it to my chest. The alarm clock on the nightstand says it's only nine in the morning. Somehow, I feel as if I slept half a day away.

I guess a few orgasms will do that to you.

I wouldn't know. It's been too long since I had one...at least, until last night...or this morning.

And that's when I remember Jeremy.

Shit.

A hard lump forms in my throat and I struggle to swallow around it. What was he thinking? He wasn't. If he was, then I just don't know. I've never been addicted to anything so I have no idea what that's like. Hard, I'm sure. The fact that he no longer exists is still hard for me to wrap my mind around.

It doesn't feel real.

Glancing around again, wondering where Shaw is, I listen closely, but don't hear any noises in the house. Then, I see a piece of paper beside the alarm clock. Leaning over, I grab it and in a neat handwriting there's a note.

Avery,

It's 8:30 and I'm going for a run. Be back in an hour.

Shaw

As I look back at the clock, I decide I have enough time to hop in the shower before he gets back. So, I walk over to the chest of drawers in the corner and grab one of his white t-shirts—I don't think he'll mind—and head to the shower.

I've just finished towel drying my hair and using some of Shaw's toothpaste to brush my teeth with my finger when I hear the front door open and close downstairs.

"Shaw?" I call out as I put everything back where I found it on the counter. I'm just getting ready to call out again when I see him in the reflection of the mirror. My smile is instant, thoughts of earlier this morning racing back, but when I see his expression, mine falls.

The bag Shaw is holding falls to the ground and his breathing increases. He looks pale, like he saw a ghost.

"Shaw?" I ask, cautiously walking out of the bathroom.

"Your fucking towel is on the floor," he sneers. His eyes aren't on me, they're focused on something behind me. When I turn around, I see the towel I used to dry off with on the floor behind me.

Nervously, due to the anger rolling off him, I take a few steps back and pick it up, holding it to my chest. "I'm sorry. I was going—"

"Were you born in a fucking barn?" He yells this time and it makes me flinch. Images of Brant flash through my mind and I feel the need to run.

"No," I say, trying to keep my voice calm and even. "I was going to pick it up." That last part comes out weak and quiet, my emotions taking over...my fear creeping in. I tell it to go away. This is Shaw. Shaw won't hurt me. But then he yells again.

"You don't fucking leave towels on the bathroom floor!"

Now, he's pacing and I swear I hear him muttering to himself. Looking around the bedroom, I try to figure out what went wrong—what I did wrong—and how I can get myself out of this. The feeling of being trapped is overwhelming, so I stand there frozen, waiting for Shaw to calm down or give me a chance to get the hell out of here.

22

I DON'T KNOW WHAT HAPPENED...WHAT SNAPPED.

Standing in the middle of my bedroom, staring at Avery in my t-shirt with her bare legs and towel-dried hair, it's a moment I've dreamed of several times over the past few months. Since we walked through my backdoor last night, I've only thought of her—her body, her words, her sounds, her skin, her hair...

But the second I walked in and saw the wet towel on the floor, flashes of Liz and past conversations—a past life—flooded my mind, pushing everything else out. She hated wet towels on the floor. It was one of her biggest pet peeves.

"Shaw! How many times do I have to ask you to pick up your damn towels? What do you think this is, a hotel? I'm not your maid!" She walks into the living room with the offending towel and throws it at me. Shocked at her outrage over something so trivial, I laugh, which pisses her off even more.

"Come on, babe, it's just a towel...besides," I tell her, standing and grabbing her by the waist, bringing her against me, "you didn't mind helping me get dirty." I kiss her neck, right at the spot that makes her squeal and she can't hold back.

The tension is gone, her anger diffused, and we're making out like horny teenagers against the wall in the hallway.

In an instant, I go from cloud nine to the pits of despair.

Anger.

Liz left me.

Anguish.

She's gone.

Pain.

I brought Avery into our *house.*

Guilt.

Our house.

Grief.

It wasn't supposed to be like this.

An excess of feelings that have nothing to do with Avery or the time we just spent together and everything to do with me come crashing down on me.

"Get out." The words tumble from my mouth, but it feels and sounds like they're coming from someone else. They sound harsh and angry, but it's not Avery.

It's not her fault.

She doesn't know.

I didn't tell her.

For fear of completely falling apart in front of her, I repeat them, knowing they might be doing more damage than I'll ever be able to fix, but unable to stop myself. "Get out."

"Why are you doing this?" Avery asks, pulling me out of the haze that fell over me the moment I walked into the bedroom. Shaking my head, trying to clear it a little more, I see the look of hurt and anguish on her beautiful face and my heart cracks, a new hole forming where Avery resides.

Unable to explain and not wanting to do this, not today, I try to soften my tone but remain firm. "Please go."

I can't look at her after...after whatever this was. I don't even know what's wrong with me and my body feels empty, my mind removed. For fear I'm going to say something else that will hurt her, I beg, "please."

"Okay." Her tone is final and sad...resolved. I turn away from her, running a hand down my face, scratching at the hair along my jaw, breathing in deeply and exhaling, but not getting any relief from the unrelenting grip my memories have on my heart. Pacing over to the window, I brace my hands on either side of it and wait until I hear her footsteps fade.

What the fuck is wrong with me?

How can I let her just walk out of here like this?

I'm an asshole. The worst kind of asshole. I had her, know how wonderful she is, and I'm letting her walk away. Because it's what's best for her. She doesn't deserve this—me.

And I sure as hell don't deserve her.

This morning just proves what I've known all along. I'm broken and irreparably damaged.

Walking backwards until the back of my knees hit the bed, I sit down with a thud, holding my head in my hands and I let the emotions that have been bubbling to the surface out.

Hot, angry tears fall and for the first time in a long time, I let them. Eventually, tears turn to angry words that spew out of my mouth—at myself, at Liz.

Screaming, I let out the repressed frustration, and slide down onto the floor beside the bed.

Why?

That's been the question I've been asking for the past five years.

Why Liz?

Why me?

Why us?

Why am I still so fucking angry?

Why, why, why?

I crawl to the wall where my phone has been charging since earlier this morning when I got up for my run—earlier, when everything was good...when Avery was here, asleep in my bed. Grabbing it and turning it on, I lean against the wall and pull the edge of my shirt up to wipe my face.

Scrolling through my contacts, I hit Avery's number and pray to God she answers. I need to apologize and make sure she made it home okay. I need to talk to her and try to fucking explain even though I can't even explain it to myself right now.

I just need to know she's okay.

The phone rings three times and goes to a recording.

"The voicemail for this number has not been set up. Please try your call again later."

"Fuck," I groan, banging my head against the wall behind me. "Fuck."

Over the next few hours, I stare blankly at nothing and let my mind go, so tired of it all. When the sun slips over the edge of the house and the early evening sets, I pick up my phone where it's been lying beside me and I try Avery again.

Same.

No answer.

When I can't stand it any longer, I pull myself up from the floor and fall into bed, pulling her pillow to my face and screaming into it. The lingering scent of her settles in my chest and I eventually fall asleep, my mind playing like an old silent movie as it alternates between memories of Liz and flashes of Avery.

This morning, when I awoke, my entire body ached like I had drank the night before into oblivion. I laid in bed for hours, waiting on the sun to rise and for it to be an appropriate time to try Avery's phone again. When she didn't answer, I sent her a text message.

I'm sorry. Can we please talk?

After I trudged downstairs and made coffee, the denim jacket she'd worn two nights ago on our way here haunted me from the bar stool. Like a masochist, I picked it up and brought it to my nose, the twisted smell of her and me was like a jolt to my system.

How did we make so much sense yet no sense at all?

And what am I going to do now that I've fucked it all up?

Since Avery wasn't answering, I thought about riding my bike over to CeCe's and forcing her to talk to me, but if she needs time, I'll give it to her. Besides, I'm still trying to muddle through my thoughts and emotions and am unsure exactly what I plan on saying once she decides to talk to me, which is why I called Sarah.

Among the many things I need to tell her is that Jeremy is dead.

So, I'm now sitting at my regular table in The Crescent Moon waiting on her to join me for breakfast and help me get my head on straight. She's always been good at that.

"Good mornin'," Wyatt greets in his unfailingly carefree way. I look up to see him sporting his typical cowboy boots and plaid bowtie, which matches the suspenders he's wearing.

No surprise there.

"Did Olivia pick out those clothes?" I ask in mock distaste. I don't really hate them but I have to give him a hard time about them.

"I can see you're even more jovial than usual. Can I interest you in a shot of bourbon with your coffee?" He's teasing, but if I asked, he'd definitely oblige.

"Nah, man, I'm good." Booze is the last thing I need this morning. My thoughts are muddled enough without it.

I'm on my second cup of coffee when my sister finally breezes in and sits across from me. Unlike myself, Sarah looks well-rested, peaceful even, and I'm envious. I'd love to feel content again. It's been so long, I don't remember what that's like.

"You sure look like shit," is how she greets me and if it were any other day, it'd make me smile. "Are you okay?" she asks, her teasing quickly morphing into genuine concern.

"No, I'm not, but I have to tell you something."

She sits up a little straighter and reaches across the table to place her hand over mine as I continue. "Jeremy...the kid, he...well, he—" Fuck, why is this so hard? It's not the first time I've had to deliver bad news.

Sarah gives my hand a squeeze. "I know, Shaw. Paulie told me about Jeremy. I'm so sorry." The sympathy in her eyes reminds me of another time and I really hate that these memories are flooding me right now. Ignoring the twisting in my heart, I try to focus on what she just said.

"Paulie? He called you or something?"

"Something," she hedges. When she's had enough of my staring at her, she relents. "You know Paulie and I spend most Sundays together."

"No, I don't know that." My tone is a bit harsher than I intended, but I'm a little confused. "Like how? Watching football? Hanging out? Are you two fucking dating now or just fucking?" I feel so stupid for not realizing this sooner. The looks and secret smiles, Paulie always doing shit for Sarah without even being asked when he's my employee, not hers...

"Don't you dare speak to me like that. What Paulie and I do during our free time is none of your business but it shouldn't come as such a surprise that we care for each other. But, that's not why I'm here and I have a feeling it's not all about Jeremy either, so spill it."

My head is still reeling from Sarah's vague confession but she's right. It's not my business and it's not why I asked her to meet me here. Thankfully, both orders of pancakes I ordered for us were just delivered, so I use the distraction to get my thoughts in order before speaking again.

Once I feel ready, or as ready as I can be, I clear my throat and speak. "I slept with Avery."

Images of the two of us together invade my mind but I try to ignore them. Flashes of skin and sounds and how it felt to be inside her keep trying to break through but now's not the time to torture myself with memories.

God, I miss her.

And it's only been a day.

One fucking day.

"Well, it's about time," Sarah replies, like what I've told her is no big deal. Now, I'm truly speechless. How can she be so calm about this?

I know she loved Liz like the sister she never had. Why isn't she pissed off right now?

"Is that all you can say?"

"It was only a matter of time before you two fell into bed together, we all knew it. What's the big deal?" She shrugs like she's talking about the damn weather. Meanwhile, I feel like I'm losing my grip on reality.

"What do you mean? It *is* a big deal. I can't believe you don't see that."

"Oh, come on, Shaw. There's no way you've been celibate all these years."

I stammer. "N-no, but..."

"So, why is this time so different? Why did you feel the need to tell me in person in a public place?"

"Because she's my employee," I lie.

"Bullshit. There's more to you and Avery and you know it. You're just too stubborn and scared to admit it."

"She hates me."

"Who, Avery?"

"Yeah." I feel the anger in my blood turn ice cold as I think back on Avery's face as I told her to leave. "She still doesn't know about Liz."

Sarah puts her head in her hands and lets out a deep sigh. "For fuck's sake, Shaw. What were you thinking? What did you do?"

"Everything was great—perfect, even—until I fucked it all up. One minute I was the happiest I'd been in years and the next, I was yelling at her for doing something that Liz used to yell at me for. It was like I had no control over my body or my words. I lashed out. I needed her out of the house so I could deal with everything I was feeling."

"Have you tried talking to her since then?"

"Of course I have and she won't answer. I don't blame her but I still have to try."

"I think it's smart of her to stay away," she states.

"Thanks a lot, sis." I know my sarcasm isn't helping but I can't help it.

"Have you thought about how you made her feel?" Sarah's eyes are blazing and I love that she's so protective of Avery. "Don't you remember why she ended up in New Orleans in the first place?"

Brant.

Shit.

I'm no better than he is. I'd never put my hands on Avery in anger but she doesn't know that. Not only have I hurt her, but I've probably scared her, too.

"What do I do, Sarah? I'm so fucking lost."

"I don't have all the answers, but when she's ready to talk to you again, you have to tell her about Liz. She deserves to know."

I nod in agreement and look at my sister. I'm reminded of times when I was a boy and so clueless about everything but she never judged me or made fun of me when I'd ask for her help. I'm hoping that doesn't change when I ask the one question I'm desperate to know the answer to.

"How can I be falling for Avery when I'm still grieving for Lizzie?"

23

Avery

WHAT THE HELL IS WRONG WITH ME? HOW DO I KEEP
managing to find myself in these situations? I feel like I'm a nice girl
who deserves a nice guy, but I'm starting to think all the nice guys
really are taken.

I thought I'd found a nice guy in Shaw, even though it took months
for him to show that side of himself. But now I don't know what to
think.

Being with Shaw at his house—in his bed—was perfect. Better
than all the dreams I'd had about him, every fantasy all rolled into one.
I've never experienced anything like that. It was more than sex; it was
passion and need and connection. Maybe even love or something that
could turn into love.

But when he started yelling at me, I didn't know what to think. I
was so caught off guard and confused as to why he'd be so upset over
a towel, but then I looked at him—truly looked at him. He wasn't the
Shaw I knew at that point. He was a man possessed. Possessed by what
though? Anger, sure, but there was more. He was desperate and hurting
and completely devastated by something. I know it sounds crazy, but I
wanted so badly to comfort him, console him, chase away his demons
for him.

Shaw telling me to get out hurt me like I've never hurt before, and that's saying a lot. Hearing him rasp out the word "please" nearly killed me.

I can't help but compare this situation with my last fight with Brant in Houston. I once couldn't imagine Brant raising his voice to me or hitting me, but he did. Shaw yelling at me didn't make me fear for my safety but it was jarring, nonetheless. It certainly wasn't what I was expecting after our amazing night together.

My phone buzzes on the coffee table but I ignore it. Shaw has been calling and texting regularly but I haven't responded in any way. I honestly don't know what to say to him. I'd like to think we could work through whatever is eating away at him but, maybe, he doesn't want that. Maybe he thinks our night together was a mistake.

And what about my job? Can we even work together now? Will I be able to look at him tomorrow, knowing what it's like for him to be inside me but also knowing what it feels like to have his wrath focused on me?

I'm so confused.

So very, very confused.

And when I think my brain can't take much more, Jeremy comes to mind and my confusion is replaced by guilt. This crap with Shaw has taken over my brain and my heart and I haven't allowed myself to grieve for my friend. I just can't believe he's gone.

I also hate that the last memory I have of him is the night in the hallway.

I wish I would've had a chance to see him the next day, maybe help him in some way.

The ache in my chest is so heavy.

Later, CeCe brings me leftover lemon cake from the coffee shop and we binge watch Friends. She doesn't ask many questions or grill me for information. She just lets me process and deal with things in my own way and my own time.

She's a good friend, probably one of the best I've ever had. I know I need to find my own place, but I'm grateful to be here right now because being alone would suck.

That thought makes me think of Shaw and the fact that he's probably alone in that big house and my heart breaks a little more for him.

After a fitful night's sleep, I wake up late and trudge downstairs to help CeCe for a few hours before our weekly Tuesday meeting at the bar. The thought crossed my mind on more than one occasion to call in sick. I might even get by with a text message to Shaw. But that's not me.

So, at noon, I'm walking up to the front door of Come Again with an anvil sitting in the bottom of my stomach. Taking a deep breath, I brace myself for Shaw—his voice, his smell, everything about him that affects every part of me.

When I step inside, the bar is eerily quiet. Paulie and Shaw are standing behind the bar deep in a quiet conversation. Kevin and Charlie are sitting at the table in the corner. The only people missing are me, Sarah...and Jeremy.

I swallow down the onslaught of emotions and steel myself as I walk across the wooden floor and take a seat in one of the empty seats at the table.

Conversation ceases and I feel like all eyes are on me. The tension in the room escalates as I feel Shaw's eyes on me, but I don't turn to see him. I can't. Self-preservation is telling me to look away and not give into my deep-rooted desire.

Clearing his throat, Shaw gets everyone's attention and starts to talk just as Sarah walks through the back door. Her presence is what we needed to balance the scales. She gives everyone a soft smile as she takes a seat on the barstool in front of Shaw, facing the rest of us.

"Sorry I'm late," she says. "I've got an early lunch next door for everyone after we're finished here."

I look from her and slowly over to Shaw, letting myself take him in for the first time since getting here. Oddly enough, the dark circles under his eyes don't make me feel better. It's obvious that he's lost sleep and I hate it. I should be glad, because so have I, but I'm not.

Shaw nods his head at Sarah and then turns his attention back to where me, Charlie, and Kevin are sitting. Paulie stands beside him with his arms crossed over his chest and his eyes trained on the floor.

"As you all know," Shaw begins, "Jeremy was found late Saturday night outside a bar on Bourbon Street. He'd overdosed and was gone by the time the police found him." He pauses for a minute shrugging his shoulders and giving a harsh shake to his head. "I've been in touch with his family and had his body sent home. It was the right thing to do, but it means that none of us will get to say an official goodbye."

Shaw's eyes dart to mine and settle there, reaching deep into my soul.

"I'm sorry about that. I know we all need a little closure. So, I thought we'd close the place down for the day. Sarah's got lunch fixed and y'all can have the rest of the day off to mourn in whatever way you see fit."

Everyone is silent, mostly lost in their own thoughts, but I'm stuck on Shaw and the sincerity in his words. The confusion I've felt since he walked into his bedroom Sunday morning is back in full force. What makes him go from this caring, thoughtful man to the one who went off on me because of a wet towel?

I don't understand it.

Maybe it's not for me to understand?

Shaw has secrets and if he's not willing to share that part of himself with me, there's nowhere for us to go from here. And I don't think I can go back to just being his employee.

When the guys finally get up to go next door to eat, Sarah follows behind them, placing a hand on my shoulder on her way by. A few moments later, the back door closes and it's just me and Shaw, who's now leaning against the bar with his head hanging down. "I'm sorry," he murmurs, barely loud enough for me to hear.

The apology is nice, but I want more.

"For what?" I ask, standing from my chair and walking in front of the bar to face him.

His head lifts slowly and troubled, guarded eyes meet mine. "For everything."

I give him a sad smile because when I look at him, I see the walls being built back up and I don't want to be shut out again. I've been behind those walls and I'll know what I'm missing out on, and I can't be here if he's not going to let me in.

Every day would be torture.

"I'm quitting," I state as firmly as I can, but my voice cracks and betrays me. "I, uh...I need to find something else." This wasn't planned so I don't have a speech planned.

Shaw's brows furrow as his face hardens. "What?"

"I can stay for a couple weeks if you need me to, but I'm quitting." I can hear myself talking but it's coming from somewhere inside that's detached.

"Why?" Shaw's voice sounds as shattered as I feel.

"You told me I should think of myself...this is me doing that."

His expression softens as he takes a deep breath and then exhales. Blinking slowly, he runs his hands down his face, cupping his hands over his mouth. Finally, he says, "You should do that."

This time, there's resolve mixed with acceptance. The pull I've felt between us is still there, but it's loosened as Shaw lets me walk out of the bar.

Once I'm out on the sidewalk, I allow myself to look back and see Shaw standing where I left him with his hands covering his face. For a split second, I think about walking back in there and forcing him to tell me the truth, making him let me in, but I want him to want to tell me.

I want him to want me enough to give me everything.

Every broken piece.

It's been five days since Jeremy's death and two days since I quit my job at Come Again.

I spent the better part of that afternoon inside the cathedral. I'm not Catholic, but it felt like the right place to be. When I walked inside and saw other people praying and lighting candles, I was drawn to them and the peacefulness I felt when I stepped inside. So, I stayed and lit my own candle.

For Jeremy.

For Shaw.

For me.

Then, I listened to the beautiful choir sing and sent up silent prayers for everyone and everything hurting in my life.

After that, I walked to Canal Street and hopped on a streetcar that took me to The Crescent Moon. I needed comfort food and Wyatt always makes me feel welcome. It's kind of been my safe place since I got to this city. When I walked in and saw Shaw's table empty, I almost took it, but changed my mind and opted for the one I sat at my first day here.

Something changed in me recently, maybe it was Shaw's words finally clicking into place...maybe I finally hit bottom and it helped me see my life more clearly. Whatever it is, it's making me want to look out for me, guard my heart better, because I don't think I can take another big hit. I've had as much heartache as I can bear.

While eating at The Crescent Moon, Wyatt and I got to talking and he offered me a job. His business partner, Tripp, is taking some time off to be with his wife who just had a baby, so he's shorthanded. Of course, I took him up on the offer.

So, here I am, on the same streetcar, headed to my first day at The Crescent Moon. When it passes the street Shaw's house sits on, I allow myself a glimpse, but that's all.

I miss him.

And if I spend too much time thinking about him, I'll just get sad and I don't have time for that today. I'm stepping off of this streetcar and into my new job.

It's a new day.

I'm a new Avery Cole.

"Hey." Wyatt greets me as I walk through the front door of the restaurant. "Let me introduce you to everyone and show you around."

"Okay," I reply, following him with an excitement and anticipation I was expecting.

When we walk through the swinging doors that lead to the kitchen, everyone is buzzing about the relatively small space but they all pause long enough to say hello.

"This is Shawn, our cook," Wyatt says pointing to a guy with longer, tied-back hair.

Between the hair and his name, my thoughts immediately go to Shaw.

What the fuck? Couldn't his name be Jerry...or Bill...and couldn't he have a buzz cut?

It's like the universe is testing me, so I plaster a smile on my face and wave. "Hey, Shawn."

"This is Dixie." Wyatt points to a lady buzzing through the kitchen like a woman on a mission. "She's the one in charge of the schedules. If you need a day off or something like that, she's your girl."

"Oh," I interject, remembering there's something I want to ask. "Do you think it'd be possible for me to only work Tuesday through Saturday? I don't mind working doubles or whatever you need, but I really need Sundays and Mondays off."

Wyatt's eyes land on mine and I divert my gaze, going back to the large stove where Shawn is cooking away like he has eight arms. After a few moments, Wyatt clears his throat and says, "sure, no problem."

"Thanks," I mutter, knowing that he knows why I asked for those days off but neither of us is willing to say it and I'm grateful. I'm not ready to talk about it. CeCe and I have barely even discussed it.

"Gretchen is our newest addition," Wyatt says, continuing the introductions. "Well, not now...you're the newest member of The Crescent Moon family." He dips his head with a big smile. "Welcome to the family."

A warmth spreads through my chest, but it's met with resistance. As much as I'm already starting to feel a part of this place, I miss everyone at the bar. I can't help it.

I also can't help comparing the differences.

Where Shaw is always grumpy and moody, Wyatt is carefree and happy-go-lucky. It's obvious he runs a tight ship, but the vibe here is so much more relaxed.

I also start comparing the similarities.

Shawn is obviously Wyatt's Paulie, or maybe that's Tripp's job, but since he's not here, Shawn is filling in. Dixie seems like a Sarah, she's the one who keeps everyone running on schedule. Gretchen is the new kid...okay, not going there. We'll just call her Charlie. I bet there's even a Kevin—the quiet one who's willing to do whatever needs done and never says anything about it.

I wonder if they all go hang out after work?

One thing that's going to be way different is working during the day and closing up shop before two in the morning. CeCe joked that I'll no longer be working on vampire hours.

"So, you'll shadow me for the day," Wyatt says, interrupting my inner thoughts. "I have a feeling you're a fast learner. Assuming everything goes as well as I think it will, you can have your own tables tomorrow, picking up Tripp's sections."

I nod in agreement. "Sounds good."

He shows me where I can stash my backpack and gives me an apron, then we're out in the main dining room waiting tables.

"How's...everything?" Wyatt asks as we're cleaning off a table, most of the restaurant empty due to the lunch rush ending and the dinner rush still an hour or so away.

I look up to see him pretending to be really interested in a few glasses he's stacking together.

"Uh, well...I guess it's fine."

"I know about the kid," Wyatt confesses, his eyes still trained on the table. "Shaw told me."

Taking a deep breath, I hold it for a second and then exhale loudly. "Jeremy."

"Yeah," he says, finally looking up at me. "You were close to him?"

I shrug, letting out a sigh. "We were...friends, I guess. I'm not sure how good of friends you can actually be with an addict." I've asked myself this question quite a bit over the past few days. How well did I know Jeremy? Not very well. If we'd been better friends, maybe he would've confided in me that he was struggling with his addiction? Maybe I could've encouraged him to find someone to talk to—a group meeting or something?

"Yeah," Wyatt says in a regretful tone. "Well, if you need someone to talk to, I'm here."

"Thanks," I tell him with a small smile. "I think the hardest thing for me right now is that I didn't get any closure, you know? I saw him one day and he was fine, the next day he showed up to work high, and then he was gone. In my mind, I still see Jeremy...he's fine, alive."

"You need closure," Wyatt confirms. "Maybe you could do something to help you feel like you're remembering him, helping people like him. That might make you feel...I don't know...better?"

I nod, thinking about it. "Maybe." He might be onto something. "It would make me feel better if I could help people like Jeremy, since I couldn't help him."

"There are some group homes around the city that take in people off the streets," he says thoughtfully.

"Yeah, like Charity House," I add. "That's where Jeremy was staying."

"Maybe go there and see if you can volunteer or something," he suggests.

My chest feels a little lighter at the thought, so I nod. "Yeah, I'll do that. Thanks, Wyatt."

"Anytime, that's what I'm here for."

His wide, easy smile forces me to return it.

"You're like a magic problem solver," I tease, appreciating the levity as I feel the black cloud that's been following me around start to dissipate.

24

Shaw

"EXCUSE ME, CAN I GET A WHISKEY SOUR?"

I glance up from the dishes I'm washing behind the bar and see a young woman smiling at me. I do a double take because she reminds me of Avery. She doesn't look like her, really, but she's about the same age, same build...just enough similarities to make me think about Avery. Not that it takes much, mind you. She's embedded so deep under my skin and even though it's only been a week since I last saw her, I feel like it's been forever—too long. Last night, I thought about calling her or texting her but stopped myself. It didn't feel right. Eventually, I'll reach out to her and explain everything, but I'm still working on getting my head on straight.

"Yeah, sure. Just a sec." Turning my head to the side, I start to call out to one of the guys before remembering I'm here alone. Kevin and Charlie aren't scheduled to come in for another hour and Paulie is next door helping Sarah. It's not the first time it's happened, but at least this time I stopped myself before yelling for Jeremy or Avery. I don't think it's ever taken me this long to adapt to losing employees, but those two were special cases and it's just not the same without them here.

Especially Avery.

I dry my hands then quickly make the requested drink. When I hand the lady her change, she gives me a blinding smile and a wink. I respond by turning my back to her and putting the whiskey bottle back on the shelf.

No thank you. Not interested.

The only person I'm interested in is Avery, but I'm afraid I've made too many mistakes with her. When I stopped by Neutral Grounds a couple of days ago, hoping to see her, CeCe said she was gone, but wouldn't tell me where.

I get it. She's protecting her friend, but it still pissed me off.

Yesterday, I had my first therapy session in over two years. For the first few years after Liz's death, I saw him regularly, but after a while, I felt like I was as good as I was gonna get. He helped me get to a place where I was a functioning member of society. I was handling the grief instead of letting it handle me.

I worked every day, took care of the house, exercised regularly, found healthy ways to get rid of the anger, managed my employees, spoke to my family...everything that was expected of me.

Everything I expected from myself.

"Surviving, not thriving," that's what my therapist told me yesterday at our session. I've been living, but I haven't been changing or evolving. Everything has stayed the same.

Stagnant.

And then Avery Cole walked into my life and shook it up. She made me start to feel things and want things I'd denied myself for so long. I'd written off even the idea of love. I didn't even think it was possible...I wasn't capable.

Even when all the signs pointed to it, I still shut it out.

Loving Liz had been so easy.

It felt as natural as breathing.

From the first day I met her, I knew I wanted it all—marriage, two kids, a house in the Garden District, and to grow old with her.

But life is twisted and unexpected. And just when you think you've got it all figured out, a pink-haired, brown-eyed girl with a heart of gold will walk into your bar and demand you give her a job.

Loving Avery is hard.

It tests every part of me, making me question everything.

"Hey, boss," Paulie calls out as he walks into the bar from the hallway.

"Hey," I reply, continuing my task at hand as I dry the glasses I just finished washing. The girl who was smiling at me earlier is now sitting at a table in the corner talking to another girl. There are a few regulars nursing beers at the bar, but for the most part, the place is quiet.

Just as Paulie approaches the bar, the front door opens and Kevin walks in, giving us both a wave. Looking at my watch, I see that it's a little before five o'clock. My next therapy session is tonight. Well, it's a group that my therapist thinks I'd benefit from sitting in on.

I'm still calling bullshit, but I'm going because fuck if I don't want to figure my shit out and get my head on straight. I want to be able to feel everything for Avery without constantly feeling guilty for it.

"I guess I'm heading out," I tell him.

Paulie nods his head, silently shoving me out the door.

He knows where I'm going and what I'm doing. He and Sarah have been my biggest supporters in this. I honestly couldn't do it without them.

"I'll see you in a couple hours," I tell Paulie, giving Kevin a slap on the back as I pass him. "Don't let the place burn down."

Once I'm on my bike, I fire it up and let it idle for second, pushing back the memories that always hit me of Avery behind me, holding on tightly as we just rode around. It's one of my favorite memories of her, always giving me a hard-on and making my chest ache at the same time.

When I pull up outside of the address I plugged into my phone, I park my bike by the curb and hop off. Walking inside the building, I hear people conversing and use that as an indicator of where I'm supposed to be. Hesitantly, I approach the open door and see a sign that reads *Grief Support Group - Moving on After Death*. Those words are enough to get my heart pounding and make my hands sweaty. I think about bolting, when a female voice calls out.

"Hello, welcome."

I can't force a smile, but I give her a tight nod. "Hello."

"If you're looking for the MAD group, you've found it." Her tone is matter-of-fact and friendly enough without being overly so.

"Mad?" I ask, taking an opportunity to look around at the small groups of people around the room, huddled around with cups of coffee and bottles of water.

"Moving on After Death," she says with a tilt of her head, watching my line of sight. "But *mad* kind of fits, don't you think? Haven't we all been mad, whether in the mental sense or emotional sense?"

I nod, because she's right. "Yeah, guess so."

"You're welcome to grab a cup of coffee or just find a seat. We'll be starting soon and I promise you won't have to say a word, unless you want to."

"Thanks," I tell her, managing something that might resemble a smile. Maybe.

"I can spot a runner a mile away."

She gives me a grin and pats my shoulder before walking over to greet someone else.

Ellen, who I later find out lost her husband six years ago, seems to be the leader of the group. After her husband died, she went back to school and got her degree in counseling, finding purpose in her grief.

That was the bar for me and the men I tried to help.

I guess we all find purpose in different places, and eventually—hopefully—we find a way to balance the grief and guilt. That's what I'm here for. I want to figure out how to let Avery in—all the way in, past all the walls and barricades.

"Grief can make us crazy," Ellen says, cutting through my thoughts. "It can make us lash out, cry out, give up. I know all of us in here lost a spouse, which is what makes this group so special. We can all identify with what everyone is going through, but you'll also find out that we're all handling it differently and that's okay. You might have lost your husband or wife and jumped right into a relationship, needing to fill the gaping wound. However, you might be wondering how you can ever love someone else. That's why we're here, to help us all understand that there are no hard and fast answers."

"I yelled at my kid last night for leaving the front door open," one lady a few chairs to my right says. Biting down on her lower lip, she shakes her head. "That never bothered me before. It was my husband's pet peeve, but I'd always just laugh it off and roll my eyes. Like, what the hell is wrong with leaving the door open? It's not like the house is going to burn down, ya know?" She pauses for a second, giving a watery laugh. "I've always been a pick my battles kind of parent, but since Barry died, I sometimes have these moments where I realize life is changing without him and I want everything to stay the same so I don't have to be reminded...and I yell at the kids over stupid shit like leaving the front door open or insist that we eat spaghetti every Monday night, because that's what he liked...and the grass has to be mowed diagonally." Wiping under her eyes, she lets out a soft laugh. "That's my crazy."

"And it's totally normal," Ellen says without pity. "I know you might feel bad after yelling at the kids, but I'm sure if you just talk to them and tell them why, they'll understand."

Another guy starts talking about how he can't get rid of his wife's clothes and she's been gone ten years.

One lady refuses to drive her husband's car, but she sits in it every day and listens to the CD he left in it on replay.

With each story, I start to feel my chest lighten. I don't open up and spill my guts, but I listen and I let their grief and crazy help me feel better about my own. It feels a lot like acceptance and that makes me feel like maybe I can look it in the face and find a place for it.

"I went on my first date," a lady to my left says as she tries to hide the smile, but Ellen congratulates her and everyone else offers her praise. Again, I just listen.

"How was it, Susan?" Ellen asks. "How did you feel?"

Susan shrugs and sighs. "Different, maybe a little foreign even. Charles and I had been married for twenty years. He was my first everything, so just being out with another man felt...weird...but good.

It'd been so long since someone had opened the door for me or held my hand across a table. Those feelings of guilt we talked about last week were still there, but I was able to push past them and start to feel deserving...I deserve to be happy and loved...I deserve to go out on a date," Susan says with another sigh.

"You do," Ellen encourages. "For those of you who haven't been here before, we've talked a lot about falling in love after losing someone. What does that look like? Feel like? I don't want to go deep into it because we're running out of time for tonight."

I glance down at my watch and see she's right. An entire hour has passed and I surprise myself by feeling disappointed by that fact. I'm not finished listening. I especially want to hear what she has to say about this last topic. I'm all fucking ears, scooting to the edge of my seat.

"I just want to say this," Ellen continues. "If you were in a happy relationship, which I can almost guarantee all of us here were or we wouldn't be here trying to figure out how to move on," she stops and smiles. "We all experienced love, maybe even the love of a lifetime, and you might be feeling like you don't deserve that twice, but I'm here to tell you that you do. And the best compliment you can give to your deceased spouse is to find love again. It's an honor to their memory, not an intrusion. Sometimes, it helps for us to put them in our position. If we were the ones who were gone, would we want them to find love?"

The entire room is quiet, thoughtful as she pauses, giving us time to mull over her question. I let my mind drift to Liz and picture her here and me gone. The sharp pain that shoots through my chest is all the answer I need.

No way.

No fucking way would I want her to be where I am today. I wouldn't want her to be lonely. I wouldn't want her to not be feeling all the love in the world. If I couldn't be here to love her the way she deserved, I would want someone to do that job for me. She deserved only the best.

"The desire for another relationship isn't to replace, but to find that happiness again."

She pauses again and I rub at my chest, trying to ease the constriction.

"Humans have an unlimited capacity to love. It's inevitable that we'll compare the next person who comes along to the one we lost, but remember we're all different. And this new person needs to be the perfect person for this season of your life. That means, they're probably not going to be exactly like your deceased wife or husband. They're going to have their own strengths and weaknesses. Let them. And let yourself love them just the way they are so they can love you right where you're at."

Ellen sighs heavily, standing from her chair.

"Who knows? Maybe we're all the lucky ones? Maybe we're going to have not one, but two great loves in life?"

25

Avery

"YOU ARE ONE STUBBORN WOMAN," CECE DECLARES when she walks into the coffee shop.

I give her an innocent-looking smile before continuing to wipe down the espresso machine. "I have no idea what you're talking about."

"Well, the dark circles under your eyes and the yawns you think you're hiding say otherwise." Her tone turns sympathetic as she continues. "You're exhausted, Avery. You've been running yourself ragged all week. Go take a nap before you have to go to The Crescent Moon. I can handle things here."

I know my friend means well and I know I should take her advice, but I have to stay busy. I like being active, so helping CeCe and working at The Crescent Moon accomplishes that. Besides, when I started staying with her, I promised I'd help out as much as possible and I never go back on my word. Plus, working all day allows me to crash when I get home and sleep soundly, which then leaves me zero time for thinking. Specifically, thinking about Shaw.

It's just too hard, even after two weeks. If I think about him, I start analyzing every moment of our time together at his house—what went right and what went wrong.

If I think about him, I realize how much I miss him.

It's later in the afternoon, as I'm busing tables at Crescent Moon, I feel my back pocket buzz. Since I only have a few customers and they're all tucked into their meals, I take my phone out and see my mama's face on my screen.

"Hey, mama, I'm at work so I can't talk long. Is everything okay?"

"Everything is fine, honey. And I'm glad you're at work because I need you to ask that sweet boss of yours for some time off."

In the short time I've worked at The Crescent Moon, my mama has fallen for Wyatt. She doesn't even know the man, but everything I tell her about him makes her love him more—the sweet southern manners, the suspenders, the bowties...all the way down to his cowboy boots. She's kind of obsessed. I actually think it might be what gets her and Daddy to New Orleans.

Last week, she conned me into taking a picture of him and send it to her so she could *really put a face with the name*. I rolled my eyes, but obliged. Her chocolate chip cookies, which I missed dearly, were on the line, and they showed up two days ago, just like she promised.

"Mama," I sigh, loving her stubbornness, but also feeling exhausted. "I know this is hard for you, but I don't know if I can make it to Oklahoma. I just started working here and I don't feel right asking for time off yet." Wyatt has already mentioned the restaurant will be closed on Christmas Eve and Christmas Day, but I'm sure other people here would like an extended holiday, too. I'm at the bottom of the totem pole right now, so I'm expecting to be covering shifts all month.

"Now, you listen to me, Avery Cole. It about killed me and your daddy to not spend Thanksgiving with you and I'll be damned if it's gonna happen at Christmas."

I still feel awful about cancelling on my parents at the last minute and I miss them terribly, but I just don't want to rock the boat here. Wyatt has been so good to me and I don't want to take advantage of his niceness. Besides, it's already so close to Christmas, I'm sure travel prices are way out of my budget by now. I already know from buying a bus ticket for Thanksgiving that the bus trip alone takes three days round trip—eighteen hours both ways. So, if I expect to spend any time at all with my family, I'll need at least two extra days off.

"Now, you need to ask off for twenty-third through the twenty-sixth. I'll forward you the email with all your flight information in just a minute," Mama says, obviously not taking no for an answer.

"Wait. What? What flight information? What do you mean?"

"The day after Thanksgiving I bought you a plane ticket for Christmas. Your daddy will pick you up at the airport and don't worry about presents. We just want you here with us. I wish you could stay longer, but I know you have a job to get back to."

My eyes fill with tears as I process her words. "Oh, Mama. You're so stubborn and I love you." I set down a bucket of dirty dishes and smile as my heart fills just thinking about seeing her. "Okay, I'll go talk to Wyatt and I'll call you when my shift ends."

"Okay, sweetie," she replies. I hear something shuffling in the background as my multi-tasking mama is off to the next thing on her to-do list. Sharon Cole gets shit done. "If Wyatt gives you any trouble, you tell him to call me."

I let out a soft giggle, wondering if that's just a sly way of her getting his number.

"Love you, Mama."

Walking into the kitchen, I place the dishes in the sink and leave to check on my customers. Wyatt, meets me at the swinging doors with a smile and a stack of plates.

"Table ten would like some bread pudding," he says, handing the dishes off to me.

"Oh, sorry, I was on my way out to check on them now," I tell him, feeling my cheeks heat up at the thought of falling down on my job. I never want to be *that* employee—the one everyone is always picking up the slack for. *I* pick up the slack.

Wyatt gives me a smile and waves it off. "No worries, I saw you were on a phone call."

"Sorry," I say again, "I wouldn't normally take it but it was my mama and I was worried something was wrong. She never calls me during the day."

"Avery, relax."

"Okay." I let out a light laugh. With another apology on the tip of my tongue, I bite it back. "This probably isn't the best time to ask you, but..." I hesitate for a second, turning toward the prep station. "Just a second." Walking over, I plate two pieces of bread pudding and pour the sweet, buttery bourbon sauce on top. Quickly, I walk back out into the dining room and take the desserts to table ten. The sweet older ladies smile up at me, one patting my hand gently.

"Can I get you anything else?" I ask.

"You know, I did change my mind on that cup of tea you offered earlier." Her warm presence reminds me of my nana and I can't help but want to be at her every beck and call. Shoot, she could change her mind a million times and I wouldn't care.

"Of course, I'll be right back."

Wyatt is still standing at the door when I get back to the kitchen. As I prep the tea, he walks over. "What were you needing to ask?"

"My mama bought me a plane ticket home," I give him an apologetic smile and sigh. "She's kind of dead set on me being home for Christmas."

"I couldn't agree with her more," Wyatt says, crossing his arms and leaning against the counter. "When do you need to leave?"

"My flight leaves on the twenty-third." I cringe, still feeling bad about already asking for a day off when I haven't even been here very long.

"Absolutely," he says without a second thought, walking around the counter to inspect what Shawn has going on at the stove. Grabbing a spoon from the drawer, he dips it in for a taste test and I have the briefest flash of Sarah...a different kitchen...a different taste-tester. My chest momentarily aches.

Damn, I miss them.

"Just let Dixie know," he continues, giving Shawn a slap of praise on his shoulder as he tosses the spoon into a basin of hot, soapy water in the sink.

"Thanks," I tell him, letting out a sigh of relief. "I didn't want to have to tell my mama you said no." The sly grin is inevitable because bantering with Wyatt comes so easy and natural.

"Ah, shit." Wyatt lets out a low whistle. "No one wants Mrs. Cole out of sorts, that's for sure."

"Yeah, she might've taken your posters out of her locker," I tease.

He's well aware of my mama's school girl crush on him. And he likes it.

"Avery," he calls out as I'm heading back to the dining room, tea for two in hand. "I meant to tell you that I know of an apartment for rent, close by, if you're still looking."

Looking down at the piece of paper in my hand, I check the address Wyatt gave me one more time. The house in front of me is gorgeous—pale yellow with large columns that frame the porch and balcony. As I glance around, taking in my serene, picturesque surroundings, I take a deep breath. The typical hot, humid days have relinquished their hold on the city for a brief moment. As December has settled in, the temperatures have dropped enough to give us all a reprieve. It's not cold by most people's standards, but after the sweltering heat of the summer and fall months, I can see why everyone is wrapping up in scarves and pulling on their tall boots.

Your blood starts to run a little thinner the longer you're here.

I notice large, grandiose trees above me have strands of beads in the tall branches. They've caught my eye from the streetcar and an older gentleman who I see from time to time told me they're leftover from Mardi Gras—*Mardi Gras Trees*, he called them.

They make me smile.

"You must be Avery," a sweet, southern voice greets from the direction of the front door. Turning, I see a pretty blonde smiling at me. Her blue eyes are obvious from where I stand and her pleasant demeanor leaves me no choice but to smile back at her.

"Yep, I'm Avery." Walking up the short sidewalk to the steps, she meets me at the bottom.

"I'm Eliza Walker," she says, offering me her hand. "Wyatt said you'd be stopping by. I was just getting ready to drop my kids off at a Christmas party." She looks at her watch and I immediately feel bad about coming at an inopportune time.

"I'm sorry," I begin, but she cuts me off.

"No." She shakes her head and gives me another warm smile. "Believe me, I meet myself coming and going most days. So, don't even worry about it. I've got about fifteen minutes before I absolutely have to leave. What do you say we check out the apartment?"

She's already walking down the sidewalk that leads to the back of the house, so I follow her.

"There's really not much to see, so it shouldn't take you long to decide if it's a good fit for you. My brother used to live here, about five or six years ago. Since then, we rented it out one time to another college kid." Stopping, she turns and rolls her eyes at me, putting the key in the lock. "Bad mistake. One we never made again."

Pushing the door open, she steps to the side. "It's mostly been used for family and friends who come through town...but we've been through it recently—fresh paint and carpet."

This is nice, much more than I expected when Wyatt told me about it. "I love it," I tell her, meaning it. It's cozy, kind of reminding me of Shaw's apartment, which I shove down to the pit of my stomach.

"We also put a brand new stove and refrigerator in a few years ago. There's not a dishwasher, but a nice big sink," she says with a small chuckle. "Oh, and you can wash your clothes in the washer and dryer inside the garage downstairs."

"I'll take it," I breathe out, immediately feeling at home in the small space.

Eliza laughs lightly. "Well, okay."

"It's five hundred a month?" I ask, repeating what Wyatt had told me.

"I was thinking more like four," she says, looking around the space.

My eyes grow wider, knowing that four hundred dollars is well within my budget. I have a little over two thousand saved up right now, keeping as much of my paychecks as possible to cover first month's rent and deposits when I finally found a place.

"Is that too much?" she asks with a frown.

"No, no...just the opposite. It's great," I tell her, taking another look around and walking into the bathroom which has a basic combination shower and tub with a small vanity. It's nothing special, but it's clean and fairly new. "Everything I've looked at so far has been either way out of my budget or in a scary place."

"I believe it," Eliza replies, sighing as she leans against the counter. "I'm sure it's a little nerve-wracking being a single woman in a city like New Orleans, but you have nothing to worry about here. We've got a great security system and my husband, Ben, is usually home in the evenings. Jack and Emmie, our twins, are always playing in the yard. So, I hope you don't mind a little noise and action."

"I think I can handle that." It really sounds perfect—too good to be true—but I feel like things are finally swinging in my favor and I don't want to jinx myself by saying so.

"Well, you can move in as soon as you'd like. If you'll stop by tomorrow, I'll have the key waiting for you."

"What about deposits?" I ask, wondering how much money I should bring with me.

"Just first month's rent will do. All your utilities are included," she adds, walking back down the stairs after locking the apartment up. "The only thing it doesn't have is a telephone, but since everyone has cell phones these days, we didn't think it was necessary."

"Yeah, no problem."

"You can tap into our Wi-Fi, though. I'll give you the password when you move in."

I know she needs to go and so do I. Glancing at my phone, it's almost five and I'm supposed to be at Charity House in twenty minutes to start volunteering.

But for some reason, I want to hug her.

"Thank you," I say instead, not wanting to freak out my new landlord before I've even moved in.

"You're welcome," she says, turning toward the house and yelling, "Jack! Emmie! Let's go!"

She smiles, pulling me in for that hug I wanted to deliver and I soak it up, feeling my chest warm. "Just think of yourself as one of the family."

"Okay," I reply when she releases me from her fierce grip and watch as two kids run out of the house, arguing about who's riding shotgun.

"It's Jack's turn," Eliza cuts in, ending their argument, rolling her eyes at me. "Kids."

Huffing out a laugh, I wave at the two of them, noticing that Jack shares his mother's ice blue eyes. Emmie has long, dark hair and big dimples. They're really cute kids. It's been awhile since I've been around any and I'm feeling like a hit the jackpot.

I love kids.

When I was growing up, babysitting was my favorite gig. Honestly, I always felt like I was getting paid for nothing. Once upon a time, I thought I wanted to be a teacher, but changed my mind when I thought about dealing with parents and not getting paid shit.

"Guys, this is Avery. She's going to live in the apartment," Eliza announces.

"Cool," Emmie says with a curious smile. "I'm Emmie." Just like her mom, she gives me a sweet smile and offers me her hand to shake before jumping in the back of the SUV.

"I'm Jack," the little boy says, with another shake, like he's twenty, instead of ten or eleven. I'm just guessing, but I bet I'm close.

"Nice to meet you both," I tell them.

"Well, we've gotta run," Eliza says turning to get in the driver's seat and then stopping. "Do you need a ride somewhere?"

"Oh, no. I'm good. Just heading back to the streetcar. I'm

volunteering at Charity House tonight."

"That's really nice," Eliza says with sincerity dripping from her words. "You sure you don't need a ride?"

"No, go," I say with a smile. "Don't be late for the Christmas party."

"Okay, we'll see you tomorrow."

Fifteen minutes later, I'm jumping off the streetcar and jogging the couple of blocks to the large house that sets behind a church. I can't be late on my first day. Even though I'm not getting paid, I still think of this as a job, people are depending on me.

Walking in, a lady with a clipboard looks up and smiles. "Can I help you?"

"Avery Cole," I tell her, a bit out of breath. "I called about volunteering."

"I'm Samantha. Welcome to Charity House," she says, taking a few steps toward me, checking her clipboard, marking something off and then looking back up at me. "We're just changing shifts, so it's perfect timing."

Samantha walks me around the large house, showing me the rooms on the top two floors that people who are trying to get back on their feet—after a stint in rehab or falling down on their luck—occupy. She explains that it's transitional housing. They come and go as they please, but unlike the temporary housing, which is located on the bottom floor, they're guaranteed a bed every night. The room is theirs until they move on, usually to permanent housing.

As we walk through the hallways, I wonder which room was Jeremy's and I think about asking, but I can't bring myself to do it. If I did, I'd probably see him there any time I was up here. As much as I want to do something to help people like him and honor his memory, I don't want to always be reminded. I'm here for closure, not to open up wounds every time I walk in the door.

"This is the pantry," Samantha says, walking into a back room that was probably once an office or even servant's quarters. Being an older house, anything is possible. The walls are lined with shelves and non-perishable foods fill each shelf. A few are a little sparse and I wonder where their donations come from. Who pays for a place like this? I'm guessing the church it sits behind might offer some contribution, but I would think it'd take quite a bit to keep a whole house, with anywhere from twenty to forty people under its roof, going on a daily basis.

"One of the jobs our volunteers do for us is organizing and maintaining the pantry. It's important for us to always have an updated list of supplies. It helps us know what we need when donors offer their assistance. We like to be specific. Although, we'll accept anything, it's more beneficial if we get the things we actually need."

"Makes sense," I tell her with a nod, my eyes still perusing the shelves. "Where do you get the necessary donations...the funds for something like this?" I ask.

"The church," she says with a nod. "They do a lot for us, but most of their donations are reserved for maintaining the house and paying the utilities. We depend on outside donors and an annual fundraiser to supply everything else. That's why volunteers are so important. Most people don't think about all the menial tasks that go undone in a place like this without help." She pauses, stepping out of the pantry and down the hall to an industrial looking kitchen. Something about it reminds me of the kitchen at the cooking school.

"This is nice," I tell her, running my hand along the cool, stainless steel.

"Private donor," she says. "Karin, our director, is good friends with several local business owners. One of them not only made the donation for everything in here, he paid for all of the remodel...sent his own guys to do it and everything." She gives me an impressed smile, then exhales as she walks out of the kitchen, but I'm left standing there.

Deep down, I know it's Shaw who did this. I don't even have to ask.

The thought of him accompanied with thoughts of his big, generous heart makes me feel weak. For the last few days, I've wanted to reach out to him, contact him, but I don't know why or what I would say. What would be the reason? If he's not willing to be honest with me, I don't see any chance for us to have anything more than the one, amazing night we shared. Because I'm not that girl.

I don't have sex with people just for pleasure.

I don't give everything to someone who refuses to give me everything in return.

I'm not going to stick around and get my heart broken.

Been there.

Done that.

As much as it hurt to walk away, I feel proud of myself for doing so. One thing Brant taught me is that I deserve someone who treats me good and I never want to put myself on the back burner for anyone ever again. The next relationship I'm in will be one based on love and mutual respect.

"Avery," Samantha calls out, pulling me from my thoughts.

"Coming." I give the kitchen one last look before walking out, meeting Samantha in the hall where she shows me the large room. There's a television in the corner, a few toys in a box, and about twenty cots.

"Today, we'll be washing up bedding, getting it ready for some new-comers."

I nod my head. "Sounds great," I tell her, needing to feel useful and get out of my head. "Point me in the direction of the laundry room."

26

Shaw

WHEN I PULL MY JEEP INTO THE DRIVEWAY OF CHARITY
House, I try to ignore the uneasy feeling in my gut. Of course, I've been here since Jeremy died but I don't stay as long as I used to. It still feels too weird being here knowing he's gone and not coming back. My head knows Karin and I did all that we could, but my heart still feels guilty, causing me to wonder what else I could've done to help him.

Walking across the yard to get to the front door, something down the road catches my eye. Under the streetlight at the end of the block, a woman is standing there, her light blonde hair swirling around her face as she waits in line for a streetcar and my mind immediately thinks of Avery.

Could it be Avery?

Could she be this close to me?

If so, what is she doing here?

Those questions lead to others that make my heart race.

Does she miss me?

Does she think of me at all?

I watch as the woman steps into the streetcar and force my feet to not run to her as I wait for it to drive away. If I would've run over there, what would I have done? Demand she speak to me? Beg her to let me explain myself?

Yes. That's exactly what I would've done and now I'm pissed at myself for not trying harder but it probably wasn't even her.

"Is everything okay, Shaw?"

I look over and see Karin standing on the front porch, eyeing me with caution. Who can blame her? Here I am, standing in the middle of the yard, clutching a large box to my chest, while staring down the road like an idiot.

For fuck's sake, Shaw. Get it together.

"Uh, yeah. I just thought I saw someone I knew," I use my chin to point in the direction I'm looking since my hands are full.

"Oh, okay. Need any help?"

"Nah, I got it."

She holds the door open for me as I step in and head straight for the kitchen and set the box on the counter.

"What do you have for us tonight?"

"Biscuits and gravy from Sarah." I take everything out of the box so Karin can store the food however she wants. I learned early on in our friendship she likes to do things in a very certain way, so I know when to step back and let her run the show.

"This smells amazing. Please tell Sarah I said thank you."

"You know I will. Got anything else you need me to do? When I was here the other day, Samantha said you had some new fixtures that needed to be installed. Have they been done yet?"

"I don't think they have, now that you mention it. They're for the upstairs bathroom. I can show you."

"Let me go get my tool box and I'll meet you there."

Karin nods then starts walking up the stairs as I head for the door. Naturally, as I jog to my Jeep, I look up and down the street, taking a chance the woman will be there again.

And then I do the same thing as I walk back to the house.

Heavy metal music blares through my earbuds as I jog through my neighborhood, pushing me to run faster, harder. When I was younger, I only ran because my coaches made me, but after Liz died, I needed a physical way to let out my frustrations and grief. Lifting weights helped but running is really what changed me.

I remember feeling so fucking stifled, like I couldn't move or breathe without someone checking in on me. My skin itched with a need I couldn't identify, my body buzzed with extra energy I didn't know how to handle. I just wanted to leave, run away. So I did. I took off running down my street and I kept going until my lungs burned and the itch was gone. I felt...free. Freer than I had in years and I didn't care about the tears that had mixed with the sweat dripping down my face. I'd finally found my outlet.

With it being mid-morning on a Saturday, there are a few more people out than when I run on a weekday. Everything in this area is decorated for Christmas now, with special holiday activities planned for the weekend, so it's not unusual to see young families bundled up and headed to the park or zoo. I try my best to ignore the tightness in my chest as I pass up the strollers and the dads wearing those baby backpack-things. It does me no good to wish for things I can't have.

It's when I start to slow my pace that I see her again.

At least, I think it's her.

Just like before, she's waiting for a streetcar but her hair is different now. It's still platinum on the top but the waves falling down her back are a mixture of different shades of purple. Still jogging, I'm able to get close enough to see her smile at a kid standing next to her and that's when I know it's her. I'd recognize that smile anywhere.

It's unmistakable.

She's unmistakable.

And definitely not a mistake. Far from it. She's more like a miracle and I need her to know that.

Before I'm able to call out to her, a streetcar stops and she steps inside. But this time, I refuse to stand frozen like I did in front of Charity House, so I run. In fact, I haul ass, catching up to the door as it shuts. Banging on the glass, I get the driver's attention and he reluctantly opens it for me.

"Thanks," I say breathlessly, paying my fare with the app on my phone, then turning to look for Avery. I know she's here, I can sense it...feel her.

On a nearly empty row near the back, she's facing the window, not paying attention to what's going on around her. When I take the seat in front of her, she's completely caught off guard, her eyes going wide when she notices me.

"Avery."

God, just being able to see her and say her name out loud calms me more than any run ever could. My chest feels lighter just knowing she's here, but then my nerves kick in.

It's really her.

"Your hair is purple."

Seriously? I finally get to talk to her and this is the shit I blurt out?

"Um, yeah, I just had it done yesterday." She twirls one of her curls around her finger and watches it rather than looking at me. I ignore the sting I feel at the way she seems to be unaffected by me or my presence and focus on accomplishing my mission to get her to let me explain myself, hoping she'll hear me out.

"I like it. It suits you." I clear my throat, trying to collect myself.

Avery looks up and pierces me with her dark eyes. "What are you doing here, Shaw?"

"I, uh, was out for a run and saw you waiting for the streetcar, so I thought I'd get on and talk to you." I wipe the sweat off my brow, pushing my hair back and out of my face. I want her to see me, all of me, and how serious I am when I say what I need to say.

She watches my movements then allows her gaze to travel over me before narrowing her eyes. "So, you thought you could just corner me on a streetcar and make me listen to you?" she asks, crossing her arms over her chest, her defenses immediately going up.

The tightness in my chest is back when I recognize my own coping mechanisms being thrown back in my face. It hurts, but I should've expected it. She said she was going to be looking out for herself, so I don't know why it surprises me. Honestly, she should. She deserves better than I've given her, but that doesn't change the fact I want the chance to tell her how I feel and try to make up for my mistakes.

"I've tried to reach out to you so many times these past two weeks," I begin, searching for the right thing to say and wishing I'd thought this through a little better. "You won't answer my texts or calls and God knows CeCe won't tell me shit. I have no idea where you're working now. How else can I get you to listen? I wasn't expecting to see you today and I sure as hell didn't plan on chasing down a streetcar, but when I saw you, I had no choice."

I watch her chew on her bottom lip and I want so desperately to rub my thumb against it and free it from its confines, but I don't. Instead, I wait. I wait to see if she's gonna give me a chance or tell me to fuck off.

When she doesn't respond, I try another tactic. "Avery, please give me a chance to explain. There's so much I need to tell you. Give me an hour," I plead. I want more. I want to take all of her time, but I'll settle for whatever she'll give me.

"I'm working today...I'm...on my way to work," she mutters, her words drifting a little and it's then I notice the way she swallows hard, her eyes still taking me in and a small ember of hope begins to burn.

Maybe she is affected by me?

I see it now in the small nuances—things I might have missed if I didn't know her so well. But I do. I've watched her so much that I've picked up on small things, like the way her teeth latch onto her bottom lip when she's confused or deep in thought...and the way she licks her lips when she's thinking about kissing me.

Fuck, I've missed her—the way she looks at me, the sound of her voice...everything.

"Where are you working?" I ask, needing to know every detail about her after feeling so detached and like she was slipping away. Just yesterday, I had the scary thought that she might've moved home. Then what? How would I have found her then? Something inside me tells me I would've...somehow, someway.

She studies me for a second before averting her gaze out the window, obviously trying to decide if she's going to tell me or not. Then she finally says, "The Crescent Moon." Her words are soft and my heart drops and then comes back up into my chest.

The fucking Crescent Moon?

"Why haven't I seen you?"

"I work Tuesday through Saturday."

Of course she does. Of course she wouldn't want to work on days she might see me.

That tightness in my chest now feels like a sharp pain.

She's been riding past my street on this fucking streetcar every damn day for the last two weeks and I had no clue.

But I'm also relieved, because I know Wyatt will take care of her. If I can't be there to look out for her and protect her, I'm glad he is.

"Let me cook for you tomorrow night...at my house. You deserve to know the truth about me, all of it and I want you to know it. After that, you can decide what our next step will be. Whatever that is, even if you never want to see me again, I'll honor your wish."

Sighing, she tortures me for a few more seconds, conflicting emotions waging war on her face before she finally whispers, "Okay."

"Okay," I repeat, releasing a constrained breath as relief floods through me.

"I found an apartment," she says, her brows pinching together as if she wasn't planning on telling me that, but she did.

"That's great," I encourage, hoping it's not in one of the shady neighborhoods she'd been looking in a couple months ago. I want to ask where, but I wait for her to share that information.

"A friend of Wyatt's," she offers, biting down on her lip again. "It's only a few blocks from your house." When she admits that and turns back to the window, I smile.

She's been thinking about me.

When the streetcar stops, she grabs her backpack and I stand, reaching out my hand to her. I know there's a chance she'll brush me off, but I'm willing to take the risk.

I just need to touch her, if only for a brief moment.

After a second's hesitation, with her staring at my outstretched hand, I'm rewarded with the feel of her soft skin when her palm touches mine.

Helping her out of her seat, I use the leverage and pull her closer to me. "Tomorrow?" I ask, breathing in her sweet scent. I just need to hear her say one way or the other. My heart needs to know.

She stares into my eyes without wavering, and I see a storm behind those deep, brown eyes. Finally, she sighs as her shoulders relax—her hand giving mine the most minute squeeze—and I allow myself to hope.

"What time?"

27

Avery

"**Excited to be leaving me?**" **CeCe asks, kicking** one of my duffle bags I have stashed behind the counter. When we got up at o'dark-thirty this morning to come down and open up the coffee shop, I went ahead and packed up my belongings. I'm moving into my apartment today...my first very own apartment. I've never lived alone. I went from living at home to living with Brant. Outside of the rooms I rented before moving in with CeCe, I've never had a place that's just mine.

"Uh, excited for a real bed and a place of my own," I clarify. "But I'll miss you."

Sighing she walks over and wraps me in a hug. "It'll be okay. You'll come slave away for me and we'll find time to hang out...you know, late at night, during vampire hours." She laughs and I hold onto her for a little while longer.

"Thank you for taking in a stray cat," I whisper.

"Any time."

We step away when the bell rings, signaling a new customer. "What about tonight?" she asks casually, smiling at the lady who's approaching the counter.

"What about it?" I ask, also putting a smile on my face for the customer.

"What can I get for you?" CeCe asks.

"Uh, a slice of lemon pound cake and a black coffee," the lady says. CeCe grabs the coffee while I get the cake. After we've taken her money and given change, she's right back at my side. "The dinner...are you nervous?"

"You could say that," I tell her, swallowing down the nervous jitters I get every time I think about showing up at Shaw's house...and being alone with him...and what he's going to say. I have my guesses, but the fact he's willing to open up to me makes my heart do funny things. "Honestly, I don't know how to feel," I admit.

"It's going to be fine," she says in a soothing tone. "Whatever he has to say, at least you'll know the truth and you can move on...one way or another."

"Sometimes, it feels like the last supper," I tell her, ignoring the hint of dread creeping into my stomach. Actually, I haven't felt very well since I woke up this morning. Too much tossing and turning, worrying.

"Don't be so dramatic," she reprimands, swatting at me with a towel. "Promise to call me tomorrow."

"I will."

After working a few more hours, I call a cab. There's no way I'm walking all the way to the streetcar with three bags. CeCe walks me to the corner and waves goodbye as the car drives away, like I'm leaving for the army instead of moving a few miles away.

Pulling up in front of the Walker's driveway, I pay the driver and hop out.

"Let me help you with that," a male voice says coming from behind me, causing me to turn around. A tall guy with dark hair is smiling at me with deep dimples and I immediately know it's Eliza's husband. Emmie looks just like him.

"Ben," I greet with a smile, brushing my hair out of my face as I pull one of my duffle bags from the trunk.

"Yep, that's me," he says, taking the bag from my hand and grabbing the other one, shouldering them both, while I get my backpack.

"I'm Avery," I tell him, waving at the cab driver as he drives off.

"Welcome to the neighborhood." His tone is easy going and playful and just as welcoming as his wife's. "The apartment might not be much, but I think you're really going to enjoy the amenities."

"Amenities, huh?" I ask, smirking.

"There's free entertainment," he says, sweeping his arm out to where Emmie and Jack are playing basketball with a few other kids their age. "Just stick around for the half-time fight. It usually occurs when Emmie steals the ball from Jack and makes him look like a loser in front of his friends." His expression is matter-of-fact and it makes me laugh. "See, she's taller than him right now. You know, that whole puberty thing..."

I laugh again, nodding. "I get it." I remember when Brant and I were younger. The first time he kissed me, way before we were boyfriend and girlfriend, we were in sixth grade and he had to stand on his tiptoes. Obviously, he passed me up before it was all said and done. My chest aches at the memory, wondering how things changed so drastically.

"Well, this is it," he says, placing my bags on the table. "Liza is at the store right now, but if you need anything, just holler...like, literally, because we'll hear you."

Chuckling, I nod. "Okay."

"And anything you don't have right now, but need, I'm sure we have extras. If we don't, my mama does and she loves taking care of people."

"That's so nice. Thank you."

Clapping his hands together, he takes a step toward the door. "Guess that's it. Keys are on the table." As he makes his way down the stairs, I hear him call back, "No wild parties and don't burn the place down."

"Got it!" I yell back, walking over to shut the door while I take the place in. It's nothing special, but it's my own space...there's a small kitchen—fully equipped—a couch and chair, bed, and dresser—everything I need. And since I didn't have to use all of my savings to move in, I have extra money to buy a few new things, like some bedding and a few throw pillows...maybe a piece of art for the walls. I've been admiring some pieces from local artists who set up in Jackson Square.

Glancing at my phone, I realize it's still early. I'm supposed to be at Shaw's at seven o'clock. Since it's only two o'clock now, I have plenty of time to unpack and take a nap. With all of the working and volunteering, I've been exhausted lately.

When my clothes are tucked away in the drawers and my toiletries are stocked in the bathroom, I walk back in and eye the bed, but opt for the couch instead. I don't want to sleep the whole day away, just thirty minutes or so...just to rest my eyes.

Opening my eyes, I realize the apartment is cloaked in darkness and my heart leaps into my throat as I reach for my phone to check the time. For all I know, it could be in the middle of the night. I felt like I slept for hours instead of minutes.

Finally finding my phone and pushing the button to light up the screen, I see that it's only six o'clock and let out a sigh of relief. At least I still have time to shower and get dressed before I'm supposed to be at Shaw's.

At Shaw's.

It's kind of crazy that just a few days ago, I thought there might never be a time when the two of us would be in the same room together, let alone, at his house. It's also not escaping me that the thought of being there dredges up memories of hot passionate sex that seem to ignite my desire.

But I push that to the back of my brain and bury it under the memories of him yelling at me, essentially exploding over a wet towel. I know it's more than that and I'm hoping he gives me all the answers I'm searching for, but I'm not holding my breath and I'm definitely not going into this dinner with any expectations.

I'm tired of being let down by people I care about. So, my plans for the evening are to go to his house, eat dinner, and hear him out. That's it. I don't let myself go past that point.

As I'm showering, I don't go overboard on grooming. It's like I'm subliminally telling myself *no sex with Shaw*. When I get out and dress, I also opt for jeans and white tank top with a grey sweater. Nothing overtly sexy or inviting.

This is just dinner and conversation.

Nothing more, nothing less.

Shoving my feet down into my boots, I glance around the apartment, deciding to leave the light in the kitchen on so I don't have to come home in the dark. Grabbing my backpack, I stop...

Ever since I've been in New Orleans, I've been living out of someone else's space. Taking my backpack with all of my most important things has become habit. But I don't have to do that anymore. Smiling to myself, I drop it to the floor by the door and pull out my small crossbody purse. It's the only thing I used to carry when I lived in Houston, just big enough for my phone and keys and a little cash. That's all a girl really needs, right?

Since I decided to just walk to Shaw's, I bypass the streetcar stop and make my way down the block. It's dark, due to winter being in full effect, but there are still people milling about. It only takes me about ten minutes to walk to his house and when I get there, I hesitate on the sidewalk for a few extra minutes.

Should I knock on the front door?

Should I go to the backdoor since I know that's the one he uses?

I take a few indecisive steps toward the house before walking toward the large front window and peeking inside. There's a lamp lit in the front room, casting a warm glow over the interior. Holding my breath, I wait to see if I can get a peek of Shaw, but there's not a direct line of sight from the window to the kitchen, which I'm assuming is where he's at, because...dinner.

Right.

I just need to walk up there and knock.

Why am I nervous?

I'm not the one who has explaining to do. All I have to do is listen. I can do that. I'm a great listener. But maybe it's the explanation I'm dreading? Is it easier not knowing?

Probably.

Is it easier to walk away and pretend I wasn't falling for him?

Maybe.

However, I want to know...I need to know. So, as bad as this may hurt the both of us, I'm ready to hear him out, even if in the end I'm walking away again.

When the porch light turns on, I jump, my entire body tensing. The door opens slowly and Shaw's standing there, watching me.

"You gonna come in...or did you want to eat on the sidewalk?"

"Uh, yeah...I mean, I'm coming...inside."

God, please save me from myself.

With my eyes trained to the ground, I make my way up the steps and onto the porch. Shaw opens the door wider, allowing me ample space to walk through. The smell of something delicious hits my nose and I want to groan in pleasure. Other than a slice of left over lemon pound cake and coffee around noon today, I haven't had anything else to eat.

Now that I'm living alone, grocery shopping is imperative.

"Shepherd's Pie," he says, closing the door behind me. "I hope you like it."

"I do," I tell him, turning to smile at him. Beneath his typical bravado, I can tell he's nervous too, probably more so than me, and something inside me makes me want to put him at ease...which puts me at ease. "It was in the standard dinner rotation at Cole Fine Dining."

"Cole Fine Dining?" he muses.

"That's what my mama always called her kitchen. If you didn't like what the staff was serving, you were always welcome to their delicious PB&J or the equally enticing ham sandwich."

"Ahh," he says with a slight nod. My eyes roam his face, looking for anything that's different about him. The dark circles seemed to have faded and even though his beard is a little longer, it's well-groomed... and tempting...I want to run my hands over it like he just did and feel it against my skin.

Stop, Avery.

Dinner.

That's what I'm here for.

"Your mama sounds a lot like mine, except yours sounds a little nicer. Mine told us we either ate what was on the table or went to bed hungry." He laughs at the memory and dips his head to his chest, hiding his smile.

My chest aches at the small glimpse and I want to see more.

"I hate when you hide your smile," I blurt out. "It's probably my most favorite thing about you...well, one of them." I feel my cheeks heat with that admission, but I suck it up and continue. "The first time I saw you smile was when you and Sarah were laughing about something. Up until then, I thought maybe you'd forgotten how."

With his chin still angled down, he raises his eyes to meet mine, the smile fading.

"All I wanted was for you to smile at me like that...and then you did. It was one of the best moments of my life." I laugh, trying to lighten the mood that's suddenly turned heavy. "It's a great smile...lights up the whole room."

Shaw grips the back of his neck and then runs his hand over his beard again, sighing. When our eyes meet again, there's an intensity there with so many unspoken words. "Avery..." he begins, but stops. "Let's eat dinner."

I want to know what he was going to say, but I can tell he needs to be in control of the evening, so I let him.

"Sounds great. I'm starving."

The table in the dining room is set with two place settings. A dish of steaming Shepherd's Pie and a basket of bread is in the middle. There's also a bottle of wine opened, waiting to be poured. It's perfect and I look to Shaw to see him waiting, presumably for my reaction.

"So, Sarah's not the only cook in the family?" I ask, walking to the seat closest to me. Shaw beats me to it and pulls out my chair.

Hello, chivalry, nice to see you.

"Thank you," I say quietly, taking my purse off and setting it on the floor.

"Here," Shaw says, bending to take my purse, putting himself in my direct line of sight and making me swallow hard. He's so close and looks so good. "I'll hang it on the hook by the door," he says, walking quickly out of the room.

"Okay."

His steps retreat down the hall but are back in just a few seconds.

"Sorry," he mutters, taking his own seat. "It's been a really long time since I've had anyone here for dinner...or well, anything...except for you."

Taking a large spoon, he serves me a helping of Shepherd's Pie and offers me a piece of bread, which I, of course, take. It all looks so good I feel like my stomach is going to jump out and take over if I don't dig in.

"Thank you."

"You're welcome," he replies in his normal gruff tone that makes me wonder what's going on in that head of his...how much has this moment been weighing on him? If I've been nervous about hearing what he has to say, Shaw must be even more so.

"Wanna talk while we eat?" I ask, thinking the distraction might be good.

Clearing his throat, he holds up the bottle of wine in question.

"Please," I tell him, watching as he pours some into my glass and then fills his up. Before taking a bite of his food, he lifts the glass to his mouth and drinks.

A little liquid courage might not be a bad idea.

"Mmm," I groan at the first bite. "This is so good."

Shaw's gaze darkens as his brows furrow. "Glad you like it," he says tightly.

We eat in silence for a few moments and I try not to make any more inappropriate noises as I thoroughly enjoy Shaw's cooking. "Where did you learn to make this?"

"My mom," Shaw says, his tone lightening back up. "We ate pretty traditional Irish food at our table. However, as the years went on and she made friends with local women, she started blending in some Cajun cooking. It's something we've all taken to over the years, but this recipe is one we don't touch."

"It's delicious," I tell him. "Reminds me of my mama's, but I think there's more potatoes, which I'm not complaining about because they're my favorite."

"Lizzie loved it too," Shaw says absentmindedly. "I kind of forgot about that until now. She'd scoop the potatoes off the top and it'd piss me off because when I'd go back for seconds, all that would be left was the meat and vegetables."

Shaw's eyes are trained on his plate in front of him and he seems to be lost in a memory.

"Shaw?" I ask, using as much gentleness and caution as I can muster. "Who's Lizzie?"

His shoulders lift with a heavy breath and then he exhales. "My wife."

My heart drops and I set my fork down on my plate, trying to process what he just said and not overreact. His wife? As in he's married...and we. . .oh, God.

"She died five years ago." His tone is flat and monotone, like these words have been written for him and he's just the messenger.

My heart drops even further, but now for an entirely different reason. Clutching the napkin in my lap, I brace myself for what's to come.

"She was diagnosed with ovarian cancer about seven years ago and fought it...for a long time. I...I loved her...love her. We were together more than fifteen years, married ten. She was my soulmate. When she died, a part of me died with her. I felt like I couldn't breathe, let alone move through this world without her."

Finally, he looks up and meets my gaze. The unshed tears in his eyes break me—heart, body, and soul. I feel a sob trying to force its way up my throat but I swallow it down. If Shaw can get through this without shedding a tear, so can I.

"The morning after...after we were together," he says, cringing at the memory and at this point, I don't know if his regret is directed at what we did or how he reacted, so I hold my breath as he continues. "Lizzie hated when I'd leave towels on the floor, especially wet ones...it was her pet peeve. Since she's been gone, I've kind of gone overboard keeping her memory alive. The wet towel thing is one of the ways I do that. At first, I'd leave them there, hoping she'd show up to yell at me," he pauses and laughs lightly. "But then, I started being a little OCD over everything...towels, dishes in the kitchen sink...leaving my shoes by the door. When all those things were taken care of, it made me feel like she was still here." He sighs and runs a hand down his face. I almost want to tell him it's enough and he doesn't have to say any more, but he continues.

"About seven months before you came to work at the bar, Sarah performed an intervention. She came to the house one Sunday, right before Christmas, and made me pack up Liz's clothes and shoes. I couldn't donate them to Charity House, because I was afraid I'd run into someone wearing them and I couldn't handle it. So, we packed them up and shipped them to a friend of Sarah's who runs a place in Tuscaloosa. And it was just the day before you came that I finally stopped wearing my wedding band...that day would've been our fifteenth wedding anniversary. It was time. And I needed that closure, but I've still struggled with it."

Pausing for a moment, he picks up the wine glass and downs the rest.

"I think the morning after we had sex," he says, lost in thought as his words pour out. "I came home from my run with breakfast and I was so wrapped up in you, thoughts of you. I hadn't thought of Liz once, not from the time I walked you through the backdoor and I carried you to my bedroom. Not one. But when I walked in and saw that towel on the floor—"

"I'm so sorry," I say, my voice quaking, sounding foreign to my ears—thick and full of emotion. Those tears I was trying to keep from shedding are now leaking out of my eyes.

"No," Shaw says, grabbing my hand and holding it firmly in his. "It's not your fault. You have nothing to be sorry for. I'm the one who's sorry. After such an amazing night, I fucked it all up by losing my goddamn mind. You have no idea how sorry I am about that...so fucking sorry."

When he sucks back his own emotions, I realize he's crying too and that shatters my heart even more. Taking a deep breath, he continues. "I've been going back to therapy, attending some group sessions and it's really helped...help me to understand my grief and get to the point where I can accept it and move past it."

My hand turns to squeeze his, unsure of where all of this leaves us but still wanting to comfort him in any way I can. "I'm glad," I tell him with all sincerity. When it comes down to it, I care about Shaw on the most visceral level. He's a good person who has been through a tragic ordeal and has every right to his grief and the walls he's erected make sense.

"Slowly," he says with a bit more composure as he tries to collect himself and rein in his emotions, "I'm realizing I can hold onto Liz's memory and love you too."

Love...

Me...

"I'm falling for you, Avery. I didn't plan on it, and God knows, I fought it, because I thought I wasn't good enough for you. I'm damaged and I come with a shit ton of baggage, but I'd like a chance to...God, I don't know. I want to make it up to you—start fresh—or just pick up where we left off...shit, I don't really care. As long as I can be with you, protect you...love you...if you'll—"

"I don't want to be a replacement," I say, cutting him off and disclose the fear trying to take root in my gut. The pieces to Shaw's puzzle coming together so clearly now.

Lizzie was his wife.

He loved her more than anything in this world.

And she died...taking parts of him with her.

Where does that leave me?

I want everything—to be with him, have him in my life, know what it's like to wake up to him and share mundane things like meals and morning coffee. . .I want Shaw's care and protection...I want to know what it feels like to completely give myself over to the simmering heat and threatening floodgates of feelings. Shaw isn't the only one who's falling.

But one thing I don't want is to be a consolation prize.

Is that essentially what he's offering? Since he lost the love of his life...he'll what? Settle for me? No, I don't want that. As much as I want Shaw, I don't want to live my life playing second best to the ghost of someone I'll never live up to, always wondering when the other shoe... or towel, in this case, will drop.

28

Shaw

I SEE HER EXPRESSION SHIFT FROM DEEP SYMPATHY
and compassion to uncertainty and caution. Her brown eyes shadowed
with so much sadness and longing. When she swallows and opens her
mouth to speak, I stop her...needing to get everything on the table...
all of it, down to the last painful detail, something no one else knows.

"I have one more thing to tell you," I start. Since I want something
with Avery I've only ever wanted with one other person, I feel like she
deserves to know the hidden secret I've been carrying with me. It's not
dirty or menacing. It's personal and made the loss of Liz so much more
than anyone else knows.

But Avery needs to know.

Because one of these days, at some point down the road, I hope to
share more with her than I've ever shared with anyone else.

Shoving down the natural response I always have to this one
particular memory, I take a deep breath...in through my nose and out
through my mouth.

"You can tell me," Avery encourages. "Whatever it is..."

"When Lizzie was diagnosed, we were at the doctor's office for
something entirely different...something so far removed from what we
left with." I close my eyes, unable to meet Avery's eyes when I give her

this piece of me, the last one. "Lizzie was two months pregnant. It was a routine visit, at least we thought it was...the doctor asked for me to come with her, but we thought it was maybe because we were going to get to do an ultrasound. Liz had gone to the first visit by herself. I was working at the bar and we had a construction crew coming to work on the cooking school...we figured we'd have a lot of visits, so it wasn't a big deal that I missed the first one."

I take a break, biting down on my lip as I let the memory of Liz's happy face when we walked into that office and saw other women in all stages of motherhood. Her excitement radiated off her. Being a mother was all she'd been talking about and we'd tried so hard for a few years. It felt like everything was coming together...we'd bought our house, had our businesses, and now, we'd have a baby...be a family.

I'd never wanted to put any more pressure on her than she'd put on herself, but damn, I wanted that baby. I might have wanted it more than she did. All I could do was support her and be there for her... answer her crazy calls at all hours of the day, meeting in crazy places to make a baby.

The sad smile breaks across my face before I can stop it.

"We really wanted that baby," I whisper. "But when we got there, the doctor dropped the bomb that changed our lives...Liz had stage four cancer and her only chance at surviving was to terminate the pregnancy and start chemo."

A slight gasp from Avery draws my eyes up from the table, where I've been focused while I get through this part of the story, and then they find hers. Quiet tears fall as she covers her mouth with a hand.

"Liz wanted to keep the baby and take her chances, but I couldn't..." I croak, my emotions catching up with me and threatening to take over. "I needed her more...I thought we'd get another chance. I never dreamed that would be the end of everything...every dream..."

"I'm so sorry," Avery breathes. "I'm...*God*...I'm just *so* sorry."

She stands and walks over to where I'm sitting, wrapping her arms around me and I bury my head in her stomach, soaking in her comfort...experiencing a level of vulnerability I haven't allowed myself in years. Instead of scaring me shitless and making my skin crawl, I bathe in it...bathe in Avery and her acceptance and understanding.

After several long minutes of us just holding each other and absorbing the truth, Avery shifts and kneels down so she's looking up at me. Regret is evident in her eyes and my stomach drops...for the first time tonight, I'm scared.

"I..." she starts and stops, teeth trapping her bottom lip as her face crumples.

"Avery," I soothe, taking her delicate chin between my thumb and forefinger, pulling her lip free. "Baby, talk to me."

"I want you...so bad. I...I think I'm falling in love with you," she says, sucking back a sob that tries to escape her. "Actually, I *know* I love you. I'm not sure when I started, but I definitely know that my feelings for you are stronger than...anything...anyone..."

I think, and I hope I'm right, that she's trying to tell me her feelings for me are stronger than what she felt for Brant without saying the bastard's name. It makes me smile. I can't help it.

"But I can't live my life being someone's second choice...second best." She finally lets out that sob and it sounds painful as it tears its way through her chest. "I know that sounds incredibly selfish of me. I should be happy to just be loved by someone like you, as good as you... that should be enough. But I want to be someone's first choice. You helped me see that. I want someone to feel about me like you felt about Liz."

The agony in her words cut me right to the bone.

"Oh, God, Avery...listen to me." My words sound harsher than I intend, but I need her to hear this and know that I'm being completely honest and transparent. "You're nothing like Liz."

The hurt and confusion on her beautiful face makes me want to stop—kiss her, hold her, soothe the broken edges—but I continue, hoping my explanation will be enough.

"Liz, Elizabeth...she was beautiful...short dark hair and blue eyes that looked like they were pulled from the depths of the ocean. She was the serious to my playful." I laugh, realizing how crazy that sounds because I'm so far removed from the person I used to be—the one who fell in love with Elizabeth Louise Franklin. "The first time I saw her, we were on campus and she wouldn't give me the time of day. I loved her before I even knew her. She had a dry sense of humor and she liked the Beatles and the Backstreet Boys."

Avery lets out something between a cry and a laugh, wiping at a fresh tear.

"It was such a contradiction to everything else I knew about her—black coffee, books about philosophy and debates about politics." I shake my head just thinking about the day I got in her car and I Want It That Way was blaring from her speakers. "Once I got to know her, I thought she was too smart for me, but it was too late. I'd fallen and there was no coming back from it."

When I see Avery's eyebrows pull together as she bears my pain as her own, letting my memories wash over her, I reach up and smooth the space between her eyes.

"She was easy to love...I chased her for a few weeks and then she was putty in my hands."

I love the reluctant giggle I get at that statement.

"You..." I begin, hoping these words come out the way I mean them and that Avery can see my heart...and that it now beats for her. "You weren't easy to love...you were hard...I fought it. But there's something about things we fight so hard against...and for...they're worthwhile. They mean more. . .because we *worked* for them."

I brush back Avery's hair—the platinum fading into a lovely lavender. "You're worth it, Avery. You're worth every therapy session and every battle I've fought inside myself. You make me believe in love and that somehow, someway, I might be one of the lucky mother fuckers who gets to experience a once in a lifetime kind of love twice in my life."

She swallows, her eyes scanning my face searching for an ounce of falsity, but they come up empty handed.

"I thought I didn't want love. Just the idea of letting myself feel so deeply for someone." I pause, correcting myself, because it's not just someone. It's her. "Letting my heart love *you*...it feels like the scariest fucking thing I've done, because I know what it feels like to lose it all. Life isn't guaranteed and I won't be able to love you without risking losing you...but you're worth it. You've made me feel again, love again... you've made me dream and hope for things I thought died a long time ago."

Her tongue darting out to wet her lips lets me know she's thinking about kissing me, stealing my breath, and, holy fuck, I want to kiss her too, but I need to finish. I need her to be certain, no questions left to ask...because once I start, I won't be able to stop.

"You'll never be a consolation prize. It's not a competition. I had Liz for fifteen years. I've mourned her for five. I'll love her forever. But I'm *in love* with you."

Leaning my forehead against hers, I tangle my fingers into her hair and breathe her in. Avery's sweet scent has always done something to me—turned me on, made me hard—but tonight it's a soothing balm to my exposed soul.

"I missed you," she chokes out, her voice sounding as raw as I feel. "I thought I was going to have to forget you...somehow." Her lips are a whisper against my skin as she leans closer. "I was afraid that it was over, you felt unreachable. But now..."

"What now?" I ask after an elongated pause, our breathing the only thing filling the space between us.

"I'm still scared," she admits.

"Me too," I confess, feeling that pull between our souls, invisible strings tangling together. "This is going to sound crazy, but I want to take it slow. I'm not willing to fuck this up again."

"I can do that," she says, a soft kiss along my jaw punctuating her words but also making me instantly regret my statement.

I do want to take things slow.

I want to do things right.

Avery deserves to be pursued.

She deserves to be shown love.

I want to give her all that, and along the way, I want to prove to her that my feelings for her are true and real. So, if that means putting aside my carnal desires, the visions of her writhing beneath me...chanting my name...so be it. I've waited this long for her. I can wait a little while longer.

"How about I take you on a date?" I suggest.

She freezes, her body going completely still.

My heart beats wildly against my rib cage.

Waiting.

Hoping.

Praying.

When I feel her lips curve into a smile against my skin, I let out a pent-up breath. I swear it feels like I've been holding it for the last hour and my chest aches, but this time in relief. Grasping her face between my hands, I pull back so I can see her eyes, and then kiss her—soundly, claiming her as mine.

29

Avery

Shaw walked me home last night.

It was late and there was a cool breeze in the air, but my body was lit up and on fire. He wants to go slow and I know that's what he needs. After everything he shared with me last night—confessions, memories, hurts, pains, his grief—I understand him.

His puzzle isn't complete, there's still a few pieces missing here and there, but are any of our puzzles ever really complete? I don't think so. Even after we die, we're still living on in someone's heart and mind. Liz is alive and well inside of Shaw.

I saw the love he still has for her and I felt like what he was telling me was the beginning of his goodbye—closure. I thought it would be my last time to be close to Shaw, breathe the same air, feel his heartbeat. Because after a confession like that, a love like they had and a wound that deep, where does that leave me?

But the more Shaw opened himself up, he became transparent, and I could see right to the depths of his being. By some miracle—a power I cannot see, a force that isn't explained—he loves me too.

He's *in love*.

With me.

Smiling, I pull my soft quilt up to my chin and twist up in it as I roll over to face the window of my apartment. My first morning here and all I can think about is being a few blocks away in a different bed, with Shaw. But I can be patient.

My mama once told me that everything good in life is worth waiting for.

I think she was talking about my virginity, but I've always held onto that truth.

Shaw said I was hard to love, which initially felt like a slap in the face, but after he explained, I got it. It wasn't *me* that was hard to love, it was the idea of letting himself fall again that was hard. After what he's been through, having a love as strong as his and Liz's and losing it all, I understand. It feels scary to me, being so consumed with my feelings for him, I can only imagine what it's like for him.

Shaw's worth the wait.

The way he makes me feel when I'm with him—safe, cherished, worshipped—is worth the wait.

I'm only twenty-three years old, but I've experienced a lot in my life. Brant made me lose faith in myself. After I left him, I wondered how I didn't see him for what he truly was. How did I not read him better? I felt like I couldn't trust my instincts, but Shaw restored that trust. Even when he tried to put up his walls and convince me he was someone else, when he worked so hard to convince me he was an asshole, and he was, but that's not all he was. I saw through his bullshit and saw *him*.

He's more than the surly attitude and gruff exterior.

The real Shaw is good and honorable. He's hard-working and kind. He opens his door to any and everybody, even a girl down on her luck in need of a job and a soft place to land. I know I was not what Shaw was looking for, but I'm starting to believe that I'm what he needs.

When my phone rings, pulling me out of my thoughts, I throw the blanket off and scramble to reach it. "Hello?"

"Hey, baby," my mama greets. "I know it's your day off but I just wanted to call and see if you got settled into your new place."

"I did," I say, sitting up and putting my feet on the floor. Looking around, I can't help the smile.

"Good," she says with a content sigh. "I'm glad. How was it? Did you sleep good?"

"I slept great." Yawning, I stand and go to the kitchen, until I remember that I haven't been to the store, so I don't have coffee or breakfast. "But, I have to go to the store. I need coffee and maybe some throw pillows," I say with a laugh, looking around at the blank slate.

"Coffee and throw pillows," she repeats with a laugh of her own. "Sounds like a good combination."

There's a brief pause on the line before she says, "You sound good... happy."

Leaning against the counter, I bite down on my lip, thoughts of Shaw still fresh on my mind and I know I need to tell her about him, but I'd rather do it in person...when I'm home for Christmas. "I am, Mama."

"Wanna tell me about it?" she hedges and I can hear the underlying question in her tone: who is it? Who's making you so happy I can feel it all the way in Oklahoma?

"I'll tell you everything when I'm home."

"Good." The smile is so evident in her voice it makes my heart ache a little at keeping things from her and also because I miss her. "I can't wait."

After a quick shower, I toss on a pair of jeans and my favorite, worn-out Oklahoma sweatshirt, feeling a smidge homesick. Sliding into my trusty Chucks, I grab my keys and a twenty and head out the door.

It might seem crazy to go to work on your day off, but I need coffee and it's the closest place I know of. Besides, I know it's good and since I started working at The Crescent Moon, I haven't had the chance to sit down and enjoy a proper meal. Any time I eat from there, it's out of a to-go container after I leave work.

My morning walk is brisk and by the time I get to the restaurant, I feel good, not nearly as worn down as I've been feeling in the mornings and I'm ready for...

My thoughts fall right out of my brain as I walk through the door and see Shaw.

His hair is pulled back in a ponytail showing off his gorgeous face.

The beard that was longer than usual last night is trimmed short, putting his strong jaw on display.

A white t-shirt stretches across his broad chest.

My eyes lock onto a bite of pancake, a drip of syrup dripping down...and his tongue swiping out to lick it off his plump bottom lip.

When he notices me, a slow easy smile spreads across his face and I do a dance of indecision, taking a step back toward the door and then a step forward toward...him. What am I supposed to do? After avoiding him at this very spot for so long, I'm in limbo over what my position is now.

Should I walk over and assume it's okay to sit at his table?

That's when I notice Sarah sitting across from him. Whatever Shaw just said to her makes her turn to see me, a warm smile shining on her beautiful face.

"Don't you know the rules, Avery?" Wyatt asks, walking up and practically scaring the shit out of me.

"Where'd you come from?" I gasp, clutching my chest. It's a bit dramatic, but shit. I'm glad I didn't need to pee, because this would be even more awkward than it already is. My eyes cut back to the table to find Shaw watching me.

"It's your day off. What are you doing here?" Wyatt asks, leaning against the hostess stand.

"Well...I," I stutter, unable to stop the ping pong game of looking at Wyatt and then back to Shaw. "I don't have coffee...or food at my apartment." Pausing, I clear my throat and try to get a grip on myself. "So, I came here. It's closer than the grocery store and Shawn will cook for me."

His eyebrow quirks as he follows my gaze, then turns back to me with a sly grin. "You sittin' with them?"

"Um, I..." My mouth gapes like a fish for a split second until I remember Shaw's words from last night.

I'm in love with you.

Shaw O'Sullivan is in love with me.

"Yeah," I reply, my eyes now glued to Shaw's as he stands from his chair.

When Wyatt leads me to the table, Sarah places her napkin beside her half-eaten plate of pancakes and stands as well, wrapping me in a hug. "Gosh, I've missed you," she says, her arms tightening before she lets go and leans back to get a good look at me. "You doing okay?"

"Yeah, I'm good."

"Are you eating enough?" she asks, giving me a motherly inspection as she tugs at my baggy sweatshirt. "Wyatt, bring Avery the O'Sullivan special."

"As you wish," Wyatt replies with a deep bow to Sarah and a wink to me.

"Is he working you too hard?" Sarah asks, following Wyatt with her eyes as he makes his way to the kitchen. I hope he remembers the coffee. Without speaking, Shaw pulls one of the extra chairs out and then leans in, placing a firm kiss in my hair with an audible inhale, like he's breathing me in. It causes my own breath to hitch in my chest and I plaster on a smile to cover up my fluster.

After I'm sitting, I take my chances and glance over at him, he's still wearing a faint smile and it makes my stomach flip. He seems happy... content...and it makes breathing easier.

"Wyatt's a great boss," I finally tell Sarah, working overtime to keep from throwing myself at the man beside me. "I've just been tired... working here, helping CeCe," I tell her. "Oh, and I've been volunteering at Charity House."

"I knew I saw you there," Shaw says, finally speaking. "A week or so ago...I was taking some food by and I saw you...at the corner."

"You saw me?" I ask, wondering when and how I missed him.

"When did you start volunteering at Charity House?" Sarah asks, genuine interest in her tone.

Turning my attention back to her, I smile, thinking back. "Maybe two weeks ago. I've been going over there a couple times a week, just doing whatever they need me to do—laundry, organizing, making up cots..."

Sarah gives me one of her warm, approving smiles as her hand moves over the table to rest on top of mine, giving it a light squeeze. "That's great. Shaw and I were just discussing putting together a Christmas dinner for the residents. Would you like to help us?"

I feel my whole face light up with her question and nod my head without even glancing at Shaw. I'm sure he's the catalyst for this idea. I love him even more for it. "I'd love to. When were you planning on doing it?"

"On the twenty-second. It'd be in the evening around six o'clock. Do you think you'd be able to get off work?" she asks, digging back into her pancakes when Wyatt shows up with my own breakfast—two pancakes with a small plate of potatoes and two pieces of bacon.

"O'Sullivan Special?" I ask, looking down at the delicious breakfast in front of me and back up at Sarah...then to Shaw, who's still watching me with a tenderness that is alarming and awakens every cell in my body.

He nods.

Sarah smiles.

"Looks really delicious," I tell them, suddenly feeling ravenous. Thankfully, along with the food, Wyatt remembered the coffee, so before digging in, I pour four creams into my cup, along with a packet of sugar.

"Four creams and a sugar," Shaw mutters, almost to himself.

Peering at him over the edge of my cup, our eyes lock again for a brief moment before I finally take a tentative sip.

When I set the cup back down and pick up my fork, I will the butterflies in my stomach to calm and go back to mine and Sarah's conversation, trying to ignore the way my skin burns under Shaw's gaze. "I'll ask Dixie to make sure I'm off early that night."

"Good," Sarah says with another smile as she beams down at her plate, then up at me...and lastly to her brother. I see the way her eyes blaze with happiness and the way she bites down on her lip to keep from spilling everything she's thinking out onto the table in front of us.

I wonder what their conversation was like before I walked up?

Were they talking about me?

Was Shaw telling her about our talk last night?

The evident pride in her eyes when she looks at Shaw tells me they definitely discussed something...and she's happy about it. I hope that means she's happy about me and Shaw. Not that I'd have to have her approval, or anyone else's for that matter, but I'd like it.

"Sorry I interrupted your breakfast," I murmur, cutting off another bite of pancakes. "I didn't mean to barge in on your—"

"You didn't," Shaw says, cutting me off. "I should've called and invited you. I just thought you might have wanted to sleep in, since it's your day off."

Our table falls into comfortable silence for a few moments and then conversation strikes back up. Shaw talks about a new hire who's starting tomorrow. Sarah throws out ideas for winter menu options at the cooking school. Shaw and I both give her our two cents worth on that, offering our services as taste testers. Just the thought of her cooking has my mouth watering, even though I'm still currently inhaling these pancakes, potatoes, and bacon.

The O'Sullivan Special.

I pause for a moment, getting lost in my head as I vaguely listen to Shaw and Sarah talk.

He laughs—openly and freely—and it makes my heart swell.

Sarah reaches across the table and gives him a playful swat.

The two of them are the real special, making me feel so warm and at home...like I belong here, with them. It's almost more than I can take without crying. I don't know what's wrong with me, maybe it's residual emotions from last night and everything Shaw shared with me, but I have to clear my throat and take a sip of my coffee to keep from tearing up.

Shaw pays the bill, even though I put up a solid argument. I tried to be sly and hand Wyatt my twenty I had stuck in my pocket, but he refused, almost looking scared of the man sitting beside me. I have to laugh at that, because even though Shaw may look dark and ominous, I know that just under that hard exterior is a soft underlayer.

"I'll see you soon," Sarah says with a kiss to my cheek as we stand in front of The Crescent Moon. "Shaw, see you in the morning." She leans in and he kisses her cheek before sliding dark sunglasses over his gorgeous eyes, giving him a very seductive vibe.

Like, I need that.

Letting out a deep breath, partially due to my full stomach and partially due to my overactive libido, I give Shaw a small smile. "Thanks for breakfast."

He turns to me, taking my hands in his, and pulls me into him, wrapping his strong arms around me. "Thank you for showing up."

"I swear I wasn't trying to swindle you out of another free meal," I tease, leaning into his warmth. The breeze around us is cool, but here in the safety of Shaw's arms, I feel like I'm nestled in a favorite blanket.

The rumble in his chest is like music to my ears and I lean in even further, absorbing him.

"Do I still get to take you on a date?"

"Sure." My response is casual, but inside I'm thinking: *you can take me anywhere...I'd follow you anywhere.* Wherever he is, that's where I want to be.

"Well, it starts now," he rumbles, leaning in to capture my lips with his. At first, it's slow and easy, like he's testing the waters. When I let out a soft moan, his hold on me tightens and the kiss deepens. With my body flush with his, he parts my lips with a swipe of his tongue. There's a lingering sweetness from the syrup mixed with hints of coffee and...Shaw. It's the only way I know to describe the taste because it's singularly *him*.

His hand slips down to my hip and curves around to clutch my ass, grabbing it possessively and sending me into a frenzy. When he pulls away with a growl, I feel my lips turn into a pout.

"Unless," he utters, low and gravelly, "we want to be picked up for indecent exposure, I'm afraid we're going to have to postpone this until I can get you behind closed doors."

"Right," I say, letting out an exasperated laugh as I fall into his chest. It's crazy what he does to me, how he makes me feel. I've never been big on public displays of affection—groping and making out—but I can honestly say had he not put a stop to our endeavors, I would've let that kiss go all the way.

The memories of our time together are still so fresh in my mind—vivid flashes of Shaw's expression when he came inside me flood my mind, making me *want*...him, everything.

Slow.

Slow.

Slow.

I have to repeat it to myself like an incantation, bringing my body under submission.

The past few days have been exactly what Shaw promised—slow and easy. It's been filled with everything from the mundane to romantic. He took me grocery shopping for my apartment and to the store to pick up a few pillows. I found a piece of art I loved on the square and he came over and helped me hang it on the wall. We've walked the park at night and taken in the Christmas lights, went to a holiday concert at St. Louis Cathedral, and yesterday, after nearly killing ourselves ice skating, we stopped and bought a tree for his house.

He said it's the first one he's put up in five years.

The thought made me both sad and happy. It's sad to think he spent all those years alone on so many nights. I know he has his family, but they all have their own lives. After being with Lizzie for so many years, he was suddenly alone. The thought makes my chest ache and I snuggle closer to his large frame lying beside me on the couch.

When it was Shaw's turn to pick a Christmas movie to watch, I was for sure he was going to go with something uber-manly, like *Die Hard* or maybe *Christmas Vacation*, but instead, we're currently watching *It's a Wonderful Life.*

I'm kind of afraid to ask him why he loves this movie so much. The main character, George Bailey, is thinking of ending it all, which makes me wonder if Shaw ever thought the same thing.

I see so many similarities between George and Shaw—a man with a good heart who does good deeds but falls on hard times...who gets a second chance.

"If I ever have a dog, I'm gonna name him Clarence," Shaw mumbles, his voice relaxed and sleepy.

"Clarence," I repeat, chuckling. "I like it. I've always given my animals human names...like Bob and Joe. Back home, on the farm, I have a miniature donkey name Clyde." I smile, thinking about his short, stumpy legs. "Clyde was also my grandpa's brother."

This time, Shaw laughs, shaking my whole body as his chest rumbles. His arms wrap tighter around me. "Was he honored or offended that you named a jackass after him?"

"Well, he passed away a while back, so. . ."

"I'm sorry," he says, placing a soft kiss to the top of my head. With my eyes on the television, I shake my head in dismay. This man, who's experienced loss so greatly, is offering me condolences and comfort for someone I wasn't even that close to and who passed away years ago. I love that about him. I love it so much I want to kiss him and hug him...I want to crawl inside his chest and take up residence, because Shaw is good. He's the epitome of a *good* man. Sure, he has flaws, but it's through the flaws that his strengths shine.

"It was the hair," I eventually say, my eyes feeling heavy as Clarence grants George's wish to never be born.

"The hair?" Shaw asks, his words just as slow and detached as his fingers brush lightly up and down my arm.

"Uh huh...my Uncle Clyde had great hair, with this fifties flip in the front," I murmur. "When my daddy showed up with the donkey, he came trotting out of the trailer with this awesome hair...the same fifties flip." I chuckle lightly, my exhaustion kicking in and forcing my eyes closed.

An indiscernible amount of time later, I wake to a blank television screen and a hot body wrapped around mine. Glancing up at Shaw, I take in his sleeping form. His beautiful face is relaxed and his dark lashes create half circles under his eyes. The dim light from the lamp casting a warm glow across his features, making him look even more glorious.

I try to look around the living room for a clock or some way to know what time it is. Even though I've been cozily sleeping in Shaw's arms, my back is kind of tight from the position we've been laying in and I need to go to the bathroom. Shifting slowly, I try to slide out of his embrace without waking him.

"Where are you going?" he asks groggily, his voice thick with sleep and sounding incredibly sexy.

"Bathroom," I rasp, turning back to him for a brief second. "And I guess I should go...home." My words are just as unsure as I feel. Shaw said slow and I don't know if me sleeping here overnight counts as slow.

"No," he groans and pulls himself to a sitting position, rubbing his hands down his face, taking in a sharp breath before he yawns. "Stay."

I'm still standing in the middle of the living room, gauging his suggestion and whether or not he really means it or if he's maybe talking in his sleep. When he stands from the couch and grabs me by my waist, pulling me into his warm, pliable body. "Stay."

"Okay."

With his head bent down into the crook of my neck, I wrap my arms around him and hold him to me. The urgency to use the bathroom taking a back seat to my need for him. After a few moments, he pulls back and just looks at me, his hand coming up to cup my face. We stand there like that, caught in a moment, for what feels like forever. His lips eventually come down to mine, tangling in a soft, slow kiss.

"Bed," he growls when the kiss turns to more. I feel him pulling back, probably telling himself the same thing I've had on repeat for the last week—*slow, slow, slow.* Turning me to face the stairs, he follows behind me, the hard planes of his chest pressed to my back, while his denim-covered legs walk in tandem with mine.

There is only sleep, but it's accompanied by our bodies intertwined—my back to his chest, his arm protectively around me, our legs twisted together.

30

Shaw

"Avery, you have a visitor."

I watch confusion cover Avery's face as she turns to Wyatt. When he uses his thumb to point over his shoulder in my direction, the confusion morphs into the biggest and prettiest smile in the world and I swear, I feel my heart grow. It happens every time she looks at me and you'd think with all the time we've been spending together lately, I'd be used to it, but I'm not.

To be honest, I don't ever want to get used to that feeling. I want it to keep taking my breath away for the rest of my life.

She practically skips over to me and places a quick kiss on my lips. "What are you doing here?"

"I just wanted to stop by and see you before I go pick up some more supplies for the dinner tomorrow night."

"Oh? What kind of supplies? I thought everything was taken care of."

"Sarah has decided Santa needs to pass out the gifts at the dinner, so I need to buy a suit for Paulie."

"Paulie?" She laughs out loud before quickly covering her mouth. "I can't believe he agreed to be Santa."

"Well, he doesn't actually know about it yet, but I'm sure he'll be fine with it. You know he'll do anything for Sarah."

She gives her head a slight shake as she looks up at me. "You're amazing, you know that?"

I wrap my arms around her waist and pull her to me, unsure of why she's giving me such a compliment but also not caring, because I just need to feel her and hold her close. "Not sure what I did that's so *amazing*, but if it means you're gonna look at me like that, then I guess I'll try to do it more often." Kissing her forehead, I inhale her scent and smile at how the smell of the home cooked, Cajun cuisine from The Crescent Moon mixes perfectly with her natural sweetness.

"Everything. If I started listing all the ways, you'd just get a big head over it." She laughs lightly, leaning into my embrace and I soak her in, letting her words wash over me and settle into my bones.

"Whatever you say, Ms. Cole." Leaning in for one more kiss to her forehead, wishing I could take it further, but since we're standing in the middle of The Crescent Moon, I know I can't. "Can I see you later?"

"Absolutely," she says, before biting down on her bottom lip.

I press my mouth to hers in a chaste, yet searing kiss. "Get back to work, you little minx," I grumble into her hair before finally letting her go.

Avery laughs and walks off, turning to wave at me one last time before heading to one of her tables.

What started off as being a simple dinner for the residents and workers at Charity House has now become a major event. This always tends to happen when my family gets involved.

The O'Sullivans don't do anything half-assed.

My guys from Come Again will be serving the food and drinks along with me, Sarah, and Avery.

Since we'd went to the trouble of procuring a suit, Sarah insisted that someone play the part. Paulie wouldn't accept any amount of money I offered, so here I am, wearing a thick, red and white costume that's making me sweat my ass off. In December. Like we all haven't had enough of that the other ten months out of the year. Because, let's face it, New Orleans gets a couple of months of cooler weather, then it's back to being hotter than balls.

Looking myself over in the long mirror, I scowl, tugging at the bushy, white beard that's covering my own, making me want to scratch my face off. After a few un-Santa like mutters under my breath, I walk out of the bedroom I used as a dressing room and down the stairs to the waiting crowd.

The smiles and laughter I receive from everyone as I ho-ho-ho myself to the large living room takes the edge off my irritation, and by the time I'm sitting in the chair by the tree, I'm actually smiling a genuine smile under the garb. It doesn't hurt that Avery is beaming at me while trying to keep her laughter at bay. The absolute joy from my family and the people I've adopted into my family make it all worth it.

I spend half an hour listening to adults turn into children for a few brief moments, sitting on my lap for goofy pictures and telling me what they want for Christmas. I'd love to be able to grant every fucking wish, but I can't.

I can't bring families back.

I can't cure diseases.

I can't stop the wheels of time.

But for tonight, me and my family, we can bring smiles to these faces and let them know that people care about them and that the entire world hasn't turned its back on them.

We laugh, we sing, we eat. Through the entire night, Avery is right there in the thick of it. In just the short amount of time she's been volunteering at the house, she's made quite the impression on the staff and some of the long-term residents. I watch them smile at her fondly, seeing what I see—warmth, honesty, beauty. She has something about her that attracts people, making them want to be around her.

"So, who's that?" I overhear one of my new guys, Devon, ask Paulie as we're cleaning up the tables.

"Avery," Paulie answers casually. "She used to work at the bar."

I haven't been very open about the progression of mine and Avery's relationship, but Paulie knows we're in one, so I wait, holding my tongue until I see where this conversation is going. The caveman in me wants to shoot Devon down with a death stare and tell him to not even look at my girl.

Yeah, that's right.

My girl.

Avery is mine.

We might be taking it slow, but eventually, I want her to be mine in every sense of the word. Some people would want to take their time, date for a few months, see how things go. But I don't have time for that. Even though she might be a spring chicken, I'm not, and I've got a lot of living to make up for.

"She used to work at the bar?" Devon asks, obviously taking a second look at her and making my hackles go up. "I just assumed girls didn't work at the bar." He chuckles, going about his business.

"Well, that one did," Paulie answers, "and she worked circles around any guy we've ever hired." There's pride in his tone and it makes my chest swell. She was a damn good worker and I can't say I wouldn't like her back, but I think it's better for her to work at The Crescent Moon. Having her at the bar every night would just put me on edge. I'd want to deck every mother fucker who even looked at her wrong, let alone the ones who wanted to comment on her tits...or insinuate what they'd like to do to her.

Avery can definitely hold her own, but I don't want her to have to.

And that's not me being a chauvinistic pig. I just want the best for her...in everything.

"She's seriously hot."

Clearing my throat, I stand up to my full height and turn on him, but Paulie beats me to the punch, not literally, but verbally. "You might want to rethink that," he says with a little more vigor than usual. Cutting his eyes at me, I see Devon do the same and his normally tan skin blanches.

"Oh...shit," he mutters, obviously putting the pieces of the puzzle together. "Boss..."

"No worries," I tell him, cocking my head to Avery, "but she's off limits...to you and everyone else."

"Got it." He puts his head down and pours himself into the task at hand, making wiping down a table look like the most interesting thing on the face of the planet.

Paulie and I exchange a look over the top of his head. When he shakes his head and gives me a smirk, I can't help but return it.

That's right, mother fucker...and tell all your friends.

At least I'm not still in my Santa suit, because that would've been awkward.

Later, after the food is stored away and the gifts have been distributed—every resident receiving new socks and underwear and blankets—I'm driving Avery back to her apartment. As much as I'd love to take her home with me, I'm trying to show some restraint. She's slept at my house a couple nights now, after watching movies late and falling asleep. But for some reason, I know tonight would be different. My possessiveness from the interaction with Devon is still flowing through my veins.

"Spend Christmas with me," I tell her, turning into the drive of the Walker's home and cutting the lights so I don't disturb them. "Sarah and I are going to Baton Rouge to Shane and Amy's. I know they'd all love to see you again...and I'd love you to be there."

She smiles softly at me, the pale light making her blonde hair look like a beacon in the night. "I wish I could," she whispers, like she's afraid to disturb the blanket of peace surrounding us. "But I'm going home. I've been meaning to tell you, but we've just been having such a great time...it never came up. I leave tomorrow afternoon."

My heart drops at that.

Home?

It dawns on me that I've kind of forgotten that Avery isn't from here. She has a home and people who love her...and..."What about Brant?" I ask, feeling rage boil under the surface at just the mention of his name. I don't want him anywhere near Avery.

"I can handle Brant," she says with confidence. "I couldn't...the last time. I wasn't ready," she sighs, her hand finding mine and squeezing it. "But I am now. I know who I am and I know what I want...and I'm not afraid of him."

"But he's..." I drift off, think all the things I want to say—an asshole, an abuser, a fucking dead man if I ever see him again.

"Not important," she finishes. "He's a bully, but he won't get the chance to have the upper hand on me ever again." She winces at the unintentional irony in her words, but I also see the strength. She needs this. She needs to face her giant. We've all got them and if other people take them out for us, we never get to be the hero in our own story.

Mine was grief.

Hers is Brant Wilson.

"But you're coming back?" I ask, allowing myself to be vulnerable and speak out my fears. Pulling her hand up to my mouth, I place a kiss, breathing her in as I wait on her answer with my heart thumping in my chest.

"Of course," she says with a small, sad smile. "Of course, I'll be back. Honey Springs will always be home, but New Orleans is now too. My roots are there, but my future is here."

I can't help the ridiculous smile that takes over my face, hiding it for a second behind her hand until she pulls it away and climbs over the middle of the seat, into my lap.

Her lips capture mine, holding them hostage, as my hands roam her body, settling on her fantastic ass. The windows are starting to fog up as we make out like horny teenagers, until the bright light at the side of the house suddenly comes on, causing us both to look up.

When we see Ben peeking through the blinds of the kitchen window that faces the drive, Avery lets out one of the best belly laughs I've ever heard. "Guess that's my cue," she mutters, shaking her head, "cock blocked again."

Pulling her back to me, I make sure she feels how much I want her. I know it's been torture, for both of us, but I also know, we're doing something right, because my feelings for her grow every day. I want to be with her forever. "Soon" I groan, grabbing a handful of her ass and squeezing, "I promise."

"That's what I want for Christmas," Avery murmurs against my lips, sounding a bit drunk on the lust that's permeating the cab of my Jeep.

31

Avery

"LIVIN' ON TULSA TIME" ALWAYS PLAYS THROUGH MY mind every time I arrive at the Tulsa airport. I chuckle to myself as I recite the lyrics in my head. Since I'm only here for a few days, all I have is a backpack, so there's no luggage to collect.

As I make my way down the corridor, I pull my phone out and call my daddy's number.

"Almost there," he grumbles without any other greeting, except for a colorful expletive.

"I'll meet you at the curb," I tell him with a chuckle.

Damn, I've missed him. Mama and I talk all the time and occasionally, he's in the background, putting in his two cents' worth, but I haven't had a real conversation with him in a while. He's always busy—bailing hay, feeding cattle, mending fences. Running a farm is no joke.

A few minutes later, as the Oklahoma sun begins to set in the early evening sky, giving me the gorgeous blue to orange sunset I've been missing, my dad pulls up to the curb in his dirty Chevy pick-up truck. Smiling, I practically run to the cab. He jumps out, meeting me halfway, a smile of his own plastered on his ruggedly handsome face.

"Hey, Daddy," I sigh, falling into his warm embrace.

"Hey, Baby." He squeezes me. "So good to see you."

"You too."

His hug is fierce, but he eventually lets go and takes my backpack from me, looking over my shoulder. "Is this all you got?"

"Yeah," I tell him, running my hands down the legs of my jeans, wishing I'd layered up a little more. It's way colder here than it was when I left New Orleans.

Thinking of New Orleans has me thinking of who I left behind and I have to catch myself to keep the sad frown from my face. Shaw dropped me off at the airport earlier. And walked me inside. Even though I told him it wasn't necessary. He stood by while I checked in and then we had a coffee right outside of security until it was past time for me to go. When I went to leave, after we'd already kissed, he pulled me back for one more. It was soul-claiming, searing...actually, I can still feel it. We haven't said the words *I love you* much since the night of our big talk, but he doesn't have to. He shows me every single day.

"Your mama is gonna be so happy to see you," he says, opening the passenger door and helping me inside before taking a few long strides to his side of the truck. Taking it out of park, we begin to roll away from the curb. "We gotta stop and get some eggs and flour at the store on our way home. She's got lots of baking planned for the two of you tomorrow...all sorts of plans."

Turning to look at me, he smiles and shakes his head a little.

"What?" I ask, pulling the seat belt over my shoulder.

"Just good to see you," he muses. "You look good, Avery. Real good." He barks out a laugh as he turns to merge with traffic and we begin our hour and a half trek home. "Your mama will be happy about that. She had herself convinced you never eat or sleep."

"Well, I do work a lot, but I also manage to eat and sleep...some," I tell him, twisting my lips in a reluctant smile. "Probably not as much as she'd like, but I do my best."

"It's all we can do," he replies quietly. "You sure you're doin' good?"

"Yeah," I say confidently, feeling completely honest in that answer. A few months ago, it would've been a lie, but I'm better than I've been in years...maybe ever. I feel like I'm figuring out who I am and what I want and I'm happy. Really, really happy.

"You've got enough money? Payin' all your bills?"

"Yes," I tell him with a small smile. "I've got a job and it pays the bills. I've made some good friends...it's starting to feel like home." The last statement is met with silence and I'm worried I've hit a nerve with the home comment, but eventually, my dad responds.

"That's good...real good," he says, eyes on the road. "That's all I want for you."

"Thank you, Daddy." Warmth floods my chest along with a fraction of relief. I won't really feel complete relief until I have a talk with my mama, but hearing him say that makes me breathe a little easier.

The local country music station that's always tuned into my daddy's radio plays on in the background as we drive along, enjoying the comfortable silence that often finds us. We've had hundreds of trips a lot like this—just me and my daddy in this old truck. It feels nice. I'm lost in thought, taking in the rolling hills and barren trees as the last of the winter evening slips into night he asks, "So, what happened with Brant?"

Not a stitch of accusation or meddling can be found in the question, only genuine concern so, I answer him truthfully.

"We got in a fight," I begin, taking in a deep breath and letting it out, my warm air fogging up the window. "A bad one. He'd been out late and I waited up for him. When he got home, I asked him where he'd been and he got angry and hit me. I woke up early the next morning, packed my bags, and left."

He clears his throat and shifts in the old, worn leather seat, causing me to look over at him. In his profile, I see the anger rolling off of his normally calm features. "He hit you?" he bites out, his eyes squinting in disbelief.

I nod, but realize he probably can't see me because the sun has completely set behind us and his eyes are trained on the open road. "Yeah," I reply, feeling no need to lie or cover for Brant. I'm done with that.

"Why didn't you tell me?" This time, his words hold so much pain and resentment and I crumble a little inside. I should've. If I was in his place and I had a daughter and something bad happened to her, I'd want to know.

"I'm sorry," I tell him.

"You should've told me," he scolds. "I would've..."

He would've. I know. He would've moved heaven and earth to make it right, but I couldn't let him do that. I needed time and distance from what happened. Because now, on the other side, I can honestly tell him, "it's okay...I'm okay."

Glancing briefly at me, taking one hand off the wheel, he grabs for mine and pulls it to him, placing a rough kiss on my knuckles. "You're my baby...always will be. If he ever even looks at you wrong again, I'll handle it."

That's what scares me, because my daddy's way of handling things is old school. An eye for an eye and a tooth for a tooth.

"Please don't worry about it," I plead softly. "I'm okay and he's been put in his place once."

"By who?" he asks, our hands dropping to the seat, but he continues to hold mine in a tight grip.

"Shaw." His name feels like a breath of fresh air on my tongue.

"The bar owner?"

I smile and nod, closing my eyes as my free hand comes up to my lips, remembering. "Yeah, the bar owner," I finally say, my thoughts going back to that night. "Brant came to get my car. He was awful... said awful things to me and tried to make me go with him, but Shaw stopped him from taking me and got a nice right hook in." I laugh a little at the memory of Brant's nose dripping blood. It's a bit sardonic, I admit, but it gives me a little vengeance.

"I'd like to meet this Shaw," my daddy says quietly.

"I'd like that too."

I think they'd get along great, just picturing it puts a smile on my face. Slipping my phone out of my pocket, I send Shaw a text to let him know I made it safely. His response is immediate.

Shaw: I miss you already.

Me: I miss you. So much.

The rest of the trip home is spent in alternating silence and small talk. My dad catches me up on everything I've missed at the farm. We had twenty new calves, two of them died. This was a good hay season and he and my grandpa, who's pushing eighty-freaking-years-old, kept what they needed for the winter and sold the rest. My mama and nana are getting a new paddle boat out of the deal. Apparently, they want one to use in the pond.

I love that my parents and grandparents are so passionate about farm life. And I love that they're okay that I'm not.

When we get to town, we make a quick stop at the grocery store for flour and eggs.

I see seven people I know on my quick trip to the back of the store. Every person wants to stop and ask me about Brant.

"How is Brant?"

"Are y'all plannin' on gettin' married anytime soon?"

"I hear he's been very successful in Houston."

"We're so proud of him."

"Are y'all home for Christmas?"

"We missed y'all at the tree lightin' ceremony."

"So, you think you're gettin' a ring?" Judy the cashier asks and it's the straw that breaks this camel's back.

"No, Judy," I say with mock regret and a heavy sigh. "The only thing I want from Brant Wilson is for him to fall off the face of the earth." With a sweet, surgery smile, I swipe my debit card and enjoy her dismay—blinking eyes and a mouth open so wide it could catch flies.

"Are you two not together?" she asks slowly, as my answer begins to sink in.

"Let's just put it this way," I say, leaning over to grab my brown paper sack and staring her right in the eyes, so there will be no confusion on where I stand with Brant. "I wouldn't piss on his leg if he was on fire."

She hands me my receipt with a look of shock plastered on her face, probably thinking how crazy I am, because even after all these years, everyone in this pea-picking town still thinks Brant Wilson hung the damn moon.

Walking out the glass door, I make it a point to turn back and smile at Judy who's still standing there, staring at me like I've grown two heads. I just smile and wave, calling back over my shoulder. "Merry Christmas, Judy."

When we turn off the main dirt road onto the long gravel drive, I see the front door open and my mama steps out onto the porch. Before my daddy barely has the truck in park, I'm opening the door and jumping out, making my way across the crunchy grass and into my mama's waiting arms.

"Welcome home, Baby." She sighs and I hear the emotion in her voice. "Welcome home."

"Thanks, Mama," I reply, returning her tight hug. "Gosh, I missed you."

"Oh, I missed you too." She sniffles lightly, but pulls me back to get a good look at my face. "You look great," she says, her face beaming. "Look at you, you're practically glowing."

"I'm just happy to see you," I tell her, feeling my cheeks heat under her scrutiny. "You act like you haven't seen me in years."

"It feels like it," she teases, but her eyes are still taking inventory and critiquing every feature. "But you definitely look different."

I laugh, shaking my head. "I thought you might like it," I say, twirling a strand of hair around my finger. "Purple is your favorite color."

"It looks good on you," she smiles, lifting her brows and reaching out to brush a strand away from my face. "But it's more than the hair."

Standing there for a few more seconds, her analyzing me and me doing the same in return, storing her up for a rainy day. My daddy finally makes his way onto the porch with my backpack and the grocery sack in tow, breaking up our reunion. "How about we take this inside where it's warm," he suggests, leaning in to give my mama a kiss on her cheek.

I've always loved the way she closes her eyes when he kisses her.

Once inside, we all head straight to the kitchen for a late dinner. My grandparents amble in the back door a few minutes later and the gang's all here.

After hugs and kisses and a spanking from my nana for standing them up at Thanksgiving, we all sit down at the table.

Looking around at everyone, I smile, but for the first time ever, I feel like something is missing.

Someone.

I suddenly want to stop dinner and tell them everything. I need my family to know about Shaw and how much I love him. But instead, I bow my head and wait for my grandfather to say grace, remembering the last time I was at a family table and saying grace.

Thanksgiving feels like so long ago. So much has happened since then. And again, I want to tell them everything—things that just wouldn't have felt right being shared over the phone, hundreds of miles away.

"Dear Lord," my grandpa begins. "Thank you for bringing our Dandelion home safely." I smile at his use of my nickname, one I haven't heard in so long but makes me feel warm inside. "And Lord, thank you for watching over her when she's not here. Bless this food and the hands that prepared it. Amen."

"Amen," we all say in unison.

"So, tell us about New Orleans," my nana says with a waggle of her eyebrows. *New Orleans* comes out like a scandalous secret and it makes me laugh.

"Well," I begin, taking a piece of meatloaf and a scoop of mashed potatoes, feeling like I could literally eat the entire loaf. It's been a long day and I haven't had a full meal since last night. "It's great," I finally continue. "The people are so nice and the city is just full of history and culture...and life." I feel my face light up as I describe my new city.

"We should go, George," she says, nudging my grandpa who grunts and takes a scoop of peas. "I've always wanted to go to Bourbon Street."

Again with the waggling eyebrows and seductive tone coming from my nana who sports purple hair, but in a lighter, silvery shade, I laugh.

"Nana!" I exclaim, trying to imagine my her on Bourbon Street with all the half-dressed, drunk people.

"What?" she asks, practically offended that I'd be shocked about this. "You think your nana doesn't know how to let her hair down?"

"Oh, I'm sure," I say, giving her a wicked smile across the table. Actually, if I had to pinpoint where my wanderlust came from, I'd probably have to attribute it to her. She's always been fun and adventurous. The older she gets, the more she doesn't give a shit about what people think or say. I really love that about her.

"We should all go to New Orleans," my mama says, looking across the table at my daddy who nods as he takes another bite of food. He and my grandpa are men of few words, and even fewer words when there's work to be done or food to eat.

Priorities.

"I've been wanting to meet that sweet boss of yours," she sing-songs, noticeably avoiding my dad's glance in her direction. If I had to guess, he's on to her little long-distance crush.

"He tried to send you some bread pudding," I tell her. "But I didn't check any luggage and it wouldn't have made it past security."

"You tell him thank you for even thinking of doing that...so sweet," she mutters, smiling fondly down into her plate of half-eaten meatloaf and mashed potatoes.

When we've finished eating and the dishes are all washed and dried, my grandpa and nana make the short drive to their house with promises of seeing us tomorrow.

"I'm turning in too," my mama sighs. "We'll have plenty of time to catch up tomorrow. I have an entire day of baking planned for us."

"Sounds perfect," I tell her, standing in the doorway of the living room admiring the Christmas tree. "It's so pretty," I whisper.

"I missed you being here to help me with it," she says, walking up and wrapping an arm around my waist. "I sure am happy you're here."

"Me too, Mama."

I watch as she walks to her bedroom down the hall. After she's gone, I pull out my phone from my backpack, snap a pic of the Christmas tree, and type out a quick message to Shaw.

Me: The only thing missing is you.

A few seconds later, I add on **Good night.**

Glancing at the time, I'm sure he won't see it for a while. It's only ten o'clock and the bar will be open for at least two more hours. Turning toward the stairs, I feel my phone vibrate, not with an incoming text but a call. I take the steps two at a time until I'm in my bedroom and breathing heavily. "Hello?"

"Hey." His smooth, deep voice pours over me like hot caramel on a scoop of vanilla ice cream.

"Aren't you working?"

"Why are you out of breath?"

Our questions come simultaneously and I let out a quick laugh. "Ran up the stairs so I didn't disturb my parents."

"Already in bed, huh?"

"Farm life," I say with a huff, like that explains everything.

"Right," Shaw replies and I wish I could see him.

"I thought you wouldn't get my text until after the bar closed, sorry I—"

He lets out a soft laugh, interrupting me. "I've been cooped up in the office all evening. Paulie sent me here because he said I'm obviously not on peopling terms tonight."

"Shaw O'Sullivan not on peopling terms?" I gasp in mock shock. "Well, I've never."

His husky laugh sends shivers down my spine. I love the way it vibrates every cell in my body when we're together. I fall down on my bed, which looks exactly like it did since eleventh grade when I got a room makeover for my birthday—yellow quilt, paisley curtains, a big fluffy pink rug in the middle of the room. It's colorful, just the way I wanted it.

For a split second, I try to imagine Shaw here, with me and I feel an intense blush creep up my cheeks, even though no one can see me or know what I'm thinking. It just feels naughty and dirty.

God, the things I'd do to him.

"Avery?"

"Yeah?"

"I miss you," he says with a heavy sigh. "I got too used to seeing you every day and being with you. I'm trying not to be a pussy about this, but I don't like it when you're gone."

My heart squeezes.

"Maybe you can come with me next time," I tell him quietly, like I'm trying not to disturb the pictures of Audrey Hepburn and Marilyn Monroe on the wall across from me.

"I'd like that."

"Good."

After a few seconds of silence, he adds, "Pretty Christmas tree."

"It is...but I'm not sure it's prettier than ours. Although, I might be a little biased."

He sighs again and I eat it up, devouring every word, sound, emotion that's coming across the line. Just a few days. I can be without him for a few days. But I don't want to.

"Call me tomorrow?" he asks.

"You bet."

"I better go check on the guys." I hear some rustling of papers and then a few seconds later and increase in noise. He must have opened his office door. The sounds of the bar pour into our conversation and I smile. I miss that place.

"I think when I get back, I'm coming back to work for you...at least one day a week. I miss it too much."

He grunts, sounding a bit like displeasure. "Uh, we'll discuss that when you're home."

My back goes a little straight at that, but I let it go. "Okay."

"Call me tomorrow," he says again.

"Okay."

"I love you."

Those three words climb their way inside my head and wiggle down into my heart, making me feel like the Grinch as it seems to grow three sizes.

"I love you," I tell him, feeling every inch of those words in return.

The next morning, the smell of bacon and pancakes greets me and lets me know I'm home. Everything about the light filtering into my room to the sounds of the old house make me smile. I do miss this place when I'm gone, but not as much as I miss Shaw.

The thought has me grabbing my phone from the bedside table and smiling down at our text messages from last night. When my mama calls up the stairs, I set the phone down and shake my head.

"Are you gonna sleep your life away?" my mama calls, forcing me to set the phone back down on the nightstand and smile. Some things never change.

"Good morning," my mama's cheerful voice sings from the stove as I make my presence known. She's already dressed for the day and flipping a pancake onto a mound that's already prepared beside her. When she turns to look at me, she smiles brightly. "So good to have you home."

"So good to be here," I reply, stealing a pancake and leaving behind a kiss on her cheek.

"Eat some bacon, too," she instructs, forcing a plate into my hands with two thick slices.

Bacon.

I grab an extra one and instead of her swatting me away, she smiles even wider. Feeding people makes my mama happy.

"Thanks for breakfast," I tell her after I clean my plate and start for the sink to do the dishes.

"Go wash up," she instructs taking the empty plate from me. "We've got a lot to get done...and we need to talk."

The way she tacks on that last *we need to talk* has my stomach turning. Her tone and change in demeanor can only mean one thing.

My daddy ratted me out.

32

Shaw

"THINKING OF MAKING THE SANTA LOOK PERMANENT?"

I look up and watch my sister and Paulie sit down at my table. "What are you talking about?"

Paulie laughs while Sarah grabs a napkin and tries to wipe at my beard. I quickly take it from her and roll my eyes. Beard or not, eating a beignet at Café Du Monde is a messy business. You can do your very best to be as careful as possible but it will all be for nothing. As soon as you take a bite or hell, breathe out through your nose, that delicious powdered sugar is going to get all over you.

"Fuck off, both of you. It doesn't do any good to wipe my face in between bites; I was waiting to be finished before cleaning myself up."

"Hey, it's Christmas Eve. Watch your mouth," my sister scolds.

I respond by rolling my eyes again and flipping Paulie off while he hides his snicker behind a cup of café au lait.

"What are you two up to today?" I ask. Although, I assume Sarah and Paulie have been seeing each other for quite a while, it's only been recently that they've felt comfortable enough to be around me in a more than friendly manner. They're both adults and can do whatever they want but it's still kinda weird seeing them like this. Ultimately, though, if they're happy, I'm happy.

"Just doing some last-minute Christmas shopping. What about you?" Sarah's plate of fresh beignets is delivered and she takes one before passing the plate to Paulie.

"Same. I'd like to get Avery a couple more gifts, and I also need to go speak to Maverick at the Blue Bayou."

"Oh, yeah? You have a new project in mind?"

Maverick Kensington is a well-known jack of all trades here in the Quarter. He does great handyman and contract work but he's also a real estate genius. It's the latter trait I'd like to speak to him about today.

"Well, yes and no," I hedge, dipping my finger in some of the powdered sugar before licking it. "I'd like to talk to him about some real estate stuff."

Sarah and Paulie share a curious look before Paulie speaks up. "You planning a remodel or expansion?"

"No, nothing like that." I take a deep breath and admit something I haven't even mentioned to Avery. "I'm thinking about selling my house."

Sarah lets out a deep breath. "Wow, Shaw. That's a big step. Are you sure you're ready for that?"

"I know I'm ready for Avery to be in my life permanently and I'd like for us to start fresh. I don't want her feeling like she has to tiptoe around the house, afraid of doing anything that might mess with Liz's memory."

"Has she mentioned feeling that way?"

"No, but I know she wouldn't say anything even if she did feel it. I want to embrace this new lease on life that I have and buy something that's for both of us."

"Well, I think that's great, I really do." Sarah pats my knee. "I love that you're thinking of Avery and what you both need to make your relationship work. But, Shaw, you own a house in the Garden District. Do you know how hard those are to come by? Why don't you rent it out or turn it into an Airbnb or something? One of these days, the two of you might need a bigger place." Her eyes twinkle when she says this and I can't stop my smile from forming.

I want that. I want a family with Avery so fucking bad I can almost taste it. I know it's too soon to be thinking that way, but I'm no spring chicken, so whenever she's ready, I'm ready.

"I've thought of that and yeah, having a private backyard is great for a family, but right now, I think we need something closer to the Quarter. Later, if we need something bigger, we'll move again." I shrug my shoulders to emphasize my lack of worry because I'm not worried. Not one little bit. Avery is my future and I find great comfort and contentment in that. It's something I haven't felt in a very long time, so this time around, I'm going to embrace it fully.

After my chat with Sarah and Paulie, I make my way toward the Blue Bayou Hotel. As I'm walking through Jackson Square, a painting catches my eye. The swirls of color making out a picture of the Square give the canvas texture and movement and I can't stop staring at it. It's a beautiful representation of the part of New Orleans Avery and I both love the most, so it's only right that it be hung wherever we end up living together. Without another thought, I pay the artist for the painting and excitedly watch as he carefully wraps it in brown paper.

I can't wait for Avery to open it.

"Hey, Shaw!" Carys greets as I step inside the lobby of the quaint hotel. "I was actually gonna call you later and ask a favor, but you've saved me a step."

"What can I do for you?"

I wait for her to ask her favor while she chews on the inside of her cheek. "Well, now I kinda wish I was talking to you on the phone because I feel bad asking."

"What difference does it make if you ask me in person or on the phone?"

"If I ask you over the phone, I don't have to see the disappointed look you're going to give me and you don't have to see how awkward I look when I ask."

"I'm really not following you, Carys, but if I promise to not make a face of any kind, will you just ask me what you need to ask?"

"Ok, fine." She closes her eyes tightly and blurts out her question.

"We're having a party here on New Year's Eve and we need a couple of bartenders. You wouldn't have to stay long...I just need a couple of people to run a cash bar then, pass out champagne at midnight. But I know it's last minute and I should've asked you first to begin with and I know you have your own business to run, so it's totally okay for you to say no."

She opens one eye to peek up at me and I keep my word by not reacting with any kind of expression. When I feel like she's suffered and waited long enough for an answer, I reply. "Sure, I'll do it."

"You will?"

"Of course, I will. I have enough employees to spare, so it shouldn't be a problem to cover my bar and yours."

"Oh, my gosh," she gushes in relief. "Shaw, thank you so much. I owe you one!"

I wave my hand at her to blow off her words. "Don't worry about it and don't be worried about asking me for help. We help each other out, remember? Speaking of, is that boyfriend of yours around? I need to ask *him* for a favor."

"He's out back, putting up more lights in the courtyard. Go on back. I'm sure he'd love the break."

"Thanks."

I find Maverick in the courtyard just like Carys said, hanging lights as high as he can reach while being on a ladder by himself. I swear, he and Carys are cut from the same stubborn cloth.

"Let me help you with that," I call out, jogging over to him after laying my painting on a nearby chaise lounge.

He looks down at me from under the arm that's holding a string of lights. "Oh, hey, man. Thanks."

We spend the next few minutes hanging the remaining lights in silence so that, I'm assuming, he can concentrate on what he's doing. I don't mind. Sometimes it's just nice to work without talking. That's how I used to do it, before Avery came along, of course.

I can't help but smile, thinking about the ways she's touched my life in such a short amount of time. And, I know it's selfish of me to think this, but I really wish she was here with me instead of Oklahoma with her parents. I wasn't prepared to miss her this much.

Once Maverick has finished hanging the lights and has put aside the ladder and tools, he hands me a bottle of water and motions for me to sit in one of the courtyard chairs.

"To what do I owe this honor, Mr. O'Sullivan? Surely, Carys didn't call you over here to help me."

"Nah, I stopped by to talk with you about something I've been thinking about and she used the opportunity to ask me to help."

"What can I do for you?"

"Well, I'm thinking about selling my house in the Garden District and buying something in here in the Quarter. I thought you might know of something available."

He smiles knowingly at me as he sets his empty water bottle down by his feet. "As a matter of fact, I do. My business partner, Shep, and I have been working on renovating a building nearby and turning it into a duplex. Each apartment will have two stories with updated everything while keeping that classic New Orleans style. Does that sound like anything you'd be interested in?"

"It sounds fucking perfect, actually. When will a unit be available?"

"We're hoping for mid-January, early February at the latest. I could open one up and let you check it out sometime next week," he says, still eyeing me with a speculative smile, like he wants to ask more, but he doesn't. "Would that work for you?"

I try to ignore the excited buzz under my skin and smooth back my hair. "It works so well, I'm tempted to think it's too good to be true," I tell him honestly.

"Then don't think of it as being too good to be true, think of it as being *meant to be*."

Meant to be.

Yeah, I like the sound of that.

33

Avery

"**W**HY DIDN'T YOU TELL ME, **A**VERY?" MY MAMA ASKS, her eyes and voice both watery as we stand at the kitchen island, waiting on our pies to finish baking. Over flour and Crisco and pumpkin, I laid out every dirty, ugly, hurtful detail of mine and Brant's last night together, as well as the time leading up to that night.

She knows everything.

And the way she's looking at me with such extreme pain in her eyes makes me think she's feeling every slap and cut and bruise.

"I didn't know how," I confess. "I think I was still trying to protect Brant, which sounds ridiculous now...and you and Daddy. I knew you'd be hurt and disappointed and I just couldn't tell you...but I should've. I regret that now. But the way you were always trying to get me to call him and fix things...I just didn't want to hurt you."

"Oh, Avery," she sighs, shaking her head as she peers out the large window that's above the kitchen sink. "I thought..." Letting out a harsh laugh, she continues, "I thought you two were just having a lover's quarrel. Never in a million years did I think he'd ever lay a hand on you." She turns, her eyes rimmed with red and unshed tears settling in the corners threatening to spill. "My baby. And I had him here in our home over Thanksgiving, telling him I just knew the two of you would work things out, because you're meant to be."

A sharp cry escapes as she places a shaking hand over her mouth. "I should've known."

"No, Mama," I tell her, comforting her the only way I know how by wrapping her in my arms like she's done to me on so many occasions. "There's no way you could've known. The Brant you knew...that I knew...he would've never done anything like that. But he changed. He's not the same person he was...that's why I left."

Her body shutters and she drops her arms to my waist, pulling me into her warm, motherly embrace. "I'm so glad," she says a steely strength returning to her voice. "I'm proud of you for getting the hell out of there."

I don't say anything, but those words make me feel good. They help heal the lingering scabs leftover from Brant's wounds.

"And I'm so happy you're happy," she adds. "I'm not gonna lie. The age difference between you and Shaw does give me pause, but you've always been an old soul so I'm not surprised that yours found another.

"Shaw's not *old*, Mama," I tell her, swatting a dish towel in her direction as I laugh at her wiggling eyebrows. Her eyes lock on mine and we share a moment of understanding—she's happy as long as I'm happy. I know that. "He's not perfect," I admit, "but he's perfect for me. You'll see when you meet him."

"I'm coming to New Orleans soon." She sniffles one last time, wiping under her eyes as she pulls back and straightens her spine. "I want to meet him...the man who stole my baby's heart."

My eyes blink slowly...once, twice..."I'd like that."

"He's special," she adds with a nod. It's not a question, it's a statement. "Mother's intuition," she says with a soft chuckle. "Every time you say his name your face lights up brighter than Mr. Henson's ridiculous Christmas lights."

"Is he going for the Griswold Award?" I ask her, picking a piece of leftover pie crust off the wax paper and popping it in my mouth. I'm weird. I like unbaked baked goods.

"Stop that," she chides, swatting at my hand and making me smile.

"You'll get worms."

I laugh, shaking my head at her. She's told me that ever since I was a little girl, but I haven't had them yet. "You'll love Sarah too." I tell her, sighing as I walk over to the oven for a peek. "She's so great...and loves to bake and cook. The cooking school will be a highlight of your trip. Well, after meeting Wyatt."

"Now, if he was a little older," she muses, "and I wasn't married to your daddy."

"Mama!" I toss her an incredulous look over my shoulder. "He's married too, you know."

"Right, that sweet Olivia."

I swear she knows more about my boss than I do.

"He can park his boots under my bed any day," she mutters. "That's all I'm sayin'."

"Oh, my God. I'm going to pretend like I didn't hear that."

We spend the rest of the afternoon baking and enjoying each other's company. Around noon, we make my daddy and grandpa some lunch. My nana comes over and helps us whip up a batch of her gingerbread. With all of the Brant stuff behind me and my parents, and I'm sure soon, my grandparents, in the know, I breathe easy.

If it wasn't for missing Shaw, it would be a perfect Christmas Eve.

But I decide early on in the evening that it's okay to miss him. I needed this trip, a few days away, to solidify what I already knew.

He's it for me.

And this will be the last holiday we spend apart, if I have anything to do with it.

Later in the evening, my mama and nana decide to find a Christmas movie to watch, and lo and behold, what do they turn on but *It's a Wonderful Life*.

"Oh, this is my favorite," Nana says, settling on the couch.

"I really love it too," Mama says, sitting down beside her. "Come on, Avery." She pats the seat beside her and I do as she asks. "You've seen this one, right?"

"Of course," I answer absentmindedly, with my thoughts on Shaw.

"It's a classic."

"We're all here to help each other get through life," my mama says with a sigh.

"This is Shaw's favorite Christmas movie," I tell them quietly. "We just watched it a few nights ago."

"Oh," Nana says, sitting up straight to look over at me. "I have something you should give him."

"What?" Mama and I both look at her inquisitively because there's really no telling what's about to come out of her mouth.

"I was at Mildred Smith's house the other day and we were sorting through some boxes she's had stored away for some years now and inside were some old books. She gave them to me since she doesn't have the room for them and when I was putting them away on my shelf, I found an original copy of *The Greatest Gift*," she says thoughtfully. "It's what the movie is based off of."

"And you'd let me have it?" I ask hopefully. I've been thinking about what I could buy Shaw, but had come up empty handed. He's one of those people who buys what he wants when he wants it. Plus, I haven't had much time to shop.

"Absolutely," Nana says, leaning back into the couch and training her eyes back on the television. "It'd just collect dust on my shelves and you'll have to go through them when I'm dead anyway. You might as well have it now."

"Nana!"

"Mother!"

Mama and I both exclaim in unison.

"What? Everyone dies eventually."

"Good Lord," Mama huffs. "Can we please just watch the damn movie."

I try to hold back my snicker, but fail. Between Mama cussing on Christmas Eve and Nana talking about dying, I lose it.

"What's so funny?" my daddy asks as him and Grandpa make their way into the living room. "Oh, *It's a Wonderful Life*. My favorite."

We all sit and watch the movie, Nana offering her colorful

commentary and Grandpa grunting his displeasure at her talking during the movie. It's perfect.

Christmas morning is slow and easy. Mama makes breakfast, Grandpa and Nana come over bearing gifts, and Daddy stokes a nice fire. We put a vinyl of Frank Sinatra's Christmas hits on the record player and everyone casually sings along.

Mama bought me a new backpack, which is much appreciated because mine is beginning to look tattered. Nana brought me the book she mentioned last night for Shaw and she made me a new knitted scarf. Mama and Nana both love the cookbooks I picked up for them at the airport. Daddy and Grandpa are happy with their pralines. It's not much, but it's enough. All that really matters is we're all together.

"I'm putting the rest of your Christmas gift in your backpack," Mama says as we clean up the living room and get ready for a late lunch.

"The rest of what gift?" I ask, confused.

"Your daddy and I wanted to give you some money...just something to put back for a rainy day or if you need anything for your apartment." She gives me a stern look when she sees the reluctance on my face. "We want you to have it. Besides, your nana and I got a new paddle boat and your grandpa and daddy got a new tractor, so it's only right that you have a little something extra too."

"Thank you. I love you," I tell her, wrapping her up in a hug.

"I also want you to always have a way to get out of a bad situation," she whispers. "Avery, promise me that you'll always tell me...let me help. And your daddy. That's what we're here for."

"I promise," I tell her. "I will."

"I love you."

That night, I sleep easier knowing my secrets are out in the open and my family knows about me and Shaw. When I lay my head down on the familiar pillow and listen to the whistling wind outside my childhood bedroom window, I feel at peace—my past and my present... and future...all merging together.

The next morning, I get up early wanting to spend as much time as possible with my mama and daddy before they have to take me to the airport. I'm making my way around the side of the barn after helping my daddy put out feed for the cattle when I see a truck turn off the dirt road and make its way up the long drive.

As it gets closer, I begin to make out the details—big wheels, shiny chrome that has no place on these dirt roads.

Brant.

My stomach begins to drop, but then I stop it. No way. If he's stupid enough to come out here, then I'm ready for him.

"Avery," he says as he climbs out of the truck and lands on his feet with a bounce. Everything about him is the same as usual—well-manicured and in place. He looks like the same old Brant, but his shine has dulled in my eyes. I see the tarnish beneath the surface. Nothing about him holds any appeal to me anymore. But it's his smile that puts me on edge. It's assuming and presumptuous, like he came here expecting something. But I have nothing for him.

Has he forgotten what our last two interactions entailed?

"Brant," I reply, steadying my voice.

"My mama said you were in town. Why didn't you call me?"

His question catches me off guard and I'm sure the confusion is painted on my face, but I ask anyway. "Why would I call you?"

"Well...because," he starts, vacillating mildly. "I thought we might need to talk things out...figure out a way to get us back on track."

That's when the steel rod in my back finds its place and I snap my head back in a boisterous laugh. "Oh, Brant. There is no us...I'm not sure there ever was an us. There was a you and when things didn't serve your purpose...well, we know what happened after that," I say, not willing to go there. I've re-hashed that night enough for a lifetime.

"It was a mistake, Avery." When anger seeps into his words, I take an instinctual step back, never wanting to be on the wrong end of his wrath ever again. He winces when he notices my retreat and stops where he's standing. Hands in the air in surrender, he continues, "I'm sorry...I don't know what got into me, but I can promise you that it will never happen again."

"You're right," I tell him with a nod. "It won't, because we're over and I hope I never have to see you again."

"We were good together," he argues. The features I used to find attractive contort as he wrangles in his exasperation. "You know we were. Why would you throw away all those years?"

I let out a harsh laugh, part of the indignation directed at myself. "I stayed with you for too long...waiting on things to get better. I think I was afraid to look like a failure," I admit. "When you started putting your job and status ahead of me, I knew it wasn't going to work..." I pause, taking a breath and collecting my thoughts. "I loved someone who no longer existed...I loved the idea of you, but I didn't love you. How could I?"

His stare is now glazed over as he begins to tune me out—not really listening to anything I'm saying—just like he used to do when we were still together and it pisses me off even more.

"Love is based on trust, Brant," I huff, wondering why I'm even wasting my breath to explain this to him when it's obvious he's a lost cause. Heaven help the woman who eventually falls for his bullshit. "We didn't have that. It took me a little while longer than I would've liked for me to believe it...but we were over long before you hit me. That was just the nail in our coffin."

The way he flinches at my words makes me cock my head in disbelief. It's the first time he's ever looked even remotely regretful about his actions. But when he opens his mouth again, saying, "You don't mean that," I realize he's delusional, only believing what he wants—what serves him and his purposes. For some reason, he still thinks that's me.

Well, it's not.

"Yes," I say, feeling a lethal smile spread across my face as I steel myself and dig in my heels, ready for a fight, "I do."

"Avery," he pleads, going to take a step toward me when my daddy makes his presence known at my side.

"I believe it's time for you to go," he says sternly.

"With all due respect, sir, this is between me and Avery."

"Not anymore," Daddy says, coming to stand beside me. "I think it'd be wise of you to get back in that pick-up truck and get on out of here. I'd hate to have to call the cops the day after Christmas." With his eyes glaring holes through Brant's head, he sucks air through his teeth as he inhales deeply. "The way I see it, you're trespassin'."

"Mr. Cole," Brant starts, throwing on that Golden Boy charm.

I hate to break it to him, but that ship has sailed.

"I'm gonna give you to the count of three...one..." he pauses, giving Brant a chance to turn and run, but he just stands there.

"Two."

Brant's eyebrows lift to his hairline and he expels a humorless laugh, hands going up in the air as he turns around and climbs back in his truck.

"The next time he shows his ass around here, I'll shoot first and ask questions later."

34

Shaw

FUCK SLOW.

I know I'm the one who set that pace, but I only did it so Avery had time to make sure I'm what she wants and for me to make sure that what I thought I felt for her is real.

Check all the fucking boxes.

I know she wants me.

I know she loves me.

I know I'm better when I'm with her.

I know I'm fucking head over heels in love with her.

And after wearing a dull spot on this shiny floor of the arrivals gate, I know I'm done with slow.

Due to winter weather up north, flights everywhere are delayed, including Avery's. By the time she landed in Dallas to make her connection, most flights were being cancelled. Fuck that.

I need Avery with me.

Tonight.

I spent half an hour on the phone, calling every damn airline until I found a flight for her to get on and paid for it. She can get credit for the return flight her mama had bought and use it on another trip home. The only other option was me driving my ass to Dallas to get my girl. One way or another, she's going to be back in my arms tonight.

And in my bed.

Glancing down at my phone, I cringe when I realize the battery is at ten percent.

Fuck.

Today has been a shit show of epic proportions. Charlie got the flu, and according to his doctor, he'll be out for the next week, at least. Kevin sprained his ankle playing basketball at the community center on Christmas Day. He's working, but is fucking slow as molasses. So, we're working with a busted-ass crew. The one night I need all hands on deck since I'm here waiting on Avery, everyone decides to fall apart.

Fortunately, Sarah closed the cooking school this week, so she's covering the bar with Paulie. The last time I talked to them everything was being handled. I trust them, but shit if I don't hate it when I can't be there.

But I hate missing Avery more.

It's actually one way I knew I really fucking love her—when she and her happiness became more important than the bar or business. For the last few years, that bar has been my life and my lifeline. It's given me purpose and something to wake up for every day. Avery changed all that.

She's now the reason.

She's my purpose.

She's what I want to wake up every morning for...and next to.

Checking my phone has become a compulsive behavior, but I stuff it back into my pocket. I'm trying to save at least a little battery for when Avery calls me to let me know she's landed. It's not like I won't know when she finally makes it. I'm standing right here by the exit. But I just need to hear her voice and know that she's safe...sooner rather than later.

"You're waiting on someone special," a sweet elderly voice says from beside me, pulling me out of my worry and frustration and causing me to look up. A pair of smiling eyes on a wrinkled-with-time face look up at me and the wistful look has me wanting to please her, so I nod.

"Your wife?"

I offer her a small smile, the term digging deep down into my gut, searching for the right emotion and finally settling on longing. For the first time in over five years, it doesn't cause me grief.

"Girlfriend?"

Giving her a soft chuckle, I let out an exhausted sigh and run a hand down my face. "Would it sound crazy if I told you she's more than a girlfriend, but not my wife?"

"Soulmate," the lady says with a knowing nod. "I've had two in my life...well, three, if you count Frank." Her words are thoughtful as she loses focus and begins to speak softly. "John, my first husband, he died in Vietnam. I thought I'd never love again." She sighs and looks back up at me. "But then a few years later, I met Bill, and we've been married for fifty years."

The beaming smile on her face is full of pride and love.

"He's not getting around so good these days, so he's making laps around the airport until I tell him to pick me up. I'm waiting on our youngest daughter, she's flying in from Dallas."

"That's where my...my Avery," I say, deciding that's the only way I can correctly describe her, "that's where she's flying from. Well, Tulsa, originally...and then she was delayed in Dallas. Have you heard from your daughter?"

"She called me an hour or so ago to say they were finally boarded on the plane, but they were waiting to be cleared for takeoff."

Avery's phone must have died because I've tried her several times and it's gone to voicemail. I thought maybe she was in flight and had it turned off, but she probably didn't have time to charge it before getting on the plane.

We stand there for a few minutes, watching the exit for arrivals.

"So, who's Frank?" I ask, remembering she named someone else.

"Oh, Frank's my Jack Russell Terrier." She smiles sweetly. "We've been together for eleven years. He usually goes everywhere with me, but he's keeping Bill company in the car."

I want to laugh at the fact that she considers a dog to be one of her soulmates, but who am I to judge that? If Avery has taught me anything, it's that we can have more than one soulmate and we never know where love will find us and who will bring it into our lives.

"He sounds great," I tell her, giving her my profile and hoping my thick beard hides the twitch of my lips.

"Oh, he's the best," she muses. "Smart as a tack. And listens way better than my Bill. Well, Bill is nearly deaf. Lost most of his hearing in a plane crash."

"Plane crash?"

What the fuck?

"He used to be a pilot," she says proudly. "Mostly just personal aircraft. He was flying to Baton Rouge one day to visit his brother and had engine failure...landed in a swamp."

"Holy shit," I say before catching myself. "Sorry."

A rueful chuckle escapes her. "Oh, honey, I said more than that." She's quiet for a moment. "And just to think, a plane crash is how I lost John."

My heart sinks.

"That's..." I begin but get caught up in my own thoughts and fears.

What would I do?

What if Avery got sick like Liz?

Am I prepared for that?

Am I ready to experience that kind of heartache?

Isn't that what I've been protecting myself from all these years?

"It was an ironic twist of fate," she finishes for me, very matter-of-fact. "After John died, I was afraid of flying, nights, knocks on my door...Saturdays. But eventually, I realized I didn't have to be. The world kept turning. Everyone else goes on with life and I had to do the same. When it's our time to go, it's our time to go, whether we're thirty thousand feet in the air or have our feet planted firmly on the ground. Years later, when Bill crashed his plane, I had the worst flashbacks, old memories that paralyzed me. I wanted to tell him he was never allowed to fly again, but I couldn't do that. We have to live our lives...we have to keep on taking chances and doing what we love. If we don't, we're not really living."

I nod my head, but my mind is still in limbo, reeling from the whirlwind of fear and concern.

Movement catches my eye as a rush of people begin to make their way out of the arrival gate. I watch as a pretty, blonde-haired woman—probably in her mid-forties or early fifties—comes up to the lady I've been talking to and gives her a tired hug.

"Mama," she sighs. "I told you to wait in the car with Daddy. What are you doing here?"

"Shush," the older woman says. "I might be eighty, but I'm not dead...I'm still running circles around your daddy." She laughs, patting the face of her daughter, who I can now see resembles her mother so much.

"It was lovely speaking with you," the older woman says, turning to me. "I hope your Avery shows up soon."

"Thank you," I tell her. "Have a good night."

Both women give me a small wave and make their way to the baggage claim.

"Shaw," a voice from behind me has me whirling around. Avery is standing a few feet away—tired, a little rumpled from a day's worth of travel, but gorgeous all the same. "I figured you'd have given up on me by now."

"Never."

Her lips twist to the side and she bites down on her bottom lip.

"What are you doing standing all the way over there?" I ask in a husky tone I almost don't even recognize as my own. "Get over here."

Letting her backpack slip off her shoulder and into her hand, she walks toward me, standing toe to toe before dropping her bag to the floor at our feet. "I missed you," I whisper, slipping my hand under her hair and around her slim neck, running my thumb along the line of her jaw. "How in the world did three days start to feel like three months?"

"I thought it was just me," she says, laughing slightly, leaning into my touch. When she turns her lips to my hand and kisses my palm, it sends an electric jolt straight through me. I was planning on kissing her, tasting her—just a little, enough to get me home—but now I'm thinking that might not be a good idea.

I want her too bad.

Too much.

Once I start, I might not be able to stop.

Placing my lips on her forehead, I breathe her in. "Let's go home."

She wraps her arms around my torso and I fold her into me, relishing in her closeness and the rightness of her, us. This is right. We're right. She's worth the risks.

The drive home is quiet. I keep glancing over at Avery, because I can. Fuck, I missed her. The closer we get to our exit, the heavier her eyes get. When she's telling me about some gingerbread her nana sent home to me, her words slow to a slur and then she's silent.

Reaching over, I brush her hair away from her face so I can see her better—the soft lines of her face, her button nose, pouty lips...long lashes that lay so peacefully on her pale cheeks. It's then when I realize she looks more than tired and I wonder if she's been feeling okay. She looks a little thinner...her cheekbones a little more pronounced.

It's probably all the working and moving and everything she's been dealing with over the last month or so, but it still makes a pebble of worry settle in my stomach. Keeping my eyes on the road, I run my hand gently down her arm and find her hand, lacing our fingers together, needing her touch.

When I pull into the drive, I carefully lean over to wake Avery with a soft kiss to her cheek and then the side of her mouth. Her eyes flutter open and she looks around. "Your house?" she asks, trying to gain her bearings.

"Is that okay?" I guess I should've asked, but I need her, damn it.

"Yeah," she replies, more awake as she lets out a soft yawn and stretches a little, exposing the creamy skin of her stomach and making my dick stand to attention.

He's a fucking horny bastard.

Give him an inch of skin and he'll take a mile.

I clear my throat and move to open the door, but turn back to her. "I can take you home if you'd rather sleep in your bed." I'll hate every second of it, but I will do that if that's what she wants.

"No, I want your bed." I know I'm a little rusty, but I'm pretty sure there's an underlying meaning there, something along the lines of *I want you*. Or maybe that's just my dick's wishful thinking.

Regardless, her in my bed is enough, even if it just means sleep.

Yeah, keep telling yourself that.

Jumping out, I grab her backpack and then jog around to open her door. When I reach for her hand, she smiles up at me and leans into my shoulder. Something about this moment makes me think of the first time I brought her here...when I had her like a seven course meal on my kitchen counter and then took her to my bed for dessert. That was one of the best nights of my life until I went and fucked it all up.

We will not be having a repeat of that disaster.

Turning the key in the lock, I open the door and let her walk ahead of me, flipping on the light above the island. "Are you hungry?" I ask, setting her backpack down on one of the barstools and walking around to the refrigerator. "I can make you something."

"I already know what I want." Her tone and words are full of confidence and fuck if it's not the sexiest thing I've ever heard, better than any porno I've watched, that's for damn sure. My hand pauses on the refrigerator door and I breathe in the cooled air, willing my dick to calm the fuck down.

This is not a sprint.

It's a fucking marathon.

Maybe a literal *fucking* marathon.

Yeah, that's not helping.

Clearing my throat, I turn toward her and see her eyes devouring me. Maybe she's remembering what we did in this kitchen too?

Maybe she's remembering the way I spread her wide for me and made her scream my name?

"What do you want, Avery?" I ask, placing each word intentionally.

"You," she answers simply. "I've been thinking about it and I know you said you want to go slow—"

"Fuck slow," I tell her, repeating the words I told myself earlier. "I want what you want...when you want it...how you want it...I just want you."

There's a stretch of silence but Avery's expression speaks volumes—need, want...love. Closing the distance between us, I reach out for her waist and pull her to me. The baggy sweatshirt she's wearing is definitely in the way and has to go. When I take the bottom hem of it and pull it up, she stretches her arms over her head and allows me to pull it off. I just need to see her, feel her.

Avery must need it too, because as soon as her arms are free from her shirt, she goes for mine, tugging at my standard white t-shirt. Saving her the time, I yank it over the back of my head and toss it on the floor with hers.

"Better?" I ask, pulling at the loops on her jeans to get her closer.

Instead of answering with words, she sighs and it sounds like relief, like she's been in a desert and just got her first drink of water. Wrapping her arms around my neck, she pulls herself up to me and kisses my lips...softly, tenderly, until her teeth come out to play, nibbling on my bottom lip and starting a frenzy.

I grab her ass and pull her up to me and her legs wrap around my waist, our mouths battling for dominance.

"I missed you," she says breathlessly between kisses. "Not just the past few days."

"I know. I missed you too."

"It's like you took me to heaven and then dropped me back to earth...I—I've never felt the way I felt when I was with you," her voice takes on an insecurity I haven't seen from her in a while, if ever. "You made me feel things *nobody* ever has." The way she emphasizes *nobody* makes me swallow, feeling jealous and possessive. I don't like thinking about *anybody* else touching Avery...or making her feel anything.

"Nobody else matters," I growl. "I'm getting ready to erase any memories of anyone else from your mind...all that will be left is *me* and the way *I* make you feel." It's not a threat, it's a promise, and I'm getting ready to make good on it.

Her soft skin against mine is enough to make me weak, but I need more. I need her completely naked and laid out before me. I carry her out of the kitchen and up the stairs. When we get to the bedroom, I walk to the bed and drop her legs. "All of this needs to go."

Without any words of acknowledgement, Avery does as I ask and strips bare. Her eyes never leave mine as she slowly sits down on the bed and slides back, but I pull her legs until her ass is at the edge of the bed.

"What are you—" she starts to ask, but when I kneel between her legs, she knows.

Bracing herself on her elbows, she never looks away. No awkwardness or insecurity, just Avery...naked, vulnerable, and mine.

I place a gentle kiss on the inside of her thigh and am rewarded with a tremor reverberating through her body. Brushing my scruff against her smooth skin, I get another shiver followed by a moan. As I work my way up to her sweet pussy, I feel the anticipation rolling off of Avery and I smile into the tender, wet skin, flicking my tongue out to taste her.

"Oh, God."

I glance up to see her eyes close and her head lull back. Her perfect breasts are on full display, giving me a front-row seat to what I'm about to do to her...shattering her just so I can collect all her pieces.

"Look at me, Avery," I demand, slipping two fingers inside her tight, hot center. "I want to see you when you come."

Pumping my fingers in tandem with the movements of my tongue, she struggles to obey my command, but eventually manages to give me those big, brown eyes. The same ones I could die a happy man staring into. The ones that own my soul and see beneath the hard surface I try to put up. She's melted the cold exterior and pulled me back to life.

When I suck her clit into my mouth and curl my fingers to reach her sweet spot, Avery cries out, not holding back and I eat up her pleasure.

"Let me hear it, Baby...I want to hear you."

"I'm coming," she moans.

I quicken my fingers, imagining my cock in their place and feeling it stiffen, pressing against my jeans as it begs to be let free. As much as I want to be inside her, I need this. The picture she's painting for me is a masterpiece—head thrown back, gorgeous tits, one of her hands pulling at her tight nipples, the other twisted in the quilt beneath her. When her legs begin to shake and she cries out again, I feel the walls of her pussy clench.

"That's it," I coax, leaning down to devour her one last time, taking everything she's giving.

When she's sated, breaths coming in labored spurts as she tries to make her way back to earth, I take the time to get rid of my pants and boxers...and socks, because that's fucking weird. Stroking my cock a few times, I stand back and take her in, appreciating every dip and curve of her body.

"Shaw." Avery's voice sounds detached, but still needy, pleading. "I want you...I *need* you inside me."

What the fuck was I waiting for? Why have I been denying myself this woman?

She doesn't have to ask me twice. Moving her up the bed, I kneel between her open thighs and rub my cock into her wetness, using it as lubricant. Leaning forward, I place my lips on hers, kissing her soundly. Avery groans and then lifts her hips, searching for what she wants. "Inside," she demands. "I need you inside."

"You want my cock?"

Her eyes open and lock with mine, going wide and then hooded.

"Yes," she says slowly, quietly. "I want your cock...inside me." The way she repeats the words makes me think she's trying them on for size for the first time, finding confidence as she goes. A wicked smile crosses her pretty mouth and it makes me impossibly harder.

"This isn't going to be soft...or easy," I warn, feeling my need to feel her and make her feel overcome my need to be gentle. "I've been dreaming about fucking you for weeks...months. Finally having you and then going cold turkey has only made me want you more. I promise

I'll make love to you later, but right now..." I pause, steadying my voice, "I'm going to fuck you."

That wicked smile is back and she runs her hands into my hair, giving it a pull. "I don't want soft or easy...I want hard. I want you. I want whatever you want to give me." She repeats some of my words from earlier and it makes my love for her grow, if that's possible. I love that even though we're so different in so many ways, we're compatible... we complement each other...and where it matters the most, we're the same.

"Hold on tight."

She takes the warning to heart and wraps her arms around my neck as I push my way inside her. The tightness from the first time we were together is still there, the perfect way we fit...the way her body stretches to take me in and wrap around me in the most delicious way makes me want to bust a nut before I even get a chance to move. Distracting myself with a searing kiss, I begin to move, relentlessly pounding into her.

Avery's cries from earlier are nothing compared to now. She's literally screaming out her pleasure as the bedframe begins to rattle the walls, while I thrust into her.

"Oh, fuck," Avery cries. "Oh, my God...Shaw." A series of incomprehensible chants and moans fall from her lips as she presses into me, seeking friction.

Pulling myself up on my knees and out of Avery, my cock weeps at the disconnect, but is quickly satisfied when I bring her up to me and plunge back inside. My hands grip her hips and pick up speed. Avery's hands reach up to grab her tits and I take a hand off one of her hips to give her clit the attention it deserves.

Literal cries rip from Avery's chest and I almost stop because I think I'm hurting her, until she makes eye contact with me, that intangible cord between us being tugged, as we fall into a visceral experience. Sweat pours from my forehead and drips down on her body while I plunge my cock into her, over and over, finally succumbing to the coiling in the pit of my stomach.

Tingling at the base of my spine.

White light exploding behind my eyes.

Avery tightening around me.

My body erupting.

Small pulses, milking my cock.

Spent, I fall forward, bracing myself on my arms to keep my weight off Avery. She's panting too, eyes fluttering, as she whispers words of adoration and praise. The emotions that rise in my chest are unexpected and nearly knock me back on my ass. "I love you," I whisper. "I love you so fucking much."

"I know."

Her slow smile and gorgeous eyes practically put me in a trance. But when she darts her tongue out to wet her bottom lip and then traps it between her teeth, I feel my cock come back to life while it's still inside of her.

Avery's eyes widen in surprise and I can't hide my smile. It's a bit smug, I admit, but honestly, this is all her. She does this to me. She makes me feel like I could fuck her all night.

"Round two?" I ask, thinking for a split second that I should let her sleep after such a long day, but the selfish, greedy bastard in me wins out. She nods slowly and I grab her legs, twisting her onto her stomach. "Get on your knees."

We'll make love...later.

35

Avery

JUMPING OUT OF BED, I RUSH TO THE BATHROOM AND brace my arms on the toilet as I begin to dry heave, only this time, they're not just dry heaves. The contents of what I ate yesterday come back to haunt me, or should I say the lack of what I ate yesterday.

As my forehead breaks into a sheen of sweat, I kneel down onto the cold tile of Shaw's bathroom and lean my head over to rest on my arm, waiting.

It's mostly bile.

Maybe I should've eaten something last night.

Maybe I picked up some nasty germs on the plane?

My flight home was packed and there was a kid sitting behind me coughing and sneezing. I haven't felt any other symptoms, but the flu doesn't always show up in typical fashion for me. Sometimes, it's chills and body aches. Other times, it's the stomach stuff.

A knock at the door has me scrambling to flush the toilet and climb off the floor, but I don't make it before Shaw's standing in the doorway.

"Avery?" His tone is questioning and hesitant.

"I'm fine," I tell him, pulling myself back to a standing position and going straight for the faucet to wash my hands and rinse my mouth out. My toothbrush is downstairs in my backpack. I'm definitely going to need that. After mine and Shaw's...sexcapade? Love fest? Fuck fest? I'm not sure what to call it. But after that, we showered together and I dressed in one of his t-shirts and fell fast asleep.

It was singularly the most erotic, passionate...orgasmic night of my life.

Swishing the water around in my mouth, I chance a glance up at Shaw to see him squinting his dark eyes at me in the mirror. "What's wrong? Are you sick?"

There's an edge of worry that I hate. I'm not stupid. I know where Shaw's mind probably goes when people get sick. After him losing Liz, he's always going to be skeptical of a cold or anything out of the ordinary. I'm well aware of what I'm getting into when it comes to him. He's not perfect, but he's perfect for me.

After borrowing his mouthwash for one more good rinse, I spit and wipe my mouth on the towel beside the sink, making sure to fold it and put it back exactly where I found it. Turning to him, I let out a breath, willing the queasy feeling to go away.

"I'm fine," I tell him, shaking my head at the lingering feeling of unrest. "I should've told you last night that I was feeling a little sick." The regretful smile I give him doesn't do a lot for the stern look he's giving me. "I hope I didn't give you anything."

I'll feel horrible if I passed on something to him.

Walking forward, Shaw touches the back of his hand to my forehead. "You don't feel warm...if there's no fever, you shouldn't be contagious."

"Maybe a stomach virus?" I ask, leaning into his touch.

Wrapping his arms around me, he pulls me into his chest, a protective air swirling around us. "We should get you in to a doctor... get you checked out."

"I'm fine. I think I just need some rest..." I pause, breathing him in. The way my body responds to him after a night like last night and how my morning started is crazy to me. I wasn't lying when I told him I've never felt anything like what he makes me feel. No one has made me lose control like he does. No one has ever made me come...ever. I'm embarrassed to admit that part—embarrassed that I spent four years of my life having sex with Brant and never being satisfied. The only orgasms I've ever had have come at my own hand.

Kissing the dark ink on his chest, I let my lips rest there for a second before asking, "Tell me about these?"

Shaw's hands slide gently up my back and to my shoulders, gathering my hair and pulling me back so he can see my face. "Promise me you're okay."

"I promise."

"You'll go to the doctor if you don't start feeling better."

His statement leaves no room for discussion, so I nod. We stand there for a few moments, him waring with his memories and me willing him to drop it.

"This is a Celtic tree of life," he finally says, a broad hand running over his defined pectoral muscle. "The endless knots represent how nature is eternal. Everything, and everyone, is woven together without end...life is continuous and it just keeps going and going..."

He trails off and I know without him expounding that the tree is something he got for Liz and I think it's beautiful. Leaning forward, I place a soft kiss over the symbol.

"What about these?" I ask, pointing to more of the black that paints his upper torso.

"More Celtic symbols...a Trinity Knot...Triquetra," he says with a lilt to his voice. "All of the men in my family have one." He sighs and turns his head, examining the ink. "After Liz died, I did a lot of things to feel anything besides grief. Getting fresh ink was one of them. Most of these hold a meaning, but some are just random symbols."

"They're all beautiful," I tell him, letting my fingers trace the patterns. "I've always wondered what they meant, so thank you for telling me."

"Avery," Shaw says, taking my hand and placing it over his heart. "You know that you own all of me, right? Every part. Even the broken pieces. They're all yours."

The honesty and conviction in his words nearly make my knees buckle. I take a deep breath and force myself to meet his dark gaze, giving him back what he deserves in return. "Thank you," I tell him, my voice thick with emotion. "Thank you for trusting me with your heart...all the pieces. I promise to take good care of them."

Crushing me to his chest, he wraps his strong arms around me, cradling my head and stroking my hair. His lips rest on my hair and he breathes deeply. "I have something for you," he whispers. "It's downstairs. I wanted to give it to you for Christmas, but I didn't find it until after you were already gone."

"I have something for you too," I tell him. "It's in my backpack."

We stand there for a few more moments, soaking in the closeness, the sense of our beings intertwining is tangible.

"Do you feel like you could eat some breakfast?" he asks, his voice low and rumbly, a vibration that goes straight to my core.

"Pancakes?" I ask, feeling like I could definitely eat some pancakes. I'd like more of Shaw and what he was serving me last night, but pancakes are a good place to start.

Later, after Shaw feeds me and I help him clean up the kitchen, I walk over to my backpack and pull out the brown paper package... tied up with string...yep, I'm cliché like that. The book doesn't feel very substantial, but it's all I have and I hope he likes it.

"I would just like to preface this by saying you're kind of hard to buy for," I tell him, chewing at the side of my thumbnail out of nervous habit. Shaw's such a simple man with simple desires. Most things that people buy would be such a waste on him. "This isn't much, but—"

"Avery," Shaw says cutting me off with his words and his stare. "Give me my present."

Handing it to him, I feel a blush bloom on my cheeks as my heart starts to beat faster. It's nothing. It's an old book I got from my nana. But it's the first gift I've ever got him, outside of food, and I'm nervous.

Unceremoniously, he pulls the string loose and tears into the paper. When the cover of the book comes into view, he pauses for a beat, eyes scanning the worn paperback.

"It's noth—" I start, but Shaw cuts me off.

"It's perfect," he says, smiling up at me knowingly. "I've always wanted a copy. Where did you find this?"

The heat in my cheeks increases and I start to pick at a thread on my backpack that's lying beside me on the counter. "My nana...so, I didn't even spend money on it. Which now that I think about it, makes it kind of a gift from her instead of me," I ramble.

Shaw's low chuckle draws my eyes back up to him and the award winning smile he's giving turns my whole body to lava. The blush on my cheeks is probably spreading down my neck and chest.

I feel flush.

Maybe I *am* coming down with something.

"Your nana, huh?" Shaw asks, pulling his gaze from me and back to the book as he turns it over in his hand, using his thumb to flip through the pages. "Wow. I really love this, Avery. Thank you."

"Well, I know how much you love the movie and you remind me so much of George...so, I thought you might like the book."

"I love it." His eyes shine when they look back up at me. "Don't ever feel like you have to buy me something, but any time you want to give me something like this...something that means something...don't hesitate. It's perfect."

Letting out a sigh of relief, I smile back at him, biting the side of my lip. "You're welcome. Oh..." I pause, digging back into my backpack and pulling out the Country Crock container. "Here, this is also from my nana...basically, she's my supplier."

He chuckles, taking the container. "Butter?" he asks with a sly grin. "Is this some twisted foreplay? I can think of a few uses..."

"Gingerbread," I tell him, fighting back a smile. The playfulness in his tone is mixed with heat and it's making me want to pull him back upstairs and back to bed, where he can bring my body under submission and make me come again...over and over...

"Avery," Shaw's voice is low and guttural. "What are you thinking about?"

I focus my gaze back on him, swallowing at the vivid imagery playing in my mind. "You."

"What about me?" he asks, coming to stand between my legs.

"And me," I admit, my tongue darting out to lick my lips.

"You want me to fuck you again?"

The blunt question catches me off guard, but only for a split second. I'm learning that Shaw likes to talk dirty and I like it too.

"Yeah," I reply, my eyes dropping to his mouth.

"With my mouth?" He leans in and brushes said mouth over my jaw, sending tingles up my spine. "Or with my cock?"

"Uh," I swallow again, fighting to keep my breathing in check. "B—both."

"That's what I thought," he murmurs, his soft facial hair brushing against my collar bone and doing delicious things to my insides.

Hot.

Melting.

Compliant to his every whim.

"Just as soon as I give you my gift." His tongue swipes out to lick the base of my neck, then he peppers kisses to the swell of my breasts, which are only covered by his white t-shirt. My nipples strain against the soft fabric.

"Okay," I practically moan, not even remembering what I'm agreeing to.

When he pulls away, my eyes flutter open as the cool air hits my heated skin. "Wh—where are you going?" I stutter, watching him walk away in nothing but black boxer briefs.

Maybe I've died and gone to heaven?

There was a moment last night when I felt like I had departed this world for the next? Maybe heaven looks like Shaw's kitchen?

He's gone for a moment and then walks back into the room with a small black velvet bag in his hand. It's his turn to look unsure of himself, but I know beyond a shadow of a doubt that whatever is in that bag is going to be perfect. Because it's from Shaw.

He could give me the toy from a cereal box and I'd be happy.

When he hands me the bag, I look up at him expectantly, thinking he'll preface it by saying something, but he doesn't. He just watches me intently. My hands fumble a little, but I finally manage to get the drawstring loosened and open my palm to shake out the contents.

A ring...not like a *ring*-ring...but a small gold ring with hands that encompass a heart and a crown. "It's beautiful," I gush. "I love it."

Shaw picks it up from my palm and takes my right hand, slipping the ring down my finger. "It's a claddagh ring," he says, that same lilt from earlier making an appearance and making me squirm in my seat. "It represents friendship, love and loyalty and when it's worn like this," he says, his eyes coming back up to meet mine, "with the heart facing inward...it means that the person wearing the ring is in a relationship. That I've captured your heart." His fingers fiddle with the gold band, adjusting it to his liking. "And one day...when I ask you to marry me, you'll switch it to this hand," he says, picking up my left hand, "turning it where the heart faces outward, letting everyone know you're engaged."

He's so sure in his declaration and it brings tears to my eyes that go unchecked, because I don't feel the need to hide from Shaw. He's the person I want to spend the rest of my life with...good times, bad times, happy times, and sad times. I want it all with him.

"Thank you," I whisper, afraid to disrupt this moment. His head bows down and kisses my right hand where the ring sits and then the left...and then my lips, sealing his promises.

"Avery," Wyatt calls into the kitchen as I'm loading up a tray with orders. "You've got a visitor...and he's grumpy and ruining my dining room vibe."

I smile at him, shaking my head. I've come to learn that Wyatt and Shaw go way back. He knew Lizzie and has been a friend to Shaw over the years. However, he does love giving him shit and I really love that about him. "I'll take care of it," I tell him with a wink.

"Not in my restaurant," he growls under his breath. "How many times do I have to tell you people? No sex on my tables."

Shawn turns to roll his eyes at Wyatt from where he's manning the stove, and Sasha, one of the newer employees lets out a shocked laugh, probably wondering if Wyatt is being serious or not.

"Right, no sex on the tables," I tell him as I back my way out of the kitchen doors, hollering "clear" over my shoulder just in case anyone is coming in.

After I deliver the orders and make sure all of my customers are taken care of, I walk over to the table Shaw is occupying. "Hi," I say in my most professional voice. "I'm Avery and I'll be your server today. Can I start you off with something to drink?"

Shaw's eyes start at my waist and rake up my body, paying special attention to my breasts, which are covered by a tight-fitting black shirt. "I'll have the special."

Leaning over the table, I place my hands at the edge, closing the distance to Shaw's mouth, my lips hovering over his. "My boss said no sex on the tables, but he didn't say anything about the chairs...or under the table...or the bathroom..." I trail off, wanting nothing more than to devour him. How dare he walk into my restaurant looking better than anything on the menu. I have another four hours on my shift. It's not fair.

When Shaw's hand touches my thigh, I jump and cover my mouth to keep from laughing, turning to make sure no one is watching. "As long as you're on the menu," he mutters, his hand inching up to cup my ass, "that's all that really matters."

"Is this what you came in here for?" I ask, my lips back in the vicinity of his. "Did you come to harass the help?"

"Yeah, I did," he answers matter-of-factly. "I also wanted to check on you." His tone shifts and his eyes take me in again, but this time, they're more concerned than heated.

"I'm fine," I sigh, leaning in and finally pressing my mouth to his, lingering for a moment but not deepening the kiss. There's no need to start something we can't finish. "I promise."

"No more throwing up or feeling nauseous?" he asks, sitting back in his seat to get a better look at my face.

"No." Okay, I haven't thrown up again. I really think that was a fluke, but I have still been feeling nauseous, but I think it's just my body telling me I need some rest. The last month has been crazy and I haven't been eating the best, except when I was at home. My mama made sure I had three square meals every day...plus snacks. "Don't worry about me," I insist, putting on the most convincing face I can muster.

After a few moments, Shaw finally sighs his surrender. "Fine."

"Is that the only reason you came in?" I ask, pulling up a chair and taking a seat. I haven't had a break since I got here today, so I know Wyatt won't mind if I sit and talk to Shaw for a minute.

"The main reason," Shaw replies with a nod, crossing his thick arms over his chest. *I wonder if he's been working out more lately?* His muscles seem more defined, which I'm not complaining about, but I hope he's not turning to his punching bag because of me. I don't want to cause him stress or worry.

"What else?" I ask, wanting to change the topic and talk about something else.

"New Year's Eve," he says and I smile.

I love New Year's Eve.

"What about it?"

"Well, Carys, who owns Blue Bayou Hotel, asked me to come bartend for a party she's hosting. I know it doesn't sound glamorous, but I think it'll be fun. I only have to be there for a couple hours. Plus, there's the bar, which I plan on tending to earlier in the evening." He sighs again and this time he sounds regretful. "I know it doesn't sound like too much fun—"

"It sounds great," I tell him, cutting him off. "All I care about is being with you...so, sign me up. I've been wanting to get back behind the bar and see Paulie and the gang."

Shaw runs a hand down his face, smoothing the facial hair in an effort to obviously calm his thoughts. "Avery," he starts, but hesitates. "I don't really want you working the bar."

"Why not?"

"Other than the fact that it drives me crazy with worry?" he asks, like that should be enough.

"You have nothing to worry about. We both know I can handle myself." I can't help it, but my tone turns defensive. I don't like people telling me what to do.

"I don't want you to have to handle yourself. And I also don't want to have to kick a bunch of drunk guys' asses for coming onto you or putting their hands where they don't belong."

Scooting my chair closer to him, I place my hands over his, forcing him to look at me. "I'm not saying that won't happen...the guys coming onto me part," I clarify, because the last thing I want is for Shaw to fight anyone, especially over me. "But you don't have to worry about it. I'm coming home with you. They might touch, but they'll never have me. And they'll walk away wishing they hadn't."

His eyes go from dark and brooding to blazing. "You can't talk to me like that in public," he warns, the corner of his lips turning up into a devious smile. "Walking out of here with a hard-on is going to be a little embarrassing." His voice is low as he leans forward and slyly guides my hand to his crotch. From anyone else's perspective, we're just holding hands, but I feel the steely length under his jeans and fight the urge to moan.

"There's nothing little about that," I reply without thinking.

"Oh really?" he asks, playfulness seeping into his words. "You think my cock is..."

"Big," I finish for him. "And beautiful."

"Fuck," he groans. Standing abruptly, he shoves his hands into jeans and lets his chin fall to his chest. Breathing in deeply, he expels it and levels me with his stare. "I gotta go."

"Okay," I say, standing and placing a soft kiss on his jaw. "Want me to come..." I linger on the word, knowing what it's doing to him, "over to your house tonight?" My question earns me a predatory smile.

"You better."

It's a threat and a promise all rolled into one and it's going to be all I think about for the next four hours.

"Cole," Wyatt calls out my last name like he does everyone else from time to time, like he's a coach on a football team. "Back to work."

"Duty calls," I tell Shaw, leaning in for a quick peck before sashaying away.

Yes, I sashayed.

I sashayed all the way across the dining room.

36

Shaw

AVERY STAYED THE NIGHT AT MY HOUSE LAST NIGHT,
but like the last few mornings, she's already gone, leaving my bed feeling
cold. I could kill Wyatt for opening so fucking early and making my
girl have to wake up before me.

I'm glad to have her here at night, but I like her in the morning
even more.

Plus, I have to put my eyes on her. Since the other morning when
I woke up to her getting sick in the bathroom, I've been worried, my
mind running wild with worst case scenarios—flu, infection, food
poisoning, stress...cancer.

I can't help it. And that wasn't even one of Liz's symptoms. She
didn't start vomiting until she was taking chemo. It wasn't pretty. It
drained the life from her. Thankfully, the doctors were able to give her
a prescription that helped her and she eventually started keeping food
down again, but they couldn't fix her, couldn't cure her.

My phone ringing pulls me out of my depressing thoughts.

"Hello?" I answer.

"Hey, boss," Paulie says. "Sorry to bother you this early, but I was
wondering if you needed me to meet the delivery guys this morning
or if you're planning on it. We're probably gonna need all the beer we

can get."

"No." I sit up and run a hand down my face. "I'll be there. Did you remember to order the champagne for the Blue Bayou party?"

"Yeah, twelve cases, four for them and eight for us."

"Think we're gonna be okay tonight? Is Charlie feeling better?" I ask, walking to the closet to pull out some jeans.

"He said he's good. Doctor cleared him for work."

"And Kevin?"

"Also good. Still limping a little," Paulie says with a chuckle. "Fucking dumbass."

I huff a laugh and prop the phone between my ear and shoulder as I throw on my jeans, walking to the bathroom to brush my teeth, pausing when I see the piece of paper balanced on the faucet.

Good morning.
I love you.
—A

"Boss?" Paulie asks.

"Yeah, sorry...what were you saying?" I ask absentmindedly.

"Thought maybe I lost you."

"Nah, I'm here," I tell him. Lost my fucking heart to a girl with purple hair and the prettiest brown eyes I've ever seen. But I'm definitely here. All of me. All in.

"I guess I'll see you this afternoon," he says, also sounding distracted.

"Yeah, we'll be there until eight...y'all will have to take it from there, but we'll be back to help clean up."

"Don't worry about it," Paulie says. "We'll get it. The new guys need to pull their weight. I'll compensate them nicely for working on a holiday. It'll be all good."

"Sounds good, man."

"See ya later."

The phone goes dead and I drop it to the counter, running my thumb along the small piece of paper, flipping it over and then back, her simple words doing crazy things to my chest—tightening, burning, expanding.

She won't be at the bar until she gets off her shift from the restaurant, and I hate that she's going to be working practically an entire day, but I hate the idea of her being alone without me even more. So, it'll be fine. She'll be fine.

She'll be with me and I'll make sure nothing happens to her.

If she seems off still, I'll lock her in my office and force her to take a nap or something.

Before I leave the bedroom, I tuck Avery's note into my bedside table. I'm keeping that shit. Pretty sure no one's ever written me a note before, and even though it's such a simple thing to do, it means a whole fucking lot.

When I finally make it to the bar, I go through my usual rituals of wiping down the already clean counters and put on a pot of coffee. Taking the clipboard we keep next to the register, I start going over the inventory, making sure everything is stocked while I wait for the delivery.

"Good morning," Sarah calls from the back door.

"Hey," I say, glancing up at her and then quickly back to the shelves, turning the labels to face out like I like them. A bit OCD? Sure. But it's my fucking bar and I can do what I want.

"Are you dusting the bottles again?" she teases, walking over to the bar and placing a box of my favorite donuts on top.

"Shut up," I tell her, sounding thirteen instead of thirty-eight... thirty-nine in another month, just a month before Avery turns twenty-four. It's so strange that the first day she walked into my bar, her fifteen year and one month age gap felt like the Grand Canyon. But now, all these months later, it feels like a small, rambling creek. It's there. But it's more of a characteristic of our relationship than a deciding factor.

"How's Avery?"

That's Sarah's new first question. It's actually starting to feel like she maybe cares more about her than me, and I'm totally okay with that.

"Good…she still seems tired, but swears she's fine," I sigh.

"You know you can't overreact every time she sneezes, right?" The teasing tone in Sarah's voice is gone and in its place is my older, wiser sister who only wants the best for me. "She's not Liz."

"I know," I tell her with a hardness I don't intend but can't help.

"I'm sure it's just the traveling and working overtime to make up for her time off. Give her a break and let her be human."

"Uh huh," I answer aloofly, letting her know this conversation is over.

The back door opening ends the conversation. "Hey, Shaw," Mark, our delivery guy, calls out. "I've got your booze."

Setting the clipboard down, I walk to the end of the bar and around to Sarah, placing a kiss on her head and grabbing a donut. She sighs, giving me a small smile. "I just want this to work," she confesses.

"I know."

The rest of the afternoon flies by. Customers start flooding into the bar way before usual, well usual for an average day. New Year's Eve is a different ball game. People make drinking a sport, but I'm not complaining. Days like this are what give us the boost we need to make it through winter.

Avery shows up around six-thirty and immediately grabs an apron and makes herself comfortable behind the bar, shooting me a smile and a wink. I walk over to her before she can get distracted with customers and place a searing kiss on her lips, loving the way her body molds to mine. "You don't have to work," I tell her, my lips lingering near her ear, causing her to shiver. "Maybe you should take a nap in my office…I could join you."

It's a cheap shot, but I'm not above bribing her.

"You're an evil, evil man," she says with a teasing smile. "But have you seen this place?" Her eyes light up as she ties her apron strings tight around her slim waist. I can tell she's excited to be back and the truth is we could use her help. She's an awesome bartender.

"Hey, kid," Paulie greets, leaning over to give her a side hug. "You showed up just in time."

"Put me to work," she says, beaming at him. "I stopped by CeCe's and got a double shot of espresso. I'm ready to go."

I laugh, shaking my head and loving the view as she turns to walk to the opposite end of the bar, jumping head first into the surge of customers. Normally, I'd hang in the background, watching the crowd and the bar, only inserting myself where I'm needed, but not tonight. Tonight, I'm tossing bottles right next to Paulie, Charlie, and Avery, while Kevin, Devon, and Sarah keep the place in order and fresh glasses stocked up. It definitely feels like old times and the whole vibe has me wearing a smile.

Lately, I've found myself smiling more. I used to smile all the time. The old Shaw was full of fun and games. My brothers and I always joked around with each other. I've missed that version of myself, but the last five years felt like he had slipped too far away.

Until her.

Avery.

She's tired. I can see it in her eyes, but her own smile is something I wouldn't trade for a million bucks. And even though I want to tell her to stop and rest...I can't deny her this.

Besides, it's fucking New Year's Eve.

When I was twenty-three, I was probably wasted by this time of night.

The fact that working a bar with her friends is what makes Avery happy is one of the things I love about her. I'd love her even if she was a little wild, but I'm not sure we'd mesh as well as we do. She's the calm in my storm, sunshine on a cloudy day...the missing piece of my puzzle... my complicated, jagged, messy puzzle. Somehow, she makes me make sense.

A couple hours later, Avery and I are jumping in the Jeep to head over to Blue Bayou. "You sure you're up for this?" I ask, trying to gauge how she's feeling. "Don't feel like you have to work. I can handle the drinks."

"No," she says with smile that's genuine but a little forced. Her hand comes up to hide a yawn and she laughs. "I swear, I'm good...I think my coffee is wearing off, but CeCe is supposed to be here and I want to see her." We stare at each other in the dim light of the cab of the Jeep for a few moments before I lean across and cup her cheek in my hand. Leaning my forehead against hers, I rub my nose along her soft skin before kissing her.

"Besides," she says, her words coming out a little dazed from the kiss, "I really love working beside you." Her tongue swipes at her bottom lip and she drops her gaze to my mouth. "You're even sexier when you're in bartender mode. It's ridiculous really...should be against the law," she mumbles.

A growl rumbles in my chest as I pull her to me and devour her mouth, just for a moment...just enough to let her know what I plan on doing to her later, as we ring in the new year properly.

37

Avery

AFTER SHAW INTRODUCES ME TO CARYS, THE OWNER of the hotel who is shockingly young, and her very attractive boyfriend, Maverick, we settle in behind the bar that's set up. Shaw's in the zone as he organizes the liquor bottles and takes mental inventory, like he's at Come Again, and it makes me smile. I love how anal he is about his business.

I wasn't lying when I said it's sexy. If I'm being honest, it's hot as fuck. And pretty much makes me want to jump him, especially when he does this fancy bottle flips that I've never quite mastered.

"Teach me how to do that," I tell him, catching him off guard.

"What?" he asks, eyes hooded when he looks down at me and I wonder if he's still thinking about our mini make out session in his Jeep before we came here.

That was also hot and made me want to fuck.

"The bottle flip...teach me some flair," I tell him, waggling my eyes.

"Oh, Avery," he says, leaning in until his lips are ghosting my ear, "I've got so much flair to teach you...it'll take years."

I swallow, eyes drifting closed. "Like, forever?" I ask on a whisper.

"That's what I'm counting on."

"What's a girl gotta do to get some service around here?" CeCe's voice breaks the trance between us and Shaw stands abruptly, clearing his throat.

"CeCe," he says with a curt nod and his signature stare.

"Shaw," she says with a knowing smile. "Avery."

When she says my name there's more seductive undertone that makes me blush. Yeah, she busted me getting all worked up. So what? It's not like she hasn't encouraged this every day since I met her.

I believe it was CeCe who instructed me to *tap that*.

"What can I get for you?" I ask, loving being on this side of things and serving CeCe for once.

"A whiskey sour," she says, giving me twisted smile. "With two cherries."

"Whiskey sour, two cherries. Coming right up." Pulling a glass from the stack, I go about making her drink while Shaw tends to a few other people who've walked up to the makeshift bar. "So, what's your plan for the evening?"

CeCe snort laughs. "You're looking at it," she says, arms wide. That's when I notice the stunning black dress she's wearing, making my black shirt and black jeans with matching apron feel like a homeless person's attire.

"Shit, CeCe. You look smokin' hot."

"This old thing?" she asks with a sultry smile and flip of her hand. "Well, I never get to go out, so I figured why the hell not, ya know?"

"Hey," I tell her, handing her the drink...and a bonus cherry, "flaunt it if you got it."

"You're a workaholic," she says, frowning as she accepts the glass and then takes a sip of the amber liquid, popping one of the cherries in her mouth. "But seriously, any time you want to come and work my counter, I'll let you. I miss you."

"I promise I'll start coming back over soon. My schedule should even out after the holidays. Maybe I can even help you out this coming Sunday or Monday?"

"Sure," she says, her response coming slow as her eyes leave me and drift to something...or should I say *someone*. A taller guy with perfectly coiffed blond hair just walked into the courtyard, garnering the attention of most people, including my friend who can't seem to peel her eyes off him.

"Who's that?" I ask, glancing at the guy who has a smile for every person he passes. I watch for a second as he works the space like a celebrity, charming the panties off most of the women and getting fist bumps or man hugs from the men.

"CeCe?" Looking back at her, I notice she's kind of frozen in time, but her eyes are now glued to the ground and her sequined black shoes. When she finally cuts her eyes back up at me, she acts like she wants to disappear.

"Hey," I whisper, stepping around the bar and into her space. "You okay?"

Her normal olive complexion is pale and her eyes are wide, like she's seen a ghost. "Fine," she hisses, looking nervously over her shoulder and then back to her glass that's still mostly full.

The guy, with his expensive suit and crisp white shirt, makes his way closer and I feel CeCe tense at my side.

"How's it going, CeCe?"

His voice is deep and smooth, perfect around the edges. There's definitely an Ivy League education behind all that CEO persona and something familiar in the way he says CeCe's name. He knows her...like *knows* her. Don't ask me how I know, I just do.

Call it friend's intuition.

Side-eying her as I slowly make my way back around the bar, she stiffens and gives me a wide stare, before finally turning her tentative gaze to the man at her side. "Shep," she says with a clipped nod, finally taking another sip of her drink.

I want to tell her bottoms up and pour her a double, because she obviously needs to loosen up...or maybe some liquid courage.

His eyes rack up and down her body and I hear his heavy exhale.

"Haven't seen you in a while," he says in a cool way that only people with swagger can manage. "Whiskey, neat," he says to Shaw as he steps in beside me. When the glass of amber liquid is placed in front of him with a napkin, he dips his head in appreciation at Shaw and then smiles at me while dropping his voice to a low, silky utterance. "See you around, CeCe."

When he walks away, I get a whiff of something expensive—cologne that makes me think of the French Riviera, which I've never been to, so I have no real life experience on what that smells like, but if I had to guess, it smells like Shep.

Okay, I obviously need some help.

"Who was that?" I whisper once he's far enough away he can't hear and Shaw is at the other end of the bar, pouring a few beers.

"Shepard Rhys-Jones," CeCe says with a huff that's half lust, half hate.

"Spill," I order, taking a towel and wiping down the bar in front of me so I look busy.

"That's a story for another day," she says with a sigh. "I just don't have the mental stamina to relive it right now."

Her dramatics make me laugh. "Are you kidding me? This from the girl who wanted every sordid detail of my sexual encounters..." I hiss. "You basically were selling me off to the highest bidder so you could get a juicy story...and you think I'm going to let this slide?" I ask incredulously. "No, no, ma'am. I'm going to at least need the basics."

With another huff, CeCe glances over her shoulder and then back at me, downing what's left of her drink. "Fine. We..." she pauses, waving a hand in the air like I'm supposed to interpret, and I already think I know, but I'm going to need hear her say it.

"What?"

"Had sex," she says, obviously annoyed she's being forced to admit it.

"Was it horrible?" I ask, a bit confused because the man I just saw looks like he can deliver...in every way.

"God, no." She shakes her head in disgust that I would even think that. "Not at all..." As her words drift off and her eyes linger over her shoulder, her tone softens. "Quite the opposite. It was the best lay of my life."

"So, why not talk to him?" I ask with a hint of frustration. This isn't CeCe. She's normally sure of herself and confident. And I hate knowing she's always alone. And that guy seems really nice...and really rich, not that that matters, but I want the best for her.

"It's been over a year since I saw him last," she admits solemnly. "He...I don't know. He rocked my world and then disappeared. I thought..." Shaking her head, she looks down at her dress, smoothing out invisible wrinkles. "I thought there was something between us. Obviously, I was wrong. It was stupid. I should've known someone like him would only be interested in a weekend fling." Looking back up, she makes eye contact and laughs it off, but I see the pain there. This little confession gives me answers to several questions I've had about CeCe.

Why is someone like her single?

Why does she never date?

Why does she seem to be obsessed with love yet never goes after it for herself?

Shepard Rhys-Jones.

"Seems like he's reconsidering," I tell her, thinking back about the way he looked at her.

"Doubtful," she mutters, pushing off the counter and throwing herself back into work. "Maverick, Carys' boyfriend is Shep's best friend. They own a business together...he's probably just in town for business."

"Or a repeat performance," I quip, raising an eyebrow in her direction.

"Well, he'll need to find a new actress for the starring role." She huffs, shaking her head. "Because it won't be me."

"Thought you weren't opposed to a weekend fling," I hedge, trying to get to the bottom of her response to seeing him.

"I...I'm not." She shrugs, turning her back to me. "For other people, maybe even for myself at one time or another, but not anymore. Not with him."

Aha. Okay.

About that time, a tall guy with a big smile and even bigger dimples walks up to the bar. "Can I get two glasses of wine and two beers?"

"Sure," I tell him, returning his smile.

"Hey, CeCe," he says with an even bigger smile.

"Deacon!" CeCe's expression morphs from a regretful scowl to one of complete elation. "I was wondering if you and Cami would be here!" She hugs him and his large arms wrap around her, hugging her back. "Avery, you've got to meet my friend Cami. She's the one who did the paintings in the shop."

"Oh, wow," I say, setting the two wines down and reaching for two beer glasses. "I'd love to."

"Here," CeCe says, grabbing the wine glasses. "We'll help you carry these. Follow me, Avery...is that okay, Shaw? Can you spare your girl for a sec?"

Shaw gives her a nod, followed by a wink in my direction. I smile at him and then follow CeCe and Deacon over to a group of people. Cami, I'm assuming by the way she leans in and kisses Deacon, is tall and blonde. Her shoulder length hair is done up in perfect curls and when she turns to greet me, her blue eyes dance with happiness.

"I'm so happy to meet you," she says, pulling me in for a hug. "Sorry, I'm a hugger."

"It's okay. I just hope I don't stink," I say with a laugh. "I've been working all day."

"Nonsense," she says, shooing my apology away. "Besides, Deacon and Micah own several restaurants, so we all know what it's like to slave away and smell like food and booze at the end of the day."

"This is Micah and Dani," CeCe says, motioning to a guy who's almost as tall as Deacon, but has darker hair and green eyes. Dani, the woman by his side, is gorgeous with her long auburn hair. The warm smile she offers me makes me feel immediately at home, like I'm among friends instead of strangers.

"Hey," Dani says, stretching across the middle of the group to hug me.

"So, how do you all know each other?" I ask, looking at CeCe.

"Cami and I became friends years ago when she was going to

college."

"Yep," Cami says, chiming in and pulling CeCe into a side hug. "And we've been friends ever since. She still has one of my earliest works hanging in her shop."

"It's true," CeCe says with a proud nod of her head. "I was a fan before being a Cami Benoit-Landry fan was cool."

We all laugh, falling into easy conversation, but I eventually excuse myself, not wanting to leave Shaw alone. Plus, I just miss him when I'm away from him. But I continue to watch everyone mingle as we serve drinks and I'm filled with wistfulness and warmth at how everyone's lives are so surreptitiously entwined.

CeCe is best friends with Carys.

Carys is with Maverick.

Maverick's best friend is Shepard Rhys-Jones.

CeCe and Cami are friends.

Cami is married to Deacon.

Deacon's brother is Micah who owns Lagniappe, a restaurant around the corner.

Dani is married to Micah.

Micah and CeCe and Shaw all have businesses in the French Quarter and rely on each other for promotion and business.

It's a web of people who quite possibly could have never met, but they did...and their friendship is beautiful and it kind of makes me teary-eyed when I think about it, which is ridiculous, but I've been feeling quite ridiculous a lot these days, my emotions always getting the better of me. So, I roll with it.

"You okay?" Shaw asks, walking back over to the bar after talking in the corner with Maverick and Shep.

"Yeah," I tell him, folding the bar towel I've been using and placing it in front of me. "What were you men folk talking about?"

"Men folk stuff," he says with a sly smile.

I nod. I want to ask him if Shep mentioned CeCe, but I wouldn't betray her trust like that. I just have to hope that it all works out. If it's meant to be it'll be, right?

"You gonna make it until midnight?" he asks, walking around and placing his hands on my hips, pulling me against his chest.

"Not if you keep doing that," I moan, leaning into him, feeling every bit of exhaustion from the day...and Shaw's semi-hard cock. Yep, that doesn't help.

"Maybe we should pop this champagne and pour the glasses. We could be home before the clock strikes midnight."

"Can we do that?" I ask, turning in his arms.

Shaw shrugs, glancing over my head at the people milling about. "Seems like everyone is pretty well buzzed. It looks like our job here is nearly done."

So, we do. At eleven thirty, we start popping open the champagne and filling glasses that are set out on a long table. When it's done, Shaw finds Carys, letting her know where to find the remaining booze and that all the champagne has been poured.

Once we're in the Jeep, my head falls back on the headrest and I really feel the day. A few minutes later, we're making our way out of the French Quarter. Shaw takes a few side roads to avoid the busier streets and then cuts across Canal until we're in the Garden District.

When we pull into the drive, the clock on the dashboard reads eleven fifty-eight.

"Midnight on New Year's Eve is my favorite," I tell him, turning my head to see him looking at me.

"I could take or leave it, but you might be able to convince me otherwise."

"Challenge accepted," I tell him, using my last bits of energy to crawl over the middle and into his lap. Our kiss starts out slow and sweet, but quickly the spark is lit and our breaths come hot and heavy, until the windows of the Jeep are fogged and we're grinding into each other, chasing our release like horny teenagers.

No, not again. Please, God, no.

For the third time in about thirty minutes, I vomit into the toilet. This time, though, not as much comes out, which is good, I guess, but these dry heaves that are tagging along can fuck right off.

I'm sure I'm not the only one praying to the porcelain god this morning, with it being New Year's Day but the difference is that I didn't drink alcohol last night. I barely even ate, just a few appetizers that were being served at the hotel. Even though I was tired when we got home, I felt fine, fine enough to let Shaw ravage my body while I ravaged his in return. I certainly didn't feel as badly as I do right now, which really bums me out because I was looking forward to spending the morning in bed with Shaw since neither of us have to work.

And, as hard-headed as I am, even I can admit defeat. After weeks of being tired and sick to my stomach, with the occasional early morning trips to the bathroom, I know it's time for me to go to the doctor and find out what the hell is going on.

Another round of dry heaves hit me just as Shaw opens the door and rushes to my side. He carefully gathers my hair and holds it back from my face and neck, his fist a makeshift hair tie. I know he's so worried about me and I can only imagine what seeing me like this is doing to him. He never left Liz's side when she was sick so, I know this is something he's done way too many times before.

"How long have you been in here?" His voice is soft, as if the volume will determine whether or not I throw up again.

I answer him with my head still in the bowl, just in case. "About thirty minutes or so."

"Avery, honey—"

"I know," I interrupt. "I'll go to the doctor, I promise, but it'll be a few days before I can get an appointment. Everything's closed because of the holiday."

"Not everything. I'm taking you to the emergency room as soon as you feel like you can leave the bathroom."

My shoulders slump because I was really trying to avoid going to the hospital, but I know Shaw's right. At least this way, we'll know what's going on and how to deal with it rather than worrying about it until I can make an appointment.

I'm going to be really pissed if I'm told it's just a virus and there's nothing I can do about it. Not that I want to be diagnosed with anything serious either, I just want to feel normal again.

I manage to take a quick shower and brush my teeth before Shaw practically carries me to his Jeep. I didn't feel like eating anything but that didn't stop him from tossing a bag of dried cereal and a couple packs of crackers in my backpack, though.

Such a thoughtful, caring man. I don't know what I'd do without him.

He squeezes my hand three times before giving me a quick smile as he drives. He's being so brave and strong for me, but I can tell this is killing him. He's scared, like he's reliving his worst days and it breaks my heart. I don't know if anything I can say will set his mind at ease, so I return his squeezes with three of my own before bringing our joined hands to my mouth for a kiss.

The emergency room is packed and I'm afraid we'll be waiting here for hours before seeing a doctor, but I'm surprised when we're taken to a curtained area shortly after speaking with a triage nurse. I have a feeling the prompt attention is due more to Shaw's demeanor than my symptoms, but I'm not complaining. The nurse tries to ease our worries buy agreeing it's probably *something viral* or the flu, but informs me they're going to run some blood work just to be on the safe side.

"I fucking hate the smell of hospitals," Shaw groans once the nurse is gone. I hate that I'm putting him in this position. I can only imagine how he must feel being here and suddenly I wonder if this is the hospital that treated Liz during her illness.

The question is on the tip of my tongue when an older gentleman wearing a white coat steps into the sequestered area and sighs heavily as he takes a look at the computer beside the bed.

Walter D. Briggs, MD is the name on the tag that's attached to his coat.

"Miss Cole," he says in a business-like tone mixed with genuine care, "let's see what we've got going on here, shall we?" Turning to me, he offers a gentle smile and then glances to Shaw, giving him an understanding nod. "We've seen a lot of flu cases lately, plus multiple viruses going around. I'm sure it's nothing, but we always like to be on the safe side."

I inhale and exhale deeply, feeling a sudden rush of panic. Needles are my least favorite thing about going to the doctor and I've never been a patient in a hospital before.

Deep breaths.

"Are you feeling sick now?" he asks.

"Um...I'm still feeling tired...a little weak," I tell him, really trying to listen to my body so I can get whatever this is nipped in the bud. "But I don't feel nauseous at the moment. It kind of comes and goes. I really hope I don't have anything contagious though because I work in the food industry and I've been around people nonstop for the last few days."

"Well," he says, wheeling a small stool over beside the bed, "that's an even better reason for us to be thorough, we don't want an epidemic now, do we?"

"No," I tell him with a small shake of my head.

"Any abdominal pain?" he asks.

"No."

"Fever?"

I glance over to Shaw and see him watching me intently. "Not that I know of."

"Good." He eyes me with an educated stare. "The rest of your vitals seem good. Blood pressure is a little low, but that could be due to fatigue. I'd like to run a full panel on you, just give everything a good look. It shouldn't take more than a couple hours. Our lab is a little backed up, but we'll expedite it as fast as we can."

"Okay," I tell him, swallowing down the nerves.

He pats my hand, giving it a light squeeze. "I'll send the nurse back in to draw some blood."

Suddenly, my stomach feels queasy again. When Shaw stands and begins to pace in the small space, I feel like this is probably all for nothing. I probably have some virus they can't give me anything for and we're going to spend the better part of the day in this hospital, a place Shaw hates, for nothing.

"If you want to go, I can call you when I'm ready to leave," I tell him, trying to give him an out.

He spins around, eyes glaring with an incredulous look on his face. "I'm not leaving you."

His words mixed with their delivery has me holding my breath. This is so much more for him than a regular visit to the doctor. Shaw is fighting demons. Our routine visit to the ER is a battle for him. "Come here," I order, holding my hand out to him. I don't want to make him sick, but if he was going to get something from me, it happened last night.

Slowly, he walks over to me and I wrap my arms around his torso, pulling him into me and resting my head on his chest as I run my hands up his back. Breathing deeply, I coat my lungs with the smell of him, finding solace even as I'm trying to give it. Eventually, he returns the hug and wraps his arms around my shoulders, dropping his head down to rest on mine. We stay like that until a throat clearing draws us apart, but even then, I'm reluctant to let him go.

"Have you had anything to eat or drink in the last eight hours?" she asks, setting her kit down on the cart and walking over to the monitor to type something into my chart.

"No," I tell her, shaking my head. "Whatever I had last night, was before ten o'clock and it's gone now." I give her an awkward laugh, raising my eyebrows to insinuate that I threw it all up without having to say that.

"Okay." She types a few more things in and then walks over to the bed and asks me to lie back and relax my arm.

I want to be a baby about this. I want to cry for my mama. I want to tell her to forget about it and that I'm feeling better. But instead, I suck it up and lie back, closing my eyes, and thinking about the way Shaw manhandled my body last night before we went to sleep.

After a couple pokes, she releases the tight band from around my bicep, drawing what blood she needs. "I'll be back shortly," she says, gathering her supplies and heading for the opening in the curtain. "If you start to feel sick, push the button."

Shaw's hand loosens from mine the second she's out of the room and he cups my cheek. "Are you sure you're okay?"

The worry etched on his face breaks my heart into pieces, but I force a smile before replying, "I'm fine. I promise." Placing my hand over his, I fight back a yawn. "I could use some crackers or something... maybe even a small cup of coffee if the nurse says it's okay?"

His expression changes a little—brightening with purpose. He grabs my backpack and pulls out the dry cereal and a package of crackers he'd insisted on earlier and hands them to me. "I'll go ask the nurse about the coffee and if she says it's okay, I'll go find a vending machine or cafeteria."

"Thank you," I tell him, bringing his lingering hand to my mouth and kissing it softly.

"I'll have my phone on me and turned up. If you need me or anything changes...call me. I'll be here."

I smile again, but this time it's more genuine. "Go. I'm fine." Lying back in the bed, I curl onto my side. "I'm going to close my eyes for a minute while you're gone."

Lying there, I try not to think about Shaw or Liz or what might be wrong with me, and let my mind drift. The white noise of the bustling hospital on the other side of the curtain pulls me into a semi-unconscious state.

"Miss Cole."

Opening my eyes, I slowly sit up, realizing I might've actually fallen asleep for a minute. Glancing over beside the bed, I see the coffee Shaw promised, but no Shaw.

Dr. Briggs is sitting on his rolling stool at the foot of the bed. With an iPad in one hand, he reaches into the breast pocket of his white coat and pulls out a pair of reading glasses, perching them on his nose as he scans the small screen. "We have a few of the results back from the blood work and I think we might have the answer we're looking for."

"Okay," I reply, sitting up fully and feeling more alert with this news. Hopefully, it's something easy and he can give me something and send me on my way.

"Should we wait for..." he lingers, gesturing over his shoulder.

"Shaw?" I ask. "No, it's fine. He's probably just in the bathroom or taking a phone call. Let's just get this over with."

He smiles gently, his eyes crinkling around the edges. "Okay." Setting the iPad on the edge of the bed, he crosses his arms over his chest and commandeers a thoughtful expression.

"The blood test we just ran came back positive for pregnancy." He just lays that down between us, no inflection, no emotion...just factual. He is a doctor, after all. I'm sure what he's saying makes perfect sense in a doctor's world. But his words do not make sense in mine.

"I have an implant," I repeat, my hand instinctively going to my left arm and rubbing at the spot I remember the implant being inserted. He already knows this. I just wrote it down on the admittance papers I filled out when I got here. "I have..."

I try to breathe normally. Maybe this is a mistake?

He pulls his brows together and then places a thoughtful finger on his lips. "Well, I'm going to guess the implant is no longer effective."

No longer effective.

That nauseous feeling creeping up on me has nothing to do with sickness and everything to do with what Dr. Briggs is saying and how he's looking at me and the raw adrenaline coursing through my body.

I'm feeling lightheaded.

"Would you like to wait on Shaw before I continue?" Dr. Briggs asks, his voice sounding farther away than it should. "Is he your..."

"He's my...my Shaw," I tell him, placing my head in my hands and leaning onto my thighs, thinking about doing what I've been told to do if you feel faint and put my head between my legs.

Breathe, Avery.

Just breathe.

"Should we wait for Shaw?"

"No," I blurt, sitting straight up and making the blood rush from my head. "No, please..." I glance at the curtain and feel my face drain of color. No Shaw. I can't tell him. What's he going to think...feel? This entire day has already been too much for him and all I wanted was to get a diagnosis and go home and sleep it off, but that won't be happening. I won't be sleeping this off.

"Are you sure?" I ask, slipping off the bed and pacing the same spot Shaw had been pacing earlier. "I mean, there's a chance it could be a false positive, right? That happens. I've heard of that happening..." I ramble, biting at the edge of my thumbnail. "Can you maybe do another test?"

Calmly, Dr. Briggs stands and places a gentle hand on my arm. "Let's have a seat and talk about it. Everything is going to be fine."

When I look up and meet his eyes, I think for a split second that he's right and everything is going to be fine, and then I remember Shaw...and that he might come back through that curtain any moment and then everything will definitely not be fine.

38

Shaw

ALL THE WAY DOWN TO THE CAFETERIA AND BACK, which felt like miles away, I sent up silent prayers to a god I'm not sure hears me anymore. Thankfully, Avery was sleeping when I slipped back into her makeshift room, so I stepped back out in the waiting room to give Sarah a call. And if I'm being honest with myself, I just needed a way to ground myself. The longer I stood in that small area, breathing in the sterile air, the more I felt myself slipping into that black abyss of grief. Memories have been hitting me like a battering ram ever since we walked through the sliding glass doors.

I remind myself over and over that this is Avery and Avery is not Liz.

Walking back into the triage area, I pocket my phone. Since we'll probably be here a while, I wanted Sarah to know we wouldn't make it for breakfast, but she didn't sound too disappointed until I told her why. When I told her Avery is not feeling well and that we're at the hospital, she turned into over-protective-mom-mode Sarah. I promised to call her as soon as I know anything and that seemed to keep her at bay, for now.

Hopefully, there's nothing to tell her.

When I round the nurse's station that's positioned in the middle of the chaos that is the ER, I see the nurse who's been with Avery since we got here and she's rolling a machine toward Avery's room. "What's that?" I ask, panic rising in my throat.

"Oh," she says, glancing from me back to the curtain and then back again. "Uh..." she hesitates for a moment and it makes me feel sick to my stomach. Maybe Avery is contagious and I got whatever she has, because I feel like I could throw up right about now.

"Is she okay? Why do you need that?" I point to the machine. "What is it?"

The questions spill out of me in rapid succession.

"Shaw?"

I hear Avery calling for me and it's then I realize I've raised my voice above what's acceptable for the hospital and a few people are watching me, probably wondering if I'm going to be a problem. Spinning on my heel, I run toward the curtain and throw it back. Avery is sitting on the bed and her eyes are rimmed in red.

"What's wrong?" I ask, running a shaky hand through my hair. How the hell did everything fall apart in the few minutes I was gone? The last time I saw her, she was sleeping peacefully and the nurse was on our side, guessing it's the flu or a virus. So, why does everyone look like they have horrible news to tell me? "What's wrong?" I repeat, looking back to Avery and then going to her, taking her face in my hands.

"Well," Avery starts, worrying her lip between her teeth as her brows pull together. She's trying to keep from crying and I can't stand it. I want to rewind to last night when we were wrapped around each other and everything felt perfect, like we were getting this incredible chance at happiness. I don't understand what I did to deserve a second chance like Avery, but fuck if I'm not grateful for it. So why does it feel like it's slipping between my fingers?

"Just tell me," I plead, losing my grasp on all rational thought. "What's wrong?" This time I turn to see Dr. Briggs standing beside the nurse and the ominous machine she rolled in beside her. When I look back to Avery, she's staring at the doctor, her silent plea for help filling the small space. Slowly, she drops her eyes back to her lap where her hands are twisting the bottom of her sweatshirt. After a few moments—enough time for me to jump to every horrible conclusion known to man—she finally says, "I'm pregnant."

Releasing her face, I stumble back, cocking my head to the side and blink rapidly as I try to wrap my brain around those two words. *I'm pregnant.* Avery's pregnant. "I'm sorry?" I ask, barely recognizing my own voice. I'm not sure what I'm feeling, but the strongest emotion is disbelief.

How can this be?

"Pregnant," Dr. Briggs confirms. "We got a couple of the blood tests back. One indicating high levels of HCG, which is the hormone the body produces when pregnant. We're not finished running all the panels, but since Miss Cole's symptoms line up with the regular symptoms of early pregnancy, we're fairly confident the only thing she's ailing from is a growing fetus." The light chuckle that follows his explanation sounds nearly joyful, but it's not registering with the loud rush of blood pulsing in my ears.

Sitting down in the chair, I cradle my head in my hands and run my fingers through my hair again, pulling a little, just hard enough to cause pain, anything to make sure I'm awake and not dreaming.

Avery's pregnant.

Looking back up at her, she's staring at me with a void look on her face and I feel my stomach drop again. "I'm sorry," I tell her, standing back up and walking over to her, crouching beside the bed, realizing what a dick I'm being, making this all about me. "Are you okay?"

"I don't know," she answers honestly. "I thought...I'm really sorry. I thought I was covered."

"It seems as though Miss Cole has a birth control implant that tends to only be effective for the first three years. Since it's been a little over four, it's probably that its efficiency declined, leaving her susceptible to pregnancy." Dr. Briggs' even, medical tone gives me a chance to process and at least get a grip on myself. I need to be present for Avery. She needs me. I'll figure out my own shit later, so I nod so he at least knows I heard what he said.

"We're going to do an ultrasound to see if we can determine how far along she is and then we'll need to schedule an appointment to have the implant removed. We'll also need to find you an obstetrician. You'll more than likely be a high risk pregnancy due to the implant being present during conception," the nurse adds. "We'll give you a minute to change into the gown. As soon as the OB on staff makes it up here, we'll get the ultrasound done and get you discharged so you can go home and rest."

Avery just nods, eyes back on her hands in her lap.

Once we're in relative privacy, I pull her into my chest. "It's going to be okay."

"I'm sorry," she whispers, her words cracking with emotion. "I know we haven't discussed this and it's probably—"

"We'll talk about it later," I tell her, cutting her off. I don't want to discuss anything besides what's right in front of us. "Let's get you in this gown and do the ultrasound."

A brief moment of relief floods my body, as I convince myself that pregnancy isn't life threatening, and isn't that all that matters? But then my mind betrays me and retrieves the memory of me and Liz in a similar situation, waiting on an ultrasound to hear the heartbeat of our baby. One that we never got.

"Are you okay?" Avery asks with watery eyes and voice. "I know this is hard for you."

The fact that she understands and is so empathetic makes my heart split—one part still mourning what's lost and the other part loving the girl in front of me.

"Don't worry about me." I give her a small smile, willing the tears to stay away. Not right now. Not today. Instead, I focus on helping Avery pull off her sweatshirt and replace it with a hospital gown that I frown at in disgust. A few minutes later, the nurse is back and a new doctor is following her.

"I'm Dr. Cambridge," he says with a wide smile. "I hear congratulations are in order."

Avery manages a forced smile and lays shaky hands on her

abdomen as she leans back in the bed. My eyes follow her touch and suddenly it all starts to sink in.

There's a baby in there.

Something Avery and I made.

We might not have planned on it, but it's here and there's no going back.

"Let's see what we can find out, shall we?" the doctor asks, pulling up Avery's gown and tucking her yoga pants down to her panty line. The flat stomach on display makes it all seem surreal again. How can this be? She looks fine...normal...definitely not pregnant.

After he squeezes some lubricant on her skin, he takes a wand and begins moving it around on her stomach as sounds immediately start to fill the room. Moving to see the screen, my eyes grow and then squint when an image of a small, bean-shaped object comes into view.

And then the loud thud of a heartbeat.

Swooshing.

Beating.

Swooshing.

Beating.

Looking down at Avery, she's entranced for a second, but then she squeezes her eyes closed allowing huge tears to cascade down her cheeks. I grab her hand, hoping she'll look at me but when she doesn't, I lean over and kiss the wet skin of her cheek and then her hair. "I love you," I whisper.

She'll be okay.

We'll be okay.

Liz has been gone for six years.

Five was my milestone for getting my shit together. I gave myself those years to mourn and wallow in my sorrow. Sometimes, it was a daily battle with memories and despair, feeling like I was barely treading water.

With everything going on lately—Avery, the baby, the memories, today's anniversary—the heaviness I felt in my chest this morning made me feel like running, so I did. I climbed out of bed before daybreak and ran until my lungs burned and my legs felt like mush. Then, I went back home and showered and dressed, while Avery was still sleeping. Before leaving for the cemetery, which is where I spend every January 15th, I set a coffee cup under the Keurig, turning it on and placing a decaf coffee pod in it, with four creamers and one packet of sugar beside it, for when she's awake.

I think of leaving her a note, but I wouldn't know what to say. We haven't talked a lot in the last two weeks. She's been giving me my space and I've selfishly been taking it. At night, I pull her to me and she melts into my touch. It's those moments, in the dark and quiet, that I know we're going to be okay. When I place my hand on her still flat stomach and she places hers over mine and we have silent conversations. She understands my reservations and fears and I understand hers. They're different, but ultimately, we're in this together.

On my way there, I welcome the cool January air as it bites my skin, letting me know I'm alive. As I drive my bike up as close as I can get to where Liz is buried, I drop the kickstand and turn it off. Once the roar of the engine is out of the picture, I'm met with a familiar serene silence.

Walking over and squatting down in front of the grave, I run my hand along the cool surface of the headstone, feeling the inscribed words beneath my palm.

Elizabeth Louise Franklin-O'Sullivan

February 22, 1980—January 15, 2012

"To live in the hearts of those we love is never to die."

I pull out the small candle and lighter from my pocket. Digging out the old one from the last time I was here, I place it on the ground and drop the new one in its spot. Lighting it, I watch for a while as the flame flickers and burns, protected from the light breeze by the large slab of granite.

The day I picked out what would mark her final resting spot, I felt like I wanted to erect a goddamn wall. The small pieces of stone just didn't seem to suffice for a person who held such a large piece of me.

"I'm sorry it's been a while," I start, brushing off the dead grass along the bottom edges, squatting so I'm eye to eye with her name.

A bird chirps from a few feet away, perched on the top of another grave and steals my attention. We have a standoff for a few minutes—she stares at me, while I stare back—before the black wings take flight. Raven hair flutters through my mind, my fingers, although they're still on the hard surface of the headstone, feel like they're touching silk. For a split second, I feel like she's right there with me. Closing my eyes, I take advantage of the audience and speak my peace.

"I miss you, every day," I whisper to her. "There was a time I felt like curling up beside this grave and dying alongside you. If that meant I could be close to you again, that's what I wanted. But my promise to you—to live, love, and keep breathing—kept me from it." I let out a rough laugh. "You knew what you were doing. You knew I could never break a promise to you, even in death."

Taking a moment to collect myself, I look around for the bird but it's gone—taken flight with the wind. As I exhale loudly, I picture Liz doing the same...flying high, free from pain. "Thank you," I say, turning back to the stone, both hands resting on the rough top edge. "Thank you for showing me what it's like to love and be loved in return so fully. Thank you for not letting me give up. I'm not sure what you had in mind when you made me promise to keep living and loving, but I feel like you've had a hand in the turn my life has taken...so, thank you for that too."

The sting in my eyes makes me stand abruptly, wiping the back of my hand across my face. Glancing down at the flickering flame and then back at the words on the stone, I smile faintly. "You're not going anywhere," I promise her. "I'll always love you...you'll always have a place in my heart."

Sweat drips down my brow and I blink it away, licking my damp upper lip before continuing to pummel the bag. My arms beg for a reprieve, but I continue to pour every last drop of energy into the treated leather.

"Should we tape a face onto the bag?" Sarah's voice startles me, but I get in a few more punches before leaning into the bag and letting my body go limp. "Seems like you've got a lot of pent-up frustrations. Anyone in particular?"

My mind goes to Avery.

She's who I'm hiding from.

I can admit that now.

Between the therapy sessions and my group sessions, I'm becoming well-versed in owning my shit. After yesterday's group meeting, I stayed late to discuss the baby with Ellen, who thinks it's the best thing to happen to me since Avery.

My head has been in a constant state of confusion for the past few weeks. Worry, fear, anxiety—they all plague me, making me think the worst. But I'm also happy...so fucking happy. And I wish I could tell Avery that, but every time I think about opening up to her, I just freak out and find something to do. The fear of saying something to fuck all of this up is paralyzing me, keeping me from saying anything at all.

What if I jinx it?

What if my own insecurities and fears bleed over to her...and the baby?

What if I speak all the negative shit floating around in my head into existence?

"How've you been holding up?" Sarah asks and we both know what she's referring to. The anniversary of Liz's death isn't one we celebrate or call attention to, but Sarah recognizes it in her own way, just like I do.

"I'm fine," I tell her, out of breath from my punishing workout.

"Then what's eating at you?" Her shoes make a sharp noise as they tread across the apartment floor. "You've been spending more time up here than the bar and home put together. Avery has called a few times to check on you. She's worried...and so am I."

When she sighs and pulls out one of the chairs at the table, I push away from the bag and grab my sweat towel, scrubbing it through my hair and down my face. I should've had a talk with Sarah last week, but I didn't. If bottling up emotions was an Olympic sport, I'd be a fucking gold medalist.

"I have something to tell you," I admit, sitting down on the weight bench and dropping my head between my shoulders.

"Okay," Sarah replies, shifting in her seat.

When I look up at her, she's mimicking my position—elbows on knees, hands folded. Her eyes are boring into mine, like she's trying to use x-ray vision to find the answer.

"Avery's pregnant."

Sarah's eyes flare, her head cocking to the side like she didn't hear me correctly, but then a smile splits her face and she stands, cupping her mouth. "Shaw," she whispers in awe, tears springing up and threatening to fall. When she moves toward me, she freezes, realizing I'm still sitting and I haven't stood to accept her impending congratulations. "What's wrong?"

"Me," I say with a huff, throwing my towel to the floor. "I'm what's wrong. I can't get out of my fucking head long enough to be happy about this..." Standing, I place my hands on my knees and breathe deeply. "I can't forget the past long enough to be happy about the present...about the fucking future. Maybe I won't ever be able to."

Her hands go to her hips and she's leveling me with the stare that reminds me so much of our mother. "Are you finished?"

I stare at her, void of any emotion, waiting for her to tell me to get over myself and move on with life.

"Let me tell you something," she says, walking forward and grabbing my shoulders with as much force as she can muster. "Your past is what's going to make you the best partner for Avery and the best...I mean, *best*...father to that baby. Don't lose that. No one is asking you to forget Liz. The fact that you had her and lost her taught you so much about love, things not many people are privy to. You have to go through extreme heartache to truly realize all there is to lose and all you're willing to do to keep it."

"There's something else," I tell her, my tongue thick with emotion as I try to swallow down the regret from what I'm about to say—what I've kept from her and everyone else all these years. "Liz was pregnant... that's how we found out about the cancer. We went in for an ultrasound and left with an appointment to terminate the pregnancy. I thought we'd get another chance. She wanted to wait, but she was scared. I couldn't make the call for her so she made the ultimate decision, but I know she was completely heartbroken over it. I've wondered many times over the years if we did the right thing. What if Liz had the baby? Would she have had more of a will to live? Would it have changed the outcome?" My voice cracks and I feel unwelcomed tears slide down my cheeks, mixing with the sweat and seeping between my lips in a salty intrusion. "I did want the baby...I mourned it, when Liz was sleeping, I'd go downstairs and pull out the ultrasound photos and just think about what it was...a boy or a girl. It really didn't matter, but I felt guilty and selfish for wanting Liz more than the baby."

I huff, taking a breath and finally meeting Sarah's gaze, which is also filled with tears of her own.

"I was so torn."

"It's okay to feel that way," Sarah says quietly. "But you have nothing to feel guilty over. Getting Liz immediate care was the best thing for her, I'm sure. Don't beat yourself up over something you can't change and don't let it keep you from appreciating what you have now. She was being strong for you...just like you were being strong for her. None of that was fair; we all know that."

Sarah's silent for a moment, soaking in this new revelation, before she speaks again. "Now it's time for you to be strong for Avery...and this new life the two of you have created."

Bending down, I grab my towel from the floor and cover my face with it, wiping away the evidence of my emotions.

"What am I doing?" I ask—Sarah, God...the Universe. "It's like I'm an imposter, living someone else's life...or maybe I'm cheating and stealing someone else's forever. I've already had my love and that's gone...Liz is gone."

I know the second the words are out of my mouth they're complete and utter bullshit. I need Avery like I need my next breath. If that makes me selfish, then so fucking be it. Whatever I did to deserve a second chance like her, I want to keep doing it for the rest of my life.

I want her for the rest of my life.

And our baby.

"But Avery is here...and this baby is here. And they need you."

I start to nod and tell Sarah that she's right—I know she's right—when a soft voice calls from the open door. "Shaw?"

Sarah and I both turn, my face contorting when I see Avery's broken features. "Avery," I say, going to her and hoping like hell she'll hear me out and not run.

Please, God, if I have one more unanswered prayer left, don't let her run.

Clearing the distance to the door in a few long strides, I jog down the steps, jumping the banister to come to land in front of her, spreading my arms wide to block her path. Her chest heaves with unshed tears, emotions, hurt. "Why did you say that? You don't want me? You don't want our baby? If that's how you feel, tell me now. Tell me so I can make plans. Don't—"

"I love you," I tell her, trying to think of the right thing to say. "I'm a dick. I didn't mean any of that. I might've at one point. I thought I'd had my one chance and didn't deserve another, but I want you...I want every part of you. I want us. I want this baby."

The tears finally pour down her beautiful face, unchecked. "Why did you say that?" she demands, her voice rising as her emotions pour out of her.

"Because I'm scared shitless. I'm so fucking afraid that my life is on repeat and I'm going to wake up one day and everything standing in front of me will be gone."

When her face starts to relax and she allows herself a deep cleansing breath, even though it comes out on a loud, unbridled sob, I sag in relief. "Why didn't you tell me? You have to talk to me," she demands, stomping her foot in anger.

I'll take angry.

I'll take a fight.

As long as she's here.

"Don't make me worry that you're going to freak out on me and bail," she says with vitriol, her finger jabbing into my chest to drive home her words. "I need you, Shaw O'Sullivan. So, if you need me...if you want me and this baby, then you're going to have to promise me you're in this for the long haul." Her small frame is shaking as she takes a deep breath, closing her eyes. The finger she was pointing pulls away as she balls up her fists and places them on her hips, looking at me with fire and determination in her eyes. "Don't hide from me. Whatever you're worrying about, I want to know. It's the only way we can work through it. You can't just bottle it all up. It's not healthy. And I need you healthy...and here. Because I can't do this alone."

Finally, she stops and takes a breath and relaxes one her of her fists, bringing her hand up to smooth her hair out of her face.

God, I love her.

I love her for calling me out on my shit and for not letting me get by with hiding. I love her big heart and the way she gets me, even the confusing parts. And she loves me, even the imperfect, scared parts.

"I love you," I tell her, reaching over to take her hands in mine, forcing them to loosen and lace with mine. "I love you so much and I'm sorry for hiding from you. Never again," I promise. "I'm going to be here for everything...forever. You're going to be so sick of me, you'll beg me to leave."

She fights back a small smile and rolls her eyes as a few more tears slip out. "Doubtful," she says, shaking her head.

With my eyes locked on hers, I pull her to me, my hands framing her beautiful, tear-stained face. "I love you, Avery Cole. And one day,

I'm going to get down on one knee and ask you to be my wife. And we're going to bring this baby into the world and it's going to be the most loved baby on the face of the planet."

"You promise?" she asks, wrapping her arms around my waist.

"I do."

Her body finally melds into mine and I hold her to me, not too tight, but enough that she starts to laugh lightly. "You're crushing me."

"I told you you're gonna get sick of me."

Sarah's head pops out from the door upstairs and she gives me a knowing, proud smile. I kinda forgot she was up there, but I don't care. She of all people deserves to see this moment, to bask in the beauty of my life coming full circle.

I'm not fooling myself. I know there will be trials and tribulations, but losing Liz and finding Avery has taught me that I'd rather experience love and loss than to never have loved. What kind of life is that? The mundane, orchestrated semblance of one I was living before Avery showed up in my bar and rocked my world, that wasn't living...that was merely existing, and I'm never going back to that.

I'm going to love Avery for as long as I'm allowed.

I'm going to be a dad.

I'm going to live it for me...for Liz...for Avery and our baby.

EPILOGUE

THREE MONTHS LATER

Avery

"I'M NOT EVEN KIDDING, THE DRIVER FLAT-OUT refused to pick her up. He said all the cabs in town have banned her and to try Uber or Lyft instead!" Kevin wipes his eyes as he finishes his story, even though he's still laughing.

"Pissy Missy struck again, I presume?" Shaw asks, walking up to where I'm seated at the bar.

"Yeah, she showed up last night," Paulie says.

"Maybe she needs her own special bar stool set aside for when she stops by?" I suggest, thankful I've never had to deal with this particular regular.

"Fuck that," Shaw replies. "I say we have some adult diapers on standby instead."

"Speaking of diapers," Sarah interjects with a wink. "Have you two registered for baby stuff yet?"

"Can you give us a minute to just enjoy being pregnant?"

'Enjoying' might be putting it lightly. Shaw and I can't keep our hands off each other is the real truth. I thought we were passionate before but then my pregnancy hormones kicked in and now, I'm ravenous for him. All. The. Time. Not that he's complaining, of course.

"Hey, Avery, you mind passing that over this way?" Paulie asks, nodding at the empty mug left by a customer.

"Not at all." I reach over to grab the mug but Shaw stomps around me and snatches it out of my hand before slamming it back down in front of Paulie.

"What the fuck, man? You can't get the mug yourself? Do you seriously need a pregnant lady to do it for you? *My* pregnant lady, to be exact?"

Shaw is absolutely seething at his old friend but I remember to swallow my giggle before placing my palm against his chest. "Shaw, it's fine. *I'm* fine. You can't keep me from doing things, you know this."

"Like hell, I can't." He faces me and places his large hands on either side of my small but round belly. "I'll wrap you in fucking bubble wrap if I have to." His growl against my ear sends shivers up my spine...and then back down to my vagina.

Standing on my tiptoes, I place a soft kiss on Shaw's jaw. He's started wearing his beard more trimmed and cut close, showcasing the strong lines of his face. I'll take him in any form or fashion, but when he smiles at me like he's doing right now, I'm a goner.

That smile is my weakness.

"You're gonna be the death of me," he sighs, visibly relaxing.

"You're gonna be fine," I remind him gently, escaping into our own little bubble for a few seconds.

"Y'all are gonna need to take this into the office," Paulie says, disgust thick in his tone.

We all laugh, the tension defused. For now.

"I have an errand to run," Shaw says, glancing down at his watch. "You'll stay here and let these dipshits and Sarah keep an eye on you while I'm gone." He tries to boss me around, but he knows it's not gonna work.

"Sure." I tell him, taking a seat at the bar.

Once I hear the backdoor shut, I hop off the stool and grab my purse off the counter. "I'm walking over to CeCe's. I'll be back in a while."

'Tis better to ask forgiveness than permission, I always say.

"Don't get me fired," Paulie says, continuing his work behind the counter.

"Have fun," Sarah calls. "And tell CeCe we said hi."

They're used to this process. They're used to me pacifying Shaw. I think even he knows I'm not going to sit here waiting on him to get back, but he has to say it anyway. The one concession I've allowed is him dropping me off at work every day. Boy, was that a battle of wills.

At first, he wanted me to quit my job and just stay home every day. We fought. Like, real honest to goodness knock-down-drag-out. He sulked. I stewed. And then we met in the middle.

I'm only working three days a week. He drops me off. I spend the rest of my time with him, either here or at his house. I occasionally go to my apartment, but usually just to chill when Shaw's busy and I'm not.

One of these days, I'll take that final step and officially move in with Shaw. I'm not sure what's holding me back, but I figure I'll take the next couple months to figure that out. Maybe it's because that house was his and Liz's. It holds a lot of memories for him, both happy and sad. And I'm not sure where I fit in. But I know I belong with Shaw. And I know before the baby gets here, I'll figure my shit out and make his home mine.

"There's my baby mama," CeCe calls out as I walk in the front door of Neutral Grounds. A few of the customers look up and I blush and shake my head. The way she talks about my baby and my pregnancy, you'd think she really is the other parent. She's insistent that she be my child's godmother. I don't know the protocol for that, but I'm assuming, since Shaw's Catholic, he's going to have strong opinions about who the godmother and godfather are.

He has strong opinions about everything else. I'm sure that will be no exception.

"Hey, CeCe," I call back, giving her a wide smile.

"Your regular?" she asks, finishing up a drink she's making and already pulling out a cup for mine.

"Yes, please," I reply, leaning over onto the counter. "Unless, you want me to make it myself."

"No, actually," she says, distracted with her work. "I'd like you to sit down, but since I know that's out of the question and you don't like taking orders from people, I'm going to let you stand there and look pretty while you're growing my baby."

Rolling my eyes, I prop my cheek into my hand and watch her work.

After a few minutes, she walks over and places a drink in front of me. Typically, with the weather turning back humid and hot—even though it's only the end of March—I'd be drinking an iced coffee or cappuccino, but not today. "One deliciously nutritious green smoothie... extra on the nutritious," she says with a proud smile.

Honestly, I'm not sure who's worse, her or Shaw.

Just as I'm getting ready to take my first drink, my phone rings and my mama's face pops up on my screen. "Hey, Mama."

"Hey, baby," she says in the same giddy tone she uses every time we talk these days. It's like we have an ongoing inside joke or secret. To say she's excited about the baby is the understatement of the century. She's beside herself, as is my nana. As for my daddy, well, he's coming around. I think he's excited about the baby, but just having a hard time wrapping his mind around his baby having a baby. Plus, he hasn't had the chance to meet Shaw in person. The age difference was a little bit of an issue at first, but the more time that passes and the happier I am, the warmer his feelings toward Shaw grow.

"I'm at CeCe's. Can I call you back later?" I ask, giving CeCe a wink.

"Hey, Mrs. C," she calls out, loud enough for my mama to hear.

"Tell CeCe hello and thank her for taking such good care of you and my baby," my mama says.

"I thought I was your baby," I reply in mock defense.

"Oh, hush," she says. "You'll always be my baby, but you're grown and you're giving me a new one to love..." Her voice drifts off and gets higher pitched and I roll my eyes, because I really don't want to have to go through this again.

"Mama," I say, trying to get her attention and get her to snap out of this sappy mood.

"Oh, I know, I know," she replies, sniffling and putting on a brave front. "I'm sorry."

"Y'all are still coming to visit in a few weeks, right?" I ask, giving her a distraction.

"Yes, your nana wouldn't let us miss it for the world. I'm pretty sure she's already got her bags packed and her gambling money put to the side. She's convinced she's going to win enough to pay for a nursery."

I roll my eyes again and shake my head. They're crazy. All of them.

"I love you, Mama. Give everyone else my love."

"Love you too, Baby."

A few seconds later, after another round of goodbyes, I pocket my phone and pick my drink back up. CeCe and I chat between her constant flow of customers and just as I'm getting ready to leave, my phone rings again. Assuming it's my mama, I pull it out of my pocket and push the button to answer. "What'd you forget to tell me?" I ask.

"I need you to meet me somewhere. Sarah is waiting for you at the bar. She's going to bring you to me," Shaw's deep voice says, catching me off guard in more ways than one.

"Uh, okay."

"I thought I told you to stay put?" he asks, his voice like silk being pulled over rough edges.

"I thought I told you to quit telling me what to do?"

His deep rumble of laughter makes my body tingle and I wish I could teleport myself to wherever he is. It's crazy that I miss him, even though I just saw him a little while ago.

"I'm heading to the bar right now," I tell him, ending the call and sliding the phone back into my pocket. "I've gotta go. Shaw needs me to meet him...somewhere," I inform CeCe, realizing I never got where I'm supposed to be going.

"Call me later," she says.

I wave at her and toss my mostly empty cup into the trashcan on my way out.

When I get to the bar, Sarah is waiting on me with an anticipatory smile. "Ready?" she asks, thumbing over her shoulder in the direction of the back door.

"I guess," I tell her with a semi-nervous laugh. "I don't know where we're going."

"I know. Follow me."

We walk out into the alleyway and get into her small, black sedan. Somehow the car fits her to a T—understated yet strong, elegant without being stuffy. She starts up the engine and backs out, still giving me a knowing smile. "So, no hints?" I ask, buckling my seatbelt.

"Nope."

"Shaw's instructions?" I ask, already knowing the answer.

"Yep."

We drive in silence for a few minutes. She makes a couple turns and before I know it, she's pulled up in front of a red brick house, or maybe it'd be better described as a cottage, with black shutters and a white door. I glance over at Sarah and she nods her head toward the structure.

"Am I supposed to get out?" I ask, frowning at her in confusion. "Where's Shaw?" I glance around the street and don't see his bike or the Jeep anywhere, but I trust Sarah and I know she wouldn't just dump me out and leave me.

"Just go inside," she says, her eyes growing soft as she cups my cheek.

"Okay," I tell her, unbuckling the seatbelt and opening the door. I glance back a couple times as I walk up to the door, which I now can see is cracked open. The surrounding houses are all painted in the vibrant colors I love so much, retaining the old world feel of the city. With one last backward glance at Sarah, who's still sitting in her car by the curb, I push the door open and walk through.

White walls and exposed brick, matched with hardwood floors

and tall ceilings, greet me. The space is beautiful, even though there aren't any furnishings or decorations. It's been restored, but whoever did the work kept the integrity of the original structure.

"What do you think?" Shaw asks, making me jump and cover my mouth. Letting out a laugh, I turn back to the open space and then back to him, noticing the windows and how they let the sun shine in just perfectly.

"It's beautiful," I tell him.

Taking a few steps toward me, but not close enough for me to touch him, he says, "Well, then it's a perfect fit for you."

Confused, and trying not to jump to unrealistic conclusions, I tilt my head and ask, "Why are we here?"

Shaw sighs, shoving his hands down into his jean pockets, making his forearms flex in a delicious way. As his eyes roam the space and then land back on me, I notice a glint of irrepressible happiness. "I was thinking about buying it," he says. "For us."

For us.

My gaze darts around the space, my mind going into overdrive as it places me and Shaw here...his big couch and my paintings...the quilt my nana made me and his stack of books by the window...Shaw's cooking and my coffee...our baby.

"For us?" I ask, my voice cracking.

"Me, you..." He pauses, taking a step close and placing his hand over my stomach. "This baby...*us.*"

My vision is muddled with unshed tears. He should've known better than to spring something like this on me, my emotions are all over the place.

When Shaw drops from view and I follow his movements, realizing he's kneeling before me with my hands in his, I hold my breath.

"Avery Cheyenne Cole," he begins, smirking. "I called your mama the other day and asked her what your middle name is. It's pretty... maybe if we have a girl, we could name her that."

"You called my mama?" I ask, emotion now taking over my entire being.

"I called your dad, too." Shaw clears his throat and his face goes serious. "I just wanted him to know that I'm going to take the best care of you. And that you and this baby, and any more babies we have in the future, will always come first in my life. I want to make you happy. I want to live my life loving you." He drops my hands and pulls a ring from his pocket, his focus on the stunning diamond shining in the perfect afternoon light. "Avery Cheyenne Cole, would you do me the honor of being my wife?"

Those visions from earlier come flooding back and I see myself five years down the road...and ten...and fifteen...and at every stage, Shaw is there, by my side. The answer to this question has been nestled in my heart for a few months now, just waiting to be released.

"Shaw. . .Brady O'Sullivan," I begin, stumbling over my tears for a second, but pausing to breathe and clear my throat. "This house is beautiful...and you are a beautiful man. I fell in love with your heart long before I fell in love with you. I know this road hasn't been easy, but it's our road and I'll walk it every day with you. There is nothing I want more than to be the mother of your child...or children," I amend with a small laugh, "and be your wife."

He stares at me for a moment—could be seconds or minutes—our eyes locking, millions of words and promises being said through single breaths.

This is it.

Shaw is it for me.

For better or for worse.

In sickness and in health.

As long as we both shall live.

Acknowledgements

Acknowledgements are always hard because we'd never want to miss thanking someone who helped us along the way. So, forgive us if they get lengthy...and on that slim chance we might forget to mention YOU...thank you. Just know we value each of you for who you are.

To the VIPs in our lives—our kiddos, family, friends, and readers. What is life without amazing people to share it with? This is a lesson Shaw O'Sullivan learns throughout Come Again. We always tend to sneak pieces of ourselves into our books and this one is no different.

First, we'd like to thank Pamela Stephenson for being our beta reader! She's always there from the beginning, watching and reading as the story takes shape. We appreciate you, Pamela!!

We'd also like to thank Nikki, our editor. Thank you for taking on this BEAST and for always helping us make the hard calls when it comes to cutting scenes and making the book the best it can be.

Our proofreader, friend, and drinking buddy, Mrs. Karin Enders. Thank you for everything! From beta reading to proofreading, we appreciate your time, effort, and camaraderie!

A shout-out to our friend, Kat Tammen! Thank you for spending an entire day reading this book! We appreciate your feedback and uncanny ability to pick out all the weird words. Love you, babe.

We'd also like to thank our cover designer and formatter, Juliana. Thank you for making the photo we love work and for making it even better. We love your creativity and attention to detail!

Also, a huge shout-out to our pimp team—Pamela, Lynette, Megan, Shannon, Candace, Stefanie, Laura, and Debbie. Thank you for always putting your two-cents worth in and giving us a safe place to bounce ideas! We love y'all!

Thank you to everyone in Jiffy Kate's Southern Belles. All of you make our days better.

Now, we hope you enjoy this story of second chances and finding love in the midst of grief.

About The Authors

Jiffy Kate is the joint pen name for Jiff Simpson and Jenny Kate Altman. They're co-writing besties who share a brain and a love of cute boys, good coffee, and a fun time.

Together, they've written over twenty stories. Their first published book, Finding Focus, was released in November 2015. Since then, they've continued to write what they know—southern settings full of swoony heroes and strong heroines.

You can find them on most social media outlets at @jiffykate, @jiffykatewrites, or @jiffsimpson and @jennykate77.

Made in the USA
Las Vegas, NV
22 July 2022